Penguin Books
The Best Stories of John Morrison

John Morrison was born in 1904 at Sunderland, England, and emigrated to Australia in 1923, earning his living as a bush worker before marrying and settling in Melbourne in 1928. He spent the rest of his working days there as a gardener, with a break of ten years as a wharfie.

His short stories, most of which first appeared in the journals *Meanjin* and *Overland*, made up the collections *Sailors Belong Ships* (1947), *Black Cargo* (1955), *Twenty-Three* (1962 — awarded a gold medal by the Australian Literature Society), *Selected Stories* (1972), *Australian by Choice* (1973), *North Wind* (1982), *Stories of the Waterfront* (1984), and *This Freedom* (1985). His most recent work, *The Happy Warrior*, a collection of articles on Australian writers, was published in 1988. His work has been published in thirteen languages, including Russian, Chinese and Italian, and many of his stories have featured in anthologies.

The award of a Commonwealth Literary Fund Fellowship in 1947, and again in 1949, enabled Morrison to write his two novels, *The Creeping City* and *Port of Call*. He now holds an Emeritus Fellowship granted by the Australia Council and, in 1986, he received the Patrick White Award for Writers of Distinction.

The Best Stories of John Morrison

Introduced by Stephen Murray-Smith

Penguin Books

Penguin Books Australia Ltd,
487 Maroondah Highway, P.O. Box 257
Ringwood, Victoria, 3134, Australia
Penguin Books Ltd,
Harmondsworth, Middlesex, England
Viking Penguin Inc.,
40 West 23rd Street, New York, N.Y. 10010, USA
Penguin Books Canada Limited,
2801 John Street, Markham, Ontario, Canada, L3R 1B4
Penguin Books (N.Z.) Ltd,
182-190 Wairau Road, Auckland 10, New Zealand

First published by Penguin Books Australia, 1988

Copyright © John Morrison, 1988
Introduction Copyright © Stephen Murray-Smith, 1982

All Rights Reserved. Without limiting the rights under copyright
reserved above, no part of this publication may be reproduced,
stored in or introduced into a retrieval system, or transmitted
in any form or by any means (electronic, mechanical, photocopying, recording
or otherwise), without the prior written permission
of both the copyright owner and the above publisher of this book.

Typeset in Galliard by Dovatype & WordsWorth, Melbourne.

Made and printed in Australia by Australian Print Group, Maryborough.

CIP

Morrison, John, 1904- .
The best stories of John Morrison.
ISBN 0 14 011741 5.

I. Murray-Smith, Stephen, 1922-1988 . II. Title
A823'.3

To the memory of a fine young man,
my grandson, Malcolm Morrison,
who was accidentally killed on 18 August 1978
at the age of twenty-two

The stories in this collection, with the exception of *All I Ask* and *Quiet Night in Station Street*, were originally published under the title *North Wind*.

· Contents ·

Introduction by Stephen Murray-Smith	ix
To Margaret	1
Tinkle, Tinkle, Little Bell	17
Easy Money	29
The Haunting of Hungry Jimmy	37
Perhaps You've Got It	51
The Battle of Flowers	59
All I Ask	87
Ward Four	94
Pioneers	106
Transit Passenger	135
North Wind	150
The Sleeping Doll	191
Quiet Night in Station Street	207
The Nightshift	214
Goyai	222
Dog-box	231
Morning Glory	243
The Incense-burner	253

· Introduction ·

The publication by Penguin Books of a new collection of the stories of John Morrison is of particular timeliness and significance. George Steiner has recently written in the London press of the new mood of humanist and social awareness that is growing in Europe, to displace the involuted and insulated literary theories and experiments of the last twenty years, and in Australia too there are signs, in film, drama and books, that the mode of the 1980s will be strongly influenced by a return to the Real, a departure from the artist as his own subject, a re-emphasis on continuity in human affairs.

Even if this does not prevail, there is no doubt that the stories and novels of John Morrison have shown a surprising historical vitality. The work of few Australian writers whose literary experience comes from the 1920s and 1930s, and whose writing is that of the 1940s and 1950s, has remained in print and grown in reputation in the past thirty years. John Morrison's work is likely to be part of the small proportion of the writing of its time that will survive indefinitely.

On the face of it, John Morrison's literary world is well removed from current literary fashion and social preoccupation. His waterside workers, once satisfying as heroes to the Left and as villains to the Right, are now a small and dwindling band. Perhaps in the 1980s air traffic controllers, with their white collars and swimming pools, will take their place as symbolic figures on the industrial scene. Morrison's backblocks 'hatters' have by now been placed in care by diligent social workers, his train- and tram-travellers have switched to Datsuns and Commodores, his Dandenongs pensioners have moved to the Gold Coast, and his farmers now rank higher in the social scale than their bank managers. Only the drunks remain.

Introduction

The world of which John Morrison writes was remote even to me, when I was shanghaied into it in the 1950s. Not *quite*, actually. That world of Morrison's young manhood, on which hang many of his stories, was the world of my childhood. But I knew nothing of his hot inland, his clanging tramp-steamers, his mist-wreathed mountain forests. What I did know a little of was another of his celebrations: the middle-class suburban Melbourne of the one-day-a-week gardener, the 'nature-strip', and the bottomless gap between the 'worker' and the rest. When reading 'North Wind' it is salutary to remind oneself that John Morrison, as a jobbing gardener, used to pedal his bicycle from Mentone to places like Kew every day for work — some twelve miles, perhaps against a north wind — and then home again after a long day. It is a world, this 'respectable' world, that he draws in delicate and damning touches: its affectations, its fear of common humanity, its shallow-rooted pretensions.

Jobbing gardeners may now be as rare a species as *Citriodora echeveria eugenoides* in 'The Haunting of Hungry Jimmy', but *that* world of John Morrison remains, though his 'Avalon' and 'Elysia', and Mr Cameron's home in Hawthorn Road may long ago have become petrol stations. For, while it is true that on one level the writer is constructing a magnificent, moving, even nostalgic picture of a Melbourne about which (since we don't talk to old people) we now know little; and while it is important not to underrate this achievement — yet Morrison is read, and will continue to be read, for quite different reasons.

There have been acute and important discussions of John Morrison's art by David Martin, Arthur Phillips and Ian Reid, which I do not want to recapitulate, partly because they are readily accessible (sources are listed at the end of this introduction), and partly because I want to write, not so much about the totality of Morrison's work, as about what we can learn of it through the stories in this collection. But I do wish to discuss three aspects of Morrison's writing which these critics refer to.

One is the strong 'ethical' content in the writing. He likes to take his characters, says Phillips, at the moment of 'ethical decision'. It is, I think, an important point, and it clearly relates in part to Morrison's North Country background (Presbyterian, both parents Sunday-school teachers) and to his affiliations

· Introduction ·

with that latter-day redemptionist institution, the Communist Party. He does believe that not only once, but many times, to every man and nation comes the moment to decide

> In the strife of truth with falsehood,
> For the good or evil side.

That a writer should have ethical considerations at the back of what he writes is not only, in my view, desirable, but inevitable. No statement or action by anyone is 'value-free', let alone those of artists, who all voluntarily elect to enter an arena. All artists are teachers, including those who deny that they are: *they* simply hold to a teaching or 'ethical' position which maintains that what they are doing is indeed 'value-free'. Since this is, I presume, generally conceded, the argument in Morrison's case must be that he strongly adheres to a perceptible ethical stance, one that colours his writing visibly.

Perhaps so. But I suggest that the interesting thing about much of Morrison's writing is that, within certain discernible 'ethical' considerations, he is so often able to suggest moral ambiguities. And the more fully fledged his stories are, the more firmly the reader rather than the writer is pushed into the judgement seat. In 'North Wind' we are worried, whether Morrison realizes it or not, at a certain obsessiveness which governs both actors, the desperate husband and the recalcitrant mother-in-law. His triumph here is to suggest flaws in the stance of the husband even though it is the husband that is telling the story. At the end, as the flames consume the weatherboard house, a black pall of uncertainty casts its shadow over all. Maybe we are expected to side whole-heartedly with Jim Thurgood, but it really isn't as simple as that. It's a strange and worrying tale.

'The Battle of Flowers' is another example. Here the moral dilemma of the gardener, caught in a malevolent helix, is explicitly one of the main points of the story, and it can easily be read as a parable, as the critics often suggest of so many of Morrison's stories. If it were to be read as a parable — and I take issue with this approach later on — it might be read as a religious parable, of the Devil leading man to damnation with mincing steps, or as a political parable, of the inability of humanity to order its world in a sane way.

No doubt somewhere or other in Morrison's consciousness or subconscious such considerations have something to do with it, but the story can be read otherwise as well, as an exercise in the genuine confusion that exists in the sphere of moral concerns, a refusal to accept an easy answer to the question Joseph Furphy posed in *Such is Life* — just which branch line do you take at what moment? (In fact, if one wanted to discuss symbols in Morrison, the place of the train and the tram in his stories would be important.) There are several moralities operating in this story, and one of them is an existentialist one. Existentialism in Morrison is discussed by David Martin in his article; for me, in relation to 'The Battle of Flowers', it is a strand in the story which admits the two gardeners, not as active agents in evil, but as observers or passive agents in a progression which is not only out of their control, but which — taking into account the vindictiveness of the Heavenly Twins — they should properly stand aside from. It is, of course, the strength of Morrison that he can deftly and economically weave so many layers of response into his work.

My third example is perhaps Morrison's greatest story, 'Pioneers', in my view a candidate for being the finest story written in this country since Lawson. Arthur Phillips has pointed out how Roy Davison, with his stern self-reliance, his disdain for 'show' and his utter competence (he himself is the only witness to it, but that is enough), 'has much in common with those neo-Puritans whom Morrison often admires'. He is destroyed, says Phillips, by 'egotism'; perhaps another way of saying it would be that Davison is destroyed by the reverse side of his own virtues: self-reliance becomes the immodesty, the brutality, which the primitive surrounds of his life have nurtured. Quite so, quite so. But over 'Pioneers' lies another cloud, an elemental cloud, which enshrouds the whole story. Bob Johnson, the observer, makes his sympathies plain, but for all that he *is* an observer, an astronomer watching galaxies collide; and in my view we are left at least as much with the feeling of 'what right have we to be here?' as with the 'ethical' judgement that Roy Davison is a prime bastard.

I do not, in other words, accept the view that John Morrison is a preacher to any significant degree, and I think that he too is subtly making the same point by including in this collection gentle stories of observation and human feeling — 'Transit Passenger' and 'Dog-box', for instance. Note that 'gentle' stories need not lack impact and meaning; the meaning is all the more puissant because (and one might even say, to the degree that) Morrison leaves the reader to work it out for himself. His view of humanity is seldom disapproving in a judgmental sense. It is distanced, regretful, sometimes sad. His overwhelming quality as a writer is a quiet capacity for detachment.

So I do not share — to take up my second point — a view of Morrison as writing 'parables'. I am sure he has no objection to his readers interpreting some or all of his stories this way, but I do not believe that he is setting out to 'write big'. I think he is too good a writer for this. He has a much less ambitious and at the same time a much more profound aim: to discuss human nature as he knows it, and to tell a good story reconstructed from bits and pieces garnered and thought about over many years. He has, in John Manifold's phrase, a 'queer affection' for the human race: never cynical, but sometimes sardonic; never resentful, though sometimes angry; never judging — or seldom judging — beyond the point to which his characters bring him.

It is the view of a gardener of men, for whom docks sprouting in the borders do not destroy a broader vision of potential beauty. It is the view of a writer who has said that 'An attitude which maintains that literature should be regarded as an instrument in the social struggle and nothing else' must lead 'straight to literary damnation'. The function of the artist, John Morrison maintains, 'is to move his audience emotionally'.

A third point the critics have sometimes advanced in discussing Morrison is the rough-hewn quality of his prose, his disdain for literary niceties, his concern that his words should be no more than hand-maidens of larger concerns. 'Old-fashioned methods of story-writing', Arthur Phillips has called them, though to be fair Phillips has also been careful to point to Morrison's 'carefully-carpentered' technique. None of the critics I have mentioned deny Morrison's literary skills, but the phrase 'old-fashioned' does keep cropping up, and it is a phrase with which I want to take issue. There are plenty of contemporary novelists and short-story writers of the highest rank who do not rely on experiment with literary *form* for part of their effects, though all, as does Morrison, tailor the choice, flow and arrangement of their words to the job in hand. It is important here to see what Morrison is doing — I nearly said 'what Morrison is aiming at', but there is a difference. He is working towards an unforced and relaxed style, not because he is in any way 'old-fashioned', but because only the achievement of such a style can carry the psychological realism which is his aim and his accomplishment.

Look, for instance, at 'The Haunting of Hungry Jimmy', where the initial aim is to reinforce the reader's understanding of the character of Hungry Jimmy, on which the rest of the story totally depends. Notice the *patience* with which Morrison rejects the natural impulse in a short-story writer to 'get on with it', and instead takes us quietly through a rehearsal of Jimmy's guttersnipe acuity. Notice, too, the quiet personal aside with which Morrison reminds us that the narrator of his first-person stories is also a participant: in 'Tinkle, Tinkle, Little Bell', where he writes, 'Not Carnation. He'd been outflanked, and he wasn't going to let me get away with it'. And observe the timing of such an interpolation, which carries with it an acute — and sometimes uncomfortable — sense of the narrator's position. And witness the ability to seize on a moment in order to set a scene and to heighten the senses of the reader, as in 'The Nightshift':

The night is full of sounds. Little sounds, like the rattle of winches at the distant timber berths; big sounds, like the crash of the coal-grabs opposite the gasworks. All have the quality of a peculiar hollowness, so that one still senses the overwhelming silence on which they impinge.

This is not 'old-fashioned' writing. It is writing that knows what literary form is appropriate to the emotion that is being created. It is only old-fashioned in the sense that the paper from which this book is made is old-fashioned.

Questions of form and style apart, John Morrison has an importance to Australians which transcends a simple 'literary significance'. Like David Martin, but not perhaps a great many others, he is a creature from outside who has lived long and thoughtfully among us as a writer. His first interest is in a

· **Introduction** ·

humanity common to all men and women, but his secondary interest, heightened of course by his coming to Australia as an adult, is in what our environment and our society have done to *us*. The experience of 'Australianness' has become a cliché in television soap-opera and in film, but serious writers have turned away from it, especially in the last two decades, for at least two reasons: because it seemed important to look at human experience in this continent in more individual terms, and (which is really part of the same) because of an increasing suspicion of, and hence incapacity to handle, generalization.

Morrison is not a generalizer, except in the sense that he will allow humanity to triumph in his stories if he can ('Perhaps You've Got It') or, failing that, will engage his readers in moral considerations. But in his stories he has, for all that, sketched in and filled in a view of a specific people in a specific place. He has asked, and gone further perhaps than any other towards answering, the most important question of all: to what degree is this society one in which people may call their souls their own?

The question is as important as the answer.

Stephen Murray-Smith

References

David Martin: 'Three Realists in search of Reality', *Meanjin*, no. 3, 1959.
A. A. Phillips: 'Short Story Chronicle', *Meanjin*, no. 4, 1962.
Ian Reid: 'Introduction', in John Morrison, *Selected Stories* (Rigby, Seal Books, 1972).
A. A. Phillips: 'The Short Stories of John Morrison', *Overland*, no. 58, 1974.

· To Margaret ·

There is a widespread idea, obviously originating in the bulb-growing industry, that all Dutchmen are good gardeners.

Nonsense, of course, and I know of more than one employer who has found it out to his cost. A man isn't necessarily an authority on sheep because he was born in Australia, or on the bagpipes because he hails from Scotland. There is, nevertheless, always the exception that for so many people becomes the rule, and Hans — call him Vandeveer — must have blown new life into the Dutch gardener fallacy wherever his green fingers took him.

Because he *was* Dutch and he *was* a good gardener. One of those inspired craftsmen who are an embarrassment to all other craftsmen who come after them. He was also something of a poet, which may not be particularly interesting, and something of a lover, which is.

It was the only case I ever came across of a gardener falling in love with the boss's daughter, and I learned all about it because I was the one who succeeded him when he got his marching orders as a consequence. I took over only a week after he'd gone, when the garden was still fresh from his talents and the household still reeling under the shock of his romance. I found a glorious garden, an employer still frozen into a bitter mistrust of all gardeners, and a confiding housekeeper who told me that 'Miss Margaret' had cleared out to relations in Bendigo, and that her mother had followed her in an effort to persuade her to return.

But of all this I knew nothing when, at nine o'clock on the first morning, Mr Cameron, master of the house, stopped to speak to me on his way out to the city. He was a barrister, with a future, I'd have guessed, in the Arbitration Court if he kept along with the right political party. A tall, dignified man somewhere below middle age, with a slow deep voice, cold eyes, and a lean handsome face that reminded me of a well-known bust of Julius Caesar.

I was older than him, with a long experience of employers, and I mistrusted him on sight. And even though, as I've said, I knew nothing of what had been going on, there were little things, even in that first brief interview, that made me wonder what I'd stumbled into. I'd been engaged through a nurseryman, and although Cameron therefore had good reason to study me, I thought there was something unnecessarily harsh and judicial in the way his grey eyes looked steadily into mine.

'Good morning, Johnston. I think I have the name right?'

'Yes. Good morning, Mr Cameron.'

He must have had plenty of confidence in his nurseryman, because there followed none of the questions I was expecting. Instead, he made it clear from the beginning that there would be no excuses in the event of difficulties or failures.

'You'll find everything in good order here.'

'It is, Mr Cameron. You must have had a good man.'

'I had.' He spoke with a noticeable dropping of the corners of his lips. 'He was Dutch. He'd had a very good training.'

I waited, hoping to learn if the Dutchman had left voluntarily, but nothing came. His eyes left me for a moment to scan the garden at large.

'I do a lot myself, though. The garden is my hobby.'

He need hardly have told me that. One day a week could never have achieved such an effect. And the place was not only perfectly kept; it was designed with imagination and richly founded. One of those lush, stately gardens that indicate an owner of fastidious tastes and all the means necessary to indulge them. Tall cypress hedges muffled the noises of Hawthorn Road, and of Balaclava Junction only a few hundred yards away. A sense of deep peace, of remoteness and isolation, had seized me the moment I'd stepped inside. There was a lively breeze blowing, but little of it penetrated the garden, and there was a greater twittering of birds than one expects to hear in a big city. I'd already observed many rare trees and shrubs, and several that were new to me. It was springtime, and a wide

· To Margaret ·

flagged path leading straight from the gate to the house, arched with roses and other climbing plants, was still dark with winter moss along the sides and littered with the fallen petals of wistaria.

Cameron nodded to indicate a small bed in the lawn not far from where we were standing. An oblong bed with an edging of alyssum just broken through, and the centre all dusted over with finely sifted stable manure as if something had recently been sown there. 'That bed is fully planted. It has linaria in the middle — dwarf Fairy Bouquet. He sowed it just before he left.'

I could see that it hurt every time he referred to the Dutchman.

'When was that, Mr Cameron?' I asked.

'A little over a week ago. You can let me know next Wednesday if there is anything you require. Mrs Briggs, the housekeeper, will give you your money when you finish. You won't meet Mrs Cameron today; she's away just now.' And with that he left me.

I didn't like him. An employer whose garden is his hobby is always a menace, but there was something else to Cameron. He hadn't once smiled. I was looking forward already to the day when I would find it necessary to challenge that Julius Caesar stare.

Mrs Briggs gave me morning tea. She just brought it out to the front porch, called me, and immediately went inside.

But at lunch-time I got the story. I'd decided that, as none of the heads were at home, I might as well eat in pleasant surroundings, so had taken my billy to the porch again. Soon after I'd finished eating she came out quite deliberately and joined me for a yarn. I suspected that the reason why she hadn't talked at ten o'clock was that she wanted plenty of time.

I had already met her, but only for a moment when, at eight o'clock, she'd given me the key of the toolshed at the kitchen door. Her appearance now on the porch bore out the impression she had left with me: a flurried, ageing little woman scared half out of her wits by a difficult household in which she had stayed too long. I knew the type: too near the end of her working days to venture into fresh fields, and still too useful to be thrown onto relations or into an old people's home. I was to find, however, that there were circumstances that made Mrs Briggs a rather special case.

She wore a white apron over a black frock, and had grey hair, a pinched, mousy little face, and hands all puffed and twisted by rheumatism.

She said she had come out to see if I'd like more tea, but when I told her I'd had enough she showed no inclination to go in again. She smiled the kind of smile you get from a person who is naturally pleasant but has little to smile about.

'I know how it is,' she said, looking at my billy as if she'd still like to fill it up. 'A man can drink a lot of tea at twelve o'clock when he's working hard.'

'I've had more than enough, Mrs Briggs.' I saw that she wanted to gossip, and added, just to give her an opening: 'You've got a nice garden here.'

Her eyes followed the path all the way down to the gate. 'Well, it should be. It's always been well looked after.'

The situation didn't seem to be one calling for much subtlety.

'Mr Cameron told me the last man was a Dutchman. What did he leave for?'

'Oh, you know how it is, he just ...' She began to fumble with her apron and gave me a confused glance, obviously torn between a desire to talk and doubt as to whether I was to be trusted. She broke out suddenly: 'Between you and me, gardener, he had to leave. There was a bit of trouble.'

She sat down in an old basket chair facing me and I waited, regarding her with an expression which I hoped was one of sympathetic interest.

'They found out there was something going on between him and the daughter.'

'What!'

One of her poor twisted hands came up in disapproval of my smile. 'Nothing wrong, mind you! I've known Miss Margaret since she was a baby, and a better girl you wouldn't find in all the world. I don't think there was a bit of harm in it. But there you are, Mr Cameron seemed to think there was, and that was the end of it.'

Up till then I'd been visualizing my predecessor as a man

· To Margaret ·

at least as old as myself, which was rather more than the age of romance.

'He must have been young, then, Mrs Briggs?'

'Hans? Oh yes, about twenty, same as Margaret. And a nice fellow he was too. You'd hardly know he was a foreigner to hear him speak, although he never had much to say. Very quiet and polite. He must have come from a good home.'

'Good-looking?'

'He was good-looking all right! I don't wonder at Margaret . . .' Mrs Briggs hesitated, and gave me another cautious glance. She knew she was talking too much, but couldn't help herself. She was enjoying every minute of it. 'They were only a couple of kids making eyes at each other. I was watching; I'd have known if it was going any further. Margaret couldn't hide anything from me if she tried.'

'There must have been something in it.'

'Oh, Hans was struck on her all right. What I mean is that there was, well, no harm in it. Margaret — '

'Just secretly laughing at him?'

'No. I think she was a bit pleased about it. He had such a nice shy way with him, no liberties. He always managed to be somewhere near the path of a morning when she went out, with a flower for her — she's a chemist in some big Government place. And she'd keep that flower fresh for the best part of a week. Oh, I saw plenty. Just little things, but they all added up. Wednesday mornings she was always up and about a bit earlier, hanging round the dining-room window, peeping to see if Hans was in the garden.'

'Wasn't Mrs Cameron awake to it?'

'Of course she was. But she was like me, she couldn't see any harm in it. And she liked Hans. She got the blame for it, though, like she gets the blame for everything that happens in this house.' Mrs Briggs closed her eyes and lifted up her hands. 'My God, if you could have heard the way Mr Cameron went on! He seemed to tumble to it all of a sudden. He brought an orchid in for Margaret one night — it was a Wednesday — and next morning wanted to know why she was wearing the flower Hans had given her. It was deliberate, the kind of thing he was always up to. Then he went for Mrs Cameron. Told her it would never have happened if she'd been taking proper care of her daughter. As if anything *had* happened! You'd have thought the girl had been led astray. Anyway, there was a fine to-do over it, and the next time Hans came he got the sack. I don't think Mr Cameron was even going to tell him what it was all about. But I told him. I told him as soon as he knocked on the door for the key at eight o'clock. So he was ready. And doesn't the very fact that he started work show that he had nothing to be ashamed of? He was putting in some seed near the gate when Mr Cameron went down at nine o'clock.'

'Cameron waited till nine?'

'You don't know Mr Cameron yet! You wouldn't get him to change his habits, not if the world was on fire. Everything's got to be done exactly the same every day of the year. He'd think he was giving Hans a bigger shock, too, if he went down at his usual time — he's like that. Anyway, it didn't take him long. I was watching out of the window. The pity was I couldn't hear anything. Not that there was much said. Hans was all packed up and on his way out in a matter of minutes. Mr Cameron wouldn't make a scene.'

No, I reflected, not with his gardener.

'And Margaret cleared out?' I asked.

'That very afternoon. She came in about three o'clock when there was only me in the house, and started packing up. I tried to reason with her, but I might as well have talked to that brick wall. It wasn't only Hans, you know. There was trouble twelve months ago over a boy-friend she had. Mr Cameron broke *that* up, and he was no gardener. His father was a doctor.'

'Mr Cameron sounds a difficult man.'

'Difficult? He's a beast!' Really carried away now by her story, Mrs Briggs said this with a vehemence that startled me. 'It's never been a happy home. The wonder is he's ever been able to get anybody to live with him. I'd have left years ago if it hadn't been for Mrs Cameron. I can stand up to him a bit, but he's had her bluffed from the very day they were married. I felt I couldn't leave her with him. The things that woman's had to put up with! D'you know what he does when he really wants to hurt her?'

I shook my head.

'He calls her by her first name. Now then, would you think that was possible?'

'It's a new one to me, Mrs Briggs.'

'Yes, and you'd need to hear it to believe it. Years ago, when he had her in tears over some fiddling little thing she'd done that he didn't like, she complained that he never called her by her first name. And it was true, I never used to hear it from one week's end to another. And ever since then, when he really wants to be nasty, he calls her "Barbara". That's her name, all right, but you just ought to hear the way he says it — as if it was a dirty word. And it isn't as if he had any reason for it, because she's never been anything but a good wife to him. Too good, although he seems to think it's the other way round. I think he's always felt he'd married beneath him. None of her friends were ever good enough for him, they never come near the house now.'

'Whose relations did Margaret go to?'

'Her mother's. That's why he won't do anything about it. He says her home's here if she wants it. It's going to be awful tomorrow if Mrs Cameron comes back without her.'

And that, as I remember it, was the full story. There were a few anecdotes about Cameron, about Mrs Cameron, about Margaret, but nothing that added substantially to the picture I already had. I was more sure than ever that I would not get along with Cameron, but I went back to my work glad that I'd got the job, and full of curiosity over what was going to happen in the next week or two.

It was a pleasant day, that first one, one of those calm lovely spring days that stick in the memory. There was a nice sense of freedom, too, in the fact that Cameron had left me to my own devices, and that no curious eyes were watching me from the windows of the house. During the morning I'd disposed of all routine work such as cutting the lawns and sweeping the paths, and spent most of the afternoon lifting and re-laying a straggled edging of agathea along a wide border facing north. A warm sun played on my shoulders, and the air was full of the invigorating fragrance of spring — stocks and cinerarias and freshly turned earth.

How well it all went with the story of Hans and Margaret! I kept thinking of them both, but it was Hans who had taken the greater hold on me. He was inevitably so much more real than the girl. I'd seen neither of them, but the spirit of the young Dutchman, in the very evidence of his talents, was with me wherever I turned. I had no small pride in my own talents, but that garden humbled me. It troubled me that it was the work not of an old master, but of a young man only on the threshold of experience. It seemed to me that, as far as Hans was concerned anyway, the affair ran deeper than Mrs Briggs suspected. Hans had been speaking to Margaret, not with just a single flower offered every Wednesday as the girl went out to work, but every day, and with a whole garden of flowers. As the afternoon wore away an odd feeling grew on me that I was moving on fairy-tale ground, that I had no right to be there; that, fortuitously, I had become possessed of something to which I had no claim. Where was Hans now? And what were the chances of his ever seeing Margaret again?

On the following Wednesday I met Mrs Cameron. In approaching the house, and just before coming abreast of the gate, it was possible to see into a corner of the garden to the right of the path, and I had a fleeting glimpse of a pale blue dressing-gown alongside the bed where the alyssum and linaria had been planted. Why she should skip when she heard me coming I couldn't understand then, but by the time I'd got off my bicycle, crossed the footpath and opened the gate, she was already heading towards the house.

She evidently decided, though, that I was too close to be ignored, and after a few doubtful paces she stopped, looked backwards, and gave me good morning. She was a woman of medium height, slender, and rather nice-looking in a matronly kind of way. She had a gentle voice and a warm, friendly smile.

My sudden arrival seemed to have embarrassed her, and knowing that some women don't like to be caught in their dressing-gowns by male employees I kept striding out so that I would pass her quickly. She had to stand aside to leave room for the bicycle, and in the brief moment in which I met her eyes I saw nothing of that cold calculating detachment which usually meets the new man. There was something else. Something which I would hesitate to describe as fear, but which was certainly anxiety. Something which fitted in significantly with the need for her to stand aside for me — and with Mrs Briggs's story. It was symbolic, as if she recognized in me one more link in a chain of events which she dreaded, but to which she had become resigned.

I saluted her, and returned as courteous a response to her greeting as I could.

She moved her head to indicate that part of the garden she had just left, and made a remark designed merely to fill in the moment I took passing. 'I was admiring the viburnum. It's always very beautiful in the spring.'

Conversation wasn't intended, so I just nodded my approval, commented that the tree was in a particularly good position, and next moment had left her behind.

At the kitchen door, when I went to get the key of the toolshed, I found out why she had scuttled when she heard me coming.

Mrs Briggs came out in a state of suppressed excitement. 'You seen the seed yet, gardener?' she asked in a whisper.

'What seed?'

'Down near the gate.'

'I've seen nothing yet.'

'Go down and have a look at it!'

She thrust the key into my hand and listened to hear if anybody was approaching behind her. 'There's the very devil to pay. That seed Hans put in, it's in Margaret's name — just wait till you see it! I can't talk now, he's on the prowl. I think he's going to get you to dig it in. Don't go down straight away, he'd know I'd been talking to you. He's mad as a hatter. See you later...'

I was in a hurry to find out what it was all about, but I changed into my overalls, got out some tools, strolled round the garden, and finally came up alongside the bed near the front gate.

And there it was, surely as charming a tribute as ever was paid by a lover to his lady. Thousands of tiny linaria seedlings broken through in the warmth of the past week — *TO MARGARET* painted in letters of vivid green right across the square of rich brown earth.

It was magnificent, a perfect germination. Under the rays of the early morning sun it fairly rippled and glowed. I could have flung out my arms and leapt into the air with sheer excitement.

TO MARGARET. This was what Mrs Cameron had been

looking at as I reached the gate. I, too, just looked and looked and looked. I could feel Hans smiling over my shoulder. The whole story was instantly lifted to a higher level. How beautifully it was conceived, and with what loving care it had been executed! 'I told him as soon as he knocked on the door at eight o'clock,' Mrs Briggs had said. 'He was putting in some seed down near the gate when Mr Cameron went out.'

And Cameron was going to tell me to dig it in!

It would be like being told to strangle a baby or set fire to a church. I realized that I was no longer just a passive spectator; I was going to be involved, whether I liked it or not, and that within a matter of minutes.

It needed only seconds to decide I would be no party to vandalism, but I was still wrestling with the problem of how best to get out of it when, almost on the tick of nine o'clock, Cameron appeared. I was working near the house, and he called out to me from the front steps.

'Ah, Johnston!'

'Good morning, Mr Cameron.'

'One minute, please.'

I began to walk towards him, but he didn't wait for me and was halfway down the path before I caught up with him.

'There's a couple of little jobs I'd like you to do some time during the day.' At a point where a side path led off to the drive at the other side of the hedge he stopped and pointed to a rose branch which had broken loose and was hanging down about head-height. 'You'll find one or two like this. Tie them in, will you?'

I nodded. I had already seen them, and was annoyed that he thought it necessary to tell me what to do with them. Or was this just an idle preliminary?

'The other thing . . .' Stepping onto the lawn he looked down at the tell-tale seed-bed with an expression of hatred. 'I want you to turn this in and replant it.'

'You'd lose anything up to three weeks, Mr Cameron,' I said. 'That alyssum is well forward. It would be past its best when the linaria — '

'I'm aware of that, but we'd still get some kind of a show.' He was already moving away, but I tried again.

'You know, Mr Cameron, in a matter of five or six weeks you

wouldn't be able to read that. Once the plants get well up and begin to spread — '

'It's the next five or six weeks that I'm concerned about,' he interrupted coldly. Taking one hand out of his trousers pocket he stabbed towards the bed with a long slender forefinger. 'I don't approve of monkey tricks like that. Ask Mrs Briggs for the seed. I got some more during the week.'

'Very good, Mr Cameron,' I said. I still didn't intend to dig it in, but an overwhelming desire to follow the story for just one more week prevented me from quarrelling with him there and then. Only a few minutes later I was glad of that restraint. I heard the creak of the front door, and Mrs Briggs beckoned me over to the porch.

'The car's gone, hasn't it, gardener?'

'Yes, Mrs Briggs.'

'Talk quietly. She's in her room getting dressed. She's all right, but I don't want her to know I'm talking to you about it. She's coming out to see you about the seed. Did he tell you to dig it in?'

'Yes.'

'You haven't ...?'

'No.' I was going to add that I had no intention of doing so when she went on in the same urgent undertone:

'Well, wait till you've seen her. There's going to be trouble over that bed. You should have been here to see the way he went on about it. The things he said to her! I told her afterwards if it had been me I'd have put my hat on and walked straight out and left him. I'm beginning to think there's something wrong with him. She says that if he does touch it she will leave him. But she's said that before.'

'I'm not going to dig it in, Mrs Briggs. But somebody else will. He could do it himself.'

'He will, too. Nothing will stop him now that he knows she wants it. Anyway, she'll be out in a minute.'

'Any news?'

'Margaret won't come home. She's back in town. She's got a new job, but she won't tell her mother either where she's working or where she's living. She rang up yesterday. She says she doesn't want to make any more trouble.'

'And Hans?'

'Not a word. I'd better go in . . .'

Mrs Cameron came out soon afterwards. She'd made up her face and was wearing a dove-grey dress of some winter-weight material that swung gracefully as she walked. She really was quite attractive, and I guessed immediately from her relaxed manner that Mrs Briggs had said something to her about my attitude to the seed. She came to the point without any manoeuvring.

'Good morning, Mr Johnston. Did Mr Cameron say anything to you about the seed-bed near the front gate?'

'He told me to dig it in, Mrs Cameron.'

I tried to let her see, both by my tone and expression, how I myself felt about the matter. She was watching me carefully, no doubt wondering how much I knew.

'Don't you think it would be a pity?'

'Of course I do, Mrs Cameron. I don't want to touch it.'

'Would you be brave, Mr Johnston, and leave it for another week if I asked you to?' Her smile had quickened, but there was a shakiness in her voice that left me in no doubt as to who was being brave. 'Just to give me time to have another talk with him about it.'

She looked down the garden in the direction of the bed and made a few confused movements of one hand that finished up fingers to lips.

'It's just a bit of — innocent nonsense. Hans shouldn't have done it. But he's gone now. And it will be a nice show if it's left, won't it?'

'It's a perfect sowing, Mrs Cameron,' I assured her professionally, and with plenty of enthusiasm. 'And perfectly timed. It will come in just when the alyssum is at its best.'

'Then do leave it. I'll tell Mr Cameron I asked you to.'

'Thank you, Mrs Cameron. In that case I won't touch it.'

Something of the admiration I felt for her courage, and perhaps of what I knew, must have shown in my face, for she dropped her eyes suddenly and was in a hurry to leave me. Surreptitiously, I watched her walk around the garden, pick a few flowers, linger for a minute or two at the contentious bed, and go into the house. I didn't see her again.

Nor did I see much of Mrs Briggs. I was looking forward to

· To Margaret ·

getting all the details, perhaps at lunch-time, but with Mrs Cameron at home I decided to have lunch seated on a case against the sunny garage wall. All I got was a bit of hurried gossip from the old lady when I took my billy to the kitchen door. She told me that things had 'just about come to a head' inside.

'She doesn't tell me everything, you know, gardener, but the night before last I heard her threaten to leave the house herself if he doesn't do something to bring Margaret back. He just laughed at her. He knows she hasn't a penny of her own. I was listening in the hall. "You're frightening me, Barbara!" he said, and next minute he turned the wireless on full blast. And her sobbing her eyes out on the sofa. It's like a morgue here now. It was only Margaret that made it possible for anybody else to stay in the house with him. Mind you don't let anything slip when you're talking to them.'

'Don't worry about me, Mrs Briggs.'

I had already told her about Mrs Cameron's request not to dig the seed in. 'Anyway, next Wednesday will probably see the end of me here.'

She gave me a troubled look. 'There's not much doubt about that. He's a man that just won't be crossed.'

'I'm not Mrs Cameron!'

'That poor woman! It'll be dreadful tonight when he comes in. He'll go and look at that bed before he puts a foot inside the house. I didn't think she'd dare do it, but it's about time she stood up to him. You'd better go — she's just in the dining-room.'

Throughout the rest of the day that bed of seedlings drew me like a magnet. My work was all at the other end of the garden, but time and again I went down just for the sheer joy of looking at it. It thrilled me that Mrs Cameron had proved to have enough of the woman in her to see in it something peculiarly precious and beautiful. Margaret was her daughter, and there was nothing to indicate that she was anything but mildly amused over Hans's infatuation, but — blessings on her! — she wasn't going to see it dug in like a dead cat. I had no doubt that in the hour or so between my departure and Cameron's homecoming she would be down there, poring over it again as she had been at eight o'clock in the morning, dreaming over it, investing it, perhaps, with all the poetry and colour she herself had ever been denied in that house of tyranny.

I was old enough to know better, but I too had dreams. There was a spell on the place, and as the hours passed it grew on me, with musings that began merely as charming fantasies and ended with an element of tragedy. Everything dies, and I saw Hans's message not only as it was that day, but as it would be tomorrow if Cameron spared it, and the day after, and every day until it burned itself out.

Hans must have known that his love for the girl could never be anything but hopeless, and something out of Thomas Carlyle kept coming back to me, Louis XVI's farewell to Marie Antoinette: 'And thou, dear soul, I shall never, never through all the ages of time, see again.'

What else could Hans have been thinking when he wrote his living message? It was easy to picture his youthful face bent over the friendly soil, his fingers moving swiftly with every bit of skill that was in them.

And here it is. Hans is gone, and Margaret is gone, but the quiet garden is full of their presence, and every day that passes the symbol will grow and grow. The little plants will push out, tumbling over and filling in the spaces between the letters. And as the name itself vanishes something else will take the place of form, and the message will lose nothing in eloquence. There will be colour, all the tender pastel shades of a flower I know well, framed in the deep lilac of alyssum. And to the understanding eye it will never read anything but *TO MARGARET*. And when the hot winds of summer come, and the exhausted plants huddle closer to the earth with every shower of rain, it will still be Hans who is speaking ...

I didn't dig it in. But I took what I knew was a long farewell look at it that evening as I passed out by the gate.

On the following Wednesday it was indeed gone.

Even though I was prepared, there was a stab of something keener than disappointment as I stood on the path and looked over at the naked soil within the alyssum. It wasn't merely desolate, it was offensive. A challenge. I could well imagine Cameron observing my arrival from one of the windows: 'That'll teach you!'

To her for whom it was really intended it must have been agony, like having the mutilated body of someone well loved laid at her feet.

I went on up to the house hating Cameron from the bottom of my heart, and ripe for trouble as I'd never been ripe for it before.

At the kitchen all was silent. I had to knock twice before Mrs Briggs came hurrying in from regions beyond. The inner door was open. I couldn't see anything through the fly-wire screen, but her laboured breathing and scuffling footfalls reached me seconds before her urgent 'Sssh, gardener! I'm coming.'

She opened the door as if she were dead scared of being seen talking to me. Her eyes were red and puffed from weeping, and her hand trembled as she gave me the key.

'I don't think you'll want it for long. He's mad about that seed.'

'He dug it in?'

'Sssh! He did it that very night. She's gone.'

'Mrs Cameron?'

'The very next morning, the minute he turned his back. I'll have to get out too, it's like a madhouse. He didn't think she would. It's given him a shock — not so sure of himself — he's walking the floor half the night.' She glanced fearfully over her shoulder. 'We'd better not stand —'

It was a fair indication of the nature of the man that even in those circumstances he still waited until nine o'clock before coming out to face me. I'd made up my mind to 'have a piece of him', as the good Australian phrase goes, and had, therefore, confined my activities to a few minor jobs which could be cleared up at a minute's notice. All these activities were deliberately chosen in the vicinity of the alyssum bed.

I was sweeping up fallen leaves on the path when I heard the front door open and his long firm stride begin to approach. Right to the last second I kept my attention on my work, struggling with a growing excitement.

But the moment I looked at him there was an unexpected reaction. I felt pity. There was the same rigid arrogant stance, the same tight lines around jaw and lips, the same scowling forehead. But something else was missing. Something of last week's icy calm. I'd have known without having been told that he was losing sleep. His eyes were heavy and inexpressibly weary, and instead of the stare of stern accusation I'd been expecting there was doubt, as if he were trying to reconcile something in my appearance with something he'd heard about me — or with something I'd done.

'Good morning, Mr Cameron,' I said carefully.

He was looking past me now at the newly smoothed surface of the alyssum bed. I nodded towards it. 'I've just planted it again.'

I waited, giving him time to decide whether or not we brought Mrs Cameron into it, and to my satisfaction he just grunted. Then I caught the sudden intake of breath, the almost imperceptible squaring of the strong shoulders, the vindictive brightening of the tired eyes. And I realized that he was deliberately disciplining himself, and that any pangs of regret from which he might be suffering would not extend to me. He was as full of fight as I was, and if anything in the nature of compromise or reconciliation within the home was contemplated no mere gardener was going to be a witness of it.

'I suppose you realize', he said harshly, 'that we've lost a precious week through your failure to carry out my instructions of last Wednesday?'

This is it, I thought. No half-measures, Johnston!

'Then why the hell didn't you sow it yourself? You dug it.'

His head jerked backwards ever so slightly, but he took it precisely as I expected him to. 'I see,' he said quietly, and kept on looking at me for what became an embarrassingly long time. His face twitched as if, of all things, he was going to smile. 'So that's how you feel about the job?' he asked at length.

'That's how I feel about you,' I said.

'All right.' Still with no sign of annoyance, he felt in an inside pocket and took out a wallet. 'Half a day. That's probably more than I'm obliged to give you in the circumstances. You can put away your tools and go home.'

And that was all. Ten minutes later I wheeled my bicycle down the path for the third and last time. Near the gate I paused to look again at the little bed, speckled now with a few fallen white petals of viburnum.

For I also had left a message in flowers: *TO BARBARA.*

· Tinkle, Tinkle, Little Bell ·

Drunks — like gaspers, alarm clocks, barbed wire, the internal combustion engine, and a few other things consequent on man's determination to make his stay on earth as delightful as possible — are always with us.

Particularly on suburban railway trains.

They come in all moods: fighting, singing, sleeping, weeping. We could get along without them, especially at the end of a working shift, when all we want to do is snatch forty winks, read the paper, talk to a sympathetic friend, or just ruminate. Now and then, however, you strike one that's worth while. And almost invariably it's the fixed-idea drunk. I don't mean the fixed idea that comes out of a bottle. Superficially, every drunk has a fixed idea, but in ninety-nine cases out of a hundred it doesn't go beyond wanting to sing his favourite song, recite his favourite poem, or knock the block off some innocent who's been caught with the wrong expression on his face.

I don't mean that kind. I mean the fixed idea that comes up from deep down and has plenty behind it. The still reasonably articulate drunk losing control of something he's forever wrestling with when stone cold sober.

Like the fellow I met one day on the Lilydale line.

He was already there when I boarded the train at Hawthorn, occupying the end of a three-seater in a not-overcrowded Tate carriage. Another passenger was in the window-seat, with the two of them so correctly disposed that it was evident the middle seat had just been vacated. My eyes were on it as I got in, but something in the way I was being observed by the man on the end warned me, and in the nick of time I sheered off and sank into the only other empty place, which happened to be on the long cushion directly facing. Quick as my reaction was the fellow was right on to it, for when I lifted my head after composing myself I found him waiting for me. Yes, waiting for me. I'd done something he didn't approve of and, true to his kind, he wasn't going to let me get away with it.

He was a man of about fifty. Fairly well dressed: grey lounge suit, black shoes, crisply laundered white shirt, tie in good taste, greying hair still slicked in a neat side-parting. Altogether a type that could reasonably be described as respectable. On the rack over the window-seat were a few things that fitted him: hat, brief-case, a Myer-wrapped parcel, and a bunch of carnations. He did have too much drink in, though, and he did have blue eyes. I've always found blue eyes a bit unpredictable. Lit by the fires of alcohol they can be quite disturbing.

They disturbed me that day the instant I looked into them. They weren't resting on me, they were fixing me. And slightly narrowed by a sneering smile that said everything.

I turned away, but in the absence of anything to read it wasn't easy to pretend, and when a few seconds later I faced him again he was still on to me. I risked a return stare that time, but primed as he was he had no trouble in seeing me out, and we rocked along to Glenferrie in a silence which I felt was beginning to hold possibilities.

Every other nose in the compartment, except one, was buried in a book or paper, from which I gathered I'd be left for dead if anything developed. Perhaps they'd had enough of Mr Carnation, and regarded me as a heaven-sent diversion.

From the one exception nothing could be hoped for. It was a little girl perched on the end of the two-seat cushion, just across the alleyway from Carnation. A rather demure little girl, with her mother in attendance. It was around Christmas time, and they looked as though they'd been to a break-up party. Mum was nursing a clown's paper hat, and a shopping bag with a packet of fancy biscuits and a toy-carton sticking out of it. The little girl's hands, resting in her lap, held a toy bell, a miniature of the kind they ring in school playgrounds.

The only time between Glenferrie and Auburn that Carnation took his attention off me was to glance at the girl. He did it as if suddenly recollecting something, and seemed to be disappointed to find that she was talking to Mum. There was the beginning of a smile on his face, but it vanished on the instant, and he came back to me more intense than ever, his brows thoughtfully puckered. Possibly the little girl had been involved in whatever was going on before my arrival, and I was being held responsible for interrupting it.

At Glenferrie I thought for a moment that relief had come. One passenger, the man on my left, got out, and two people came in. They were a young couple, but in my preoccupation I didn't immediately observe that they were together. The girl took the seat next to me, while the youth sat down between Carnation and the man in the window-seat. Everybody looked them over, then went back to their reading. Girl and youth sat stiffly, exchanging weak smiles. Sitting together can be very important to the young, and they were silently commiserating with each other. The girl even went so far as to stand up and look along the carriage to see if there was a double-empty somewhere else. Evidently there wasn't, and she resumed her seat with a shrug of the shoulders that communicated itself to me like a message. Opposite us, her companion was making faces at her: 'Never mind, sweetheart, somebody will get off in a minute.'

Carnation was missing nothing. To my own relief he was taking quite a bit of interest in the newcomers, and manifestly getting a perverse pleasure out of their discomfiture. He looked down at the young fellow's knees alongside him, then at the girl, deliberately connecting them. His smile was more than smug; it was malicious.

The solution was too obvious to be ignored, but before I could act the girl herself took the matter in hand. She was quite pretty, and leaning forward with an engaging smile she asked Carnation if he would change places with her: 'You wouldn't mind, would you?'

Carnation did mind. I believe he'd seen the request coming, and had been fairly licking his lips in anticipation. He didn't speak. He just slowly shook his head, staring heavily at the girl with an insolent 'so-what're-you-going-to-do-about-it' kind of grin.

She tried again, no doubt thinking he was just teasing her.

'Please? And you come over here.'

'I'm all right where I am.' Then, to clear the decks for real action, he transferred the dispute to her escort. 'I've been sitting here all the way from Flinders Street.'

'That's all right, sir,' said the young man brightly. 'Don't worry.'

'Worry? I've got nothing to worry about.'

I couldn't see the girl's face, but felt her slide back into the seat resigned to defeat. No doubt she was a bit red in the face.

It's true, of course, that all the world loves a lover, even on a suburban railway train. So I acted.

There was no need to say anything. I just tapped the young fellow on the knee, got up, and stood aside for him to move over. He protested, of course, but he did take it, probably under some urging from the girl, for when I sat down alongside Carnation she rewarded me with a dazzling smile. It isn't often you get a chance to play Santa Claus to young love.

At the same time I was well aware that I'd made an enemy for life. Trying to appear unconcerned, I occupied myself with filling my pipe, but was painfully conscious of the deliberate slewing of my new neighbour's head and the heat of those unpredictable blue eyes. He kept it up for a long time. Until, indeed, my pipe was filled and I'd taken the first few puffs. I was getting a bit browned off myself by then. A few newspapers had been lowered along the opposite seat, and the young couple, now hand in hand, were watching the situation with some anxiety.

So I faced him. Surely *all* the world loves a lover...

Not Carnation. He'd been outflanked, and he wasn't going to let me get away with it. The blue eyes were fairly sizzling. The corners of his mouth drooped sardonically. He didn't say a word, but he might as well have shouted it at me: you think you're smart, eh?

I shrugged my shoulders and turned away so as not to blow smoke into his face. After a few more tense seconds he relaxed, and took a careful survey of the compartment, finishing up with the little girl with the bell. The back of his head was towards me, but he must have been smiling, for the child giggled, then looked down self-consciously at the toy in her lap.

'Go on, dear,' he urged in a wheedling voice, 'ring it again.'

The child fidgeted and looked up to make sure that Mum

• Tinkle, Tinkle, Little Bell • 21

wasn't forgetting her. She certainly wasn't afraid of him, though, and it seemed that the little bell also had been involved in whatever comedy was taking place before I joined the party.

'Go on, dear, ring it.'

The child giggled again, and snuggled a little closer to her mother.

'It's all right. It's a nice sound. I like it. Softly tolls the little bell — ever teach you that song at school?'

Mum also was quite unconcerned. 'Tell him no,' she prompted pleasantly. 'It's only little Russian girls who learn that song.'

'Aha, Mummy knows!' Carnation began to hum 'The Volga Boatman', but broke off after the first toneless bar and went back to the bell. 'Aren't you going to ring it? Come on, just one more teeny weeny little shake.'

Everybody was now watching. One or two disapprovingly, but all the others looking as though they were ready to laugh. I also had relaxed. He seemed to have forgotten me, and the little bell didn't seem to be a very dangerous fixed idea.

'One more little ring, just to please me . . .'

'Go on, darling, make the gentleman laugh again. We're getting off at the next station.'

That wasn't so good for me, but it brought results. The child looked at Mum. Then, rather impishly, at Carnation. He made the appropriate gesture, and thus encouraged she rang the bell. No half-measures. She did it just as a child would in such circumstances. Swiftly, vigorously, and with reckless daring. Then, overcome by shyness, she buried her face in Mother's coat.

It was a pleasant tinkle, correctly elicited and charmingly performed. Everybody chuckled, even the two who had been keeping straight faces. Several heads bobbed up over the back of the seat to see what all the fun was about.

The effect on Carnation was astonishing. He gave a shout of joy, rocked with laughter, throwing his head back against the cushions, stamping his feet, and slapping his thighs.

'Darling, you'll kill me! Do it again — do it again! You've got no idea — tinkle, tinkle, little bell! So help me bob it was exactly like that . . .'

All eyes were on him, but nobody seemed to be particularly

startled, only amused. Apparently they'd seen it before. I had no idea what it was all about, only that Carnation evidently connected the ringing of the bell with some side-splitting experience all his own.

He went red in the face, laughed so much that he began to cough, and was still spluttering into his handkerchief when we pulled into East Camberwell. Mother and child got off there. It was almost an affectionate farewell, with Carnation coming out of his mirth long enough to congratulate the mother on having such a charming daughter, and the child herself turning in the doorway to blow him a kiss.

The after-effects lasted all the way to Mont Albert, with a few passengers joining here and there, but more leaving, so that the compartment was gradually getting empty. The courting couple had slid down to the end of the long seat, nicely removed now from further embarrassment.

I myself wasn't only relaxed — I was beginning to enjoy Carnation. At the same time I knew that anything could happen once he got the little bell out of his mind. My hopes rose, though, soon after we left Box Hill, when he got his breath back again.

'Tinkle, tinkle, little bell!' He fetched me a hearty nudge in the side with his elbow. 'You've got no idea how funny that was. Children — the innocence of them! If Mummy only knew!'

This set him off once more, and I had to wait until he'd finished coughing into his handkerchief. 'There's something good behind all this?' I suggested encouragingly.

'Good?' He looked me full in the face. 'You're telling me! Listen . . .' He stopped, threw a glance at the courting couple, and changed his mind. 'No, I can't, not now. But, oh dear, if you only knew!' And off he went again into another prolonged chortle.

Apparently there was an element of ribaldry in the story, which immediately set me wondering how far he was going, or how far the courting couple were going. Speculation on these points made me forget my own danger, and it came as a shock when, just after leaving Blackburn, he returned to the attack. All had been quiet over the last few miles, with only ourselves and the young people left in the compartment.

Tinkle, Tinkle, Little Bell

'That wasn't a very nice thing you did on me, you know,' said a peevish voice right into my ear.

All the fun was over. His mouth drooped again; the blue eyes were heavy-lidded. I realized also for the first time that he'd been putting away something more potent than beer.

'You aren't angry with me, are you?' I countered cheerfully.

'How would you feel if somebody did that on you?'

'You'd have done it yourself if I'd given you time,' I said diplomatically. I nodded discreetly towards the far corner. 'Just look at them — you wouldn't be a nark, would you?'

While I'd been pleasantly ruminating he'd been brooding, for he was right back to where he'd started from, the drunk with a grievance. 'How do you know I'm not a nark?'

'That little girl — the bell...'

'That's got nothing to do with it. I'm talking about what you did when they came in. You made a nanny out of me.'

'I had no intention of doing anything of the kind.'

'You're one of these little gentlemen, aren't you?'

'I think you would be too...'

'You reckon?' He smiled, a slow twisted smile full of bitter disbelief. He shook his head. 'No, cobber, you're wrong. You wouldn't get me giving up my place to a woman. Not if she were ninety. Not if she were pregnant.'

'I think you do yourself an injustice.'

His smile became a snarl. 'You'd know, of course, wouldn't you?'

I had time to digest that one, because at that moment we ran into Nunawading and the young couple got off. Two men came in, took the same seats, and promptly resumed a conversation of their own. Carnation returned immediately to the business in hand.

'Eh?'

'What was it you said?'

'I said: you'd know, wouldn't you? I'd give my place to a woman?'

'Well, wouldn't you?'

'No!' It would be difficult to convey the decisiveness he put into the one word. He continued to stare at me after it was uttered, his lips holding the pout, his blue eyes cold as ice.

'You're a bit sour on women?' I suggested.

'I've got good reason to be sour on women. Chivalry — don't you talk to me about chivalry!' He began to act, taking on a flat humourless smile, dropping his voice to an ingratiating whine, making stagy gestures with his hands. 'Allow me, madam! After you, lady! Take a seat, Miss! Wipe your feet on me — bah, don't you come that fair sex business with me! They just burn us up. Listen, I'll tell you something . . .'

I realized by now, of course, that I was doomed, but only to boredom. Something else had become the target.

'Go on, I'm listening.'

'It cost me ten thousand quid once, giving my place to a woman.' He waited, leaving plenty of time for the enormity of the misfortune to sink in.

'Ten thousand pounds?'

'Ten thousand pounds, every cracker of it.'

'How?'

'In a Tatts queue.'

I began to see. 'She got your ticket?'

'She got my ticket. Ten thousand quid. One Saturday morning in Flinders Street. You know what it's like in there on Saturday mornings. She could have picked on anybody, but it had to be me. The old, old story: she had a train to catch. Would I mind if she went in front of me? Always the little gentleman — I let her in. And she got the ticket I'd have got: ten thousand quid. I got the next one, one off the winner. Wouldn't it?'

'Wouldn't it.'

'You still think I'm a nark?'

'I never did think you were a nark. I can understand your feelings.'

'You still think I should give up my place to a woman?'

'No!' Disputation in such circumstances would have been suicidal.

That satisfied him so far as I was concerned, but he remained sunk in reminiscent gloom, no doubt going over for the ten-thousandth time all the things he could have done with those ten thousand pounds. I kept silent, watching his bowed head, the sad profile of his face. Presently he began to smile, as if his thoughts had run into pleasanter channels. He shook his head, muttered to himself, chuckled, then remembered that I was still there.

'Tinkle, tinkle, little bell! I got my own back that time.'

'The bell?' I prompted, no longer bored.

'Not that one. No, another little bell, exactly like it. Tinkle, tinkle ...' His joy got the better of him, and once again he slapped his thighs and burst out laughing. 'I fixed her!'

'Who?' The miles were slipping past, and I badly wanted the story now.

'The one in the waiting-room. Listen ...' He glanced indifferently at the two men, then stood up and peeped over to see who was at the other side of our partition. Reassured, he sat down again and got his chuckles under control. 'Ever had a blood-test?' he demanded unexpectedly.

'No, I can't say I have.'

'They put you through it if they find sugar in your water. To see if you're a diabetic. Well, I had one once. Specialist in Collins Street, my local quack sent me in. Poky little place up on a top floor, but everything very — you know, pukka. You ever been ...'

'I've never been to a specialist.'

'Always by appointment. No waiting, like the hospitals. Receptionist — present your letter — nurse — nice waiting-room — "Please sit down, sir, and we'll call you in a minute." Just like that. So it should be, you're paying plenty. Well, in I went, first up one morning. Nobody else there. Cosy little room with a radiator going. I needed that, too. I'd come all the way in from Coburg on a tram, and there was a frost. No breakfast either, they've got to do these tests on an empty tummy.

'Nine o'clock comes, and right on the bat up pops the nurse. "This way, please, Mr Jackson." Into another room, only a few yards down a passage. "Take off your coat, please, and roll up your sleeve." One good prick, and a few drops of blood into a test tube. Same thing on the lobe of one ear. She didn't have to tell me what was next. I'd seen the bottle on the trolley the minute I walked in. Hospital bottle, with a little bell alongside it. Mustn't forget the bell! Sure enough, up it comes: "That will do for now, Mr Jackson, except ...", and she points to the bottle. "I'd like a specimen of urine. I'll leave you here, and when you've finished just ring the bell and go back to the waiting-room. I'll call you again in half an hour."

'Good enough. I rang the bell — it was exactly like that little girl's — then went back to the waiting-room. Still nobody there, so I turned the radiator to my feet so that I was getting the full good of it, and settled down for a nice quiet read. Still with me?'

'Yes, I'm still with you.' His speech was a bit thick, but easy to follow. He had it all so pat, indeed, that it was evident I was listening to an oft-told tale.

'After about five minutes in comes another patient. Female, young, pretty, and got up like a mannequin. A real show-piece. Blonde, big eyes, good figure. Natty little hat and the latest cut in overcoats. Umbrella, gloves, handbag, all matching. And a scent that filled the whole room the minute she walked in. Right, now get on to this. I was in the box-seat, fair in the middle of a big settee, out of any draughts, and with the radiator really giving me the works. There were three armchairs on the opposite wall, but they weren't getting anything. Follow?'

'Yes . . .'

'And this piece looked as cold as a frog, for all her get-up. So I did what any gentleman would have done. And, mind you, this was after the ten thousand quid business. I still hadn't learned. I didn't even think. I just threw her a bright smile and moved along to the end of the settee. I also wished her good morning. But d'you think she'd play? Not on your life! She just gave me a stare as much as to ask what the hell I was doing there, and who the hell did I think I was talking to. No smile. No good morning. She just stalked across to one of the armchairs, the one farthest away from me, laid her stumpy little umbrella across her knees, crossed one leg over the other, and ignored me.'

As the story developed Carnation had become increasingly earnest and coherent. The memory of the experience evidently rankled deep.

'How long ago did this happen?' I asked, and he read me like an open book.

'Not so very long ago! Don't you worry, I'm awake to these birds. She'd have sat beside me all right if I'd been a young buck. I just didn't interest her, that's all, so she wiped me off like a dirty rag. She did worse than that — she insulted me.'

'Insulted you?'

'She pulled her skirts down!'

'Well . . .'

'Spare me days, you must have had it done to you some time! If there's one thing I'm hostile on it's these women who sit down facing you, wait till they catch your eye, and then pull their skirts over their knees. That's what this one did. There was only the two of us there, you know, that's what made it bad. I'm not saying there was anything wrong with her legs — they were well turned, believe me — but I was old enough to be her father. Anyway, that's what she did. Then she gave me a cold stare, as much as to say: "Now then, Jack the Ripper, find something else to look at!" Wouldn't it have annoyed you?'

'I think it would.'

'It annoyed me, but I let it go at first. She had the drop on me if I started anything. But after a minute or two I got the idea of seeing how much of a bitch she really was. That's my form, you know — keep on paying the rope out. Particularly since that ten thousand quid business. Get me?'

'Yes, go on.'

'Well, I leaned forward and turned the radiator sideways so she would get the good of it too. And I gave her another bright smile. "I'm taking it all," I said, "and you look cold." Now, you tell me, did I do the right thing?'

'Of course you did.'

'But d'you think she'd come in? Not on your life! Up goes her little nose. "I'm quite all right, thank you," she snapped. And that was it. I gave up. I even apologized for intruding on her, turned the radiator back where it was, and got stuck into my book again. Pretended to, anyway. I was too mad to read. She'd made me feel like a bloody pervert, and she knew it. I didn't look at her again, but I could feel her sitting there all the time. She had me so worked up I was scared. I felt that if I as much as moved she'd scream for help.' Carnation broke off to look out of the window. 'Was that Croydon we just went through?'

'Yes.'

'I'll have to hurry. I get off at Mooroolbark. Well, after a few minutes in pops the nurse: "Miss Bandbox, will you come this way please?" And up gets Bandbox and follows her out. Golly, it was like getting a boil off the neck. Everything nice and peaceful again. I just lay back and closed my eyes, and got thinking of what I was going to do the minute I got out — head for the nearest restaurant and order bacon and eggs and a whole pot of tea. I was even looking forward to the nurse calling me again. You know what nurses are like, it's their job to pet you a bit. You know it's all blarney, but it's nice just the same. And this one had a real nurse's smile — worth a pint of anybody's blood. It was quiet, too, quiet as a church after the door in the passage closed. You could have heard a pin drop.'

The brakes were going on. Carnation threw a glance at the luggage-rack, reminding himself of his belongings. 'Then I heard it! Very faint, but I heard it — the little bell!' He drew in a great breath and once again began to rock and splutter. 'Tinkle, tinkle . . .'

I don't really know how funny it is, but he'd prepared the ground so well that it got into me. The image of Bandbox was too vivid. I also began to chuckle. That pleased him, and as we ran into Mooroolbark he lurched to his feet, grabbed me by one shoulder to steady himself, and puffed his whisky-laden breath right into my face.

'I had her! I knew — she was all mine, all mine! When she walked in, all stiff and dignified, I was right on to her. I didn't move. I just gave her the works from where I was sitting. The smile on the face of the tiger . . .'

He staggered as the train came to a standstill, and I got up to help him collect his possessions. Time was running out . . .

'How did she take it?'

'Take it? She couldn't take it. She tried, mind you. She even got to her seat and put her leg up again. But she couldn't get off the hook. I just sat there watching her with a nice matey grin . . .'

'So?' I had him by one elbow, piloting him towards the door.

'She shot through. Gave it away. I don't know what tale she put over the girl at the desk, but she didn't come back. I fixed her.'

He was on the platform. I handed him his bunch of carnations. 'Goodbye, friend, and good luck!'

'So-long, cobber!' He stepped backwards as we moved off, and wagged a wavering forefinger at me. 'See you take a lesson — never give up your place to a woman — never . . .' I lost sight of him.

Who am I to judge? Ten thousand pounds is a lot of money.

· Easy Money ·

We've worked all night, loading 'small' flour into the *Jaipur* at Berth Eight Victoria Dock.

Just before seven o'clock, finishing time, the foreman comes along the deck and speaks to Clarrie Carr, our hatchman. I'm standing a few yards away and can't hear what he says, but I do hear Clarrie's reply:

'Ask them yourself. That's your job, not mine.'

The foreman casts a doubtful eye over the six of us. We're up level with the deck at the for'ard end of the hatch, stowing between the beams, which have just been placed in position. He picks on Clements, not because he's nearest, but because he looks the least aggressive. He shows bad judgement.

'How about you fellows? Will you work a breakfast hour?'

'Better see the gang-leader,' says Clements. 'He's on the wharf.'

'I've seen him. He says it's all right with the wharf hands.'

'It always is with them hungry bastards.' A lascar seaman places a piece of bamboo matting against the nearest beam, and Clements expertly hits it with a bag of flour. 'Hear that, you blokes?'

They all stop, looking at Clements and the foreman.

'We've got to work a breakfast hour.'

'I didn't say you'd got to,' protested the foreman. 'I'm asking you.'

'You've got the wharf-crowd in, haven't you? That's eight. And two deck-hands —' The winch drivers, perched one at each side of the foot of the mast, keep expressionless faces, as if they can't hear a word. They haven't been lumping flour all night. 'That's ten out of a gang of seventeen.' Clements turns his back. 'As far as I'm concerned the answer's no. I've got a good bed waiting for me.'

29

Payment for every hour worked after seven o'clock without a meal break is 13s as against 7s 8d ordinary nightshift time, but 'breakfast hours' are still not popular these days. Not with the men who work below, anyway; we've always had it when seven o'clock comes.

In this case, however, and with the exception of Clements, nobody minds much, because it looks like a bit of easy money. There have been rumours all night of a big lift going into the empty after end of our hold. It means that the ship would have to be moved round to the big crane at the end of the dock, during which time we could do what we liked — at 13s an hour. They can't dump us and start us again at their own sweet will, as they did in the old days.

Clarrie looks at me and Bob Grainger. 'What about it?'

'I'm easy,' I tell him, 'but a seven o'clock finish would do me.'

'Me too,' says Grainger. 'Let 'em get one of the other gangs. Hatch Four's still working, isn't it?'

'Tell him we'll work it, and be done with it!' shouts Mick Anstey from the other side of the deck. He's flinging bags of flour off the tray as if he has a personal grievance against each one of them. 'Standing there nattering like a pack of bloody old women. It would be two hours before we got finished. The tug isn't even here yet. Twenty-six bob for standing by for twenty minutes while they land one lousy case. By cripes, I'll be in that!'

The foreman goes off to tell the supervisor, while we throw the last bags into the spaces between the beams.

'How many more d'you want?' asks Clarrie.

'Half a tray'll be enough,' someone tells him.

We wait, half asleep on our feet while the empty tray swings out over the wharf. The morning sun is too bright on eyes red and weary under the heavy dusted lids. Nobody is smoking. Men smoke too much on nightshift. We've smoked ourselves sick. What we want now is something hot and strong in the mouth, like good coffee. A smell of it coming from the galley — the officers' galley — under the superstructure makes us lick our dry lips.

Lascar seamen, busy on their early morning tasks, drag their slippered brown feet to and fro along the deck, still steaming

· Easy Money ·

from the hosing it received an hour ago. All the length of the dock a cloak of mist covers the dark water, as if a fire is burning under it. It's Sunday morning, and very little noise comes from the sleeping city. We hear the tramp of the gang from Hatch Four as they come for'ard to the gangway and clatter ashore — finished. It makes us feel lonely.

The half-tray, about fifty bags, comes aboard. All six of us swarm around it, and in a final flurry of white dust the last bags thump into place. The English first mate comes out to stand watching us and enjoy his first pipe as we put hatchboards on at the for'ard end and take them off at the after end, covering up the flour, and exposing the deep black hole where the big lift is to go. I experience a thrill of pride as I look at the white shingle wall of the 'break'. There are fifty thousand bags of flour in that end of the hatch, and they've been built up with a face as straight and snug and tight as the side of a house. The after end cargo, to be taken in at Geelong, comes out first at Surabaya, but our flour isn't likely to shift while the vessel runs the last leg of the voyage to Semarang, two hundred miles or so further along the Java coast. There's an art in building a 'standing break', and by tacit consent the placing of those outermost bags is always left to Anstey and Clements, one working from either side of the hatch. They'd be picking at each other if they were both here now, but Mick is at the galley door with Clarrie's big billy, looking for coffee. He gets it, as he always does, and we gather round him with our pannikins on the covered end of the hatch.

'How did you blokes manage to live before I joined the gang?' he grumbles as we fill up.

George Blair and a few other wharf hands, not knowing we have coffee, come aboard with their two-gallon community milk-can full of tea. Bags are opened and left-overs from supper brought out.

It's good sitting here in the warm sunshine after the toil of the night. One's legs get weary walking to and fro for nine hours over the yielding bags. The last night is always the worst, filling out under the deck-head. Even when you know there's enough clearance you keep your head down, over-conscious from long experience of the steel ribs above. There's a saying that you can always tell an old wharfie by the bald patch on top; a man keeps forgetting until he's had the skin taken off a few times.

However, the hot coffee and tea put new life into us, restore the flavour of tobacco. Some of the younger fellows curl up on tarpaulins and coils of rope and go to sleep. The rest of us get talking. Conversation turns on the practice of giving men their pay in envelopes, commenced on the waterfront only last week.

'By God, it was funny at the 'Pound last Thursday!' laughs George Blair. 'See all the envelopes lying on the floor? I'll lay the odds there wasn't one man in ten took his packet home.'

'The women'll soon be on to that —'

'Depends on where you live,' says an old wharf hand seriously. 'Women in Port and Williamstown know the wage rates as well as we do. A bloke living in Heidelberg or Murrumbeena's got an open slather. His missus never meets other wharfies' wives down the street to check up with.'

'A married man that taps his pay's a bastard,' says Clarrie.

'Depends what kind of a missus he's got, doesn't it?' says Mick Anstey. 'I know blokes that would be flat out getting the price of a smoke back if they took the whole packet home.'

'Well, what's wrong with standing up for what they're entitled to? I don't care whether they lack principle or guts — they're no good either way. I take my wad home every week just as I get it, hook two quid out in front of the wife, and give her the rest.'

'What about when you have a bad week?'

'I do the right thing. My missus trusts me. If there ain't enough I take less.'

'There's never enough for mine,' says one of the winch drivers gloomily.

'Then you know what to do about it —'

'And if she finds out about the pay envelopes, tell her you're a staff man, a gin-block winder, a yardarm bungerupper — anything. What would she know about it? We had a bloke in the last gang told his wife he had to work a year's probation before he got full money.'

'He must have lived out in the scrub —'

Stories tumble fast one over another. Appreciative chuckles run around the group of idle men.

'Remember Sam Wollan? Worked the *Troja* with us. He hardly took a cracker home for a month. Told his missus he'd broke a winch and had to pay for it out of his wages —'

'That's nothing. I know a bloke that come on the wharf and peeled off ten bob every week for six months. Told his wife he had to provide his own truck, rope-slings and crowbar.'

'That still ain't as good as a bloke I know. Whenever he wanted a bit extra he'd tell his wife he'd been working the port side of the ship — less dough. And when she wanted to know why, he gave her such a lecture on stanchions and goosenecks and shackles and overhead plumbs that she wished to Christ she'd never opened her mouth.'

'Bill Revelle's wasn't a bad lurk. His wife got talking down the street one morning with some other wharfie's wife. It come out that Bill and the other bloke had put in exactly the same hours, and when Bill got home that night his wife tackled him. Wanted to know how he'd got a quid less than the man up the street. Bill did some quick thinking — looked at her like she was mad. "And I suppose", he says, full of sarcasm, "Mrs Bloody Brown didn't tell you Charlie was working the *Oronsay* at Prince's Pier, and I'm on the *Woniora* up the river? Spare me days! You could jam the *Woniora* up the *Oronsay*'s funnel. You think they're going to pay the same dough for that lousy little packet?" And away he goes to square off with Charlie before anything else comes out.'

'And what a bright crowd you've got there!' Clarrie Carr's voice rises. 'Sam Wollan — Spider O'Neale — Mallee Robertson — Darky Hands — I know every lousy one of 'em. Hands' kids are always hanging round my joint for a square feed. One day last week . . .'

He gets a fair hearing. Logic and decency are all on his side, and they know it, for all their rough jesting. The debate comes right back to a question of ethics. And dies out, for there is nothing to argue about. It's Sunday morning, anyway, and we've been working all night. Two more men have stretched out and gone to sleep. I place my rolled-up coat under my head and lie back pleasantly relaxed, watching four seamen up in the trucks of the for'ard mast leisurely stowing the derricks of Hatch Two. There's no sensation of movement, but I know we've left the wharf. A few minutes ago I heard the churning of the propeller of the tug as it backed in to take the tow-rope. There was a shouting of orders from the bridge, a dragging in of shore-lines, a shuffle of slippers, a chatter of outlandish voices.

Tommy Swain, a young fellow who came to the waterfront only three months ago in search of the big money he'd been reading about in the newspapers, remarks, with a casualness that deceives none of us: 'I bet they don't keep us hanging around too long on thirteen bob an hour.'

'Why?' asks Mick Anstey coldly.

'Seventeen men at thirteen shillings an hour! Not to mention the buck. It's a packet, isn't it?'

'You think the shipowners might not be able to afford it?'

'Well, it is a lot, isn't it? And we're doing sweet nothing.'

'You think the national economy might not be able to afford it?' Anstey's voice is loaded with irony. Sparring up for the kill. We all know his form. He forgets that the young generation has to learn what makes the clock tick, just as he had to.

But George Blair, who has held a good gang together for a long time, gets in first. 'Take it with an easy conscience, son,' he says in his gentle way. 'I'll work out what the freight charges on this flour come to if you like. It would pay a lot more than thirteen shillings an hour if it was properly whacked up. You earned thirteen bob an hour all last night, but you didn't get it. I've been on this waterfront twenty-seven years. The shipowners would never get out of my debt, not if they kept me in blessed idleness all the rest of my bloody life.'

Anstey knows he has been headed off. 'The shipowners ain't paying this anyway,' he says stubbornly. 'They're still on the ten per cent cost plus, ain't they? D'you think they care? I've seen gangs sitting around waiting for cargo for three hours —'

'Breakfast hours?' Tommy Swain, still incredulous — and hopeful.

Half a dozen voices support Anstey.

'Too right in breakfast hours!'

'You ain't seen nothing yet, son.'

'I've seen men sent out to load cargo that wasn't even consigned —'

'I've seen cargo put into the wrong ship —'

'I've seen men sent to ships that wasn't even there —'

'Wharfies would have been shot for treason if they'd done some of the things shipowners done.'

'Best I ever saw was on the old *Echuca*. We worked all one morning putting in cargo for Sydney — Number Two Hatch, I think it was. And at one o'clock the buck put his head over the top and told us to take it all out again — the ship was going to Adelaide!'

'They should have left it in and said nothing, brought it back in the ship. What difference would it have made? They drag stuff all over the world —'

Bob Taylor, one of the winch drivers, looks at his mate. 'You was on that *Time* job at Twenty-one Dock, wasn't you, Peter? When we filled up the 'tween-decks with empty drums —'

Peter nods sleepily. 'When we was all sent down to Yarraville?'

'That's it.' Bob raises his voice to take in the entire company. 'By cripes, that was funny. They ordered us to Yarraville — eight o'clock start Monday morning. Four gangs. And the bloody ship had been lying up in the dock since the Friday night. It was ten o'clock before we got the hatches off.'

'And that's when your pay would have started — in the old days!'

Anstey comes in again. He knows all about the old days, when there was no such thing as easy money. He looks around truculently. 'Stone the crows! I'm sitting here with fifty thousand bags of flour under my ginger. Who grew it? Who milled it? Who brought it here? Who put it into that hatch? And whose bloody flour is it? Don't ever talk to me about easy money! I know who gets the easy money —'

Nobody takes him up, so he spits hard across the deck and retires into a sulky silence. Half a dozen separate conversations begin, a drowsiness settles over the whole for'ard end of the ship, and I fall to reflecting on all the wealth of the earth that passes before the eyes of the men of the waterfront. High up against the blue sky the four seamen are still messing about with the derrick heads. They work slowly, clumsily, under an incessant bombardment of orders from a serang on the deck below. Two white seamen would have the job done in fifteen minutes.

And who is going to blame those brown men? Indians, those of them that we see, anyway, are not cheerful people, like the eternally laughing Javanese. They have little to be cheerful about. In the handsome, serious faces of those four men up there one can see something of the sorrow of four hundred million outraged people and their ravaged country.

Perhaps, more intimately, they're thinking of the comrade who will stay behind here, perhaps forever, when the ship sails. The one who was knocked into Hatch One last Wednesday morning when a shackle came out of the yardarm runner, and who hasn't yet regained consciousness. What fearful thoughts will be his if ever he does open his eyes again? White ward, white sheets, white nurses, white-coated doctors ...

I remember seeing him standing stockstill, looking thoughtfully into the half-filled hold just before he was struck — looking at the thousands and thousands of bags of beautiful white flour — perhaps he came from starving Bengal —

Half an hour later I got a glimpse of his dark moist face as they swung him over the side on a cargo tray to the waiting ambulance. It was twisted into a stiff ironic smile, as if something far more terrible than a loaded tray had hit him in that last conscious second. I can guess what it was, too — he looked an intelligent man. We found out long ago on the Australian waterfront.

That's why we can lie here with easy hearts, taking a bit of easy money.

• The Haunting of Hungry Jimmy •

Melbourne author Bernard Cronin, a dear old friend of mine now dead, once remarked to me, 'Ted, I never did meet a rich man who didn't want to be richer.' He went on to suggest that no great intellectual equipment is needed to rule from a roost in middle Collins Street; only a primitive astuteness, a resilient social conscience, and an utter dedication to the making of money. Jimmy Boon had all three.

Jimmy was the youngest of a large family living a street away from me in Mentone, and I found his performance worth following from the Sunday morning on which he confronted me with a dead rabbit when I was working in my garden. I already knew him by sight as a lively urchin selling *Heralds* of an evening at the railway station. I also knew a bit about him from stories brought home from school by my own children. Jimmy was twelve then, but already an opportunist, with a reputation for tight dealing in those little transactions which take place in all playgrounds. I'd heard of him charging other children two lollies for a ride on his first push-bike, and trading a pair of very surplus white mice for a quality biro pen — the latter subsequently retrieved by an irate parent.

I gave him a shilling for the rabbit that Sunday morning, and was quite captivated when, with a cheeky grin, he bailed me up for an extra penny when I asked him to skin it. The dexterity with which he did that marked him as an expert; I couldn't have stripped off a glove quicker.

'Are there many around?' I asked him.

'There's a few,' he replied guardedly.

'In the golf links?'

'You can get 'em there as well. Anything you want doing?'

Which struck me as a precociously clever way of throwing

me off the scent of his business secrets. A very alert boy indeed. His eyes were on the drive, which was littered with weeds and clippings from the border I'd just cleaned out.

'Not really,' I said.

'I'll shift all that for two bob.' He was irresistible.

He was also a born worker. His energy and efficiency won my respect. 'Do you do much of this?' I asked him when, half an hour later, I was paying him off on a drive as clean as a billiard table.

'Only when there's not much on at the links. Anything else?' He was looking around hopefully.

'Not today. Bring me another rabbit next week.'

'If I can get one.' He was conceding nothing.

On the following Sunday he turned up with two rabbits. 'One and ten the pair, mister.'

I said that one was enough. He said the one I picked would be one and twopence on its own: 'It's a big 'un. Take the pair for one and eight?'

I didn't, out of sheer stubbornness, but before he left he sold my wife half a dozen eggs at a few pence below shop prices and offered to cut my front lawn for one and sixpence. I decided I was dealing with a budding financial genius, a conviction which was reinforced next day when I learned that he had two dozen hens which he fed on the cheap by picking up off-cuts of cabbages and the like at the local greengrocer's and mixing mash with dregs collected from milk bottles left around the school playground.

The best lurk of the local hopefuls was, from my inside knowledge, caddying at the golf links, either at Kingston Heath or Royal Melbourne. Jimmy's short stature, however, put him at a disadvantage, and he'd found he was rarely among the chosen. So he'd given it away, and was spreading his activities over an area as impressive in its dimensions as it was in its infinite variety. You never knew where he was going to pop up: dragging a billy-cart loaded with empty bottles for sale at the bottle-yard, selling programmes at the railway station on Saturday race-days, calling ice-creams and chocolate in the intervals at the local Hoyts, pushing his bike on an early morning newspaper delivery, letter-boxing handbills for the shopkeepers.

He was only thirteen when he had a round of lawns that he

• The Haunting of Hungry Jimmy •

cut at weekends, using his own rotary mower pulled from job to job on the very daddy of a billy-cart constructed by himself out of bits and pieces from the tip. The mower also was probably salvage. It was always breaking down, but Jimmy had picked up plenty of experience watching his big brothers tinker with their auto-bombs, and invariably got it going again. It made a fearful racket, and led to his first skirmishes with the law. Somebody laid a complaint about his disturbing the peace on a Sunday morning right in the middle of church services, followed a week later by another complaint about his waking people up too early on working mornings.

A third complaint came soon after when, through his father, he was ordered to reduce the number of hens he was keeping and dismantle some of the ramshackle pens that were beginning to give a drunken lean to the dividing fence.

By then Jimmy had abandoned the rabbit branch of his business complex but, as an old customer, I was possessively lined up for a *Herald* one evening at the hotel on the beach front. As — with transparent slowness — he fumbled for my change he wanted to know if I'd be interested in some cheap fish next Sunday morning: 'Fresh flathead, straight from the Bay. I get 'em down at Keeford's.' (Keeford's was the boats-for-hire at Beaumaris.)

I was still interested in him, but no longer to the point of involvement. Only a few minutes previously my drinking mate had pointed him out as a promising little roughneck who had won the coveted hotel pitch by defeating another youngster half as big again as himself. I'd decided not to continue too close an association with a boy who had already earned himself the nickname of Hungry Jimmy.

He left school at fourteen. I heard that his father, a builder's labourer, wanted him to go on for a further two years at Caulfield Technical School, with the aim of an apprenticeship in plumbing or electrical fitting at sixteen. Jimmy, however, eager to get into immediate wages, had his way and took his first job, telegraph boy at Mentone post office. At the end of four weeks he was sacked when some citizen reported him cutting a lawn while he was supposed to be still out on a delivery. It appeared that he was already under observation for the excessive times he was taking on assignments.

It was then Daddy Boon's turn to prevail, and for the following eighteen months Jimmy struggled to keep his lawn-mowing contracts by working two or three hours before and after school. With travelling times thrown in, that made pretty long days for a youngster. But he was tough, and, at an age when boys usually do launch into real growth, was fast putting on height and weight — and muscle. So much so that I wasn't surprised when I came across him 'jockeying' for Les Binns, a Cheltenham carrier with a twice-daily run between Melbourne and Mordialloc.

'What happened to Caulfield Tech., Jimmy?' I asked him.

'Aw, that?' He sniffed contemptuously, and paused in the act of lowering a crate to the roadway in Mentone Parade. 'There's no dough in school. I'm getting paid for this.'

'This' didn't last much longer than his first job. I was never able to find out what happened, presumably because Les Binns was a mate of Jimmy's father.

'Jimmy Boon?' Les was an easy-going type, and chuckled when I tried to draw him out on the subject. 'Yes, he wasn't with me for long. He'll get on, that kid. Too smart for my little firm. What won the last race?'

Which I took as a gentle reminder that you don't dob a cobber's son in. My guess is that Jimmy was caught out running a few small deliveries of his own on the side.

He never had another full-time employer. The lawn-mowing had given him connections, and he'd gradually acquired some expertise in gardening. As I've already indicated, he was a real worker, and in the kindly climate of Melbourne speed and neatness count for more than horticultural know-how. We were in the post-war boom years, with full employment, and big wages in industry. Young men weren't attracted to what had always been the Cinderella of manual occupations, and some skilled tradesmen were themselves able to hire labour to do the unprofitable chores in their gardens. Admittedly, gardeners' earnings also were on the up, but they still lagged, and anything went as long as there was plenty of it. Jimmy gave plenty. In no time he'd built up a full week of garden maintenance, and word was going around that Jimmy Boon did more work in an hour than most of the local potterers could do in half a day.

The Haunting of Hungry Jimmy

For about eighteen months, up to his eighteenth birthday, he steadily consolidated. He was an ant, a bee, a spider, a money-spinner. People aren't fussy in the hunt for maximum values for outlay. He was Hungry Jimmy from Parkdale to Cheltenham, but he got the work. No forty-hour week for Jimmy Boon. He was at it from the crack of dawn to the setting sun, weekends included. From all the evidence, his only recreation was a Saturday night appearance at the local cinema with Elsie Parker, who lived only two blocks away from him. Elsie, often referred to as a 'big lump of a girl', kept house for her not-very-bright father (who got an occasional pick-and-shovel job from Jimmy), several junior brothers and sisters and an ailing mother who nevertheless supplemented the family income by taking in bits of homely dressmaking. There was much speculation among the local wits on who really paid for Jimmy's weekly treat, and on whether the recreation extended any further than escorting Elsie home after the show. He was never seen drinking at either the Mentone or the Royal Oak, but his long working hours and tireless pursuit of fringe benefits were subjects for further fruity discussion in both bars, with some credit given for the fact that at least he wasn't depressing rates of pay. On the contrary, and acting on the immemorial precept that the value of any commodity is the most that you can possibly get for it, he very soon began to jack up his prices. With the exception of one or two seasoned experts he was, at seventeen, probably the best-paid gardener in the district. Details of his techniques came out one day during a heated argument in the Royal Oak when someone quoted him on the relative merits of natural manures and artificial fertilizers.

'Jimmy Boon a gardener!' exclaimed Alec Fraser. 'He wouldn't know the difference between a forkful of horse-shit and a forkful of bloody spaghetti.' Alec, who boasted an apprenticeship served on the estate of a Scottish earl, ran a small nursery out on the Warrigal Road and employed a few men on maintenance and landscape work. 'Get-rich-quick Jimmy; he's just a rip-tear-and-bust merchant. I've lost two good jobs over him in the last month. All right, he keeps up to award rates, but there's more ways than one of undercutting. I pay my men full money, and I've had Councillor Baxter's garden for six years and never a complaint. And what does Jimmy do? He comes along, asks Baxter what time he gives, and when Baxter says one day a week Jimmy looks round with a sniff and says he'll eat it in half a day. So bang goes me. I told Baxter he wouldn't get the show my man was giving him and he says he doesn't care much about flowers since his wife died; he just wants the place keeping tidy. Another job Jimmy knocked off was Yanko Private Hospital. I had old Bob Grimm doing it. Two days a week. Bob's getting up in years now, but I'd have kept him on as long as Sister Drew was satisfied. Jimmy's got it now. One day a week, and where the hell am I going to send Bob?'

From which flying start Alec proceeded to enlarge on the tale of Jimmy's misdeeds: 'He was getting all his seedlings from me to begin with; wholesale, that's a third off. Now he's growing all his own in the old man's back garden, and trying to cut me out of my corner with the florist at Cheltenham. The only shop where I've been able to get a display. I'll tell you something else he did. Sister Drew wanted a show of phlox along that main border of hers. Jimmy told her it was cheaper and better to grow phlox straight on from seed. Said he'd need half an ounce, sowed the whole half ounce at Yanko, and planted all his other gardens with the thinnings at one and six a dozen. That bloke would skin a flea for its hide. Remember that caterpillar plague on the cypress hedges last year? Jimmy read in the *Herald* about the new malathion poisons, bought a large bottle, told Arthur Nevinson he had a small job to do, borrowed his knapsack pump for the weekend, sprayed half the cypress hedges in Mentone at ten bob an hour, then took the pump back to Arthur without having the decency to sling him a bottle of grog.'

Another man who nursed a personal grievance against Jimmy was my friend Neil Campbell. Neil was a professional photographer and commercial artist living in Cromer Road, Beaumaris. Apart from an affection for trees in general, there were two in which he had a small commercial interest. One was a well-bushed variegated agonis in Beach Road, the other a very beautiful young lemon-scented gum in Plummer Road. Both trees were occasionally used by Neil as backgrounds in outdoor commissions for wedding and fashion shots. The owner of the agonis, a Dr Barnard, exacted a small fee, but in the case of the eucalypt Neil's enthusiasm had made him *persona grata* with Captain Moriarty, a retired master mariner who had christened his home 'Lawhill', after the famous old windjammer in which he had once served as a junior officer. Little of the tree was yet visible above a cypress hedge on the frontage, but when you stepped inside the garden you found it was forked unusually close to the ground, and magnificently placed against a background of dark camellias, with glimpses here and there of the fine white ironwork of an old colonial-style verandah. There was something almost erotic about the slender, naked white limbs of the tree. 'Just look at it!' Neil had exclaimed on the day he took me in to see it. 'It's like a nymph, isn't it? Inviting you ...'

Early in the 1960s Neil went into a business partnership with an old friend in Sydney, and when he and his wife came to my place for a farewell dinner the conversation naturally turned on his feelings about leaving Beaumaris. Apparently it wasn't only a matter of business. He was glad to be getting out.

'Mentone and Cheltenham are closing in on us, Ted,' he said despondently. 'When we first came here Beaumaris was a green suburb, big blocks of tea-tree scrub everywhere, and full of birds. Look at it now. They all want city-style gardens, and the first thing they do is clear out the native trees. It seems to be in the blood; Australians still want a bit of the Old Dart. To remind them of what? That damned Jimmy Boon's just knocked off my nice agonis.'

'He must have muscled in on Dr Barnard?'

'Barnard died, and his widow went to live with her daughter. Jimmy canvassed the new people, got the maintenance job, and talked them into getting rid of all their trees on the front. See the idea? The less trees, the more beds for his seedlings. Change over twice a year, and more labour for upkeep. He's after the trees wherever he gets a foot in. Takes the big ones down free on condition he keeps the firewood. Grubbing's a charge. He's made a deal with some wood merchant down Moorabbin way. Hires a chain-saw, cuts the tree up himself into one-foot blocks, and this dealer comes along with his truck and carts the lot off at a nice profit for both of them. I'm getting the hell out of it before he picks up Moriarty's garden and murders my lemon-scented gum.'

On the very day he turned eighteen Jimmy took out a driver's licence, bought a utility truck, and became an employer of full-time labour. In the words of another fascinated observer, he took off like a rocket. The groundwork had been well scouted. He'd got on to an industrial development near Black Rock where a large quantity of sandy topsoil was available free for the removal. At the same time, back of the Nepean Highway at Parkdale, there was a housing subdivision where clean filling and top-dressing were in demand at £1 a yard. With a front-end loader at one end of the line, two lusty labourers spreading at the other, and Jimmy driving like a bat out of hell between, it was only a matter of weeks before he was able to put down a deposit on a tip-truck and advertise in the *Mordialloc City News*: 'CARTING. Sand, gravel, soil. Rubbish removed. No job too small. Quotes free.' He even had a phone number, that of his girl-friend, who took the calls and did the necessary paper work. She was turning out to be a girl after Jimmy's own rapacious heart, leaving her mother now and then to attend to the phone while she herself went along to do a bit in Jimmy's back-garden nursery.

Finding lusty shovel hands and a reliable driver for the tip-truck presented no problems. There are competent labourers everywhere, men with no special skills and a casual attitude to life, but willing enough workers where there's good money with no responsibility attached. In very little time Jimmy had five of them on the receiving end, with himself in the utility checking up now and then and holding down the best of his garden maintenance department. This latter, however, soon began to wither as the housing estate opened up new vistas of conquest: fencing, concrete paths, landscape gardening.

It was the day of what was known as the 'spec. builder'. With an acute housing shortage, and suburban councils at their wits' end to meet demands for accommodation, regulations were not always strictly enforced, and almost any ambitious carpenter with a bit of capital to pay wages, and reputable enough to get materials on credit, could set himself up as a builder, with no end of buyers ready to move in almost before the paint was dry.

The Haunting of Hungry Jimmy

Such a climate of urgency, limited funds — and 'she'll do, mate!'— was made to order for the small-fry marginal operators, and Jimmy Boon prospered. Working along the rapidly extending line of development east of the Nepean Highway, and with a foot already in with the builders through his cheap filling and rubbish removal, he became, in the local paper: 'JAMES BOON. Landscape Gardener and General Cartage Contractor.'

One truck, two trucks, three trucks ...

Few of the working-men home buyers could afford professional garden design, and were easily talked into rough-and-ready jobs by the builders concerned. That usually meant Jimmy Boon. Jimmy's landscaping at first amounted to little more than clearing away the building rubble, appropriating any left-overs of sand and metal, blinding what was left of the site with an inch of clean top-dressing, scattering a few pounds of grass seed, perhaps laying a concrete path, and planting several commonplace shrubs. Later he recruited a man with some knowledge of garden lay-out, an invalid pensioner, but who nevertheless was able, for a modest fee, to supervise the growing number of odd-bods on Jimmy's payroll.

At twenty-two Jimmy Boon was directing one of the most extraordinary rag-tag-and-bobtail business complexes at the northern end of the Mornington Peninsula. He had five trucks on the road, plus two utilities, plus a late-model Holden in which he did the round of enterprises extending from Frankston to Moorabbin. His headquarters were now the home of his prospective father-in-law, whose vacant block on the side was cluttered up with salvage building materials, set off by the cannibalized carcase of Jimmy's first tip-truck on the frontage. With a full-time job now as yardman, an economically promising marriage in prospect for his eldest daughter, and a son-in-law-to-be with an office already built on to the back of the house, Charlie Parker must have felt that the world was really beginning to smile on him.

In 1965 Captain Moriarty died, and his home — with Neil Campbell's beloved lemon-scented gum — came on the market. Nobody was surprised when Jimmy Boon bought it, got married, and moved in. Rumour had it that he'd gone heavily into the red to attain this triumph, but his ability to come out on top was never doubted. It was the time also when it was observed that he was beginning to make occasional small donations to shrewdly chosen local appeals, both sporting and charitable, such as football clubs and elderly citizens' functions. Cynical gossip at the pubs suggested that he might be trimming his sails for the City Council.

My own first thought when I heard of Jimmy's acquisition of Lawhill was of Neil Campbell and his nymph-like eucalypt. I was glad that Neil was no longer around to witness what I anticipated as inevitable destruction. Every few days, in my journey to the city, I made a point of going down Plummer Road, following with a rising horror the domestic application of Jimmy's moronic ideas of home and garden design. The first shock came when I and several motorists were held up one morning by a wire line stretched taut across the road, one end of the line being attached to a tip-truck, the other to the first tree of Lawhill's encompassing cypress hedge. Trust Jimmy to find the shortest way home. When I passed again in the evening the hedge, pulled out tree by tree as cleanly as a dentist would pull out teeth, was gone, and Lawhill's secret garden lay exposed to the world.

Stopping the car, I sat for some minutes looking across at it, trying to fix an image of it before it vanished forever from the face of the earth. It had got a bit ragged since the death of the captain, but that only added to its snug, lush, old-world charm. In my racing imagination there was a shrinking fear in the two windows peeping through the screen of camellias, just as, in the uplifted limbs of the white tree, there was a suggestion of outraged innocence, like a lovely young girl suddenly caught naked.

I said then a silent goodbye to it, but week by week the respite — of the tree — was extended while Jimmy went to work on what he, no doubt, regarded as modernization.

Using cheap bricks, and his wife as a labourer, he built a low wall to replace the hedge. Diagonally across the big lawn he cut out and concreted a car drive, with a loop on the front of the house for turning, and access to a metal pre-fabricated garage on the side where the captain had had a picturesque fernery. In the centre of the loop he constructed a crude rockery topped by a white plaster stork that made a startling con-

· The Haunting of Hungry Jimmy ·

trast to a pair of rainbow-painted gnomes pointing the way to the front steps. All the camellias were cut down, hedge-like, to the exact level of the verandah decking, and the house itself transformed from a quiet green to a brick red — which might have been nice enough but for a dazzling new iron roof. Along the sunny side of the garden every sizeable tree was removed, leaving only a few small shrubs as backing for what was obviously intended to be an annuals border in the best Melbourne suburban tradition. The general Jimmy Boon effect was finally topped off by white-painted, drip-catching clam shells placed under every garden tap.

Through it all the delicate white tree lingered on. If trees could speak ...

The haunting? I've come to it.

Two things happened simultaneously. Hungry to get into the really big time, Jimmy (it came out, and was the talk of the town) invested much too heavily in the minerals boom, got caught in the collapse, and had to put Lawhill back on the market. About the same time Neil Campbell came to Melbourne to look for suitable premises for his company, which was extending to Victoria.

One morning a big red and white FOR SALE notice appeared on the front of Lawhill, and soon afterwards, late on a Friday afternoon, I picked up Neil at his city hotel to take him home as a weekend guest. Several years had passed since he'd left Melbourne, so that he was eager for a sight of old familiar scenes. I wasn't surprised, therefore, when he asked me to take the winding road along the sea front to Mentone.

Conversation moved easily from family affairs to work, and from that to local gossip, which latter soon brought us to Jimmy Boon. Neil was vastly interested, and informed me, before I'd completed my story, that he was doing some jacket-designing for a Sydney publisher and wanted a good colour photograph of his lemon-scented gum while he was staying with me. I told him that it was now well grown, and also that he could get a wide-open shot of it from the street, with, at foot, a gorgeous little gnome in blue breeches, scarlet jacket and yellow pixie hat. He was not amused.

'Still want to see it?' I asked dryly.

'No.'

But as we took the last curve in the road at Beaumaris he changed his mind and we swung into Plummer Road.

Jimmy couldn't possibly have timed it more cruelly, for even as we came abreast of Lawhill a utility loaded with lemon-scented one-foot blocks was creeping slowly out at the gates. Even the tidying-up was almost completed. It wouldn't have been quite so bad if the tree had been felled in the captain's time; in the tranquil colonial house something would have been left. As it was, the background of red and silver and lollipop gnomes was not only aggressive, it was obscene. I looked down on Neil, who, leaning across with his chin almost on the steering wheel, was staring tigerishly past me at the figure of Jimmy Boon, industriously stoking a bonfire of twigs and leaves on the loop of the drive. A column of pale blue smoke was going straight up into the calm evening air.

Two or three minutes passed before Neil spoke. 'The lousy bastard! The lousy bastard!'

My sympathetic pat on the shoulders stirred him into life. He went to get out of the car, and shook me off when I put out a restraining hand. 'Let go, Ted! And you stay there...'

'You can't do anything.'

'I know that. I just want to have a word with him.'

'You'll buy into a brawl. At least let me get out...'

'I won't buy into any brawl. And I don't want him to recognize you. Stay in the car.'

So I remained where I was, watching with some anxiety as Neil crossed the road and slowly walked up the drive to the scene of operations. From that distance even the sound of their voices didn't reach me and most of the pantomime that followed had me completely bewildered. Neil did most of the talking, with gestures not all comprehensible but indicating a steadily rising indignation, while Jimmy, leaning on a garden rake, looked increasingly sheepish and worried, like a mischievous schoolboy caught red-handed by an irate master. Neil's first gesture, in response to something Jimmy said, was to put both hands over his face and keep them there for some seconds, as one would moan 'Oh, my God!' But I could make nothing whatever of his tapping his heart a few minutes later and spreading both hands in another gesture that took in the whole of the Lawhill property.

· The Haunting of Hungry Jimmy ·

It went on for about fifteen minutes. Twice Neil clapped both hands to his head in disgust, walked away a few paces, then went back, as if another aspect of the enormity of Jimmy's crime had just occurred to him. Every second I expected Jimmy to explode, but he appeared to be getting only more and more crestfallen. When at last my friend gave up and began to walk back to the car Jimmy's eyes never left his back. He still hadn't moved when Neil was getting into the car.

'What on earth were you pitching him?' I asked as Neil, a bit breathless from excitement, settled down beside me.

'I fixed the hungry bastard,' he exclaimed with grim satisfaction. 'I gave him something that'll haunt him to the end of his days.'

'All right — what?'

'I told him he'd just cut up the only known tree of its kind in the world — for firewood.'

'That would worry Jimmy. So what?'

'It worried him by the time I finished. He tried to tell me it was only a lemon-gum.'

'So it was . . .'

'Sure, I said it was a lemon-scented gum all right. But a very special one. I asked him hadn't he ever heard of the hybrid *Citriodora echeveria eugenoides* — something like that. I'm good at names. What the hell would he know?'

'Go on. So?'

'I told him only two of them had ever been found, and that the other one, years ago, had turned out to be the best wood for violins since Stradivarius. That wiped the grin off his face. Stradivarius has the jingle of money even for Jimmy Boon.'

'He believed you?'

'Take a look at him now.' I did. Jimmy had been joined by his wife. Both were watching the car, transfixed, like the two gnomes. 'I told him old Moriarty had turned down a dozen big offers for it. I told him the tree was registered with the International Society of Ichthyologists — entomologists — archaeologists — oh, some bloody thing. He'll have forgotten by now. I told him he could look out for a stinking letter when word of what he had done got to the Geneva headquarters of the society. I told him I was Australian agent for a famous Berlin firm of violin-makers, and that somebody had drummed them that this joint was on the market. I told him they'd cabled me in Sydney to get down here on the first available plane, with a blank cheque — repeat, blank cheque.' (That mysterious pat on Neil's heart-breastpocket.) 'I told him — Ted, for chrissake step on it before I think of something else to go back and tell the bastard.'

I stepped on it. A final backward glance showed Jimmy and his wife still stuck on the front of the house, watching us as if we were driving off with the body of their first-born.

• Perhaps You've Got It •

I first met Bernie and Megan O'Flynn when I retired after an illness and bought a small property at Montrose in the hills near Melbourne.

My wife and I took the place on sight, chiefly because it was pleasantly situated. It is one of two weatherboard houses on a back road only ten minutes' walk from the shops, but with unimproved blocks all around, and a fine view of Mt Dandenong.

I spoke to Bernie and Megan on the day we went to inspect, and that also had something to do with it. There was no sign of life around the next house when we arrived, but when we came out to the road again Bernie and Megan were waiting for us, innocently engaged in raking up leaves under a yellowing maple. Obviously they'd popped out to have a close look at their prospective neighbours.

They were a cosy-looking couple, seventyish, both on the plump side, both bespectacled, both ruddy-complexioned in the way of people who spend a lot of time out of doors, and both dressed for the part, jeans and serviceable old cardigans. It was Bernie who stepped over to me when I gave them goodday, while his wife remained where she was, taking a hard look at Helen, who was ahead of me and already seated in the car with the agent who had driven us up.

Bernie's stare, while friendly, was equally searching. No doubt feeling that he could do worse than have two other oldtimers come to live next door, he began by remarking that it was 'a nice little place'. I agreed.

'It's very quiet, if that's what you're looking for,' he went on, with a glance up the timbered hillside. 'Hardly anybody ever comes down here.'

I nodded approval, and asked him who owned the adjacent blocks.

'Nobody seems to know,' he said. 'Some big shot down in town, I suppose. They'll lie for a long time yet. There's a road surveyed along the back, but it's a bit steep down from the bitumen, and the council's got enough on its plate for years to come.'

Not much followed, but in the space of a few minutes he did a good job for the agent. It was evident that he and his wife were terrified of the vacant house falling into the hands of someone who would disturb the peace.

Well, I bought it, and there was never any reason for regret. It was a comfortable little house, sound and convenient, and with an established garden. And as neighbours the O'Flynns were just right, friendly but never intrusive. On the first day, only minutes after the departure of the removal van, Megan set the pattern by knocking on the door to ask if there was anything we required: 'The baker and milky will call in the morning, but if there's anything you want now...' There wasn't, but it was an encouraging start, particularly as Megan took herself off as soon as Helen explained that everything was under control.

A slightly formal exchange of visits soon after we'd settled in gave us an opportunity to get to know each other, and for the women to show off their housekeeping. Through these little tea parties we learned that Bernie and Megan had emigrated from Ireland as a young married couple almost forty years ago, that Bernie had worked for the PMG for thirty years as a linesman, that there had been no children, and that a foolish investment had robbed them of all of their savings except enough to provide a roof over their heads in their declining years. The last detail came out only in passing, and was dismissed by Bernie with a remark which nicely summed up his basic philosophy: 'I often say to Megan there's plenty that haven't got even that much. Happiness is a funny thing, you know. You don't always know when you've got it.'

The O'Flynns lived on their age pensions, supplemented by vegetables from their garden and eggs from their hens. Not much, but they considered themselves fortunate in being able to put by a little each week towards some new comfort. Now and then in their idle yarning there would be a reference to something big that they would like: a holiday up north, a replacement for their early-model fridge, a concrete path in from the front gate, a septic tank in place of the primitive bucket, new spouting, new iron for the rusting roof. But the subject of needs was never dwelt on at length, and was usually dismissed with the familiar Australian: 'Never mind. One of these days we'll win Tatts ...' They'd been taking tickets for years, but had never drawn even a minor prize.

The garden was the great joy of their lives. Only a post-and-wire fence separated the two properties, and, with our house raised on much higher stumps, we had a commanding view of most of the O'Flynns' outside activities. Theirs was a higgledy-piggledy bits-and-pieces garden after the fashion of elderly people: a small patch of lawn back and front, vegetables along the side nearest to us, and an intricate mix-up of narrow paths, shrubs and flower-borders, with a few sizeable trees to give spots of shade. A free-for-all garden full of old favourites such as hollyhocks and foxgloves, and in which there was always a splash of colour somewhere.

Bernie and Megan spent hours in it every day, although Megan was often to be seen sitting contentedly with her knitting on an upturned box close to where Bernie was working. I gathered that she knitted quite a lot for a charity down in town.

Bernie also had his ruminating perch, but it was a fixed one — the stump of a fallen tree near the fowlyard on his bottom boundary. He used to begin every day there, letting the hens out to scratch over the vacant block while he enjoyed his first pipe. It seemed to have the soothing effect on him that contemplation of a bowl of goldfish has on some people, although it came out that the custom was utilitarian in origin: 'The first day I let them out a damned dog killed two before I could get out of the house. So I keep an eye on them. You can't beat a bit of open-range picking for chooks. Anyhow, I like watching them.'

There were pickings for Bernie and Megan, too, on what was always referred to as 'the back block'. Like much of the immediate surroundings, it was part of a long-abandoned orchard, and there were still some ragged old apples and apricots that gave Megan fruit for jam-making. There were also a few well-grown eucalypts, the fallen debris of which provided a supply of kindling wood. I believed, however, that the chief value of the little wilderness to the O'Flynns was the sense of protection, of privacy, which it gave them.

That meant something to Helen and me also. There were no dividing fences below, so that it was like living on the edge of the bush. We spent many a pleasant hour sitting on our verandah contemplating the quiet trees and watching the comings and goings of all kinds of birds, particularly around a huge cherry-plum whose branches overhung our garden.

The block was also a fine playground for our grandchildren when they visited — open places to scamper in, trees to climb, secret places to hide in — and another of Bernie's dreams of sudden wealth: 'If ever I win Tatts I'll buy it.' Land, septic tank, holiday in Queensland, refrigerator, new verandah, new spouting, concrete paths — 'if ever I win Tatts'.

One day he did. Family business had taken Helen and me to Adelaide at the time, so we missed the initial impact. A letter from a local friend, however, put us in the picture.

'Big deal over here,' he wrote. 'Your old mates have had a win in Tatts. Not the big one. Five thousand dollars, but that's a million to the O'Flynns. They're a bit scared of all the commotion it's stirred up. The track down from the township is worn bare, and all the bots and bites in Victoria are on to them. Bernie tells me there's been begging letters in the mail every morning. All the same, he's a happy man. I had to go in for a cuppa, of course, and it was a pleasure to listen to him and Megan.

'They haven't started to spend it yet, but they're having a marvellous time working out priorities. Five thousand dollars should get them pretty well everything they need. Bernie's going to get a quote for a septic tank, and Megan's tickled to death over the prospect of a new fridge. She couldn't get a silly grin off her face all the time we were talking.

'Bernie tells me that neither of them has had a good night's sleep since they got the news. They keep waking up, thinking of what they're going to do with the money. Still, they'll settle down once the spending's done. It couldn't have happened to two nicer people. You'll get the whole story when you come back.'

We did. An hour or so after our return, Bernie knocked on the door, and while Helen went over to fetch Megan and I got out a bottle and glasses to celebrate, he plunged straight into it: 'Five thousand dollars! You know, Bob, I just can't get used to it all...'

He began by telling me, with much irrelevant detail, how he and Megan had received the news: 'We was just going to sit down to a bite of lunch', and went on from there to Megan's reaction. 'I thought she was going to flake out on me.' Then the reactions in the township. 'Everybody was very nice about it, but there was a few from outside tried to hook it off us. Them get-rich-quick wallahs. Buy shares in this, buy shares in that. They was wasting their time. I was bit once.'

It turned out to be a twosome for us. Helen got captured by Megan for a cup of tea and Megan's version of the event, while Bernie rambled cheerfully on about all the things they were going to buy with the five thousand dollars. It was pleasant listening, but later, when he was gone and Helen and I got to comparing notes, it became evident that the O'Flynns were already running into difficulties over those priorities.

It was noticeable also that the field of requirements had suddenly extended. Naturally enough, I suppose, Bernie was primarily concerned with outside matters such as roof and septic tank, while Megan had her sights set on a new fridge and floor-coverings. But the few sheets of new iron had become a whole new roof, and talk of linos had given place to talk of wall-to-wall carpet for at least the bedroom.

'I asked her if they'd thought of going away for a little holiday,' said Helen, 'but she told me they'd worked out that there wouldn't be enough left by the time they had all they wanted. They're going to get a price for repairs to the front verandah, and Megan says the kitchen stove has just about had it. I always understood it was a good stove.'

It was a pattern which developed with rather startling speed in the following weeks. Megan got her new fridge and Bernie had the verandah redecked. There were also some odd purchases of tools, clothing, linen and kitchenware. But the really big spending became bogged down over questions of what came first. In the beginning the septic tank had been the main project, but Bernie was now taken with the idea of a major structural alteration to the house. They had a skillion roof, which meant that the house got pretty hot in summer. Bernie argued that, as much of the iron was coming off in any event, they might as well build a pitched roof, with insulating pads laid over the ceilings.

Megan also was prepared to carry on with the old outhouse bucket, but thought the money would be better spent on repainting inside and out, and on some modern furniture to replace the cumbrous stuff they'd got by on all their married life. She was digging in over a new stove too, and, according to Helen, had begun to find fault with the washing machine.

Gradually we became aware of an element of discord creeping into the O'Flynn establishment, with Megan trying to enlist the sympathy of Helen, and Bernie trying to win me. We thought it all very human and amusing at first, but stopped joking about it as the days passed and we saw ourselves being drawn towards a domestic squabble.

We observed that both Bernie and Megan were tending to avoid coming over when we were both in the garden. From where I was occupied, I would see Megan come in by the side gate and, after a surreptitious glance in my direction, head straight for the house. Bernie showed a corresponding craftiness in making sure Helen was not around when *he* felt like a session. There was also less circumspection in their approach to the subject of the windfall. They were becoming obsessed with it to a point where it was crowding out other interests. They could never get to it quickly enough. Needs and complaints were not only proliferating, they were changing direction. Talk was less and less on the money itself, and more and more on each other.

It's human nature to discover faults once grievances creep in, and Bernie and Megan O'Flynn were seeing each other's warts for the first time in their married life. Nothing really vindictive, just a nagging resentment of their respective stubborn attitudes, concern with self masquerading as concern for the other.

'After all, he spends nearly as much time in the kitchen as

I do,' declared Megan to Helen. 'Just imagine what it would be like with a coat of that new plastic paint, a bright lino, and one of them Laminex settings. He'd even find his food would taste better.'

'That house never cools down at night in a heat-wave,' said Bernie to me. 'There's only a few inches between iron and ceilings. I've seen her sitting up in bed gasping for air.'

Common to both of them was a time-worn refrain: 'But you know what women are,' from Bernie, and 'You know what men are,' from Megan. It was a bad business all round, because we'd grown so close to the O'Flynns that we couldn't be indifferent to the notes of discord going up from the other side of the fence. Our efforts to keep out of it meant that traffic between the two blocks slowed down and became very much one-way, with a reluctance on our part to down tools for a gossip when we saw one of the O'Flynns heading across. It was useless trying to keep them off the subject and mentally exhausting trying to avoid saying anything which could be repeated in support of their separate grievances. In short, we became sick and tired of the O'Flynns and their five thousand dollars.

How did it end? One morning I saw Bernie engaged in a long conversation with two city-dressed men on the back block. Soon after lunch on the same day he came over to where I was reading on the back verandah. He looked upset, and wasted less time than ever on preliminary civilities.

'Bob,' he announced, 'I've bought the back block.'

'Fair dinkum?'

'Fair dinkum.' There must have been a note of irony in my voice, because he shuffled uneasily. 'Well, I did use to talk about it. You know.'

I remembered the two strangers I'd seen him talking to in the morning. 'You've actually bought it? You're not just thinking about it?'

'No, I've bought it. The agent's coming up tomorrow with a contract.'

It was wintertime, and my eyes were on the sour black earth under the cherry-plum where a small mob of scarlet-and-blue rosellas had just flown in to feed on the litter of fallen fruit-stones. When I turned again towards Bernie, I found him watching me anxiously, even a bit guiltily.

'Do you reckon I did the right thing, Bob?'

'That depends on two things. Megan, for one —'

'She wasn't too happy about it at first, but she come around.' I noticed that his hand, resting on the little table between us, was trembling with excitement. Look, Bob, we had to do it. Did you see them two blokes over there this morning?'

'As a matter of fact, I did.'

'Well, they was looking for survey pegs. They're the agents from Box Hill. I saw them from the kitchen window and I went down and chatted them. They told me the block was going on the market. The owner wants a bit of quick cash, and they've already had an inquiry about it. You could have knocked me down with a feather. I had to act.'

'How much did they ask?'

'Four thousand dollars.'

'Four thousand!'

'You don't have to tell me. I know it's hot: it'll clean me out. But what's a man to do?'

'What about the roof, and the septic tank and —'

'They'll just have to keep,' Bernie shrugged his shoulders philosophically. 'What you never have you never miss.'

The idea immediately took on an extra dimension, and he seized on it eagerly. 'After all, we did have it, you know, before we got the money. And we were doing all right, weren't we?' He was looking desperately for vindication. 'Bob, tell me straight, d'you think we're doing the right thing?'

'It's the wisest thing you ever did in your life, mate,' I said heartily. 'Go over and fetch Megan and we'll wet it. It's a great day for the Irish!'

• The Battle of Flowers •

People called them 'the Heavenly Twins', not because they were pious or beautiful, but because their surname was Haven. Theresa and Isabel Haven — the Haven Twins — the Heavenly Twins — quite simple.

They lived at Beaumaris, in Coolibah Avenue, an unmade street running back from Beach Road into a wilderness of heath, tea-tree and bracken fern. A street with only two houses in it, the red-tiled brick veneer of the Twins, and a picturesque old weatherboard occupied by a retired business couple. 'Avalon', as the Haven home was called, was the property nearest Beach Road, and used to stand out from the faded greens of the surrounding scrub like an oasis in a desert. As the Twins' gardener for many years I was immensely proud of it. It was one of the show gardens of the south-eastern suburbs. It enjoyed a fame that extended throughout Melbourne. Photographs of it adorned the pages of home and horticultural magazines. Artists painted it; fashion designers used it as a background for their latest outdoors creations. Nurserymen courted the sisters' orders so as to be able to mention Avalon in their catalogues. Year in and year out every flower show south of the Yarra carried a winning exhibit from 'the Misses Haven'. I was employed by them only one day a week, and Beaumaris is a long way out from the city, but I kept the job because I was well paid, and because for me also it was a good advertisement. I used to lay out gardens at that time, and I found that reference to Avalon always helped considerably in getting me contracts.

At the beginning of the feud the Twins were, I suppose, about forty years old. Both were tall, as women go, but whereas Isabel was fair, soft-voiced, and gracefully rounded as a woman ought to be, Theresa was dark, deep-toned, and rather bony in structure. Isabel dressed brightly, with a preference for greens and yellows; Theresa kept to sober browns and blues. No one knew better than I, though, that beneath these contrasting superficialities the Twins were as alike as the proverbial two peas. I never learned anything of their childhood or youth, but it must have been a strange one, for they had come to maturity in the frigid harmony of a mutual selfishness that chilled me. Neither of them ever seemed to get an idea that rose above the level of poppies and pansies. From the shelter of an adequate independence they viewed the outside world without interest and without pity. They took in no newspaper, and were genuinely bewildered by the occasional echoes of turbulence that managed to penetrate Avalon's encompassing cypress hedge. They kept no maid, received no visitors, and went out only rarely to shop in Mentone or walk sedately along the foreshore. They lived only for their garden, treated me with civility because it was the fruit more of my talents than of theirs, and paid me two shillings over the award rates because I knew it as well as they did. They also paid a record commission on seedlings and manures, which was something they didn't know. Perhaps they wouldn't have cared, either, for nothing was ever too good for the garden, whether it was work or expense. All weeding was done by hand, all watering between sunset and sunrise. Every newly planted seedling was provided with a little tin shield until it took root; dahlias for exhibition were shaded from the sun by worn-out umbrellas; aphis were removed from rosebuds with little camel hair brushes; snails were hunted at night by torchlight. They bought their roses in Adelaide, their rhododendrons in Sassafras, their ranunculi in Geelong, their tulips in Macedon. At competition-time people used to say that the place didn't look quite real, that it was like a scene in a fairy-tale. There wasn't a blade of grass nor the petal of a flower that didn't appear to have been skilfully placed in position.

The feud, no doubt like most feuds, had its beginning in a trifling difference. Early one summer, when plans were being made for the autumn display, I discovered that the sisters were not in agreement concerning the long border that ran along the south fence. Isabel wanted to keep to the old subjects that

The Battle of Flowers

had helped to take so many prizes: phlox, petunias, asters and zinnias, backed up by groupings of herbaceous perennials. Theresa wanted to change over to foliage plants: alternanthus, iresine, pyrethrum and begonias, with a background of dahlias and amaranthus.

When the spring show was over and ready to be pulled up I asked Theresa what she proposed putting in. I asked Theresa only because she happened to be the first one I saw that day. Had Isabel come out first I would have asked her, for I'd always been careful to treat the sisters with equal respect.

Theresa replied that she would let me know about the border next week, explaining, without a sign of irritation, that she and her sister had not yet made up their minds about its composition.

On the following Wednesday it was Isabel I saw first, and I immediately asked her if a decision had been reached in regard to the long border. She looked at it thoughtfully.

'Would that aspect suit foliage plants, Johnston?'

I assured her that it was as suitable for foliage plants as for flowers, and after some further reflection she said that she and her sister were still of two minds on the matter.

Wednesday came around again, and this time the two women approached me together. When I brought up the question of the south border they looked at each other half sheepishly, half defiantly, and I realized that they were as far from agreement as ever.

'I'm afraid —' began Isabel.

But Theresa broke in in the abrupt manner which was characteristic of her: 'We'll let you know later, Johnston. Come, Isabel.' And without any further remark the two of them turned their backs on me and went into the house.

An hour afterwards Isabel came out and told me to dress the border in readiness for planting. I did so, but a week later was again obliged to ask what was going on. Theresa was alone. She frowned, and directed an impulsive and aggressive glance towards the windows of the house, as if wondering if her sister was watching. Then, with an unmistakable emphasis on the pronoun, she informed me that 'we' had decided on a foliage display.

I didn't see Isabel at all that day, but on the following Wednesday she came out while I was engaged in planting. Her usually serene face was sulky.

'What is your private opinion of all this, Johnston?' she demanded after wishing me good morning.

'It'll be a change at least, Miss Isabel,' I said cautiously.

'A change!' She gave me a withering stare and went off without further comment.

From that day the south border became Theresa's private preserve. Isabel washed her hands of it, and took control, with equal exclusiveness, of the several beds set in the big lawn. The first division of interests I had ever seen at Avalon. Up to that time the enthusiasm of the sisters had been disposed mutually and impartially over the entire garden. Now each had a clearly defined section of her own into which the other was careful not to intrude. In all other respects everything continued as usual, but for Theresa the flower beds in the front lawn had ceased to exist, and for Isabel there was no longer a border alongside the red gravelled drive. It was difficult for me, because when a three-cornered discussion took place we used to talk as if there were a couple of vacuums in the garden. I had a good job to hold down, and was too long in the tooth to mention the south border in the presence of Isabel or the flower beds in the presence of Theresa.

Autumn came, and the sightseers peering over the low front hedge were more numerous and enthusiastic than ever. Theresa triumphed, Avalon taking first prize in the *Herald* competition and second in the one run by the municipal council. According to press comments on the winning gardens, Avalon had never been more beautiful. The *Herald* said that the foliage display was a refreshing innovation, and prophesied a 'revival in popularity of these comparatively neglected plants'. Another paper said that the Misses Haven had struck a new and dignified note in show borders, and referred scornfully to the 'rather tawdry brilliance of the overrated phlox and petunia'.

All this, it will be understood, was bad for the sisters. They weren't the kind of women who make a confidant of an employee, but I'd known them too long not to be able to read them. On the Wednesday after the judging I observed a change for the worse in the humour of both of them. Theresa was full

The Battle of Flowers

of a smug self-satisfaction that got the better of her whenever she looked towards her sister or the big lawn. Isabel sulked, but she sulked with dignity, with lifted head, tightened lips, and a glint in her eyes that indicated she was already nursing schemes of revenge.

But nothing happened during the winter, except that the division of responsibilities, which had begun with the south border, was gradually extended throughout the entire garden. In addition to the border, Theresa took over the rockery near the main gates, as well as lawn, fernery, fruit trees and herb plot comprising the back garden. Isabel kept the front lawn with its show beds, the border against the house, the shrubbery along the north side, and the fish-pond which made the centrepiece of the small circular drive in front of the loggia. Whether or not this arrangement was a formal one I cannot say; what I do know is that by the end of the winter it was being observed as meticulously as if it were the substance of a written agreement. The sisters still associated at odd times, but were careful never to approach me together. Even so it was the devil's own job discussing my work with one or the other of them as if half the garden didn't exist. I was glad, therefore, when one day Theresa instructed me to divide my time equally between her and her sister, she herself to take the mornings and Isabel the afternoons. I showed no surprise, because I didn't feel any. The existing state of affairs was disorderly, and Avalon was no place for disorder.

'My sister and I think it will be much better that way,' remarked Theresa without the slightest sign of embarrassment. 'You will be able to organize your work more effectively.'

The dignity with which those two women carried on their wretched dispute was pathetic. Always it was 'we' or 'my sister and I'. They must have known that I comprehended everything, yet neither by word nor act had either of them yet attempted to enlist my sympathy. Unbending and utterly impersonal, each tried carefully to preserve my respect not only for herself but for the other. They did this, indeed, so successfully that for a long time I believed that reconciliation was always just around the corner. Every Wednesday morning I went out to Beaumaris in the full hope of seeing them come out by the loggia talking and laughing together in the way they used to before those infernal irisenes and begonias sprouted up between them.

But it was a forlorn hope, for as the months of winter and spring and summer wore away the breach between the sisters gradually widened. And all the time Avalon became more and more beautiful. Under the driving power of a rivalry which had taken complete possession, the Heavenly Twins excelled themselves.

Maintenance of existing standards was sufficient for neither of them. New features were introduced: alterations in lay-out, new shrubs for old, the latest and most expensive items from the nurserymen's catalogues. Hardly a week passed that I didn't have to take a labourer with me to carry out extra work.

All these changes, however, temporarily robbed Avalon of some of that lush fullness which had been its greatest charm, and I for one wasn't surprised when, in the second year, the garden failed to receive even a mention in the competitions.

The result was a serious and immediate quickening of the feud between the sisters. A new shed was built against the back fence and equipped with a complete set of new tools, even to a lawn mower. These were Isabel's. Theresa retained the old outfit, quite a good one, which was kept in a partitioned section of the woodshed. Never at any time now were the two women to be seen in the same part of the garden. One of them was always in attendance on me, according to whether it was morning or afternoon. If in the morning Theresa and I were busy in the front garden, Isabel kept to the back. If in the afternoon Isabel and I worked in the back garden, Theresa kept to the front. If in the middle of morning or afternoon I had to change my field of operations, the odd sister instantly shifted also. Sometimes, when several moves were necessary during the four hours, I used to feel like the belled gardener of a convent.

Often during the last year I had wondered how they got along together in the house. I began to see evidence now that the quarrel had reached far beyond the garden. In the morning, a few seconds after the postman's whistle blew, Isabel would come down the drive for her mail; directly afterwards Theresa would fetch hers. Instead of one bread box on the little side porch there were now two. Between twelve and one o'clock

The Battle of Flowers

Theresa was in the garden; between one and two, Isabel. From which I concluded that they had ceased taking their meals together.

For me the situation still bristled with embarrassments, but this complete estrangement was at least an improvement on the earlier state of affairs. I knew now exactly where I stood. In the mornings Isabel simply didn't exist; in the afternoons I remembered her and forgot she had a sister. At twelve o'clock Theresa made my tea for lunch and paid me nine shillings. At five o'clock Isabel paid me nine shillings. At ten-thirty Theresa gave me morning tea; at three-thirty Isabel gave me afternoon tea. I knew to an inch the boundaries of the two territories, understanding that it would be treachery to pull a weed out of the shrubbery before twelve o'clock, or stake a fallen plant in the south border after one. At noon I used to put all Theresa's tools away in the woodshed, and at one o'clock solemnly wheel out Isabel's new lawn mower. One afternoon Theresa went out shopping and forgot to turn off a hose which was playing on some shrubs newly planted against the back fence. It was still running at five, because under the eagle eye of Isabel I just didn't dare touch it.

I got accustomed to it all, even began to enjoy it. No skin off my nose if they had nothing better to do with their lives. I was making a nice thing out of commission on all their new purchases, and life had acquired a new and novel excitement. On Wednesday mornings I used to go in at the gate of Avalon in a mood of lively anticipation, like going into a theatre. If those two women could have seen themselves as I saw them they'd have patched up their differences in a matter of minutes.

In the spring there came a sensational development. The adjoining property, 'Yantara', with its wild old-fashioned garden, was put up for sale and Isabel bought it. She didn't take long to make up her mind. The very day after it was advertised she asked me if I had any vacant days. I replied that I never had vacant days, but might be able to farm out some of my other jobs if she wanted more time.

She looked me straight in the eyes. 'I'm thinking of buying Yantara, Johnston. If I do I'll go to live there, and will want the garden thoroughly overhauled.'

I nodded casually. Nothing that she or her sister did was

likely to surprise me now. 'I'd have to employ labour, Miss Isabel. That place is in a bad state.'

'I'm not afraid of expense. We might go in and look it over next week. It would be a month or so before I got possession, anyway.'

She asked me if I would be prepared to take over Yantara permanently one day a week, and I agreed. Sooner or later I was going to be involved in a quarrel with one of the sisters, and I saw clearly that Isabel with a brand new garden was likely to provide the richest pickings. I'm a family man, and I couldn't see anything better for those two crazy women to squander their money on than filling the bellies of my children.

Theresa said nothing about the matter that day, but on the following Wednesday asked me if I knew 'about Miss Isabel'. I replied that I did.

'Has she engaged you to look after Yantara, Johnston?'

'Yes, Miss Theresa.'

Eyes on the ground, she considered that for a moment. Here, I thought, is where Johnston comes to the parting of the ways!

But to my surprise she suddenly raised her head and gave me a challenging stare. 'I will, of course, require a full day at Avalon just the same.'

'I was hoping you would,' I answered, keeping a straight face with difficulty. 'There's really no reason why I shouldn't run both places.'

She was still staring, but the challenge had now become a warning. 'Perhaps there isn't. But I shall rely on you to keep up the reputation of Avalon.'

I assured her that she need have no anxieties, but when she glanced significantly to where the tangled wilderness of Yantara showed above the dividing fence I understood that this was to be the final round as far as I was concerned.

That afternoon Isabel and I inspected Yantara. And, believe me, it *was* a wilderness. The back lawn had run to seed long ago, while the front lawn had been cut ever and ever smaller until it ended along all sides in a fringe of grass plumes, milk thistles and overgrown shrubs. A coprosma hedge on the frontage had pushed down the rotten fence and reached far out over the footpath. Climbing roses and bougainvilleas draped the walls of the house and ran exuberantly up the tiles. From somewhere at the back a cluster of dolichos shoots had reached the chimney stack and trailed at a drunken angle like a feather stuck into a top hat. Every footpath was pitted and weedgrown. Under the fruit trees in the back garden part of last year's crop still lay rotting in a mush of horse-radish and New Zealand spinach. A mouldy smell hung over the entire property.

'There's one thing about it, Johnston,' remarked Isabel cheerfully, 'the place is rested. It ought to respond quickly.'

We talked it over, schemed, visualized. She was like a general planning a campaign. She'd been in before, of course, and knew in detail what she wanted doing. Dig and re-lay the back lawn. Get a motor mower onto the front lawn. Bring the hedge down to five feet so that it was level with Avalon's. Out with the dolichos, the plumbago, the sparmannia, the old roses, and every other tree and shrub except this and that and the other — the liquidambar, the sophora, the protea — she knew her trees almost as well as I did.

New water-channels, new gravel for the drive, a new front fence and gates, a rose pergola ...

She looked towards the pink bunches of Leonie de Viennot on Avalon's big pergola and at the rare magnolia flowering beyond it, and for the second time that day I saw the light of battle in a woman's eyes.

'We'll make a garden of it, Johnston,' she said grimly.

'We will, Miss Isabel.' I felt a twinge of guilt, though, on encountering the same searching stare with which Theresa had raked me.

'I expect,' said Isabel with unmistakable emphasis, 'that you will serve me here as conscientiously as you did in Avalon.' The feud had quickened my perceptions, and I did not miss the smile that flickered for an instant on the determined lips — only on the lips. The sisters were beginning to drop their guard.

Although I could not but feel flattered that both of them had decided to keep me, it was plain that the new situation could not last long. But in the meantime my pickings looked like being fatter than ever, and as the imp of avarice awakened within me I flung myself into the struggle with real zest. Let the devil take both women if they wanted it that way, and all strength to Johnston.

Isabel applied herself to the new enterprise with tireless energy, tackling the house itself with no less thoroughness than she did the garden. Within forty-eight hours of its evacuation Yantara was invaded by a small army of workmen: carpenters, painters, plumbers, tilers and plasterers. In order to fully enjoy — and capitalize on — the proceedings, I took sick for a fortnight and stayed away from my other jobs. The weather was dry, and in the middle of the back lawn we had a bonfire that burned for days. I had a good labourer with me, and at the end of those two weeks the late owners of Yantara would never have recognized their old home. On the frontage the hedge, brown and leafless from its severe cutting, stood straight and even as an oblong box behind a new green-painted picket fence. You entered by an ornamental wooden gate bearing a brass plate with Yantara's new name: Elysia. Freshly turned beds stood out like ink spots on the shaved and yellow lawn. White polished gravel covered a drive drained by open channels and spanned by three sets of double pergolas placed at regular intervals. All the main borders were edged by red tiles instead of the conventional jarrah boards. Behind the tiles spread the bare soil with an apparently indiscriminate array of stakes marking the position of new shrubs and trees. Perusal of the labels on those stakes, however, would have shown any practised eye with what care they had been arranged. Isabel, no less than I, knew to a foot how high each tree would grow, and, before they were put in, the two of us had set out all borders with twigs cut to an approximate scale. Each subject was given the room it would require at maturity, no more and no less. In the meantime all the spaces between were to be filled in with annuals and herbaceous perennials.

One evening, when remodelling was completed and the last of the workmen had left the house, Isabel surprised me by giving me a tip. She coloured a little as she held it out, a one pound note. Neither she nor her sister had ever done such a thing before; no doubt she realized I'd recognize it for what it was, a bribe for favours in the struggle with Theresa.

'You've worked very hard, Johnston,' she said with one of those gentle smiles I'd seen so rarely since the feud began. 'Let us hope Elysia is a success.'

'It will take time, Miss Isabel, but the foundations are laid.'

• **The Battle of Flowers** •

'Time? You might as well know now that I intend to enter for the autumn competition.'

'This year?'

She knew very well it was absurd, but — 'this year!' she repeated with childish petulance, and went off without giving me time to say another word.

So, I reflected, Avalon is to be my garden after all. Theresa will win, and Isabel will put the blame on me.

Avalon was already off to a flying start. As soon as Isabel moved out Theresa told me to dismantle the rose arbour and take up the crazy paving from the front lawn.

'We can get rid of all this rubbish now,' she said maliciously.

She let the sundial stay, but two of the flower beds were levelled and grassed over. Jealous of Elysia's distinctive white gravel, she dispensed entirely with her own drive, extended the lawn right across to the south border, and laid a footpath of glazed bricks edged with lavender bushes in a series of graceful curves from the main gate to the loggia. So as not to leave a chink in her armour, she painted house and outbuildings, and put up a little greenhouse to counter Isabel's up-to-date fernery.

In January I found it necessary to ask for more time in both gardens, for, with the labours of the sisters now divided, one day a week from me was no longer enough for either Avalon or Elysia. Theresa, whom I approached first, gave me a day and a half. Isabel gave me two days, and when Theresa heard of it she also gave me two days. It occurred to me that if the feud persisted, and the financial resources of the sisters were equal, they would ultimately reduce themselves to mutual beggary.

As I expected, Elysia was unplaced in the autumn competition. Avalon got third place in the municipal event and only a commendation from the *Herald*. Both women, however, took it in good part.

'I suppose we could hardly expect to recover in one season, Johnston,' said Theresa. 'We'll get full points for the alterations next year.'

I believe Isabel thought the tip had proved to be a good investment, that I had been guilty of some kind of sabotage. She was far too experienced to have seriously anticipated success, and didn't attempt to hide her satisfaction over the failure of Avalon.

'This was the only year I was doubtful of, Johnston,' she told me with a particularly friendly smile. 'We'll be getting results by next autumn.'

We! Theresa and I versus Isabel and I. I felt like a man running guns for both sides in a South American revolution.

All through that winter and the following spring the rivalry of the Twins took greater and ever greater possession of them. Each became the victim of a fixed idea, lived for but one purpose. They began to neglect themselves personally, taking to going about in shabby clothes, and shoes down-at-heels, unpolished and unlaced. Holes and wrinkles disfigured their stockings, frocks which I remembered having seen on them years ago were suddenly resurrected. A smell of camphor hung around both of them. They gave up wearing gloves in the garden, so that their hands became as soiled and roughened as my own. Nothing in the whole sorry business shocked me as much as the sight of those once immaculate women toiling away with their disordered hair straying down over their foreheads and inches of petticoat showing below their frayed and faded skirts. And how they did work! At one time a certain feminine delicacy had characterized their choice of operations; now they stopped at nothing. When I clipped Avalon's hedge it was Theresa who raked up and wheeled away the rubbish. In Elysia Isabel chased me away from the incinerator, telling me that that was something to which she herself was quite capable of attending. At each side of the dividing fence I became exclusively the skilled gardener, with a woman for labourer.

When spring came again, Elysia had taken on a beauty already comparable with that of Avalon. Side by side the two gardens bloomed and glowed, like two lovely and jealous women. Each, however, had a distinctive charm of its own. Avalon was a handsome matron, Elysia a dancing nymph. A contrast curiously appropriate, for I'd never been able to rid myself of an illusion that Isabel was younger than her sister. The slender fingers of new roses reaching up fence and pergola, and the brighter green of her restored lawns, became her, just as the deeper tones and fuller shadows were becoming to Theresa.

In the exhibition flower beds of Elysia, the Moorabbin soil

• The Battle of Flowers •

I had used for top-dressing produced a show of stocks that fairly made Theresa writhe. She wanted to know why they were better than Avalon's. I told her.

'Then please see that we have fresh soil for *our* stocks next year, Johnston,' she said curtly. 'I expect you to keep me informed of these details.'

That was the kind of thing I had to put up with every week at each side of the fence. When I tried to defend myself by saying that I was considering expense I was given clearly to understand that this was no business of mine.

'I'm not in the least concerned about costs,' said Theresa. 'I want Avalon to keep its reputation as the best suburban garden in Melbourne, and I'm quite prepared to pay for it.'

'I leave it to you, Johnston, to get me the best,' said Isabel. 'If I find I can't afford it I'll tell you so.'

So I gave them the best. The riot of spending quickened. Avalon and Elysia became bottomless sinks into which poured the money of those two foolish women. With only a modest competence to begin with, they must have known that they were endangering the security of their declining years. Real estate values at that time were in a state of chronic collapse, and neither property would have brought half its normal price on the open market. I felt sorry for the Twins, but it wasn't my place to advise them — they'd have regarded it as an impertinence anyway. It was a state of affairs I just couldn't do anything about, except help myself to the pickings. And help myself I did. I became master of the art of egging them on. I got hand in glove with a nurseryman who allowed me one-third commission on all purchases, and between the two of us each sister was kept discreetly informed of what was going on at the other side of the fence. Some weeks I earned more in commission than I did in wages. Occasionally I had a prick of conscience, but only occasionally. Those were hard times, and thirty-three per cent profit on luxuries was surely quite legitimate in a society which approved one hundred per cent profit on the things whereby men live. For the first time in my life I was a good and respectable citizen by the very standards set by those who had attained the highest positions in the land — I was getting some money without working for it.

In the second year of the sisters' separation the inevitable happened — I was kicked out of Avalon. Neither garden received an award in the autumn competitions, and I suddenly found myself suspect at both sides of the fence. Perhaps I'd have lost both jobs had it not been for one of the morning papers. True to newspaper policy of being strictly impartial on every issue which is of no importance, it came out with an article which damned me in Avalon and blessed me in Elysia:

'The Misses Haven appear lately to have engaged themselves in friendly rivalry. So much the better for the community. In the new Elysia one can already discern that touch of genius which made, and for so long sustained, Avalon as the pride of the south-eastern suburbs.'

It was on a Wednesday, but, except at midday when she filled my billy for lunch, Theresa shunned me. At five o'clock she came out with my pay, wearing the air of one who has an unpleasant duty to perform, but is determined not to flinch from it. Consistent to the very last, she sacked me with brutal directness.

'I'm sorry, Johnston, but I won't require your services any more. I've engaged another gardener.'

'You were pretty quick about that!' I exclaimed.

'Surely you aren't surprised?'

I wasn't. Nor was I particularly upset. I just didn't feel inclined to let her get away with it so smoothly.

'In a way I am, Miss Theresa. I was expecting something like this last year, but now —' I stopped and waited.

She gave me a resentful stare. She was as dowdy as usual, but dignity simply oozed out of her. 'Really, Johnston, I would prefer not to discuss the matter.'

I nodded indulgently. I wanted to say something more, but at the moment could think of nothing which would be sufficiently crushing without being grossly rude also. I couldn't repress a smile, though, as I turned away, the contrast between her grand air and her folly was so ludicrous.

'You're laughing at me, Johnston!'

I flung her a pitying glance over my shoulder. 'Goodbye, Miss Theresa,' I said quietly. Something of what I felt must have shown in my face, for she suddenly blushed and hurried away towards the house.

Isabel was at no pains to hide her satisfaction when, next day,

The Battle of Flowers

I told her what had happened. 'Good! You'll be able to concentrate all your interest on Elysia now.' It came out so spontaneously that I couldn't keep my face straight. It didn't even occur to her that the fact that I'd lost two days' work might also be of some interest to me.

'That's one way of looking at it, Miss Isabel.'

In all innocence she returned my smile, and in that moment we reached full understanding. A pact was signed. No more subtleties and pretences. We were, frankly and irrevocably, in league against Avalon. It was to be a fight to a finish, a battle of flowers.

In the following week my successor appeared at Avalon, and at the end of his first day we wheeled our bicycles out at the respective gates side by side. He was middle-aged, hatchet-faced and taciturn. I tried to engage him in conversation, but Theresa must have given him a lively picture of the state of affairs, for he glanced back at the windows of the house as if he were afraid to be seen talking to me.

'You've come into a good job, mate,' I said cheerfully.

His face was full of suspicion; goodness knows what he'd been told about me. 'It ain't in bad nick,' he replied without warmth. The next instant he added: 'It's been a bonzer day, ain't it?' and before I could say another word he was on his bicycle and riding away.

All right, I thought, if that's how you want it, that's how you'll get it. You're for Theresa and I'm for Isabel. Look out for yourself —

I discovered later that his name was Egan, and, to give him his due, he was a good gardener. Watching week by week over the fence, I observed no basic alterations in Avalon, but on everything the new man did there was an unmistakable stamp of the expert.

Twelve months of comparative calm passed away, with Elysia gradually and surely approaching the ripe beauty of Avalon. The sisters had pretty well reached their limits in competitive planning and settled down to a kind of trench warfare on the show benches. In this way the struggle had passed largely into the capable hands of Egan and me. He also had absorbed some of the animosity of the sisters, and espoused the cause of Theresa as enthusiastically as I espoused that of Isabel. We entered every horticultural show from Caulfield to Frankston and from Brighton to Dandenong. We exhibited almost everything for which there was a class. We didn't speak to each other, but when judging was over would hang smirking around our respective vases, or saunter past each other with disdainful sidelong glances. Other growers began to whisper of conspiracy, for between our professional ability and the intensity of our mutual dislike Egan and I were irresistible. Where one failed the other would almost invariably succeed.

Theresa was fortunate, for she had found a man after her own resourceful and indomitable heart. She drove Egan even as Isabel was driving me. Under the urge of the rival Twins he and I forgot everything we had in common. It became a matter of personal prestige with both of us. We took to spying on each other over the fence, jealously observing the progress of subjects being groomed for exhibition. Had Egan given some indication of a sense of humour I might have preserved my own. As it was, his sour face coming out night after night at the gate of Avalon gradually got under my skin, and I lost sight altogether of the funny side of the floral feud. I credited him also with the stiff-necked arrogance of Theresa, and developed a sympathy for Isabel which bordered on affection. Isabel was still womanly, still soft-spoken and softly lined. No less indomitable than her sister, she nevertheless had a smile that melted, an air of crucified virtue that aroused in me all the protective instincts of the damned and dominant male. She was a drear and woebegone figure as she moved now against the rioting colours of that magnificent garden. Sometimes I would see her standing motionless for minutes on end, facing the dividing fence and utterly lost in thought. Against that fence, and hidden by a shrub, was a box with a path trodden to it across the border. I never once saw Isabel near that box, but I didn't move it and I didn't fork up the path. It was easy to imagine her mounting up in the solitude of evening or early morning to see what was going on at the other side.

I myself didn't need a box to stand on. On tiptoes I could look over the fence at any point, and the sight of Theresa moving among her flowers like a general among his troops used to exasperate me. Her parting words: 'Really, Johnston, I prefer not to discuss the matter' kept coming back to me. I thought

The Battle of Flowers

of a number of things I could and should have said to her at the time.

Isabel must have perceived this change in me, for the old formal relationship of mistress and man began to weaken and collapse. At morning and afternoon tea times she now brought out a tray for two and called me up to the front verandah where a rustic table stood in the shelter of climbing roses. She never mentioned Theresa, but all our conversation moved cunningly around a mutual hatred of Avalon. Those were the times when I was able to take stock of what the quarrel was doing to her. Constant sulking had drawn deep downward-pointing lines on her face. Grey hairs fringed her forehead. She sighed frequently, and there was a heaviness below her brooding eyes that indicated broken sleep. Her soiled fingers looked grotesquely out of place as they lifted silver teapot and fragile china. I never enjoyed her hospitality, for the tea was always weak and the cake usually stale. From this, and certain other signs, I gathered that she was beginning to feel the financial pinch and had been driven to economies in housekeeping. She used to leave the front door open, and looking into the hall was like looking into a coal cellar. Blinds of all rooms except two were kept down so that the whole house, apart from bedroom and kitchen, was in perpetual darkness. A smell of dust and old clothes drifted out of it. I used to wonder what the end of it all was going to be. In the meantime I'd given up laughing at the conflict of two foolish women, because two foolish men were now also involved.

Suddenly, as if the sisters were afraid of a stalemate developing, there came the war of weeds.

One fine spring day I trenched along the north border of Elysia, and a month later had the finest crop of docks that ever grew in a decent garden. For the uninitiated I should explain that the dock reproduces itself from the root as well as from seed. Dig up a healthy dock, chop the root into six pieces, bury them all six inches deep, and in due time you will have not less than five vigorous young plants.

Had Egan — or Theresa — been satisfied with a mere handful I might just have dug them out and thought no more about it. But he, or she, had made a positive welter of it. There were hundreds and hundreds. They must have been thrown over before I dug the border because they were all thoroughly worked in. The result was altogether too good. Mother Nature, however prolific, is always haphazard, and there was an ordered touch about that sowing that moved me to instant suspicion. Egan!

I could hear him working just at the other side, and after only a moment's reflection I stood on the bottom rail of the fence and looked over.

'How're you off for docks?' I demanded harshly.

He gave me a sour smile, the first time I'd ever seen his lean face relax. 'How're you off for nut-grass?'

'I'm not concerned about nut-grass —'

'And I ain't concerned about docks. Suppose we don't say nothing about nothing?' As he spoke he flicked a little heap of brown nodules with his fork. 'I been on this muck for the last five weeks. It didn't fly in.'

Isabel!

'That didn't come out of here,' I said loyally.

'Maybe it didn't.' Egan's lower jaw stuck out a bit further. 'And them docks didn't come out of here.'

Argument was manifestly useless. It required but little imagination to see the implications. Like rockets Avalon and Elysia had soared upwards together, reached their zenith, and gone immediately into the downwards plunge. The whole nature of the struggle was changed in an instant. I'd always taken a pride in my craft; to me, those gardens were still something much more than the battle-ground of two jealous sisters.

'You bloody vandal!' I said to Egan.

'You're a dirty cow for starting it,' he retorted.

Isabel waved me over to the verandah as I stepped down.

'He says we're throwing weeds over,' I said, watching her closely.

'We? — surely you wouldn't do that, Johnston.'

'I certainly would not, Miss Isabel.'

'Are you suggesting I did?'

I was, of course, suggesting precisely that, but her effrontery momentarily staggered me. 'They say one of us did, and I give you my word it wasn't me.'

'Then it was neither of us.'

'They're giving us docks in exchange.'

'I said it was neither of us. However, show me.'

Together we went over and looked gloomily at the invaders.

'They must have got the nut-grass in with a load of manure,' I said, just to let her see I was prepared to play along. I still didn't believe her, but the way she was looking at those docks stirred me to pity.

We could clearly hear Egan digging away at the other side.

'We didn't get these in with manure, Johnston!' Isabel's lips were set in a thin hard line. Right or wrong she was going to fight back! A new excitement gripped me; at a word from her just then I'd have scaled the fence and made it war indeed.

'No, Miss Isabel, they didn't come in with manure.'

'It's a bad weed, Johnston.'

'I know worse ones.'

'Ah! — for instance?'

'Oxalis. I have a garden full of it down at St Kilda. I dig out a bucketful every Friday.'

'You burn it all, of course?'

'I've *been* burning it.'

Our eyes met. She was smiling now, a slow malicious smile. She was different from the Isabel of even five minutes ago. I knew I was in the process of selling my soul to the devil.

'I think I can rely on you to do the right thing, Johnston.'

She could, even as Theresa could rely on Egan.

We began with dock, nut-grass and oxalis, but, as in all the conflicts of men, each side was forever seeking new and more potent weapons. Egan and I knew our weeds as well as we knew our onions, and Avalon and Elysia forthwith became the innocent repositories of all the pests of our other gardens. We used to give them to the sisters, who pelted them over the fence as soon as our backs were turned and the shades of night had fallen. Every day we arrived with gunny-bags more or less full, like condemned men carrying their own blocks. The fact that even in those circumstances we could still meet in the street without smiling was a fair measure of the depth of stupidity to which we had fallen. We used to flourish our bags at each other with a 'this'll slay you!' kind of expression, spit contemptuously across the plot of grass between us, and stalk in at our respective gates with jaws set and noses in the air as if we were doing something altogether heroic. I can laugh at it now, but was far too embroiled to see the funny side of it then.

By the time the autumn shows came around both gardens were beginning to wilt under the new offensive warfare. Those women started something when they pitted Egan and me against each other, for the petty squabble of two female novices is a vastly different thing to the deadly clash of experts. We wasted neither energy nor materials. Nut-grass, sorrel, dock, onion weed, perennial phlox suckers, finely chopped couch-grass, oxalis — everything that passed over that fence was a gardener's headache. We knew exactly what to use, and when and how to use it.

In a few months there was a patchiness in exhibition beds and ribbon borders that damned whatever chance either place might have had in that year's 'Best Garden' competitions. Surface-rooting plants like asters and petunias won't stand being fiddled about with, and we had a choice of disturbing them in getting the weeds out or of letting the weeds overwhelm them. It was among these easy victims that the invaders skirmished with particular zeal, as if they had entered intelligently into the evil spirit of the new game. Here and there patches of naked soil soon marked places where they had driven us to the necessity of making a clean sweep.

The effect on perennials, and on choice subjects such as dahlias and gladioli being prepared for the show benches, was equally disastrous, for neither Egan nor I had time to look after them. Five hours out of every eight were now spent with fork and rubbish bucket. The consequence was that a general air of neglect began to settle over both gardens. Weeds made headway on the shaded portions of paths, hips matured on the roses, lawns got tufty around the edgings, withered blooms still clung to the spring-flowering shrubs.

And still no sign of weakening from either of the sisters. Now, if ever, was the time to call a halt, for it was plain even to outsiders that we had embarked on a career of mutual and deliberate destruction. Whispers of the quarrel were getting around, so that at any time of the day now I could look up from my work and see curious faces peering over the gate. (It was no longer possible to look over the ragged hedge.) One day a newspaper reporter asked me for 'a story'. I told him to go and see Isabel. Buying had practically ceased in both gardens, with a consequent reduction in my 'pickings', but curiosity over the outcome of the struggle, and an eagerness to triumph over Egan, made me reluctant to give up the job. I used to show each new species of weed to Isabel as it made its appearance, but she would merely compress her lips, glance vindictively towards Avalon, and sigh as if at the perfidy of a world utterly beyond her comprehension. 'All right, Johnston,' she would say resignedly, 'just keep on doing your best.'

That remark was typical of her non-committal promptings. Any third person overhearing it would naturally infer that I was to do my best in combating the invader. But I understood the full and exact import — and I did my best. Theresa had become the aggressor by first throwing docks into Elysia — so I argued — then let the first peace overtures come from Avalon.

One morning, only three days from the first of the autumn shows, Egan put his head over the fence alongside where I was working.

'You dirty cow!'

'What's up now, moaner?'

'You don't know nothing about this, I suppose?' He jerked his head backwards and I stepped up on to the bottom rail and looked over.

I didn't see it at first; he had to point it out to me.

So as to gain a bit of shelter from the hot summer winds, Theresa had always grown her dahlias in groups in the north border. The particular group to which Egan was now drawing my attention consisted of three plants of Jane Cowl, bearing among them several magnificent flowers many points better than anything I had in Elysia. I'd been watching them enviously for over a week. Isabel also knew about them, because I'd found the imprints of her shoes more than once at this very spot.

That morning all three plants looked as if they'd been under twenty degrees of frost. The big bronze petals drooped miserably, while the foliage was already turning black. Everything around them was normal, except for a few drops of greenish-coloured liquid spattering other foliage in a distinct trail straight to where we stood.

'I didn't do that, son,' I said impulsively.

'You never do nothing!' snarled Egan. 'You know what's on now, don't you?'

I didn't answer immediately. For the first time since the feud began I was really shocked. A wave of disgust passed over me, for both gardens had reserves of beauty that still lifted them above the war of weeds. A tattered gypsy-like beauty with a novel charm of its own. Enough still to warm the hearts of men masters of their craft. I had a sudden vision now of two little brown deserts.

'Eh?' persisted Egan.

'Eh?'

'I said: you know what's on now, don't you?'

Like a cat watching a canary, he was looking at my own dahlia bed only fifteen feet away.

'We aren't going to do this, are we?' I faltered.

'Like hell we ain't! You started it.'

I was going to deny that again, but a perverse sense of loyalty got the better of me. I hated Isabel at that moment, but I'd got thoroughly accustomed to regarding Egan and Theresa as the enemy.

'If you touch those dahlias I'll burn you out from the bloody roots up!' I fumed.

'So what do I do about that?' Egan nodded again towards his Jane Cowls. 'Say nothing and do nothing?'

'Please your damned self,' I murmured helplessly, and got down off the fence. I knew very well what I'd do if I were in his position.

Isabel had the hide to deny her guilt, but didn't waste any histrionics over it.

'We'll have to fix up a couple of sheets of roofing-iron over our dahlias,' I informed her as soon as she came out.

'Why, Johnston?'

'Egan's mad over those Jane Cowls. Somebody sprayed them with weed-killer.'

'He's blaming us, of course?'

'It was done from this side of the fence.' My anger got the better of me, and I added with plenty of feeling: 'That's something I couldn't do, Miss Isabel.'

'Nor me either, Johnston.' She gave me a frigid stare, as if daring me to pursue the matter further. 'And I'm certainly not

• **The Battle of Flowers** •

going to disfigure the garden with roofing-iron to please anybody.'

She wasn't going to disfigure the garden!

'What about the Show?' I asked. 'There's only three days to go. Suppose we cut a few flowers and put them on ice?'

'That's never satisfactory. We'll take a chance.'

She'd take a chance — with Egan next door! It was in that moment that my allegiance first began to waver. Once again I got the feud in its correct perspective, a contemptible squabble between two idle women. She, Isabel, didn't want peace, or a beautiful garden. She didn't want vengeance, because there was nothing to be avenged. She'd reached a pitch of malevolence where she wanted destruction for its own sake. Theresa also; there was a pair of them. I'm quite sure that Isabel used poison first only because she happened to be the first to think of it. Theresa would have done it with equal relish. All the lovely flowers of Avalon and Elysia had long ago become to the sisters nothing more than instruments with which to wound each other. Perhaps it was some kind of frustration working in them. I don't know, I'm not up in such matters.

What I do know is that I suddenly burned with indignation. She'd take a chance — she knew very well that there was no chance about it. She knew what was going to happen to those dahlias as well as I did. I remembered Egan's honest rage as he pointed to his Jane Cowls, flowers into which he had put the experience of a lifetime and the patient care of four months. My heart warmed to him and hardened to the sisters. I thought of his wife and mine, in their little cottages. No doubt our domestic circumstances were very similar. Two tiny pocket-handkerchiefs of gardens in which we had to grow vegetables in order to make ends meet. No dahlias for *our* women. We only grew them.

There came over me an irresistible temptation to plumb the final depths of the sisters' degradation. Isabel was still only halfway across the lawn.

'Miss Isabel!'

She turned, still scowling. 'What is it, Johnston?'

'D'you mind if I take a bunch of those flowers home?'

'Of dahlias?' She wasn't merely surprised; she was offended. 'You aren't serious, are you?'

'They'll be dying tomorrow. I thought it a pity to waste them.'

'They will not be dying tomorrow!' she snapped. 'We're going to show them on Saturday.' And with a swirl of her tattered skirts she hurried off.

I decided then and there that if those dahlias were still alive on Saturday morning I'd assassinate them myself the moment I arrived.

I didn't need to.

Egan excelled himself. He and I have lately got on to speaking terms at the local hotel, and I've learned that he did the job himself. I suspected it at the time. That bed of dahlias was no woman's work. Like Isabel, he'd fortified the weed-killer with something else so as to get quick results. (What that something was it isn't necessary to say here; the sisters may not, after all, be unique!) Egan told me he went all the way to Ringwood on the Wednesday night to borrow a big orchard pump from a mate. His reaction to the poisoning of the show dahlias was ultimately the same as mine; if they want fight, let's give 'em fight good and proper and have done with it. He set a smart pace. He took not three dahlias, but all of them. For all the use it was going to be in the next six months, he took the very bed they were growing in. He used the hard jet; black hieroglyphics were traced on the lawn all around, where his aim had strayed occasionally off the target. Isabel must have tried to effect a rescue on the Thursday, for the bed had been flooded with water. She might have saved her time.

I was always in attendance on the mornings of Show Saturdays, and at nine o'clock she came over to where I was grubbing aimlessly in a tangle of weeds.

'Good morning, Johnston.'

'Good morning, Miss Isabel.'

She waited. She wanted me to open up the subject but I was determined to make her come right out into the open this time. After the first glance of greeting I kept my head down and went on working. Her soiled shoes and slovenly stockings, only four feet from my face, filled me with disgust.

'You've seen the dahlia bed?' she asked just as the silence was becoming embarrassing.

'Yes, I've seen it. They made a good job of it.'

The Battle of Flowers

'There's nothing we can do about it, I suppose?'

'Nothing. You won't be able to grow even chickweed in that bed for twelve months.'

'I see.' She was silent for perhaps half a minute. Then: 'Johnston, we must — I would like —' her voice trailed off.

I straightened up, and the instant my eyes fell on her face I was seized with pity. Poor devil! She was a bundle of nerves. She was trying to tell me something, but all she could manage was an inarticulate twitching of her pale lips. Struggling to keep back the tears, she was mutely beseeching me. Her coarse fingers fluttered over an ancient cameo brooch at her throat. All my bitterness dissolved. I thought to myself: you're for the Bughouse anyway. The kindest thing Egan and I can do for the pair of you is to slip the skids under.

'There's a bit of scum on the drive near the house,' I said in a voice loaded with significance. 'It needs spraying.'

The instant brightening of her tired eyes confirmed my most gloomy suspicions. They lit up, like the eyes of a little girl promised a new doll.

'You will require some materials, Johnston.'

'Four gallons, and an orchard pump,' I said solemnly. 'Will you order them today?'

'I'll ring up for them immediately.'

'If you can get them out in time I'll come back and do the job after tea.' Curiosity as to whether she had a scrap of pride or conscience left in her impelled me to add: 'It's much more effective done after dark.'

She didn't even smile. 'Thank you, Johnston. I'll pay you, of course. These things have to be attended to.'

These things have to be attended to!

It was a strange experience going in at the gate of Elysia that night. I'd never been there after nightfall before, and was startled to find how completely all sense of familiarity was lacking. Stars and a crescent moon made it easy to follow the paths, and I knew to a foot the position of every bed and bush, yet they were different. I felt like a trespasser, like a criminal. Not a breath of wind stirred. Invisible figures lurked in every shadow; shocked eyes shone at me from every gloomy bush. I trod gently on the gravelled drive, but the noise was terrific. The nature of my mission must have been playing havoc with my nerves, for I remember that every foot of the way I was tensed for a scream of alarm. After all, I *was* a criminal, and I *had* come to murder. The sense of guilt and imminent calamity deepened as I passed the darkened front of the house and saw a yellow light gleaming in the window of the toolshed.

Isabel had left a hurricane lamp burning; on the bench was a new orchard pump and a four-gallon drum of poison.

There was a light also in the window of the kitchen across the drying-green, but my lady didn't come out. I was tempted to make her a more active accessory by knocking on the kitchen door and pretending I needed hot water to mix the poison with, but after some consideration I decided to spare her what little peace she had left. I also wanted to give her and Theresa a last chance, to keep control of the orgy of destruction for just one more round. No irreparable damage was yet done to either garden; perhaps the sisters would come to their senses even at this late hour.

I used, therefore, only one bucketful of poison. To this day I will swear that Theresa watched the whole operation from the front of her house. It also, like Elysia, was in darkness, but time and again I saw something moving like a black ghost on the pale tiles of the loggia. If she'd suddenly flung up her arms and run at me across the lawn I would, without doubt, have downed tools and fled all the way home, because there was an eeriness about the whole proceedings that had me thoroughly on edge.

But nobody interfered, and I went on with my crime. Standing on a big box against the fence, I directed my fire carefully at a long bed of chrysanthemums on the near side of the big lawn. For good measure I took in a chunk of the surrounding grass and a section of lavender border along the brick path. It was impossible to see anything clearly, but I knew Avalon as well as I knew Elysia, and I prided myself that Egan would see on my work the same neatness and dispatch which had characterized his treatment of my dahlia bed.

He did.

Surreptitiously on the Monday morning I watched him clearing away the wreckage and opening up the poisoned soil. He did it earnestly and efficiently, as he did everything, but there was a glint in his dour eyes that boded ill for Elysia, and an ironic smile on his shovel-chin that showed he was wide awake to the futility of further effort. Once, during the morning, I saw Theresa standing on the edge of the lawn thoughtfully studying the north border. Her face was towards me, and she also was easy to read. She was considering the next blow, estimating the consequences, weighing Avalon against Elysia — her rhododendrons against our peonies, her daphnes against our gardenias, her liriodendron against our jacaranda. Directly opposite her was a full-grown camellia loaded with fat buds, many of them already touched with red where the petals were beginning to break through. Theresa's eyes rested on it long and wistfully, and I promptly put it at the top of my list for the next onslaught.

My own little lady was in high good humour. She wished me a particularly affable good morning, gave me fresh cakes for afternoon tea, and went about all day with a smirk that made me wish to be Egan just for that night.

Rhododendrons — peonies — daphnes — gardenias — camellia —

Four weeks later, in a wilderness of scarred lawns and ravaged trees, I said goodbye to Elysia. Isabel let me mess about for eight hours among the ruins, but at five o'clock ended the farce by telling me I would have to look for another job. Hollow-eyed and dishevelled, and with that awful cemetery of a garden for a background, she was the most tragic figure I have ever seen. Her efforts to preserve a last miserable shred of dignity almost brought a lump to my throat.

With a wan smile she held out a pound note and some silver. 'Your money, Johnston.'

I looked at her in inquiry.

'Yes, there's ten shillings extra — for luck.' An odd movement passed over her, a deep shivering drawing of the breath. She shot a swift and apprehensive glance to right and left of her. This place, I thought, is going to haunt you.

I thanked her, and her wandering gaze came to rest on me. 'Johnston, I'm sorry. I — it really isn't any use going on, is it?'

'Why, Miss Isabel?' I asked mercilessly.

She made a pitiful gesture. 'There's no — no garden. You'll have to look for another one.'

Her tone was sharp, but I'd asked for it. The woman was manifestly on the edge of the abyss. I was tempted to say all kinds of things, but before I could make up my mind the situation became too much for her and she impulsively thrust out her hand.

'Goodbye, Johnston, You've been a — a fine fellow!' A convulsive grasp, a heart-rending smile, the swift glisten of tears and she was gone. Her shabby figure vanished into the house before I realized I hadn't said a word of farewell.

Egan had already departed from Avalon, two days before. He and I were the last links of the Heavenly Twins with the world of sanity. In due time life will assert itself in both gardens, but Egan and I will not be there, and only the strong will survive. No doubt some strange stories will grow up around two spiteful old crones tottering to their graves through an ever-mounting wilderness of dolichos and wild ivy.

· All I Ask ·

Nelson looked past the driver at the clock on the dashboard. Eleven pm.

That made an hour's run. Fast going, until a few minutes ago when they'd got up into the hills and started dropping off passengers here and there. Must be near the end now. All the other passengers gone. He had the back seat of the big Studebaker all to himself. Only the driver in front.

'How much further?' he asked.

'Not much. You're for Olinda, aren't you?'

'Yes. Eseama Guesthouse. Know it?'

'Mrs Furneaux's joint. Yes, I know it.'

Nelson eased himself forward so that his head was at the driver's shoulder. 'How far have we come?'

'About thirty miles. The Gully's twenty-five out of Melbourne. Olinda's six miles further on.'

'What mountains are these?'

'The Dandenong Ranges. Not much mountains about them. Never been up here before?'

'No. I just left a ship yesterday.'

That wouldn't have been hard to guess anyway. He'd been self-conscious of his blue raincoat, rollneck jersey, and cloth cap, from the very first.

'Skinned out?' The driver sounded as if he knew something of the ways of seamen.

'No. On the level. Paid off.'

'Going to have a look at Australia, eh?'

'Something like that. I'm going to try to dig in ashore. To hell with the sea!'

Nelson sniffed. To hell with the sea. The air had been getting colder. Now it bit in the nostrils. Something else besides cold.

87

The smell of trees and rotting leaves. Ferny Creek dropped behind. The driver changed gears and the car settled down for the easy run through to Sassafras. Now and then a rabbit bounded across the deserted road. Once they swerved to dodge a wombat, petrified by the headlights. Tall eucalypts stood stiff and straight at either side. The wall of scrub abruptly ceased, revealing, far in the distance, the twinkling lights of a great city.

'That Melbourne?' asked Nelson.

'That's Melbourne. You get one of the best views in the Ranges from here. You're nearly three thousand feet up.'

'It's like a landfall. Cape Town's just like that when you come in at night.'

'The driver grunted, and a few minutes later braked to a standstill near a cyclone gate set in a cypress hedge.

'This is it. Cost you five bob.'

Nelson got out and felt in his pocket while the driver unbuckled his suitcase from the carrier at the back. He was smiling to himself. The old fascination, strong as ever! The intoxicating thrill of penetrating strange places. Just a short leap this time — in distance. In other ways, far longer. A new life. Everything full of meaning. Nearly three thousand feet up. How well his mood had been suited to the pugnacious hum of the big car ever since leaving the Gully! Up — and away! How was it they put it? — above sea level! And this was it — this lofty timber, these hairpin bends in the high-banked road, these cosy doorways beaming deep amongst the leaves every time they stopped to set someone down. These black abysses rimmed with polished blackbutt spars. There came over him a soothing sense of remoteness, of flight fulfilled, like what visited him sometimes in the night-watches.

'Thanks,' said the driver. 'Through the gate and straight down. The house is on the left. I'll blow the horn to tell 'em you're here.'

Nelson went in, followed a beaten track a short distance, and came to another gate while the echoes of the horn were still leaping about the hills. From where he stood, the ground fell away steeply so that the roof of the house, some distance away, showed as a sharp silhouette little higher than his feet. Most of it was in darkness, but a door opened, throwing a broad beam of light down a wooden ramp and up a path lined with shrubs. A woman called out: 'Is someone there?'

'Yes, the new man.'

'Come right up. We're expecting you.'

We're expecting you! The words warmed him. How long ago was it that anyone had expected him anywhere?

He found she was just a girl, wearing a white apron over a brown uniform frock. She had a jolly smile, as if she'd just finished laughing at a good joke.

'Leave your bag there. Mrs Furneaux is in the kitchen.'

He followed her through a sort of laundry into the kitchen. A huge place, like the kitchen of an hotel he'd once worked at in Vancouver. Everything on a generous scale. A big range, a big draining board, big sink, big table. And warm, very warm, with a smell of foods he hadn't tasted in years.

'So, you did manage to find us?'

Not quite as it sounded. The woman was smiling as she came across to him.

'I was told to get the ten o'clock car, Mrs Furneaux.'

'Miss Tinsley is an old muddler. I distinctly told her the eight o'clock. But it doesn't matter. Your name's Nelson, isn't it?'

'Yes, Mrs Furneaux.'

She was plump, grey-haired, fussy. Motherly was the word that leapt to his mind. Not at all what he'd expected in the proprietress of a first-class guesthouse.

'Well, I'm glad you've come. We've been without a man for three days.'

Her keen eyes were taking him in from head to foot. For the hundredth time since coming ashore he wished he had an open-necked jersey and a hat.

'You *are* a gardener, aren't you?' she asked with manifest suspicion.

'Yes, Mrs Furneaux.'

Not such a big lie. Any mug could push a lawnmower, trim a hedge, and grow vegetables. She'd hardly expect orchids.

'And you understand cows?'

'Yes.'

'And fowls?'

'Oh yes.'

Cows and fowls! How Olsen, Ketchem and McNab would grin if they could hear this!

'You look a nice respectable sort of man, anyway,' she burst out unexpectedly. 'Well, I'll have a proper talk with you in the morning. Nellie will tell you what to do, won't you, Nellie?'

The girl, who had gone over to the range, nodded casually.

'And give him some supper. We look after our people here, don't we, Nellie? We're just a nice happy little family.'

Nelson bit his lip to keep his face straight. A nice happy little family — oh, mother, take me in!

'Thank you, Mrs Furneaux.'

'I must get back to my guests. We have a bridge party.'

When she had gone it was as if a warm breeze had ceased blowing.

'Sit down,' said the girl. 'I suppose you could eat something?'

'I can always eat something.'

That was how she made him feel. How everything made him feel. Hard to guess her age. Perhaps twenty, possibly nearer thirty. The skirt of her dress hung rather wide and she had a trick of standing with her feet planted far apart. Low-heeled shoes. Quaint. Like some girls he'd once seen on the outskirts of Rotterdam. Smiling all the time, as if a trifle embarrassed. Her voice, though, was crisp and confident.

He looked in astonishment at the plate of eggs and crumbed chops she placed before him. 'Is this what you call supper here?'

'Don't tell me you can't eat it!'

'I can eat it all right.'

'There's always plenty to eat here. D'you want tea or coffee?'

'Coffee, please, if it's all the same to you.'

She poured him a cup and went and sat on a high stool at the bench and began to roll butter pats. Now and then a mutter of voices came from inside the house. Otherwise it was perfectly quiet.

'When I first heard the name of this place,' he said just to make conversation, 'I thought it was Easy Anna!'

She gave a merry laugh. 'No — Eseama. It's Aboriginal; it means return.'

Return! Home is the sailor...

'Do you have to work as late as this every night?'

'Goodness, no. I'm usually in bed long before this.'

'Did you have to stop up just to look after me?'

'No, there's a party inside. I've got to help Miss Leveson and Dick with the supper. All the others have gone to a dance.'

'Who's Miss Leveson and Dick?'

'She's a sort of companion-housekeeper. Dick is Mrs Furneaux's nephew.'

'She makes him do a bit, eh?'

She gave him a glance he couldn't quite read. 'He runs the buffet for her. He's only sixteen. She's worried about him. His dad and mum are in England. She's responsible for him, and he's pestering her to let him go to sea.'

Nelson smiled comprehendingly. 'And she won't let him?'

'No. She wants him . . .'

'She's a wise woman,' he said decisively. 'The sea's no good.'

'How do you know?'

'I've had fifteen years of it. I've just blown it in for good.'

'What's wrong with it?'

'Everything. There's too much rubbish talked about the sea. What do poets know about it?' He cleared his mouth, then quoted sardonically: *All I ask is a tall ship and a star to steer her by.* Punk! I've had a gutful. I'm asking for something different now.'

'You'll get along with Mrs Furneaux!'

He went on eating in silence, now and then casting a covert glance at the girl's calm face and her shapely legs swinging clear of the floor. Nice. She had long eyelashes. Everything about her sweet and real. The first decent girl he'd been alone with in how many years?

'What's wrong — you didn't go to the dance? Did you have to stay back?'

'I could have got away. What do I want to go dancing for?'

'Don't you like dancing?'

'I don't know. I never seemed to bother.'

Funny. She must have been asked often enough. Maybe, if he stayed here . . .

She went out and was busy for some minutes in what seemed to be a sort of servery. When she came back he had finished eating, and she offered to show him his hut.

'What happens in the morning?' he asked.

'I'll call you at seven. You get up and milk the cows. Come in here first for a cup of tea.'

'It's years since I milked a cow. I was ashore in Canada once.'

'You'll be all right. Bring your bag.'

Five yards up the garden path she stopped and shone the beam of an electric torch onto a weatherboard hut. 'There it is. All your own! There's four blankets. If you want more you can have them.'

He chuckled. 'Do you look after everybody like this?'

'They're there to be used. It's cold here at night.'

'What do I have to call you — Nellie?'

'That's what everybody else calls me. You're no different.'

'Good night — Nellie! Thanks for the nice supper.'

He stood watching her until the door of the house closed behind her. Dutchy! Crumbed chops and eggs . . . four blankets . . . a smell of trees and dead leaves . . . the glow of a kerosene lamp on wooden walls . . . 'All your own!'

Ten minutes later he heard a dog bark twice, then fell asleep.

Home is the sailor . . .

In the middle of a blissful dream about Olsen and Ketchem, and a ship hull down on an enchanted horizon, someone banged on the wall of the hut: 'Mr Nelson!'

Dutchy . . .

He opened his eyes. Only the pale square of the window relieved the black darkness.

'Hello — what's up?'

'Can you drive a car?'

'Can I what?'

He sat up just to satisfy himself he wasn't still dreaming.

'Wake up! Can you drive a car?'

'Yes. What's all this about?'

'Get up and come out. Mrs Furneaux wants you.'

'What time is it?'

'One o'clock. Something's happened . . .'

'Am I supposed to work at night?'

'This is something special. Come on . . . she's waiting for you.'

'But what does she want?'

'I'll tell you when you come out. Hurry...'

Five minutes later he came up the laundry ramp still wriggling into his blue jersey. Nellie met him on the threshold. She spoke in an urgent whisper, but looked as if she were secretly enjoying a huge joke.

'It's young Dick — he's gone!'

'Dick? Oh, that nephew? Well?'

'He's cleared out.'

'Cleared out?'

'Yes, run away.'

'Run away?' For a moment he was only concerned with trying to see where he himself came into the picture.

'Mrs Furneaux missed him when the party broke up. He never goes to bed without saying good night to her. She went through to his room. And there was a note saying he'd run away to sea.'

'To sea!'

All I ask is a tall ship...

'She wants you to drive her to town. She thinks she can catch him. He must have gone down on the last service car. She's half crazy... sssh! here she comes...'

'Well, the goddam young fool!' ejaculated Nelson.

But he, too, was laughing at a secret joke.

· Ward Four ·

There was a story I read about an air crash. Two aeroplanes colliding and everybody in them being killed. It was, quite frankly I believe, based on the crash over the Grand Canyon in America in 1955. A moving story, made agonizingly real by the author's mastery of technical detail. The ultimate power, however, derived from his insight into the last thought common to all the as-yet-uninjured passengers as they spun earthwards: 'I am here, and this is happening to me.'

I am here, and this is happening to me.

And that, I remember, was *my* first thought. It must come to a lot of people when they open their eyes and find themselves in a hospital bed for the first time in their lives. Particularly if they are not young, have been blessed with robust health, and are well acquainted with hospitals as a visitor calling on sick friends.

My thoughts ran: I am in bed — it is night-time — this is a big room — it is a hospital. I couldn't see any lights, but there was light. Church-like and restful, enough to see with. At the foot of the bed a woman was standing quite still, watching me. I could see only her head and shoulders; below that all was hidden by something on the bed. I thought: and that is a nurse. She shone a torch at me, but switched it off instantly when she saw that my eyes were open. I learned afterwards that I had cried out in my sleep, and that the patient in the next bed had called her.

She came round to my side, and I got the fresh sweet smell of her as she bent over me.

'Are you all right, Mr Crowley?'

'Yes,' I replied, and immediately went to sleep again.

Next time I woke up there was more light, and a lot of commotion around the bed on my left. Subdued voices, shuffling feet, tinkling vessels. I turned my head, but could see only a white linen screen. A nurse came out from behind it and hurried over to a long bench in the middle of the floor. The sense of urgency quickened my interest, set me thinking, and kept me from falling asleep.

I am here, and this is happening to me. This is what it is like in hospital when there are no visitors.

There wasn't much pain. Just a headache, a vile taste in my mouth, and a sensation of something pressing evenly and heavily on my legs. I was lying with head and shoulders slightly raised, and saw that what I had thought to be something on the bed was just the bedclothes heaped up over a cage. I knew what that meant: it fitted in with the pressure on my legs.

So that's where the damage is. What else? Under the blankets I cautiously stretched my arms, clenched my fists. Trunk, loins, upper thighs, on all these members I was able to reassure myself without moving much. But an attempt to reach further involved putting some pressure on my legs in order to bring my shoulders up, and I fell back dizzy with pain.

Legs. Of course it would be the legs. I lay still, thinking, and it began to come back to me. Berth Sixteen Victoria Dock — the *Boissevain* — 9.15 p.m., just after we of the nightshift had started work — the 'tween-deck of Number Three Hatch — trays of flour, 60 lb per bag and over a hundred bags to the tray —

The tray that did it. Three of us on the yardarm side, swinging it like a great pendulum so as to land it as far under the deck-head as possible — 'This time! — stand by! — come orr-orr-orrf!'

The sudden realization that the dropping tray was hanging tight on the midship — men at either side of me leaping sideways — a roar of angry voices, with that of the hatchman rising over them all: 'Off midship! — off midship! — off midship! — drop it, you bastard, Sammy!' The crash, and the pain, and the heavy wire and hook settling relentlessly over my head and shoulders as I went down.

Yes, legs, of course. Fractures for certain. One? Two? No use trying to find out for myself. I'd have to wait until someone came along. I fell to wondering if my wife knew, if she'd been in yet, what time it was, how long I'd be in hospital, if my legs would get well enough again to let me go back to the waterfront. If indeed they were still with me.

This latter idea panicked me for a moment, so that I had to take myself in hand. The activity around the next bed helped me there. I heard the patient groan, and I thought: that man is worse off than me. And all those others. I was able to see now where the half-light was coming from, little lamps set in the floor at intervals all the way down the centre of the ward. Shadowy beds, each with a sick man in it. They were already here while I was lustily heaving cargo around on the *Boissevain*. Perhaps some of them will never leave.

They were finishing around the next bed. A nurse removed the screen, revealing a white-gowned doctor just walking away from the other side. Another nurse was arranging the patient's pillows, while a red-caped sister was fiddling about with basins and instruments on a trolley like a dinner-wagon. In a few minutes one of them switched off the light and they all went away. It became quiet except for the sound of heavy breathing, a snore or two, and a moan quickly broken off. In the distance a toilet was flushed and a door closed. At the nearby bench two nurses were talking in low voices. Now and then — pleasantly reassuring sound! — they had a little laugh together. I looked over at the patient on my left, the one who had just received attention, and found that he was lying watching me with wide-open eyes. Below a bandaged forehead his dark brooding face struck me immediately as being not Australian.

'How you fill?' he asked.

'Not bad,' I replied.

'You slip long time.'

'How long? What time is it?'

'Half past one. Maybe a bit more.'

'What time did they bring me in here?'

'About midnight.'

'How long have you been here?'

'Not long before you. I get knock down by a car. Break my leg and some ribs. Bust my head — damn!'

He didn't wince as he said this, so I gathered he was just cursing his bad luck. He pushed himself into a sitting position and seemed to forget me as he gazed gloomily across the ward. I could just make out his strong middle-aged profile. It was the face of a man who is troubled not by pain but by something else, something that was there before the accident.

On the other side of me a grey-haired old man lay flat on his back, peacefully sleeping.

The voices of the two nurses had ceased. By lifting my head a little I could see the sister's brightly lighted desk near the distant entrance. She was sitting there now, writing. A young doctor was standing over her, smoking, and talking to her. She looked up at him and smiled.

Over an amplifier a voice said softly and distinctly: 'Calling the foreman — calling the foreman.'

The foreman — innocent euphemism! I knew who that was. An experienced friend had once told me. It meant that a patient had died and that a certain individual was required to remove and otherwise attend to the body.

How big it all was! And how smoothly efficient.

And the same thought came to me again, but with a new significance. I am here, in hospital for the first time in my life. But last night, and all the other nights and days, it was going on just like this. This extraordinary instrument got together by men for the help of their sick brothers. All those years while I was toiling away among the tumbling cases and swinging trays it was here, waiting for me to get hurt. Yesterday, only a few hours ago, it happened, and I passed out in the noise and turmoil of a ship's hold. And when I awake I am here, in this peaceful bed, washed, stitched, bandaged, drugged. Everything has been done.

Everything has been done. I fell asleep again.

Dreams. The kind of dreams that come to people in trouble. Stupid, turbulent dreams, full of menace and violent movement.

The picture was one I knew well. A reproduction of an old print in a book that had been lying about at home for a long time. The French Revolution. The storming of the Bastille. Voluminous-skirted women, wild-faced and dishevelled, dragging a cannon. Men marching. Tramping feet and slowly revolving wheels. And in it all there was some kind of rhythm that increasingly excited me. And a man's voice shouting. A voice that woke me up trembling, and that I knew was real even before I opened my eyes.

'Joan! Joan! Where are you, Joan? Oh, you bitches! — you bloody bitches!'

And there it all was, passing across the foot of my bed. Big wheels turning indeed, the wheels of a trolley-stretcher. Marching women, nurses. Somebody else knocked down by a car or hit by a swinging tray. The procession passed quickly, going all the way down to the end of the ward where there were two beds with wooden frames rigged over them. Another nurse was already at one of them, with the light turned on, throwing back blankets and sheets.

The patient, after that one great shout, had fallen silent, but seemed to be feebly struggling. I couldn't see much for the people around him: two wardsmen, two nurses and a sister, followed at a little distance by a doctor and a young fellow who was no doubt a student, both in white gowns.

All down the ward patients had stirred, with here and there one of them sitting up to look. The grey-haired man on my right slept on. The foreigner on my left was still awake, and following the trolley with angry eyes.

'That iss a bad man, that,' he muttered as if to himself.

'He must be badly hurt,' I suggested.

'He still don' have to say things like that,' he said.

I felt a bit that way myself, but didn't want to talk. The headache was still bothering me, and my mouth was poisonous. I'd have given anything for a cup of tea. I just wanted to lie quietly with my head on one side watching what was going on around the new patient. They must have had him tied down to the stretcher, because there was quite a struggle getting him over on to the bed. Wardsmen, nurses and doctor all took part, so that for a few minutes the scene was one of confusion and involuntary noises. The gasps and exclamations of the nurses came to me clearly. In the middle of it all the patient began to shout again: 'Joan! Joan! Get away, you bitches! Leave me alone — Joan!'

He had a strong clear voice, not at all like that of a man gabbling in a delirium. He sounded as if he knew very well what he was saying, and expected an instant response. Once, as a nurse reeled backwards for a moment, I got a glimpse of his heavily bandaged head, his face turned yearningly in the direction of the entrance. They were tying him down all right. The nurse who had been thrown aside had returned to the attack and was swiftly making a knot in a strip of linen while a wardsman held on to one straining arm. Other nurses were securing him at the other side and at the feet.

The foreigner was still muttering indignantly: 'How much good for him could his Joan do now?'

How much indeed? Possibly she doesn't even know about it yet. But this is a place, I reflected, where there are no strangers, only hurt people.

He became quiet. Perhaps the doctor did something to him, because I saw him bending over the bed. The two wardsmen came away, wheeling the empty stretcher. Then the sister and a nurse together. The third nurse worked on, and as the ward became quiet again I fell asleep.

More dreams. Shouting again. People running. There was a long road, path, alleyway, just an impression. Far away at the end of it a man was shouting, and I was under some desperate need to get to him. There was a woman with me, running also. A woman I recognized, but hadn't seen for years, and who had never meant anything to me. She was urging me on, and weeping.

When I opened my eyes the sister was just passing the end of my bed, running back towards the new patient. I'd certainly been trying to run with her, because excruciating pains were now shooting up my legs.

Another struggle was going on around the bed under the frame. The powerful voice rang through the ward: 'You bitches! Oh, you cruel bitches!'

He seemed to have got one hand free. Two nurses wrestled with him on the far side. Their panting voices came to me clearly:

'Oh, Elsie, he's got hold of me!'

'Bite him, Lynne! Bite him —'

Lynne must have done so, for he gave another great bellow, and one of the nurses jumped backwards just as the sister reached them. Thus reinforced, they got him secured again and his struggles ceased. The sister was bending over him, talking to him in a firm, urgent voice:

'Mr Anderson, listen to me! Listen. I think you know what you're doing. You dare to hurt one of my nurses —'

My nurses! The words sent a glow of satisfaction through me.

From the bed on my left there came the voice of the foreigner: 'Why don't they knock him on the head!' and I knew he was feeling just as I was.

Straight across the ward from me a man had got out and was sitting with his bare feet resting on the floor, hands on the bed at either side of him, ready to launch himself to the rescue. The sister caught sight of him and instantly hurried to him.

'Mr Joliffe, get back into bed this moment! How dare you —'

'That bloke's dangerous, sister. He'll hurt one of them girls.'

'Nonsense! We can look after him. Come on, into bed with you! And don't let me catch you —'

Male footfalls sounded at the other end of the ward, and another man appeared. He also wore a white gown, but I didn't think he was a doctor. Perhaps a technician of some kind. He was carrying a coil of what looked like sash-cord, and went to work on the new patient, rigging a contrivance that lifted a splinted and bandaged leg and kept it suspended from the wooden frame. The man lay quietly watching him with glistening eyes. One of the nurses came away. As she passed me I could see, even in the bad light, that her face was flushed with exertion, her hair disordered, and her uniform pulled all askew.

The ward became still again. The sister had set out on a leisurely round of the beds, stopping at each one for a moment, sometimes to flash a torch, sometimes for a few quietly spoken words when she found the patient awake.

I was having a fair bit of pain now. Not only the head. My legs were bothering me. I must have started something trying to run in that dream. The bed was comfortable, though, and there was no desire to move. I thought: if only it were morning and I could get a cup of tea. Around me were all the odd little sounds of sick people sleeping, or trying to sleep. And the distant sounds of the hospital itself: 'Calling Dr Blacklaw — calling Dr Blacklaw —'

Blacklaw — Blacklaw — like Blacket, my mate on the waterfront. Jim Blacket, 'Big Jim'. And I was back again in the 'tween-deck of the *Boissevain*, going over every detail of the accident. The midship wire, running off too much and too late, coiling down over my head. The whole ship lying across my legs. Big Jim, leaping in and sending bags of flour flying right and left as if they were feather pillows: 'On top there! Hold everything! — hold everything! — hold everything!' Confusion piling on confusion, and the sudden lapse into another restless sleep.

This time it didn't last long, and the awakening was a gentle one. Quiet voices talking close by my bed, and the red cape of the sister brushing between me and the foreigner.

'Mr Skevic, you were told not to sit up!'

'I can't lie down, nurse.'

'You *must* lie down —'

'My back. It aches.'

'My dear man, you must expect to be aching somewhere, otherwise you would not be here. Come on, down you go!'

The bed rustled, and I knew she was tucking another rebel in. 'You want to go home soon, don't you?'

He said something I couldn't make out, to which she replied in a shocked, half-amused whisper: 'Oh dear, that's a dreadful thing to say! Wait till she finds out you're in hospital — and how are you, Mr Crowley?'

She had turned round and was looking down at me.

'Not too bad, sister. I suppose you couldn't give me something to shift a sore head?'

'What's wrong with your head? Don't you want it any more?' She had a jolly face. 'Yes, I think we can do something for you. Have you much pain anywhere else?'

'Not much, sister.'

'All right, I'll send you something for the head.'

It was on the tip of my tongue to ask her about my injuries, but I restrained myself, and lay watching her as she continued her tour along the ward. It took her quite some time. At one bed, where more work was going on behind a screen, she lingered for so long that I began to worry. I thought: she's got involved again, what's a headache in a place like this?

She came out again at last, though, checked the last of her patients, and a few minutes later a nurse came to me with a glass half full of white liquid.

'Mr Crowley, are you the man with the headache?'

I recognized her as one of those in the tussle with the noisy patient, the one who had passed me with her hair disordered and her uniform askew. She'd tidied herself up and was quite pretty.

'No, don't try to sit up, Mr Crowley. I'll hold it for you.'

A strong little hand slid under the back of my head, and she smiled down at me as if I were the only patient in the ward who meant anything to her. I swallowed the stuff and relaxed. I wanted to say something to her before she went away, something that would please her.

'Do you get many like that?' I asked, indicating the bed with the frame over it.

She seemed surprised. 'Like who?'

'That bellowing bull down there.'

'Oh, him?' She gave a merry little laugh. 'He'll be all right when he wakes up.'

And she was gone, leaving me with a feeling that I'd been very nicely ticked off, and thinking, not for the first time in the last hour or two, that a man who has never been in hospital has a lot to learn about women.

Skevic said something. I observed that he was sitting up again, his eyes following the nurse with an expression both surly and sceptical.

'You'll have sister after you again,' I warned him.

'Damn the sister!' he muttered. 'What difference does it make, anyhow?'

'Have you been in hospital before?'

'Hospital — no! I have never been in bed before.'

'Never been ill?'

'Never.'

'You have to do as you're told here, you know.'

'Do as I'm told?' His frown deepened. 'All my bloody life I do as I'm told!'

What was it the sister had said to him — 'She'll be sorry when she knows you're in hospital.' I was tempted to say something further, to try to get him to talk, but he so obviously didn't want to talk. He just wanted to sit there brooding. He looked lonely and lost.

I thought: when a man is well he can hold all kinds of prob-

Ward Four

lems at bay. By all manner of makeshifts and strategems and dissimulations he can sustain a secret little world of his own within the big world. Nobody finds out about him. But when sickness comes his defences are down, and all the people he has mistrusted and shut out move in on him. Skevic seemed sunk in the black despair of a man who has been delivered, bound and helpless, into the hands of the enemy.

'Calling Dr Baines — calling Dr Baines —'

Whatever it was they had given me to drink was most effective, for in a very short time sleep came to me again, and when I finally awoke it was full morning. There had been dreams, something involving water, but nothing remained with me from the instant I opened my eyes. Only the water —

I lay still, squinting in the sunshine that flowed in through the tall windows across the ward. Two nurses, with masks over the lower part of their faces, were working at the near end of the medical bench. They had a trolley-tray and were setting it out with an assortment of dressings and small vessels.

Skevic was lying down with his head on one side, watching me. He wore an odd expression, a kind of intrigued half-smile, as if I'd done something amusing and he was waiting for me to do it again.

A sensation as of some liquid running down my right temple gave me a fright, but when I put my hand up no blood came away on my fingers. They were just wet. I glanced over at Skevic.

'The nurse,' he said, nodding towards the bench, 'she squirt water at you.'

I was just in time to catch her in the act of taking a sly peep at me over her shoulder. She had a little surgical syringe, and had obviously been on the point of taking another shot at me. She had a pony-tail hair-do, and the white mask over her mouth emphasized delightfully the impish sparkle of her eyes.

I gave her a smile, and with a playful toss of her head, and a swift glance along the ward to make sure the sister hadn't been watching, she went on with her work.

It was a charming awakening. There was some pain in my legs, but the headache was gone. More exciting than anything else, I could see two nurses slowly advancing down the centre of the ward, pushing a trolley from which they were distributing mugs of tea or coffee.

'How are you this morning?' I asked Skevic.

He pulled a sorry face, raised himself on one elbow, and leaned towards me. 'I want a lik,' he said in a pained whisper.

I was a bit slow in picking up the odd pronunciation.

'What you do here when you want a lik?' he repeated.

'Ask a nurse for a bottle,' I told him, secretly pleased that someone else was leading the field in that direction. A nurse was just then coming back from an errand at the far end of the ward. 'Ask this one,' I urged.

He looked frightened and angry, but must have been badly pushed, and there was no time for deliberation. Impulsively he committed himself to a desperate 'Nurse!' just as she reached us, then weakened, and lay there with his big mouth wide open.

'Well, what do you want?' she asked a trifle impatiently.

'I want — I want —'

'He wants a bottle, nurse,' I said with cold-blooded detachment.

'Oh, is that all?' And with a pleasant little laugh she reached out and pinched him under the chin. 'Of course I'll get you a bottle, darling!'

The effect on Skevic was almost electrifying. He stared after her with his dark eyes almost popping out of his head, then turned them on me. 'You see that?' he demanded incredulously.

'You've got nothing to worry about, mate,' I said. 'They're good girls in here.'

He nodded, but did not speak. Lying there on his elbow, he took in with a broad contented smile the whole of the slowly awakening ward.

The trolley had reached us and a nurse walked over and gave each of us a mug of tea. In all my life nothing had ever tasted better.

Somewhere outside in the grounds a bird was singing. The old man on my right might have died in his sleep for all the signs of life that he gave. But at the far end the noisy patient in the bed with the frame was fully awake. With his bandaged

· Ward Four ·

head resting on a single pillow he was facing towards us, watching the approaching tea-tray. His expression was sad, but quite composed. A very ordinary face, full of deep thought: I am here, and this has happened to me.

From my left came the anxious voice of Skevic: 'They kip me here till I get better?'

'Yes,' I said, 'they'll keep you here till you get better.'

· Pioneers ·

He was a farmer in a lonely out-of-the-way stretch of country between Bendigo and Weebah in central Victoria.

I got bogged on an unmade road outside his boundary fence one wretched winter evening. I should have loved every hair of his head from the beginning, because he represented my only chance of getting out that night, or even possibly the next day. It does me little credit, I know, but the truth is that I was angry with him before we came together.

His house wasn't far away. I could see it plainly, with its clustered outbuildings and a few trees, only a few hundred yards away across the darkening paddocks. Once, when several noisy bursts on the engine had only taken me in deeper, I looked over and thought I saw a figure on the verandah. But by the time he did decide to investigate I was well and truly planted, and in no humour to give him the kind of welcome he was entitled to expect. His own manner also didn't improve matters.

Eagerness and satisfaction fairly oozed out of him as he lumbered up and laid his great arms casually along the top wire. He was easy to read: he wanted company. Traditional bush hospitality is based on this need as much as it is on kindness. I understood that, but this fellow was just a little too uninhibited about it. He made no move to duck through the fence to take a proper look at the situation. He didn't even bother to sympathize with me. I was bogged, and I was his for the night. He made me feel less like a rescued mariner than a struggling fly for which the spider has just arrived.

'Too close to dark now, Mister, but we'll have you out of that in two ups in the morning.'

He gave me to understand he had a horse that would walk

off without even knowing there was a car on the end of the chains.

I hoped he was right. For the rest, there was nothing to do but thank him, express the hope that his wife wouldn't be inconvenienced, and go along.

If a neurotic is a person totally obsessed with self then I suppose he was a neurotic. But at least he was a cheerful one. He must have been over seventy. There was a tell-tale stiffness in all his movements, but his energy was terrific. In spite of the raw evening he was wearing only a flannel shirt with the sleeves cut out at the shoulders, like a League footballer. He worked his arms like paddles, and had the long-reaching stride of a countryman, setting his big boots down as if he were crushing something at every step. He just couldn't get me to the house quickly enough. The exertion was making him blow a bit, but it didn't stop him from talking. Everything he said was a complaint, but whenever he turned his great bomb of a head towards me I could see the small eyes twinkling below the flopping brim of his hat. His face was coarse, ruddy and big-boned. He had a trick of twisting his mouth to one side that called to mind a snarling dog. All in all he went well with the bleak landscape and falling night. His property was flat and almost treeless, limited on one side by a low range of fading hills and on all the others by walls of grey-box forest.

By the time we reached the homestead I felt I had the measure of him, and was wondering how I was going to last the night without quarrelling. Three times in less than ten minutes he'd put me right in my place.

The first time was when I offered him a cigarette, and he told me he'd never smoked in his life.

'I never could see what any man gets out of it. Spare me days, you go and toil your guts out to get some money, you take it into a shop, you buy a bit of dried herbs wrapped up in a tissue, and — you come outside and stick a match to it! It never made sense to me, Mister.'

The second time was when, a minute later, I ventured to suggest that the weather might be taking up.

'Taking up?' He strode on for several paces in silence, giving himself time to digest this further evidence of my folly. 'It'll take up at the end of the month, not before. The moon come in on its back. If you've been watching the weather as long as I have, Mister, you'll know what that means.'

The third time was when, not far from the house, we came to two eagles crucified on the fence-wires. I'd got the whiff of the stinking carcasses as we approached.

'Wedgetails,' he announced laconically as he undid a gate. 'I got four of 'em last week.'

To have spoken my mind would have been provocative, and therefore rude in the circumstances, so I just nodded.

He was too sharp, though, and after closing the gate behind me and going only a couple of steps he suddenly swung his head at me again.

'You wouldn't be one of them naturalist blokes, would you?'
'Naturalist? No, I'm not a naturalist.'
'I thought you was a bit quiet about them eagles.'
'I don't like to see dead eagles.'
'I don't like to see dead lambs!'
'What about dead rabbits? Young rabbits. Eagles —'
'The myxo'll look after the rabbits. Tell you what, Mister, you could walk right across this property and never see a rabbit.'
'Since the myxo?'
'Since the myxo. Them CSIRO blokes did a good job there.'

Yes, I thought, but when the same people tell you to spare the eagles you won't listen to them.

Dignity, however, was satisfied, and I let it ride there. I'd become irritated by his persistent 'Mister'.

'Anyway,' I said, 'it's time we got around to names. I'm Bob Johnson.'

He came to a dead stop and thrust out his hand. He had the grip of a wrestler. 'Bob Johnson, eh? A good plain name, like mine. I'll settle for the Bob if you don't mind. I'm Roy Davison — Roy to you. Anybody round here'll tell you all about me. They say they'd know my hide in a tannery.' He pushed his face close to mine. He had the smell of a strong and healthy man. 'Mind you, Bob, I'm not offering you much. We live plain, just me and the Missus.'

'I've never lived any other way. I'm a stranger, and you're taking me into your home.'

'That's it!' He gave my hand a last powerful pump before

letting it go. 'No man can do more than share what he's got.'

He started off again, and a few seconds later we were at the homestead.

I'd been watching it all the way from the road, looking in vain for lights. I hadn't expected electricity, but was a bit chilled now by the faint glow that came from one lonely window. I was, indeed, taken aback by the entire aspect of the place. He left me for a minute or two to 'lock up the chooks', so that I had time to take stock.

From a distance it had seemed just an average small farmer's homestead, most of it obscured by a few trees left for shelter. I remember that the first impression it made on me, on close inspection, was of deadness. It was like looking at a miniature ghost-town setting for a Western film. In the half-light it was eerie. Just the usual conglomeration of outbuildings and yards grown up over the years in the slapdash tradition of the Australian bush. But too tidy, too clean, too silent. A dog was barking as we came in, but had stopped at a sharp word from its master. Now there wasn't a sound. I'd have welcomed the snuffle of a feeding horse, the squabbling of fowls settling down for the night, or the sight of some vehicle standing in the yard. There was nothing. I felt myself surrounded by the sad and unmistakable quietness of old age, of exhaustion, of labour completed. And of decay. A working homestead should be full of rich odours: fresh milk, cow-dung, dry feed, hempen bags. Here there was nothing like it. The prevailing smell was one of stagnation, of dust and rust and moulding leather. The odour of things no longer used creeping out beneath doors no longer opened.

More depressing than any other part of the scene was the house itself. It was the smallest and most primitive I'd ever come across on an old-established farm. What kind of woman was it, I wondered, who had never attempted to create a garden? What kind of man who, even in this dry country, had never enclosed a small piece of ground for her to do so?

It was little more than a skillion-roofed shack. Double-fronted, with a doorway set fair in the middle, and four naked posts supporting a verandah from which you stepped down only six inches onto the trodden earth. The kind of shelter a selector would rush up in the first bitter years of struggle.

I knew the plan of it without going inside; the bush is full of them. Four rooms, the two front ones cut by a tiny passage leading into a living-room. Perhaps a back verandah with a sheeted wash-house at one end — perhaps. It was in one of the rear rooms that the lamp was burning. One window at the far end of an otherwise dreary wall. It stared straight out at the equally dreary wall of the barn only a few yards away.

He came back. No doubt he guessed I'd been doing a bit of sizing-up and decided he had better help me get my ideas into order before going inside.

'There's nothing much goes on here these days, Bob. But I tell you what' — head thrust forward again, eyes narrowed, and the dogmatic voice coming out of the distorted hole in his face — 'this used to be one of the best farms in this district.'

'Did you select it?'

'Yes, I did. I suppose I'm what you'd call a pioneer. I broke it in myself.' He put out his hands, palms upwards. Long years of heavy toil had given all the fingers a permanent inwards curve so that I could have laid a pick-handle in them just as they were. 'With these two hands. When we come here first all this was grey-box forest. It was just being thrown open.'

'And no bulldozers in those days!'

He gave me a pleased slap on the shoulder. 'No bulldozers! Axe, monkey-grubber and trewella-jack — and fire. Head down and bum up and go for your life from dawn till dark. Young blokes these days don't know what work is. No wonder they've got no guts.'

'You're pretty well retired now?'

'You can call it retired. I'll never stop as long as I'm on my feet. All the same I don't do much. Years ago all this was under wheat, with a little dairy herd on the side. I just run a few sheep now to give me something to do.'

'No cows?'

'No cows. Just one for the house. I've got a son-in-law only a few miles away. He's a bit of a no-hoper, but he sees we've always got a milker.'

'Your family has all gone?'

'Three daughters. All married and gone. There's just me and the Missus left. She never threw me a bull calf.'

There was a note of bitterness in this last bit that he seemed to regret as soon as it was out. He was in the act of leading off towards the house, but he pulled up again.

'Not that I'm saying she could help that. She's a bit crook these days. Not wearing as well as I am, if you know what I mean. I'm beginning to have to look after her a bit. Get up and get me own breakfast of a morning, and that kind of thing. Nothing fresh to me — I've had women on me back all me married life.' He had begun to walk again as he talked. 'Look out for the step, and keep right behind me as we go in.'

Four rooms — the two front ones cut by a passage leading into the living-room —

The woman turned out to be commonplace enough, but my first sight of her was not without impact. Lamplight dramatizes things that electricity only illuminates. I was struck first by her smallness; it was in such contrast to her great bear of a husband. Waiting for us to appear in the doorway, she was standing quite motionless on the far side of a table on which an ancient pedestal lamp was burning. Stooped, grey-haired, and with a pinched, worried little face, she looked much older than Roy. She was slightly flushed and breathing heavily as if she'd just been exerting herself. I had no means of knowing how she usually kept herself, but guessed that she had been hurrying to titivate herself up. She was wearing a dress of some dusty hue that could have been either green or blue in that weak light. It seemed to be well cut and of good material, but sat on her in the crumpled and slovenly way of a garment that has just been dragged out of the bottom drawer. Her freshly brushed, glistening hair explained the faint odour of coconut-oil that hung in the room. An odour that mingled appropriately with the mustiness of a wooden house built too close to the ground and beginning to go in its foundations.

In all this, however, there was nothing particularly surprising. What did disconcert me was the way in which she was looking at her husband. Head lifted, eyes widened, lips set in that tight straight line that betrays clenched teeth, she was staring at him as if he'd just done something altogether outrageous. By bringing me in? I saw it for only a split second. She didn't realize how close I was behind Roy. She knew I'd caught her, because she was thrown into confusion when the introduction came.

Whatever was behind it, Roy showed no reaction. Rather maliciously, I thought, he added to her embarrassment by remarking on her toilet: 'Spare me days, Ada, you didn't have to go doing yourself up! We've got a visitor for the night — Mr Johnson. This is my wife, Bob.'

She smiled instantly, but it wasn't very successful. The smile of a woman who is not only upset, but is unaccustomed to meeting strangers. It was I who had to go round the table. Her hand was thin and dry, but it took mine firmly and held on.

'We was listening to you,' she said in a faltering old woman's voice. 'We could tell somebody was in trouble.'

I expressed the hope that she wouldn't go to much bother over me. She began to make excuses for the poor fare I'd have to accept, but Roy didn't give her a chance to finish.

'I've told him all about that. Good gracious me, he knows we wasn't expecting him! Tell you what, Bob — it might be plain, but it'll be good. We'll give you the best bit of cold lamb you ever sat down to.'

'You'd better make him comfortable first, hadn't you?' Her smile had vanished. 'He'll want a wash —'

'Of course he'll want to wash. Come on, Bob. I'll show you where everything is.'

I'd been prepared for a bit of polite conversation, but he brushed her off with less consideration than one would give a housekeeper. He'd lighted a hurricane lamp, and as we moved away I could only excuse myself and throw her a glance that I hoped she would find sympathetic.

Roy's great bulk, and the poor illumination shed by the lamp, emphasized the smallness of the place. In the space of a few minutes I was shown kitchen-living-room, two bedrooms and a stuffy little parlour; it was like moving about in a partitioned box. I kept thinking of the three girls who had been raised here.

Up to four feet the walls of the bedroom were stained lining-boards, as was the ceiling. The upper part of the walls was papered in one of those pretty-pretty floral designs that went out with antimacassars and button-up boots, and was now faded and smoky. On the floor was a worn linoleum, with a fringed drugget mat alongside a brass-knobbed iron bed. There was a wardrobe, a dressing-table, a wicker chair, and a cretonne-covered stool which might have been a cut-down barrel. Nothing matched. Over the bed hung a framed text. 'I am the Light of the World.' There were two photographs. One, of a family group, was on the wall facing the head of the bed. The other, a bust of a young woman, stood on the dressing-table, with a small polished casket, and an oyster shell in which was an assortment of pins and brooches.

Everything indicated that I'd been given the main bedroom but when I protested to Roy he brushed me off with that finality which I knew by now to be characteristic.

'You leave me to worry about that, Bob. We're all right. We're only too glad of a bit of company. Did you ever sleep on a feather-bed?'

'Never.'

He reached out and patted it. 'Then let me tell you you're in for a treat. I wouldn't give you five bob for them kapok things. I'll just light this other lamp and then show you the bathroom.'

He'd apologized for the modesty of his hospitality, but it was amusingly evident that he didn't really see it that way. He was thoroughly enjoying himself.

'You wouldn't have had much to do with these things either, I'll bet.' He was bending over a little tin lamp on the dressing-table, adjusting the flame in the fiddling and exacting way of old people.

'Very little, Roy. They're just an emergency in town.'

'No wonder they're all nerves and spectacles down there. You know what, I wouldn't have that electricity on, not if they was to bring it to my very gate.'

'There's more to it than just lights.'

'And that's the very thing that turned me off it! Years ago I very nearly put in a little generator of me own. I was thinking of a milking plant. The girls was leaving, and Ada and me was beginning to find it a bit hard. And d'you know what? The minute I mentioned it she started on me. First she thought it was going to be nice having an electric iron. Next it was an electric jug — it was going to be beaut not having to light a fire of a morning just for a cup of tea. Then it was a toaster. Lights outside, back and front, so we wouldn't have to creep about with lamps after it was dark. Nothing big, mind you. Not a word about stoves or fridges. Just a few little things to make life easier.' Roy picked up the hurricane lamp again, ready to lead off. His eyes were narrowed to wrinkled little slits. And the lips were snarling. 'You know what — that's what's wrong with the whole world today. They're making it too easy. People's getting that way they don't know what to do to fill the time in. Anyway, I saw the writing on the wall, and I put my foot down. No electricity — no arguments. I settled for a little petrol engine for the dairy. That got her out of the milking, anyway. I was able to do it all on my own. She still moans about it, though — you know what women are.'

Yes, I thought, and I know what men are.

I took a few toilet things out of the small bag I'd brought from the car, and followed him out again. We had to go through the living-room, but Ada didn't speak. She just looked round to give me a shy smile from where she was busy at the stove. The table was laid, and there was an appetizing smell of hot scones.

It turned out that the so-called bathroom, which was entered from the living-room, was merely a closed-off corner of the back verandah. It was so small that Roy had to go in first, place the lamp on a bracket evidently there for the purpose, and come out again before I could go in. There was no pedestal basin and no tap. A bucket of water stood on the floor, and out of this he filled a tin dish standing in a galvanized-iron bath from which white lacquer was flaking. Everything, however, was scrupulously clean, including a towel that smelled of moth-balls. I kept thinking: three daughters were reared in this house — where did they sleep? And where now are the signs that they ever were here?

Roy returned to the other room while I washed, uncomfortably bent over the side of the bath. I could hear him and his wife talking only a few feet away:

'Aren't you going to give him some hot water? There's plenty of it.'

'For goodness sake, Ada, stop fussing. He doesn't want hot water to take a bit of mud off his hands.'

'It would be decent to ask him, anyway. It's a cold night.'

'He's young. Stop worrying.'

'What time is he leaving in the morning?'

'Soon as we get the car out. He wants to be in Melbourne by noon.'

'Will you be able to get it out?'

'It'd better come out once I hook Captain on to it! He'll pull it in two.'

'D'you know where Captain is? It'll be dark.'

'Spot'll flush him out for me. Where'd you put that linctus?'

'It's still on the back step where you left it this morning.'

All this dialogue was carried on on a surly note, in the way of two people who don't really want to talk but have to keep essentials moving.

A sudden silence fell just as I re-entered the room. I found both of them frozen in an attitude of intent listening, facing each other but completely concentrated on something else. You could have heard a pin drop. From far away on the main road — the road I should never have left — there came the faint hum of a truck.

'Sounds like the Carsons,' said Ada thoughtfully.

'The Carsons went through an hour ago,' declared Roy.

'It might be George Mills coming back. He went in this morning.'

'That isn't the Bedford. Sounds more like Andy Ferguson to me.'

'The Jensens!' Ada snapped the words triumphantly, and to make it clear that as far as she was concerned the subject was closed, she turned again to the stove, adding in a flat voice: 'Shirley was saying they all had to go in some day this week.'

Roy became aware of me standing there, and promptly urged me to come through. 'You know your room now, Bob. Give yourself a brush-up or whatever you want and then come right in here. We're all ready to sit down.'

No secrets in that box of a house. The minute I was gone Roy returned to the subject of the passing truck. Every word came to me clearly.

'Did Shirley say what they was going in for?'

'I couldn't make it out. The line hasn't been too good lately, you know that.'

'Who was she talking to?'

'May Rodney. She was telling May not to go over this afternoon because they was all going out ...'

'Shirley wouldn't say much anyway if she thought there was somebody listening in.' Eavesdropping over a 'party-line', probably the only real contact they had with the outside world. I seemed to have come a long way from my car.

I was looking at the family photograph on the wall. It fascinated me. Six men, three seated and three standing outside a slab hut against a background of tall timber. Everything in it dated and strictly formal: the composition of the picture, the theatrical attitudes of the subjects, their attire. All dressed up in their Sunday best: blue suits with short jackets and narrow-cuffed creaseless trousers, shirts buttoned at the necks, bowler hats. Bushmen to a man, and tough. I don't think I ever saw a tougher-looking bunch. Not a hint of a smile among them. Six closed mouths, six jutting jaws, six pairs of cold eyes staring sternly at the camera. It was like facing a firing-squad. They were all big men, and all similarly featured. Brothers. I held the lamp up for a closer inspection, but couldn't pick Roy.

Straight from this formidable gang I picked up the photograph on the dressing-table. And this, I thought, is the woman I just heard say: 'You can start cutting the meat.'

It was a most successful picture of a very charming girl. She was wearing a blouse, or frock, of what appeared to be black velveteen, cut well out on the shoulders — I think 'scoop-cut' is the word — and totally devoid of collar or other adornment. The angle of view was inspired. I'd like to have seen another photograph of the same girl in profile and looking upwards. Such a portrait would have emphasized dramatically the lines of a neck rising with unusual length and grace from the exposed shoulders. It would, no doubt, have caught an expression of dreamy innocence, of youthful anticipation. But it would have missed something better. As it was she was looking down at you, and turned just sufficiently to show both eyes. The expression captured was a delightful blending of surprise and friendliness, as if she'd just realized you were there and had instantly taken to you. Eyes widened, brows slightly lifted, lips barely touching in the beginnings of a smile. Every feature childishly rounded, like those of a doll. But there was something in the firm little chin that pointed straight to Ada. She would be led but not driven, defeated but never quite vanquished.

What was it Roy had said? *She never threw me a bull calf*...

Without realizing I had moved, I found myself looking down at the bed. Where she had 'thrown' the three heifers. Three times she had lain here in this stuffy room while Roy went out into the night for doctor or midwife. What must it have been like at each announcement that it was a daughter? That firing-squad of brothers glaring down from the wall...

I could hear her now, still battling on in the kitchen: 'Aren't you going to put a shirt on?'

And his arrogant, low-voiced reply: 'You just get the tea ready, Ada. Just get the tea ready. I'll look after my shirt.'

She did her best, and it was a good meal, but there was no getting away from him. And little I could do about it. He began to talk about horses as soon as we sat down, and kept on them.

The best bit of cold lamb I've ever tasted, green tomato pickles and chutney, good bread, good butter, hot scones, and — Captain.

'The best horse I ever had, and that's saying something. Know anything about the prices of horses, Bob?'

'Very little I'm afraid.'

'I gave ten pounds for him. Ten pounds at a time when any buggy horse would fetch up to thirty.'

'What was the catch?'

'Badly broken, that's all. And in the hands of a bloke that didn't know the first thing about horses.' Roy chewed a little faster, then gulped. 'I'm in the main street of Weebah one day when I see this fellow holding the horse outside a store. Fair dinkum, standing at its head like a new-chum, and there's a good rail alongside that everybody tied up on. It sort of got me in, because this thing looked as if all it wanted to do was go to sleep on its feet. It wasn't even fidgeting. I was a bit curious, so I went over and chatted the bloke. And he told me it wouldn't stand. And it wouldn't tie up. It was what we call a pull-back. I'd seen them before. You can tie them up all right, but as soon as you go near them again they just lie out on the rope or reins so tight you can't get them loose. No struggling, mind you. They just stretch back as far as their necks'll go and prop like that. One of them things you just come across now and then in horses. Anyway, I finished up buying this one. The bloke had had a gutsful of him...'

There was a lot more before Roy got to the point. He was sitting facing me, with Ada on the end of the table between us. Her eyes were on her plate, her expression one of bleak resignation. But for her I think I would have enjoyed the anecdote. Roy had a good sense of narrative, despite the note of egotism that ran through it all. At least I knew it was true, and he finished up by evoking a scene that was as Australian as it was amusing.

'I fixed him. I fixed him for keeps in less than thirty minutes.' He stopped while he cut a few pieces of meat and collected them one by one on his fork. 'About half a mile up the creek there's a greasy clay bank with a gum-tree set back just a bit from the edge. Well, I put a good halter on this horse and I walked him out there, and I tied him to that tree with his back to the creek. There was just enough level ground for his four feet. I walked away a few yards, turned round, and come back to him. Sure enough, out he stretches. He's a big lump of a horse, but there was plenty of tree too! Pull? — so help me God, you could have laid a ruler from the tip of his nose right down to his tail. Forelegs away out in front, hind-legs slanted forward under his guts, and his backside hanging out over the creek. All you could see was the whites of his eyes. You could have strummed a tune on that rope. Well, I had a sharp knife handy, and I let him stop like that till he had every ounce of his weight in. Then — one quick slash . . .'

I was glad of something to chuckle over, but Roy's eyes didn't as much as flicker.

'Bob, may I never move from this table if that horse didn't turn right over three times before he hit the water. He must have thought he'd pulled the tree on top of him. He wasn't even game to come out on my side. He went clear across the creek and didn't stop till he was fetched up by the first fence. By cripes, that cured him! You know what, you could have hitched that horse to a baby's pram after that.'

No doubt.

There followed more horse stories. Captain — Cigar — Tug — Ginger —

Good stories. They could have made pleasant entertainment if only he had allowed his wife to come in. It was her life, too, that he was talking about, but there was hardly a mention of her, never a shared smile, never once a comradely appeal for verification. As far as he was concerned there were just the two of us. She, on her part, made no attempt to intrude. She was evidently conditioned to it. But there was always dignity in her isolation, a subtle scorn in the lowered face. I felt she was drawing strength from me, knowing that I understood and was on her side. I recalled Roy's words: 'Axe, monkey-grubber, trawalla-jack and fire.'

And Ada? When *we* first came here ...

I got interested in Roy's knife and fork. The one, long-pronged and handled in black bone, might have been a worn-down carving fork. The other was a skinning-knife, the handle neatly bound with string and only a little pointed triangle left of the blade. He must have been using them all his married life. A careful man, who would look after things, the obvious things. I didn't like the thorough way he mopped his plate with a piece of dry bread, pushed it away from him, straightened himself up in his chair, squared his shoulders, and scanned the table for what was next. It was all too possessive and self-satisfied.

For an old woman Ada also ate heartily. A trifle noisily, perhaps, but with a certain fumbling daintiness.

More than once I tried to bring her into the conversation — if conversation it could be called — but each time Roy headed her off. I congratulated her on her scones, and received a melting glance of gratification. But before we could make talk on the subject he shouldered both of us out of the way.

'You know what, Bob — them scones have taken prizes at every show from Bendigo to Weebah. And where it wasn't her scones it was my cattle. Only a small herd, mind you, but it was a good one. I had a jersey bull ...'

Once, though well aware that I was taking chances, I seized an opportunity to ask her about the daughters.

'Yes, they're all married and away,' she said quietly.

'Grandchildren?' I smiled, searching for a safe line of inquiry. I didn't look at Roy, but knew he was watching her.

'We've got eleven,' she replied, 'but we don't see much of them.' She was going to add something to that, but again Roy took it away from her.

'There's only one of the girls in the district, Bob. The other two went to live in town. I never hear from them.' There was no emphasis on the I, but it was significant.

'You did say there was a son-in-law not far away.' I spoke quite without design, just to keep things moving. It was all so difficult. Something was lurking between them...

Ada picked up her empty plate and left the table. Roy flicked the cloth in front of him with the backs of his fingers.

'To tell the truth, Bob, he's not much chop. Too fond of bending the elbow, if you know what I mean. There's two things I've got no time for, that's boozers and drones. This fellow's both. Always either in the pub or hanging over a fence stopping another bloke from getting on with his work. I don't know, I can't make him out.'

'Everything in moderation,' I said cautiously. 'I take a drink myself —'

'I never tasted it. Wouldn't know what it was if you was to blindfold me —'

'I know some good men who like a beer!'

'And I know some good men who don't! Beer and racehorses — they've been the curse of this country.'

'I say! We haven't done so badly —' It was time to challenge him, but I was startled at the way he took me up.

'We haven't done so badly?' The wrinkles around his narrowed eyes were quivering. 'You fair dinkum? I broke in six hundred acres of good land — on me own. And I've met blokes that never swung an axe all their lives. This country — look, Bob, can you tell me how it is that in a country like this men go about looking for work?'

'Oh yes —'

'You reckon they want to find it?'

'My word they do!'

He fixed me with an exasperated stare. Ada had sat down again and was buttering a scone. He seemed at a loss to know where to begin on the great mountain of my stupidity. I was wondering how far I could go when he made up his mind.

'Hold on, Mister, I'll tell you a story. I get them coming through here, you know — these blokes looking for the lost axe. And scared stiff they might find it. Well, I'm out there along the track one day doing a bit of fencing when one of them slouches up. I'd had my eye on him all the way in from the road, and I know the form before he ever opened his mouth.

'"Good-day, boss!" he sings out, cheerful as you like. "Any chance of a job?"

'"There's plenty of work," I says, "but no job."

'"What d'you mean?" he wants to know.

'"I'm not an employer," I tell him. "A farm like this doesn't run to paid labour. But I'll tell you what — I'll give you a bit of work for your tucker."

'"And his head come up — believe me, you'd think I'd made an indecent suggestion to him."

'"No wages?" he asks.

'"No wages," I say.

'"Stone the crows, mate," he says, "I'll give *you* a better job than that. You come along with me and carry me swag and open the gates, and I'll feed *you*!"'

I began to chuckle, but Roy was in deadly earnest.

'You can laugh, Bob, but that's the form, take my word for it. Mind you, he wasn't boasting. He looked as if he was living off the fat of the land.'

However, the story had taken some of the nip out of the air, and one way or another he got back to his horses. When Ada got up to clear the table he also rose. I asked if I might smoke, and she immediately placed a saucer in front of me.

'We don't have any ash-trays, Mr Johnson.' The shy smile that went with this was a secret little message.

'Never been such a thing in the house," added Roy with manifest pride.

He went out and brought in a bucket of water, from which he refilled the kettles on the stove. Then, to my astonishment, he took up a position alongside Ada at the sink and began to dry the dishes. It was done so casually that it must have been routine. No doubt one of a number of little things by which he preserved an image of himself as a thoughtful husband. Not so casual was his remark on the fact that no water was laid on to the house. It had been too long in coming; it sounded defensive.

'I bet it isn't often you get into a house where you can't turn a tap on, Bob?'

'As a matter of fact this is the first.' To make sure he got the point, I added: 'And I get around the bush quite a lot.'

A movement of the woman's head was arrested just in time. I think she was going to give me a glance of approval.

'I know, they will have their little taps.' An undisguised sneer. 'And they squeal like stuck pigs when a dry spell sets in and their tanks run out. You know what — I've never once run out of water all the years we've been here. That right, Ada?'

'Yes, that's right.' I couldn't see her face, but she might as well have added: you damned fool!

I couldn't tell how, but we had begun to communicate with each other and Roy was quite unaware of it.

'Carry your water in as you want it, and you'll treat it with respect, that's what I say. Taps make it too easy. You forget about the tank outside. But you go out and stand there waiting for the bucket to fill, and you'll think of it then! It becomes an instinct to reach out and tap it. I was brought up in the Mallee...'

He was getting the dishes away as fast as she put them out. Every article in its appointed place in a cheap open-fronted dresser. Plates standing edge to edge along the backs of the shelves, cups swinging from hooks underneath. Knives, forks, spoons — each in its narrow cell forever laid — he seemed to be counting them. The context in which I was seeing it made it fiddling and childish. If only Ada had been allowed to talk...

She never was. When all was done we sat down again. I knew by the way he checked the trim of the lamp that there was to be a session. One might have thought he was setting the stage for a high-stakes card game or a seance. It was, indeed, becoming more and more unreal as the minutes passed. Not a sound came to us from outside. There wasn't even a breeze to make the house creak. I'd have given much for a homely sound such as the purring of a cat.

Ada brought out some knitting, and I made what was to be my final effort to draw her into the company.

'For the grandchildren?' I asked her.

'One of Moira's,' she replied, looking at me with smiling eyes. 'There's always something wanted, and things are so dear to buy.'

'And never as good! There's nothing to beat a hand-knitted article. I'd say that's for a girl?'

She held it up. 'A boy would look funny in it, wouldn't he?'

But at this point Roy decided she'd had a fair go. Leaning over the table to make sure he got me away from her, he pointed a thick forefinger at the knitting. 'Bob, I'm never done telling her she's a fool. Night after night she sits there straining her eyes, and they're all a darn sight better off than we are. They don't even thank her for it.'

'You know as well as I do they're thankful,' she said sharply.

'They don't go far out of their way to show it!'

'What d'you want them to do?'

'Come over and see us sometimes, Ada. That's all, just come over and see us.'

She was going to say something else, but changed her mind. She just lifted her head, gave him a defiant stare, and went back to her knitting. It looked like a brave effort to keep the family skeleton in the cupboard, but Roy wouldn't meet her.

He sighed, puffed, shifted the saucer ash-tray out to the middle of the table then back again, licked his lips — all the bogus fidgetings of a patient man driven beyond endurance.

'Look Bob,' he got out at last, 'it's a sore point, this matter of the daughters ...'

'Let it ride, Roy,' I urged. 'Every family has its problems.'

'Every family hasn't! Mine are all women. D'you know what — two of them girls has never set foot in this house since the day they left. Moira comes once in a blue moon. She wouldn't come at all if she didn't have troubles.'

'The husband who drinks?'

'It isn't only the drink. His old man left him a good farm, and he's letting it go down the drain. He doesn't know the first thing about horses, to begin with.'

The temptation to point out that we had moved into the age of the tractor almost got the better of me, but I controlled myself, satisfied that the talk was drifting into a safer channel. All his attention was on me again.

'D'you know what that man did on me once? I'll tell you. I had a horse here I used to use for breaking-in. A little bay mare with black points. One of the best deals I ever made. Picked her up for next to nothing. Another one of them blokes that couldn't solve his own problems. She'd been badly mouthed, and he couldn't do anything with her. Well, I got her, and I went to work on her, and she turned out a beauty. There wasn't much of her, mind you, but she was as game as Ned Kelly. And she had brains, I used to talk to her. I had her so she'd come to me at a whistle no matter where she was. And she'd hold anything in the brake. One day I had a colt tied on the side, and it reared up and come down with both forefeet inside the shaft. Work that out for a mess! And she got me out of it with only a bit of paint scratched off.'

There was a lot more before he got to the heart of the story.

'I wouldn't have taken eighty quid for that mare. And d'you know what happened? That bright son-in-law — he wasn't the son-in-law then — he foundered her on me! Killed her just as surely as if he'd taken an axe and knocked her brains out. He borrowed her to go in to Weebah. I wasn't in the habit of lending my horses — I don't believe in it — but I was having a bit of trouble with the girls at the time,' Roy shot a swift glance at Ada, still placidly knitting, 'and I let him have it for peace' sake. And d'you know what that half-wit did? He drove that mare full bat for fifteen miles on a stinking hot day, turned her loose in a paddock of a bloke he hardly knew, and went off to the boozer!'

He knew very well that I hadn't yet got the point, and, good story-teller that he was, he waited, giving me time to do a bit of futile guessing and build up for the shock that was to come. His prolonged stare made me uncomfortable.

'He just couldn't get to that pub quick enough. I'm not saying it didn't enter his head that my little mare might be thirsty too. He thought of it all right. But he didn't think far enough. He just decided he'd have a few beers and then come back and give her a drink when she'd cooled down. It never entered his head that my little mare might go looking for a drink herself. Any man with any heart for a horse at all would have gone over that paddock and made sure she couldn't get it, the state she was in. Well, I suppose you can guess the rest. She found water all right. There was a dam down at the far end of that paddock, and she got to it and give herself a gutful. By the time he got back there was nothing anybody could do for her. And people wonder why I'm crooked on the booze. I loved that mare.'

I could have liked him for that were it not for Ada. Still knitting, head bowed, the faintest of smiles on her face. I thought of that son-in-law-to-be coming back to tell Roy what had happened. Or had that grim task fallen to her? And how many other times? With three grown girls on the place there must have been a lot of coming and going of young men. What scenes must have been witnessed here! What bullyings and thwartings and intrigues and diplomacies! Something new was coming into the lined face over the knitting. Not malice, smugness rather. It took me back to the girl in the velvet blouse. Strength in the chin —

'Now then, Bob, do you blame me for being hostile on the booze?'

I nodded, cautiously. I wanted to get him back to horses, and keep him there. 'Horses are like children, I suppose. Only they don't grow up. We've always got to do a lot of the thinking for them.'

'Unless you get one like that little mare!' He thought for a moment, absorbing my idea. 'Yes, I think you've got something there. We've got to keep on watching them, putting things out of their way.'

A short silence fell. Then, as he began to speak again, I realized that he hadn't really been following me. He'd been deliberately leading into another apt recollection, digging again into the past. Another little tragedy, another stupid suitor, another daughter, more lost horses.

'Right in the middle of harvest it was. I had to put a man on for a few weeks, and this fellow was . . .' another sidelong glance at Ada, 'hanging around. I thought I might as well use him. One morning I sent him out to run the team in. And, mind you, it *was* a team! There wasn't a better one for miles around. Pull? I've seen them go down on their knees like bullocks. All right, out this bloke goes. It's a big paddock, and they wasn't in sight from the house, so I told him to jump on an old grey pony that was in the yard.

'Next thing I know — so help me God — he's got that team coming in at a gallop! At a gallop — heavy draughts! I was in the barn when I heard them, and out I rushed just as they come round the bend in the creek, hell for lick. I suppose he wanted to show off for Agnes. All the girls was up in the cow-yard at the time. I couldn't see him and the pony, they was away back in the dust somewhere. I dropped everything and started to run down to have a piece of him as he come in. But it was nothing to what was coming. D'you know what a Mallee gate is, Bob?'

'Yes, it's a short loose panel, just droppers and wires.'

'That's right, you foot 'em into loops on the posts. Well, that's what I had on this paddock. Now the one thing you never do when you open one of these so-called gates is — leave it lying on the ground. If you're going away and want to leave it open — as this bloke did, so he could run the horses through — you carry it round in a half-circle and stand it along the fence-line. I've seen more stock crippled through getting tangled in a Mallee gate lying on the ground — anyhow, you know what I'm talking about . . .'

'He ran the team over it?'

'He put the whole team over it! I had a big wall-eyed chestnut as mob leader, and a bit of a rogue when he was off the bit. There wouldn't have been any trouble at all if they'd been brought in quietly. But you know how it is when you push a mob of horses — something gets into them. And this Red, out he goes in the lead, thumping along like a big rocking-horse. I'm watching him, and I know he's going to break. You get that way you can read horses' minds. I knew what Red was thinking, the way he was slewing off-course and back again and throwing his head about. He was feeling good — to hell with work this morning! Out he lights for the creek again, and the whole mob after him.

'Well, that still didn't break any bones. They wasn't exactly race-horses, and the grey had no trouble turning them. But by the time they're headed for home again, they're not lined up for the opening, they're coming down the fence-line.'

'And the gate on the ground . . .'

'The gate on the ground. I could see it lying there, but I'm too far off to do anything except give a mad yell. I'm helpless.' Roy closed his eyes and shuddered. For the first time he had my full sympathy. 'Four wires — all barbed! Fair dinkum, I couldn't bear to look. I shut my eyes. I only opened them again when I heard the first thump, and a scream, and them wires twanging like fiddle-strings. Red's in them, plunging on, and every plunge brings them bloody wires further up his legs. And the rest of the team jostling up in a tight bunch. Two more went down, two others trampled over the top of them, only one cunning old mare managed to sheer off in time.' Roy stood up in his excitement. 'Bob, you got no idea what it was like. By the time I got over there one of them was up again and running round in circles, blood streaming from it backside to breakfast. The other two just kicked and tore themselves to bits. Four barbs — it was like a butcher's block. First thing I did was sing out for somebody to fetch me a gun. I had to shoot them both, and the other one as soon as I'd had a look at him. I never got a team like it together again.'

He sat down again. He was trembling.

'And the young bloke?' I asked.

'Lit out for the scrub. Turned the grey loose in the last paddock and kept going. He knew I had a gun. He left the district, and it was two years before he came back again. I heard he was around, but before I could do anything a copper come out from Bendigo and told me he was watching me. Everybody else was too!'

He fell silent. Only the ticking of the clock and the clicking of the knitting needles. It would have helped just then if the needles had stopped. They seemed to be mocking him — a bit of trouble with the girls at the time — I had to put a man on for a few weeks — showing off in front of Agnes. Never threw me a bull calf — everything came back to that, and all three of us sitting there were aware of it.

There was something to be said for Roy this time.

'I suppose you needed the warning, for your own sake.'

He gave me a bitter smile. 'Needed it? Yes, I needed it. He didn't stop long. Three weeks, and he was off again. Agnes went with him. Did a moonlight. He'd been writing to her all the time. I knew nothing about it. We've never seen either of them since.'

A few difficult minutes followed, but I managed to get him going again, watching the clock, and wondering how long it would be before somebody suggested turning in.

Ada looked as if she was prepared to knit all night. I realized by now that with her also a grievance had eaten in like a cancer. They were fighting over me, had been from the instant I walked in, and for the time being my sympathies had swung a little towards Roy. Ada's sustained silence was becoming suspect. She believed that Roy was digging his own grave with me. The timing of the occasional glances she threw at me was always significant.

Moira — Agnes — what of the other daughter? What did these two talk about when they were alone together and no sound came to them from the road?

Hoping for better luck this time, I asked Roy how many of the horses had recovered, how long it was before they worked again, and how he had treated them. It turned out a good line of inquiry, because he gradually calmed down and became absorbed in something he prided himself on, the healing of sick animals. Every farmer had to be his own vet in those days, but, as in all things, it appeared that Roy excelled. He told me how he had solved not only his own problems, but those of his less capable neighbours also.

'Send for Roy Davison, they say when they are in strife. By cripes, I've had some queer cases, Bob.'

He brought out a set of veterinary surgeon's charts. Beautifully printed in several colours, and with an ingenious arrangement of sliding panels representing the various organs, there was one for each domestic animal. They were worn with handling and obviously very old, but still in usable condition.

'I got them off an old German bloke years ago, he brought them out with him. D'you know what, that man could take a cow to pieces and put her together again, just looking at these cards.'

Perhaps he could, too. They showed where everything belonged.

'A fellow sent for me once to come and have a look at a cow with a blind tit. Now that's nothing very unusual, Bob. But this one . . .'

For over an hour I listened to stories of his veterinary exploits. I couldn't always follow them anatomically, but they were fascinating in their revelations of human struggle and resourcefulness. Animals were bread and butter in days when bread and butter were all that a small selector could expect out of life. An incapacitated animal could jeopardize so much. There were unforgettable pictures of anxious families gathered around lame horses, of 'staked' sheepdogs, of Roy riding through the night to a complicated delivery in a cow-paddock.

And never, except once, a sound from the woman. That once

was when the click of her tongue silenced Roy and set all three of us listening to the hum of a truck on the road. Apparently this was the only excitement shared by man and woman, the only game they played together. Roy won this time.

'George Mills getting back,' he announced solemnly.

Ada gave it a further moment's consideration, then nodded grudgingly and went back to her knitting.

Roy, looking well satisfied, took up again the tale of his sick animals. He was relating his efforts to save a 'sanded' colt, and he told the story with all the simple earthiness of a countryman. He explained to me how a horse in drought country, nuzzling hungrily in the withered stubble, kept taking in sand. And how sometimes the sand failed to evacuate, and kept building up in the bowel.

'Tell you what, Bob, that colt had a lump on his belly like a football.' His hands described a circle. 'You could move it about, and it was as hard as this board.' He thumped the table with his knuckles. 'He was down when I got there. Fair dinkum, you wouldn't have given two bob for him. One look at him, and I knew that whatever I did had to be drastic — and quick. Well, there was two big trees growing just a few yards from where he was lying, and somehow or other we managed to drag him over to them. I sang out for some ropes, and we slung that colt from them trees with his back on the ground and his four legs sticking straight up in the air. Then I told the woman of the house to go in and fetch me a rolling-pin. They all wanted to know what for, but I told them they'd better do just what I said and leave all the thinking to me. So out comes the rolling-pin. Ever heard of anybody doing this before, Bob?'

'Never!'

'Neither had I — but it worked! Down I got, and I rolled that lump, that football, just like it was a big chunk of dough. Every bit of weight I could put into it. It took a long time, mind you, but once it started to break up I knew that I was on the right track. Grunt? He grunted all right, but there wasn't anything he could do about it, with his four legs up in the air. I kept it up till the lump was all gone, broken up and sort of dispersed in his bowels. Then, while he was still upside down, I give him the biggest drench I've ever put into any horse, and kept him there till it had time to work. Then we let him get up. That fetched it!'

All the earthiness of the countryman, and no holds barred. I don't think Ada minded, though. Another nail in Roy's coffin. She knew I was watching her and wouldn't miss the disgusted way she wrinkled her nose and tightened her lips.

'Tell you what, Bob, that colt was working next day. D'you reckon one of them vets would have thought of that?'

'I doubt it, Roy.'

'And even if he'd thought of it, would he have done it? Them blokes don't like getting their hands dirty, you know.'

I let the slander pass, and was instantly sorry, for Roy's next words took him straight back to the daughters.

'And all I got out of it was a burned haystack.'

I could have let that go also, for it was said in the way of a man capping off a story, not beginning a new one. But before I could gather my wits it was out: 'A what?'

'A burned haystack.'

I kept silent, waiting for a clue. Roy's eyes were on his fingers, nervously drumming the table. Ada was watching him, the peaked little face full of eagerness. She didn't want him to stop. She'd forgotten her knitting, and the sudden cessation of the clicking needles added much to the tenseness of the atmosphere.

'I know that can be a death-blow to a farmer, Roy,' I observed. Somebody had to say something.

'Death-blow?' He drew in a long breath. 'Some things is so bad it hurts to talk about them.'

'Then don't.' I looked at the clock on the mantelpiece, then at each of them in turn. 'I don't know what time you good people are in the habit of going to bed ...'

'You might as well tell him now you've started,' said Ada suddenly. She put down her knitting, lying with the transparency of a child: 'To tell the truth, I was beginning to feel a bit sleepy, Mr Johnson. Would you mind if I turned in?'

Roy remained seated as the two of us stood up. I had already gathered from something he'd said that Ada was accustomed to going to bed earlier than he, but there was nothing routine about it tonight. His readiness to keep on talking was as obvious as her determination to give him the opportunity. But the little war between them was maintained to the bitter end. She began to say something to me about being up in the morning to make breakfast, and he instantly roused himself.

'Breakfast, what's special about tomorrow morning? I always get the breakfast, don't I?'

'But there's Mr Johnson —'

'I'll look after Mr Johnson, Ada.'

As the bone of contention, it was easy for me to take over this time. I did it as gently as possible, and I thought she took it fairly well, but her disappointment came through. Perhaps she'd been looking forward to a short session with me in private while Roy got through some early morning chores.

Her parting smile was loaded with appeal, as was the grasp of her dry old hand. She held on to me.

'It's been nice to have a visitor. It isn't often anybody comes here.'

'You've been very kind, Mrs Davison...'

'I hope you get your car out all right in the morning. If ever you're passing this way again...'

I promised. I'd made up my mind to send her some little gift, perhaps something to brighten that poor little dressing-table. But the promise was one of those one has to make, regardless of any likelihood of its being kept. I didn't ever expect to see her again. She went out, and all I heard of her afterwards was the scratch of a match as she lighted a lamp.

Nothing could have been more unexpected than Roy's first words when we were left alone.

'You know, Bob, she's not looking too well tonight.'

I was astonished, because the remark seemed to have been made with real concern.

'I suppose it's past her usual bedtime,' I replied. 'She did look tired.'

He shook his head. 'That wouldn't hurt her.' But, rather too casually, he added: 'She wouldn't have gone, anyway, if I hadn't mentioned the haystack. It always upsets her.'

He pondered, giving me time to throw the ball back to him. Second thoughts seemed to indicate that his anxiety over his wife was merely another device to lead me back to the haystack. It was hard to tell. Odd relationships grow up between two people who live together for a long time. Roy and Ada had probably become as essential to each other, though in a different way, as Darby and Joan.

'Perhaps you shouldn't wake it up,' I suggested.

'Wake it up?' he scowled. 'As far as I'm concerned it never went to sleep. A hundred and fifty tons of hay! — at a time when there wasn't a skerrick of grass in the paddocks. Seven horses to feed, and not a cracker to my name. By jeez, I've gone through it if ever a man did! And d'you know who did that?'

'The fellow who owned the colt?'

'The bloke who owned the colt. And d'you know why he did it?'

I shook my head.

'Because I ran him off the place with a shotgun, as I was entitled to. It was long after I fixed the colt, mind you. To tell the truth, it wasn't his horse, it was his old man's. But he used to ride it, and it was him that come tearing over here one morning, begging me to come and help him. He was a big lump of a bloke, but only seventeen at the time, and I took pity on him. Dropped everything I was doing — you know how it is with a boy and his horse. Well, I saved it for him, like I told you, and the next weekend he rode it over here to thank me. He got asked in to dinner, and that was the beginning of it. He got shook on Rose, that's my youngest daughter.'

Roy stopped suddenly, and turned his head towards the door through which Ada had gone. I also thought I'd heard a sound. He hadn't bothered to lower his voice, and must have known as well as I did that she was listening. But all he did was give me a conspiratorial wink and nod — never mind her! — and get on with the tale.

'She was only seventeen, Bob. And I was still sweating it out over Agnes, she'd only been gone a year. What would any father have done?'

'What kind of fellow was he?'

'No good! Irresponsible. His own Dad was having trouble with him. I found out he wasn't as green as he was supposed to be. He'd been away picking-up in the shearing sheds, and he'd learned a bit too much for a boy his age. D'you know what he did one day — but listen, I'll tell you what happened here first. You'll see for yourself what kind of bloke he was. I began by warning him, and I warned Rose. She was as silly as a wheel, too, but a man's got to do what he can to protect his daughters once he's stuck with them. The trouble is I was always kicking against the wind.' Another wink, another significant nod at the bedroom door. 'It was a battle of wits, believe me. They kept on beating me, no matter how I watched them. I'm not going to go into details, you're old enough to know how it is. One night I caught him. Mind you, I'm not saying they was up to anything real bad, but it was hours after she was supposed to be in her bed. I ran him off the place. I had the gun with me, and I put a charge of shot into the ground behind him as he lit out across the yard. Next night up went my haystack.'

'Are you sure it was him?'

'Am I sure it was him — right afterwards he shot himself!'

'Killed himself?'

'Killed himself. Put a bullet through his head. I suppose he hadn't properly realized what he'd done till it was too late. And he'd got scared. He knew I'd be out looking for him. So he beat me to it, very nearly blew his head right off. We found his body days afterwards in one of the back paddocks. You could even see how he'd done it. He's lying alongside the log he'd sat on, and a bit of stick still across the trigger. We'd never have found him if it hadn't been for the smell.'

'And Rose?'

'Cleared out. We got a wire from Agnes down town saying she'd turned up there. She stopped with Agnes. Got herself a job and finished up marrying a bloke with the Board of Works. I believe they're living in Geelong now.'

I don't think Roy realized what sadness there was in those two words: 'I believe.' It would have been difficult to tell what his feelings were just then. All the steam had gone out of him. He was sitting with knitted brows, casting back. Moira — Agnes — Rose — and Ada, who wasn't looking so well tonight. It made a cohesive picture, but how he interpreted it I couldn't guess. His face might have been chiselled out of stone. 'You've upset yourself talking about these things, Roy,' I said gently. 'Why not turn in?'

'I suppose you're right.' He stirred himself. 'I better go in and see how the wife is.'

There were no more stories, and it was left to Ada to round the night off.

At the last minute Roy lit a hurricane lamp and went out, saying he wanted to have a look at a sick sheep. His footfalls had hardly died away before I heard a sound behind me and turned to see Ada beckoning me from the barely open bedroom door.

'Mr Johnson — sssh!'

I went over to her, and she instantly reached out and seized my wrist. She was wearing an overcoat over her nightdress and had nothing on her feet. The smell of coconut-oil was strong. Her eyes were bright with anger.

'Mr Johnson, that was a good boy! You hear me — he was a good boy!' She was shaking my wrist in rhythm with what she was saying, dinning it into me.

'Yes, Mrs Davison . . .'

'And there was nothing wrong going on. I looked after my girls!'

'You don't have to tell me that.' I was trying all the time to disengage myself, terrified that Roy would come back and catch us talking.

'They were all glad to get out of the house.'

'I understand . . .'

A gate clashed somewhere across the yard, and I pulled free. She shook a trembling finger at me before closing the door.

'He killed that boy!'

A few minutes later I was lying in the feather-bed, staring over the black iron rail at the firing-squad on the wall. The brothers Davison.

I don't know which of those two people haunts me most, Roy or Ada.

• Transit Passenger •

By twelve-thirty he had changed his books at the Athenaeum Library, picked up his repaired watch at Dunkling's, shopped for a few trifles at Coles', and bought two singlets and a shirt at Myer's.

The rich smells of Myer's big ground-floor delicatessen tempted him to get something to take home, but there was little pleasure in eating a main meal alone, and when he came to the city he usually had something. So he made for Walton's, partly from habit — it had been his wife's favourite cafeteria — and partly with a vague idea of dropping in afterwards on one of the new cinemas at that end of Bourke Street.

Walton's was busy as usual, but he found a table. Leaving bag and hat as tokens of possession, he took his place in the queue and returned with a simple meal of vegetable soup, smoked fish with mash and green peas, prunes and custard. And coffee and biscuits to linger over with a cigarette.

He was commencing on the fish when he first saw her. A woman rather beyond middle age, wearing a smart little felt hat and well-cut brown overcoat, and with umbrella and hand-bag in contrasting browns looped over wrist. Not particularly noticeable; he wouldn't have observed her at all but for the fact that she happened to be looking in his direction as his eyes ran along the people in the race. She'd just picked up tray and cutlery, and between glances at the menu on the wall, seemed to be scouting for a place to sit. He'd completely forgotten her when a few minutes later he looked up to see her, tray in hands, confronting him from the other side of the table.

He had to push one or two of his dishes aside to make room for her, a courtesy which was acknowledged with a rather cautious nod. Nothing was said while she set out her meal, a frugal one of tea and sandwiches, settled down, and began to eat, keeping her eyes mostly on her plate with what he suspected was the uneasy concentration of self-consciousness.

As so often happens when two strangers are thrown together at a cafe table, he also began to feel the need for some communication. He was a shy man, though, so the entire meal was eaten in silence, with one or other of them glancing up now and then to scan the bustling, clattering floor. It was during the Easter school holidays, with a lot of children on the loose.

They finished eating almost at the same time, and it was then that they began to talk, when he asked her if she minded cigarette smoke. No, she didn't mind, adding with a friendly smile that she was used to it: 'My husband smoked.'

From there on they both relaxed. He told her he'd been a heavy smoker, but had cut down in recent years. 'Doctor's advice, but it's hard to take. I manage to keep it down to five or six a day.'

She nodded sympathetically. 'You'd miss it most after a meal, wouldn't you?'

'For me it's the last course. Silly, but there it is. We're all entitled to our weaknesses.' His hand went to his pocket. 'I didn't ask you . . .'

'No, thank you. I tried it once or twice, when I was young, but I never took to it.'

Silence was impossible after that, and within a few minutes they were finding out about each other. A remark by him on the surrounding commotion led to her telling him that it was one of the reasons why she had come to a cafeteria: 'It's kind of sociable. There's more to look at than in a restaurant. I like watching all the Mums feeding the children.'

'Only a Mum herself would say that.'

'Yes, I had two. I know all about it.'

He was on the point of suggesting that grandchildren had probably taken over, but stopped in time. She was obviously old enough, but pride in grandchildren and caginess about age are testy rivals in some women. 'I've graduated,' he confessed, taking it on himself. 'Three grandchildren. They keep me in practice.'

'They'll keep you in practice all right!'

'I can't complain. I don't see them very often. We live on opposite sides of the city.'

'You're lucky. Mine are a lot further away than that. Two in England and three in New Zealand.'

He expressed his sympathy and asked how long it was since she had seen them.

'I've just seen the English ones. I'm on my way home now.'

'On your way home?'

'I live in Sydney. I'm travelling with the *Orcades*, at Port Melbourne. We're just here for twenty-four hours.'

'You're just a visitor, then? Transit passenger ...'

They talked on amid a cacophony of voices, clattering cutlery and scraping chairs. It came out that her husband, a field officer with the N.S.W. National Parks and Wild Life Service had died three years before, and that there was a married son in England and a married daughter in New Zealand. The son, Robert, had failed his matriculation, gone off on a walkabout, 'taken up with' an English girl foot-loose in Italy, married her in London, got himself some kind of job as selling agent, and was now living with his family in Manchester. The daughter, Anne, was married to a New Zealand solicitor and living in Wellington.

She, on her part, learned that his wife had died some eighteen months before and that there were three children: two sons, both married and living in Melbourne, and a daughter, still single, who was a nursing sister at Bendigo.

'George — that's the one with the children — is with Massey-Ferguson out at Sunshine, but Bill is in Canterbury, only two miles away from me. He and his wife are both teachers.'

Against all recent habits, he lit a second cigarette. It was pleasant sitting there chatting with a nice woman, easy to keep putting off saying it was time to be going. Why should he? After eighteen months he still wasn't reconciled to going into an empty house, any more than he was reconciled to sitting alone in a cafe. He, too, had a special reason for preferring cafeterias; the feeling of isolation was less acute in the earthy look-after-yourself atmosphere, and never that edgy sense of being under observation oneself. Moreover, her remark about liking to watch the busy Mums probably told only half the truth. She had referred to her husband in the past tense, and had shown no reluctance to enter into conversation.

Apparently she was at a loose end until her ship sailed again. That interested him. Most Sydney people had some contact in Melbourne. In any event friendships usually formed during a long voyage; cabin-mates went ashore together at ports of call.

He was still talking about his son Bill when she asked him what Camberwell junction was like these days. Told that it was as baffling as ever, she said that she and her husband had once been involved in an accident there.

'We were on holiday here. Ten years ago. Everybody told us we mustn't miss a run up to the Dandenong Ranges.'

'You didn't get there?'

'No. Nobody was hurt, but the car had to be towed away. We had to fly back to Sydney.'

'A pity. You'd have liked the hills.' He went on to talk about the Dandenongs, where he had held two appointments as head of primary schools. Careful to keep the conversation light and not too subjective, he was giving her every opportunity to bring the meeting to an end, but she appeared to be as disinclined as he was.

'When does your ship sail?' he asked with sudden resolution.

'One o'clock tomorrow.'

'You say you don't know Melbourne. What are you going to do with yourself in the next hour or two?'

'Just look around. A bit of window-shopping.' Her expression remained friendly, but became a little more alert.

'Window-shopping! You can do better than that. Why not let me show you around Melbourne?' He leaned persuasively across the table. 'Look, we're two grown-up people, we don't have to pretend. I'm finished with what I came into town for and nobody's waiting for me at home. I was thinking of going to a cinema, but it's too nice a day for that. Let me show you our Botanic Gardens?'

They came out into the dusty yellow autumn sunshine and took a south-bound tram in Swanston Street.

'I'm always glad to get out of the city centre,' he said when they were seated. 'Even Camberwell, five miles out, is better than this. Melbourne used to have a good smell. I remember when I first came down, a lump of a boy from the bush.

• Transit Passenger •

I thought Melbourne smelled exciting, a mixture of all kinds of things: beer, paper, cooking, new clothes, hot stonework. Now it's beginning to stink like any other city. Gas, oil ...'

They got off at Domain Road and went first to the Shrine of Remembrance, strolling slowly around the base, then climbing to the top, from where he pointed to landmarks and places of interest: Port Melbourne where her ship was lying, the vague outline of the distant You Yangs, the nearer Dandenongs, the greens and whites and reds of the suburbs, the new multi-storeyed office blocks of the business centre.

Afterwards they went down, and for two hours wandered in the gardens, resting now and then when a seat with an attractive vista took their fancy. He told her much about Melbourne's notable public gardens, but most of the time they talked about themselves, with bits of conventional moralizing and philosophizing thrown in, after the fashion of elderly people.

'My daughter and her husband wanted me to go and live with them when Dad died,' she told him once, 'but I didn't even consider it. It hardly ever works out. Somebody always gets hurt.'

'True in the end,' he qualified. 'It can be successful enough while there are infant grandchildren. No baby-sitter like a Nana. And I'm not denying that's a joy to both sides. But the picture usually changes when the nips grow up. We're the most dispensable of all relations. And that isn't a complaint. Every generation has to live in the light of its times, and in the modern rat-race we've simply gone back to the tribe. The Eskimos had their own solution: when pressure was really on they used to wall up their aged or sick in an igloo and leave them to it. We're going one better. The three-generation family group is just about a thing of the past.'

'Three-generation? Two-generation families don't last long now.'

'Indeed no. There's a joke going the rounds in Melbourne: "Is your daughter still studying?" "Yes, she's doing her matric. — and living with a bloke in Carlton."'

They laughed together, and continued for some minutes on the broad issue of young and old. 'It can be hard on both sides,' she said. 'Some of the young ones can be very selfish, and some of the old ones very perverse. My husband and I had a taste of it both ways. We had his mother living with us for the last six years of her life.'

With a little encouragement she went on to tell a fairly familiar story of family disruption:

'There were two brothers and a sister, and when the mother was widowed they all got their heads together and agreed that she would live with the eldest brother and his wife and have a few weeks with the others whenever she felt like it, or whenever Stan and Eva felt like a break. It was Stan himself who came up with the idea. You can never be sure about these things, but I have a suspicion that he and his wife had it all worked out from the start. The mother got a good price for her house and put up a nice little self-contained flat in Stan's garden. And for eighteen months everything seemed to be working out all right. We all had good homes, and at that time the mother was well able to look after herself. Sometimes we had her for a few weeks, and sometimes the sister.

'Then — it's hard to know for certain just where the fault lay — she began to get restless and complain about Stan and his wife. Stan's story is that she was picking on the children, and hanging around the house too much when Eva was busy. There could have been some truth in that, but in the light of what happened afterwards I think there was more to it. Anyway, friction developed, and Mum started to come around the rest of us more and more often. In the end she didn't want to be at Stan's at all. There was an open quarrel while Arthur and I were away on holiday, and when we came back we found her with Margaret, the sister. Next thing we knew, Margaret was in trouble with her husband, and he brought Mum round to us, bag and baggage. We had her for six years. It wasn't easy.'

'What happened to the bungalow?'

'The flat? Stan's eldest boy is living in it; he'll have a wife with him soon. There was a lot of trouble over that flat. It split the family. We all felt that Stan should have paid for it, but he took the attitude that it was there if Mum wanted to live in it. Knowing perfectly well that she didn't. He said she could take it away if she didn't want to live in it. It's brick. He's a different kind of man from his brother. Arthur used to say that his mother was deliberately provoked into getting out.'

'And you?'

'I thought so too, but I tried to pour oil on troubled waters. Arthur was upset chiefly because of me. He thought I was being put upon. He loved his mother, but he wanted to be fair to both of us.'

'Was the mother difficult?'

'In a way, yes. She was a bit of a pet, but she became almost a full nursing case. She had a lot of pain. For the last two years Arthur and I never once went out together. The others practically cut us off altogether; they were afraid of being asked to give us a few weeks' rest.'

'What about your children? How did they take her?'

'They tried, but they weren't infants. They had their interests, and they were bringing their friends about the home. Teenagers aren't very tolerant. They were glad to get away. Anne — that's my daughter — had a business training and took a flat as soon as she could support herself. We never knew where Bobby was; he roamed all over Queensland and the Territory before he went abroad.'

She said this with a smile that discounted any hint of lingering grievances, and for a few seconds silence fell between them. They were sitting on a seat facing a wide sweep of lawn running down to the lake. Not many grown-ups were about, but there came up to them the babble of children feeding the water-birds.

'So that's why you didn't go to live with your daughter,' he commented at last.

'That's why I didn't go to live with my daughter. Why should I, anyway? I'm quite able to look after myself. It would have meant leaving all my friends and associations. I like my garden. And your own home is the only place in the world where you can do exactly what you like.'

He reflected that it all fitted. There was a soothing air of self-sufficiency about her. A pleasant woman, ageing gracefully.

She was watching the distant children now with an indulgent and reminiscent smile. He was tempted to ask her how she had adjusted herself to living alone, but decided it would be too personal, appear to imply something he was trying all the time to avoid. Instead, he remarked again on the general disintegration of the family unit in modern society. The women's liberation movement somehow came up, and they found themselves good-naturedly differing when he suggested that women would never free themselves from the tyranny of men until they could free themselves from the tyranny of their children: 'Some biologist has pointed out that women are the only female animals that never want to give up their young. I don't like the sound of that. Suppose we walk on a bit? We're getting too involved.'

They went down to the kiosk, settled for ice-cream instead of coffee-in-cartons, bought a stale loaf to feed to the birds, and fell to criticizing the City Council for taking so long to provide a proper restaurant in place of the one burned down some years previously.

'It was a pretty shabby old set-up,' he said, 'but at least you could sit down and have a bite to eat. We used to come here often on a weekend with our first son. I didn't tell you about him. He was a paraplegic.'

'Was?'

'Yes. He died. I don't usually talk about him, but I got thinking of him when you were telling me about having to look after the old lady. My wife and I knew what it was like having to live carefully.'

'That must have been painful. We take the troubles of old people for granted. What happened?'

'A road accident. His first car. You know how it is with them. They don't all drink, but none of them can resist speed.'

'How long did he live?'

'After the crash? Seven years. He was only twenty-five when he died. Broken spine, internal injuries. Nerves shot to pieces. He couldn't walk, couldn't feed himself —'

'You don't have to talk about it if it hurts.' He noticed a movement as if she were about to put her hand over his, but it was arrested.

'Not now. I was glad when I came home from the hospital for the last time and told my wife that nothing could ever hurt him any more. It was hard on her; we had him at home most of the time. Hard on all of us. For him — well, you hear a lot about the fortitude of very sick or crippled people, but those who live with them see them with the guard down. You can't expect them to keep up a brave front all the time. God knows Paul tried, but it used to get him down very often. He'd known

• Transit Passenger •

what it was like to be a big healthy boy. I used to catch him watching his brothers and it used to tear the heart out of me. He didn't realize what big restraints it put on them too.

'Nothing was the same after Paul's accident. There's a limit to what you can demand of boys. They did try, but he got to be terribly irritable and demanding. That was the worst part of it for Mum and me, trying to keep the family together. He was losing ground all the time because of the internal injuries. It was what finished him in the end, but by that time both the other boys had left home. Kathy went to the Alfred Hospital as a trainee nurse.'

He fell silent, watching a few cheeky sparrows picking up the last of the crumbs around their feet, then looked up to find her eyes resting on him full of compassion. 'We're having quite a weep, aren't we?'

'Not really,' she smiled.

For a few moments they contemplated the lake without speaking. The sun still showed above the city, but all the heat had gone out of it. Shadows were lengthening. A few adults were still about, but all the children were gone. Both of them were aware that the time for movement had come.

'Well, what do we do now?' he asked. 'Call it a day and say goodbye?'

'You've been very kind.'

'I could say that for you. It's been quite an afternoon for me. You just go back to the ship?'

'I think so.'

'I like the enthusiastic way you say that! Why not eat with me again? I know what a ship's dining-room can be like in port. Half the passengers missing. Alleyways buzzing with strangers. Services out of gear. I've still got that empty house waiting for me. We could be there in twenty minutes.' He was going to add something about being above the age of suspicion, but saw the fatuity of it in time. 'There's two choice steaks in the fridge. You can cook them for me if it will make you feel any better.'

She began to laugh. 'You're a funny man —'

A few minutes later, out on Domain Road, he was telling her not to make a fuss over a taxi fare: 'It's peak hour. If we went by tram we'd have to stand. I have a car, but I don't bring it in to the city in daytime. Parking's the problem. But I'll run you right down to your ship as soon as you indicate you'd like to go.'

On the way out to Camberwell he was again pestered by that inhibition which had accompanied the first few minutes in the cafeteria. The intimacy of a taxi was something rather different from a cafe table or a park bench. For the first time he was aware of the womanly smell of her, a vague scent which he couldn't identify, but which was in the same good taste as her grooming. And an occasional sidelong glance at the still smoothly filled profile confirmed that she was a decidedly attractive matron.

Her reaction when he had suggested going to nis home lingered with him. She'd obviously been on the point of a polite evasion, but a new expression had suddenly come into the watchful eyes. Penetrating, yet carrying an unmistakable twinkle of amusement. Of challenge too? — he wasn't so sure of that. He wondered what was passing behind them now. If she, like himself, was recalling some of the corny music-hall jokes about coming up to see the etchings. She was sitting rather primly, with gloved hands resting in her lap, showing little interest in the streets they were passing through, and telling him about the three women with whom she had shared a cabin. Two of them, companions, had disembarked at Adelaide; the other, with whom she had struck up a friendship, had accepted an invitation to go ashore with one of the unattached male passengers:

'She was a bit apologetic about it, because we had a wonderful day together at Cape Town. But you know how it is; she's younger than me, and he seemed a nice man.'

She went on to describe that day in Cape Town, her cabinmates, the voyage in general, but he felt that it was all just a cover-up for the same kind of unease that he was experiencing himself. She was talking too continuously, too inconsequentially, as people do when they are afraid the conversation might peter out, or veer off in a wrong direction. And why shouldn't she be a little on edge? Everything indicated a woman of ripe experience but conventional standards. Widows, no less than widowers, could be driven by loneliness, but without a doubt she must be wondering what she was let-

• Transit Passenger •

ting herself in for. He knew that the feeling of relief was mutual when the cab turned into a quiet street off Prospect Hill Road and pulled up at a modern brick bungalow set in a lush but rather down-at-heel garden. Movement helped, and there was no casting around for something to talk about.

There was the garden: 'It's got right out of hand since my wife died. I did the spade work, but she was really the gardener. We always had flowers ...'

There was the matter of hospitality as they went inside: 'I'll show you where everything is. I want you to relax and enjoy my home, just as I'm enjoying your company. It's a bachelor home now, but I try to keep it civilized ...'

There was the preparation of the meal, with her taking over the cooking while he set the table, and some wary skirmishing around the difficulties of organizing food for one only.

There was the meal itself, with more talk of food, comments on a few articles of interest when they moved into the lounge, more family confidences, a narrowing down to some details about her late husband's work, and the welcome discovery of a common area of enthusiasm.

'He loved trees. He used to get quite upset over what's happening to our forests. Do you know what clear-felling is?'

'Do I what!' She must have found his reaction gratifying. 'They take everything. Mature timber, saplings, the lot. Nothing left for regeneration. It's going on all over the green coastal strip. Hundreds of square miles of native hardwoods wiped out to make way for the quick-dollar conifers.'

'And chipwood — you know about that?'

'Yes, I know all about it. Machines, monster mincing machines chewing up whole forests on the spot for export. They're altering the entire face of Australia.'

'I wasn't much concerned about it at first. I was more worried about my husband's feelings.' She gave him a shy smile. 'I'm afraid I was — well, just a mousy housewife. But I always liked the bush, and once, when we were on holiday, Arthur showed me what was going on. It almost made me cry, and when we got back to Sydney I was as bad as him when it came to fighting for the trees.' The shy smile again. 'Can you imagine me standing between a tree and a council man with an axe?'

He returned her smile. 'I'm beginning to see you!'

'Arthur was away at the time. We were living in a quiet street, trees down each side and hardly any through traffic. But a major road not far away had to be closed off for repairs and we were part of the detour. The trouble was that when the job was finished heavy traffic kept on coming through because drivers had discovered we were a short cut out to the highway. Next thing we knew was that the council had decided to cut down all the trees —'

'To make it cosy for King Car? I could see that coming. So you got together?'

'Yes, we got together. Everybody in the street was in it, even quiet little me. It's funny how cheeky you can get when there's plenty of others. Gosh, when I think of it!' She put a hand over her face and giggled. 'I finished up tussling with the city engineer. Two policemen turned up, and four of us had our names taken for obstruction. I'll never forget it.'

'And what came of it?'

'Nothing! The council men all went away and we heard no more about it. The trees are still there.'

She'd told the story less in a spirit of pride than in the manner of one recalling a mischievous escapade. The halting phrases, the excited little shake in her voice, and the twinkling eyes were, like the giggle, all wholly feminine. It was easy for him to enter into her enthusiasm over the trees, but something else, something which had been there ever since they had settled into the taxi, was increasingly intruding, taking over. It was very peaceful sitting there, very homely, just the two of them. He began to regret having indicated the two big chairs, a few feet apart. There was the sofa. He wanted to touch her. It would have been easy to put his hand over hers, to get away from trees. Constraint was once again in the air. He found himself recollecting a remark which a friend had once passed to him: 'A man and a woman don't ever really relax with each other until they've been in bed together.'

The thought of returning from Port Melbourne to an empty house was beginning to haunt him. But she was looking at him, waiting ... 'Officialdom isn't always to blame,' he said hurriedly, going back reluctantly to the council axemen. 'What chance have trees got in a city rat-race when they can't survive even in the bush? Nothing is safe if it can be turned into dollars,

• **Transit Passenger** •

or if it's in the way of making dollars. I saw it often in the Dandenongs when new services were being put through. Most of the Departments have learned to walk cautiously, but blokes on the job couldn't care less. Supervisors want results. And sit a young bloke up on a powerful bulldozer and he'll push anything over, just to feel his muscle and hear the crash. Some of the locals are in it too. Once it took a real man to fell a tree. Not now. Any smart lout can hire a chain-saw, fell a big one near his block, cut it up, and have a whole winter's firewood inside his gate in a couple of hours.'

Trees, and more trees, with the minutes ticking away, an occasional brief silence, a personal anecdote now and then by way of a booster, a surreptitious glance by one or the other at the clock over the fireplace, and behind it all a mutual awareness that the casual encounter was moving steadily towards climax or anti-climax.

About nine-thirty she remarked that it was time for her to return to the ship, and he rose immediately.

But he was thinking of a few minutes earlier, when, looking up suddenly after stubbing a cigarette, he caught her eyes resting on him with an expression that no man of experience would misinterpret. It gave him heart, and in helping her on with her overcoat his hands closed firmly on her shoulders and he deliberately turned her to face him.

'Do you really have to go?'

For a moment he thought he had moved too abruptly, but before she could react the telephone rang. It was on a bureau only a few feet from where they were standing.

'Answer it,' she said, with lowered head. 'Talk. Give me time. It isn't easy.' But a swift pressure of her hand on his arm as she left him was full of promise.

In the morning they lay quietly talking, going over those last few minutes, as a man and woman are apt to do when the last barriers are down.

He'd been first up, slipping through to the kitchen to make tea, and returning to find her wide awake. She also had been out, brushed her hair and made up a little, and looked quite charming, if a trifle comical, in his oversize pyjama jacket.

They'd drunk their tea with him sitting on the side of the bed, then he'd lain down again. A few hours previously he'd fallen asleep thinking of that telephone call, of how he'd resented it, but of how decisively she'd turned it to advantage. He'd watched her go down the short hall, painfully conscious of the street door at the far end.

Then a great wave of relief and a mounting excitement as, without hesitation, she'd turned into the bedroom. Someone was talking to him at the other end of the line, but he was alive to nothing except that she didn't come out again, and that no light was turned on. That she was waiting for him.

Now, with only a little sunlight filtering in through the venetian blinds, she told him with some amusement that he'd crept into the room like Daniel entering the den of lions. There'd been just enough light as he approached the bed to reveal that she was lying with eyes closed, and arms and shoulders fully exposed above the covers. She hadn't moved as he undressed, but immediately turned towards him as he lay down beside her. She also was completely nude, and a prolonged shiver passed over her as he ran his hand from shoulder to hip.

Fulfilment was slow in coming, but the firmness of her body and the warmth of her experienced caresses had surprised and delighted him.

'Do you know what you kept on saying?' she reminded him.

'Probably something quite silly...'

'You kept saying "Oh, my dear, my dear! Thank you, thank you..."'

'Did I really? Well, it's how I felt. Indescribably grateful. And something else, something better, something that the young can never fully experience. I think the sweetest moment in a mature man's life is when he first knows, beyond any doubt, that a woman he — yes, a woman he badly wants — is not going to refuse him. Nothing can equal that.'

'You said "I didn't think I was ever going to hold a woman in my arms again."'

'Yes, that I do remember. It was true. At my age...'

'I'm not a young woman.'

'No. No, you're not young either. But...'

'But what? Go on.'

• Transit Passenger •

Raising himself on one elbow, he moved the hand which had been resting on her breast and gently pushed back some hair from her forehead. 'You know, you look different this morning, younger.'

'Everything's different this morning.'

They talked on. In the garden a blackbird was singing. No other sound came in to them. Once she asked him why he was smiling.

'I didn't tell you who it was that rang me last night.'

'Who?'

'My son, Bill. It was funny, although I didn't think so at the time. He knew I wasn't really with him. He kept asking . . .'

'Stop laughing! Tell me . . .'

'He kept asking could I hear him, was I still there. He . . .'

'Stop laughing . . .'

'He said: "You're not getting up to any monkey tricks over there, are you?"'

'That's funny. He would be joking?'

'Of course. Children — grown-up children — have some weird illusions about their parents. Half the cause of what they call the generation gap. They think that nothing can be very exciting after fifty, and that life can't be more than a flicker after sixty.'

They fell to exchanging some views on that. Then, in a short silence when each knew that both their minds were on the passing of time, he asked her: 'What happens now?'

She closed her eyes and gave that some thought. 'I have a ship sailing in four hours.'

'Let it sail! I'll run you down to get your cabin baggage off. Or would you rather I meet the ship in Sydney? I could fly up tomorrow.'

· North Wind ·

Beaumaris. January 14th. 1944. And as I open my eyes on the sunlit morning three thoughts leap at once into my mind: it's hot, Jean will be home tonight, and Mother Lil must go today.

Three thoughts which have hovered around my bed ever since I lay down on it seven hours ago. They were there every time I woke up, which was often. Now, out of the warm light streaming in at the window, they make final assault and take complete possession. It's hot. Jean will be home tonight. Mother Lil must go today.

These breathless mornings deep in the tea-tree scrub have an indescribable charm, and, as I lie luxuriating, Sterne's lovely formula for happiness comes back to me: someone to love, something to hope for, and something to do. Today, then, I should ask for nothing more, because Jean is my love, tonight she is coming back, and as for something to do — well, Mother Lil has to be got rid of, and there's a task worthy of any man.

She was already in bed when I got home last night, so doesn't yet know how complete are the plans for her departure. What a wicked creature she is! One of the last things I told her before going out was that she is the kind of woman who gets mothers-in-law a bad name. By then her fury had nearly exhausted itself, and she just glowered at me. I don't know what kind of reception I'll get this morning, but I'm glad that the chips are finally down, even though I'm apprehensive about how Jean will react when she arrives and finds her mother gone. Lil's influence over her daughter is quite frightening.

However, it's a risk I'm prepared to take, for no good could come of any further hesitations. That treacherous woman has been at the bottom of all the friction in this home since she moved in, and I made up my mind last week when Jean left that I would not ask her to come back while her mother remained under our roof. We should never have taken her in when her husband died. Jean herself had lingered too long under the parental roof, one of the hazards of a late marriage such as ours.

Years ago I met a man who told me that his wife made a hobby of domestic intrigue. I took him only half seriously, but I know now that such creatures do exist. Mother Lil is one of them, and being a neurotic to boot is able to deceive even her own daughter. Really, there are two Mother Lils; one for Jean and one for me. Jean's Mother Lil is the one on display when both Jean and I are the audience. When Jean is not around I get my own Mother Lil, the unadulterated scheming hypochondriac, but a bit careless, with the guard sufficiently lowered for me to glimpse both the deception and the lurking jealousy behind it which is the real danger. With Jean she's sweetness itself, the frail little old lady sitting quietly here or there with her needlework, or occupied in slow motion with some light household chore, courageously eager to help, not to be a burden to us in spite of the torments of her arthritis, her nervous stomach, her misplaced disc, her migraines, her angina. None of them, let it be noted, necessarily visible to the naked eye. She isn't yet seventy, but at her theatrical best can convincingly fill the role of a nonagenarian. An indomitable nonagenarian because — let me admit it — she usually makes the best of herself visually: good taste in clothes, hair well set, and never anything but a discreet use of cosmetics. But all of it skilfully integrated into the brave little old lady act: the carefully controlled movements, the trembling voice, the caution about what she eats and drinks, the clever pretence of losing the drift of what she wants to say, the complaints of sleepless nights, the urgent need to lie down and rest frequently. Yesterday, in her rage when I told her I was going out to book accommodation for her elsewhere, she dropped the act and really let herself go. I know now beyond any doubt what I've always suspected, that physically she's as tough as old boots and mentally as alert as a fox.

She knows now that I'm wide awake to her monkey tricks. She might also be a bit afraid of pushing me too far. I really was very angry when I stormed out, and was at no pains to close doors quietly when I came in. All the same, and significantly, she slept well, because every time I woke up I could hear her snoring. She's quiet now, which probably means that she's wide awake, waiting for me to get up, and trying to guess what my next move will be.

Surely only a morbid neurotic like Mother Lil could think evil on such a morning. We're only fourteen miles from the heart of Melbourne, but there are times when one can capture here all the drowsy charm of the Australian bush. Only a hundred yards away a bitumen road, punctuated by electricity and telegraph posts and bounded on the near side by expensive brick homes, runs along the foreshore. But our 'street' is only a sandy track meandering into the tea-tree scrub, and this block of mine one of only two taken up and built on. Nobody ever passes my gate except to call on my only neighbour, Bob Burge, a little further in. Our immediate surroundings have probably changed little since the coming of white men.

I've known a thousand mornings just like this, but the spell of them is as potent as ever. The long hot night has left me enervated, and for half an hour or so I lie still, looking at the pattern of leaves in the garden and ruminating on the weather and Mother Lil. Mostly on Mother Lil. It is recorded of M. Porcius Cato that he used to conclude his every speech in the Roman Senate with the words *Delenda est Carthago!* Carthage must be destroyed! That's precisely how I feel about Mother Lil. Whatever else this day is fated to bring forth, Mother Lil as a unit of my household must be destroyed.

Whatever else . . .

At seven o'clock I got up, prepared myself a breakfast of boiled eggs and toast, and took a cup of coffee in to her. I'd done that much for her every day of the past week. Not in any hope of pleasing her, but just to deny her the pleasure of telling Jean that my only thought in the mornings had been for myself.

On that last day I knew in an instant the line of conduct she had decided on. She was the very picture of misery. She'd thrown off all coverings except the sheet, so that it was possible to follow every line of her pinched and sprawling body. She lay on her stomach, head on one side, one arm hanging limply over the side of the bed. As if she'd been shot. Her single visible eye was turned up at me with the lugubrious expression of a chicken under the axe. She'd had the window closed all night, and there was a stale smell. Choking down my disgust, I placed the coffee on the bedside table and gave her good morning.

'We're in for another hot one,' I added.

'It was hot all night. I thought daylight would never come. Are there any aspirins in the house?'

'Do you want to take some now?'

'Get me three, will you? I used the last of mine hours ago.'

I fetched them, and stood over her while she swallowed them and sipped some coffee.

'You know I'm not going to work today, don't you?' I said by way of an opening.

'When do you get your truck back?' she asked, referring to the fact that I'd had to put my utility in for a minor repair. In a way, I'm self-employed, maintaining a round of small gardens by contract. None of them local.

'Crowdy's promised it for tomorrow afternoon.' I knew what she was thinking, so went on with sudden resolution: 'But that doesn't affect you. I'll get you a taxi.'

Her expression hardened. 'I told you yesterday I'm not going.'

'And I told you you are. It's a nice little flat, and I've paid two weeks' rent on it. It'll give you time to look around for one you might like better. A couple of suitcases will keep you going. Once you're finally settled somewhere I'll bring out the rest of your things.'

'You've got it all nicely worked out, haven't you? But I'm not going.'

'Stop kidding yourself,' I said shortly, and went out. Time enough if there did have to be another scene.

Certain now that she was going to resist to the last, I ate my breakfast with little real pleasure. I had to face the fact that she couldn't lose if she held her ground, physical force being unthinkable. Perhaps I'd have yielded there and then if something else had been at fault. As it was, courage and determination flowed into me with the morning sunshine. It was still summer, Jean was coming home, and all the world except Mother Lil was sweet and wholesome and full of promise. Even the little white kitchen gave me comfort, because Lil had kept it, as she had everything else, in apple-pie order. Not that she got any aesthetic satisfaction out of method and cleanliness, but just so as not to leave a chink in her armour. She was forever condemning the younger generation of women as a pack of useless, permissive, undomesticated gadabouts, and in the absence of Jean was obliged to lay some emphasis on her own superficial virtues. Jean herself is so artless; what chance did she have against the manipulations of a female Iago?

For that matter, what chance did I have? I had, of course, heard a few things about Lil before my marriage. For instance that she was a fanatically possessive mother and a nagging and domineering wife. But I underestimated her, and didn't anticipate a situation where, as a widow, she would so soon be under my roof. Even then it took me some time to realize that she was much more dangerous than a run-of-the-mill troublemaker; that she was positively sick-minded, and ready to embark on a long-range plan to break up my marriage and get her daughter back. With Jean well into her thirties, still at home, and unattached, Lil had never seen me as anything but a destructive intruder.

'Look out for Mummy!' her sister Jill had warned me. I thought she was only half in earnest, and she wasn't slow to remind me of that last week when she rang from Woodend to tell me that Jean had turned up on her doorstep — with a suitcase. She, for one, knows the long background of last Thursday's rumpus here: the persistent snide remarks to Jean, behind my back, concerning a certain Evelyn with whom I'd lived for a short time and who was now married but still housed in Mentone; the recurring lies about someone telephoning when I was out, and hanging up instantly when a woman's (Lil's) voice responded; the cleverly timed 'jokes' about attractive housewives whose husbands were at work on the days when the gardener was due; my increasing curtness to Lil, while Lil herself was always so nice to me — in Jean's presence. I suppose Jean can hardly be blamed for believing there must be something in it all when I finally lost my temper, called her an idiot for listening to 'that lying old bitch', and marched out, declaring 'All right, if that's what you think, I'll go to this damned woman — now! And her name isn't Evelyn!' She herself was gone when I returned hours later, repentant and half stunned with grog.

However, to get back. *Delenda est* Mother Lil! Tonight she must be gone, gone with the wind.

Gone with the wind — the wind — the wind — it was the whispered refrain to which, a little after eight o'clock, I crossed the road and went down the cliffs for a swim.

'There's going to be a north wind,' I said to her when I got back from the beach.

It was nine o'clock then. Heaven knows I didn't want to speak to her at all, but it was necessary to say something if only to show my satisfaction at finding her up and about. But it didn't take me long to realize that she had merely altered her tactics. Call it a strategic temporary withdrawal. She'd decided that she might have overplayed her hand; that I meant business this time, and in a last resort could ring Woodend and postpone Jean's homecoming. After all, it was me, not Jean, that she wanted out of the house. So she'd got up, groomed herself with even more care than usual, tidied the kitchen, and wetted down Jean's collection of ferns on the front verandah.

It was fiercely hot by then. I'd made the announcement about the rising wind casually enough, but the truth is that I was getting uneasy. Ours was a timber house, water was not laid on, and the tea-tree scrub, dry as tinder, came very close to the back and side fences. It had been a wet spring, and I hadn't managed to burn off the usual protective fire-breaks before restrictions were clamped down. Born and raised in the Dandenong Ranges and involved in many bushfires, I knew all the baleful implications of a hot northerly. The previous day also had been one of high temperatures, with many fires throughout the state, including three reported 'out of control' in the Grampians, the Otways, and at Bairnsdale in Gippsland.

All this was quite beyond Lil's comprehension. She'd never lived in the bush, and had always ridiculed any suggestion of wildfire so close to the city. To her a north wind implied nothing more than some temporary physical discomfort. She read no message in the metallic whiteness of the sun or in the first playful little puffs stirring the tops of the tea-trees.

I'd found her standing at the top of the front verandah steps, holding a watering-can, and with a bunch of freshly cut dahlias at her feet. She was too cunning to sneer at my remark about the wind. 'Yes, I could tell that,' she said quietly, 'so I thought I'd pick a few flowers before they got burned. We've got to have a bit of colour in the house tonight. Jean likes flowers.'

We! I'd read her correctly.

'Jean herself will be colour enough for me,' I said curtly, and went into the house.

She followed me, and began to sort the flowers on the kitchen table while I stood by filling my pipe. The air was charged with suspense. Too clever to take the initiative, she was carefully poised for whatever move I might make. Behind the placid face bent over the flowers I could almost hear the creakings of her tortuous mind. GOD IS LOVE, proclaimed a text on the far wall. Her property. She was very pious, went to church twice every Sunday, and never lost an opportunity to fortify her platitudinous moralizing by quoting the scriptures. Jean and I are both Christians, but I hate cant, and that text, like Mother Lil, was marked down for imminent dispatch.

'Have you had breakfast?' I asked her.

'Not yet. I'm just going to make something. I suppose you could take a cup of tea after your swim?'

'I could. I'll have it in the lounge. I want to make out some accounts.'

'I'll bring it in to you.' She allowed her features to soften a little. 'Will you have something with it?'

'Just a biscuit.' And without thanking her I went into the other room.

The accounts were just a subterfuge, for I could no more give my mind to work that day than fly through the air. Mother Lil, a searing northerly, and a temperature steadily climbing towards a century were more than enough. I recollect that at the very moment when I sat down there came the first gentle tapping on the wall. A familiar sound, but peculiarly disturbing then, falling as it did into a silence already loaded with menace. Just a branch of an old guelder rose bush growing near the window. But long experience had taught me that only from the north could so light a breeze brush it against the house. Minutes passed before it came again, hurried and furtive, like a secretly whispered warning. No other sound in all the world except the restrained movements of Mother Lil in the kitchen.

When she came in I was sitting where the light from below the half-drawn blind fell on the end of the table. Books were before me and a pen was in my hand, but I'd taken up the pen only when I heard her at the door.

'Drink it while it's hot,' she said, placing a cup of tea at my elbow. 'It'll cool you down.' She was full of such stupid fallacies.

'Is there anything you fancy for lunch?' she asked.

'Not really. Make what you like. I never eat much on these hot days.'

'I can open a tin of salmon, but there's nothing for a salad unless you can find a nice head of lettuce in the garden. I suppose you don't feel like going up to Mentone?'

'I didn't intend going out at all. I'd have to push the bike. I'll get a taxi for Jean tonight, but I'll be going in by train.'

'We've got to have something in by then anyway, and the shops would be shut. I'd go up to Mentone myself, but in this wind ...'

She left it at that, and I nodded reluctantly. The suggestion was reasonable; it was no day for an elderly woman to be out shopping.

'I'd go soon if I were you,' she said carefully. 'The wind seems to be getting up.'

'I'll go now.' Her composure worried me. I had my own plans for Jean's homecoming, and saw clearly that it was necessary to press the attack. 'We'd better have an early lunch,' I said pointedly, 'there's a lot to do.'

'And all day to do it in,' she added cheerfully. 'Don't worry, we'll have everything ready.'

That 'we' again. I stood up. 'I'm speaking of the packing, Lil. I want to order your taxi for three o'clock.'

'Taxi!' she gasped, and clapped a hand to her lips. 'Then I wasn't dreaming?'

'When?'

'This morning. I was half asleep, and you seemed to come in and say something —'

'You bet you weren't dreaming!' Her audacity staggered me. 'I told you I'd rented that flat for you in Malvern, and that I'd order a taxi to take you there at three o'clock.'

Suddenly she smiled. 'You're joking, Jim.'

'I was never more serious in my life. You've reached the end of the line here. You're going — today.'

Her smile faded. She cut a rather pathetic figure, standing with one hand clutching the edge of the table, the other with fingertips still resting on her lips. An attitude which went perfectly with the shocked reproach in her eyes.

'Jim —'

'Now for God's sake, Mother, don't let's have a scene over it. I've made up my mind to finish this business once and for all.'

'What business?'

'Stop pretending. I've warned you over and over again. You've come between Jean and me.'

'That's a lie. I've done everything I could —'

'Yes, to break us up. That's why you have to go. Anyway, you're quite capable of looking after yourself, and Jean and I are entitled to our own home. It's immaterial who's at fault. Let's say you don't fit in here. I just want you to go and live somewhere else, and I'm making it as easy for you as I can.'

She took on then what I can only describe as a haunted look. Her eyes fairly popped, her breathing quickened. She even retreated a pace, as if I were threatening her with violence. Yes, she could act. Any witness of that scene would have set me down as a monster. Pushing back her silvered hair, she cast a woeful glance around the room.

'Jim, I can't believe it. I can't believe you've got it in you to do a thing like this. You and Jean are all I have left in this world —'

'You have a sister —'

'I never got on with Nell —'

'Everybody else does! And stop trying to make a tragedy of this. I'm not sending you to the salt mines. You and Jean can visit each other.' Embarrassed in spite of everything she had done, I shook my finger at her. 'I'm just not prepared to talk about it any more. I have a few things to do, then I'm going up to Mentone, and you can start packing as soon as you like. When I come back we'll have some lunch, and you can lie down for a couple of hours. I'll order a taxi for you about three o'clock. And that's all I have to say.'

* * *

Once, in a quiet moment, I'd heard again that urgent tapping on the wall, and as I step outside an innocent baby of a north wind breathes on to my face like a waft from an oven. No violence yet, just a prolonged puff, full of the breath-catching odour of crisp-dry bracken and tea-trees. Pumpkin and rhubarb leaves droop listlessly in the green well of the garden. Bill, the dog, lies panting on his chain under an old boobialla bush. Beyond the fence the wilderness of scrub streams evenly southwards, giving off a sound like a thousand women dancing in paper dresses. An endless, hurried rustling. There's no poetry in this wind in the trees. Only menace. I've spent hours on days like this watching for smoke out there.

Between the encroaching walls of scrub the sand lies deep on the track which, where it enters from Beach Road, is fingerposted 'Erica Street'. Not much wind reaches ground level here, but little whirlpools of dead leaves frisk in odd places, and there's a growing commotion overhead in the few remaining eucalypts.

A great change has come over Beaumaris in the last hour or two. Watery mirages tremble on the road as I bowl along to Mentone. The sun, still only halfway up the eastern sky, has taken on colour and form. There's a slight haze, but how much of it is smoke I cannot yet tell. Persistent south-westerlies in winter have pushed the tea-trees on the cliffs over at a pronounced northward angle; they look now as if they are leaning intelligently into the gale, as people do. Shadows play over patches of sparse and withered grass. The Bay itself is a malignant green, white-whipped with the crests of a million wavelets streaming across from Beaumaris to Mordialloc.

These northerlies give plenty of warning. Others, like me, have read the signs, and comfort-loving humanity is already withdrawing before the tempest. Few people are about, and blinds are drawn at the windows of all houses along the sea front. Here and there a sprinkler is running, but most of the gardens were well watered last night. Now and then a fragrance of flowers and moist leaves penetrates the prevailing odour of parched scrub. Stocks and late carnations; they have a pleasant taste in gardens along here. Beach Road drowses in an atmosphere of well-to-do peace and security.

But there's a telltale black plume flying from distant

Dromana. And a reddish-brown froth mushrooming over Mordialloc. And the very devil of a north wind is working up. And if anything were to start on the Black Rock or Cheltenham side of us ...

'It's in Cheltenham,' said Bob Smailes. 'In the golf links, and building up.'

About eleven o'clock then. Smailes was officer-in-charge of Mentone Fire Station. Weary of flying grit and the glare of the road, and with shopping finished, I'd called in for a gossip with an old mate. Mentone was unusually quiet for such an hour on a Friday. The few women on the Parade hurried about their business with heads down and summer frocks hard-blown against their legs, eager to be finished and back to the shelter of their homes. As I placed my bicycle against the wall two motor-coaches full of cheering children rolled down towards the beach.

The tiled and brassy interior of the station soothed my aching eyes. Six crested helmets on the wall reminded me of youthful idolatries. Smailes and one of his men were engaged in stowing extra beaters in the box at the rear of the old-fashioned fire unit.

'Morning, Bob.'
'How are you, Jim?'
'Getting ready for it?'
'We'll be doing a bit by the look of things.'
'What's the strength of the burn at Mordialloc?'
'Grass. It's in old Taffy's paddocks, other side of the Nepean. We got the call, but didn't stay long. There was enough men to hold it.'

'They won't hold it if it gets across the creek,' growled Bob's mate. 'We should have run a line —'

All three of us jumped as a bell rang.

'That could be it!' exclaimed Bob as he ran into the office.

The other man gave me a smug grin as he reached for his tunic and belt. He was in the driving-seat and revving the engine by the time Bob had taken the call. Two more men, wearing the silly little caps of wartime auxiliaries, hurried in from the station yard and stood by.

I'd seen too much of fires to be more than parochially interested in a turn-out of the fire brigade. Peeved that the alarm had robbed me of a friendly chat, I waited for Smailes to appear.

'Mordialloc?' I asked.

'No. Cheltenham.' He gave me a sympathetic glance. 'You'd better get home, Jim. It's in the golf links, and building up.'

Often in approaching my house from Beach Road I'd had an odd sense of penetrating secret and remote places. Perhaps it was because of the usual silence. There were never many birds in my immediate vicinity, and after the early morning outburst of song what few there were seemed to be too busy scratching a living in the thin ground litter and the limited variety of food plants. The weirdly twisted tea-trees also added something to the illusion, calling to mind, with their pale and antiquated colouring, Arthur Rackham's paintings of Fairyland.

I recall now that the sensation struck me that day with disturbing force. Plunging into the sandy track was like plunging into a cave. The terrific headwind ceased, and for the first time since leaving Mentone I was able to open my eyes wide and breathe in comparative comfort. But there was something else also. A premonition of imminent danger that seized me the minute I left the road. A loss of nerve, and not without reason: the impending struggle with Mother Lil, and the certain knowledge now that there was fire in the scrub only a mile or two away. No smoke clouds showed yet in the north-west, but there was a smell, and in the last hour the light had noticeably deteriorated. Everything pointed to immense fires burning inland. Overhead a yellow moonlike sun, shorn of its beams, lay on a sky grey with smoke and, no doubt, dust from the drought-wracked Mallee. My house, seen from the garden gate, looked just as it did right after sunset on a still and overcast winter day.

Mother Lil had again changed her tactics. An opportunist of the first water, she'd seized eagerly on the new situation created by the north wind. Perhaps, in her perverted piety, she imagined that the Lord had delivered me into her hands. When, entering from the back verandah, I found no sign of life and the whole place in semi-darkness, I guessed instantly where to look for her. Knowing that she would have heard me come in, I stood for some seconds in the kitchen, waiting for the first moans.

I thought next that she would pretend to be asleep when I did go into the bedroom, but she didn't. She'd decided to put on, in full dress, a replay of the early morning act. Stretched out in a posture of utter exhaustion she presented a picture that would have deceived anyone but me. Every other blind in the house was drawn. In this room only she'd cunningly left a narrow slit of light so that it fell dramatically on her face. Once again a single anguished eye squinted up at me as I walked over to her.

'Feeling the heat?' I asked cautiously.

She heaved a long sigh. 'I can hardly breathe. I've just had an awful coughing fit. I thought you'd never get back.'

'There was a headwind all the way. Is there anything I can get for you?'

'No thanks. I just want to lie here. Is there a change coming?'

'There's always a change behind a northerly, but it's a long way off yet. The wind's still rising.'

For perhaps half a minute she lay still, drawing in her breath in theatrically laboured gasps. When that branch of the guelder rose gave a particularly loud rap on the wall she raised her head.

'What was that?'

'Just a branch outside.'

'It's like someone at the door. I heard it before and went out, but there was nobody there.'

To that I made no reply. There was a feverish light in her eyes, and she'd made the remark in the low-voiced gabble of one talking in sleep or in delirium. It came to me that she was drawing on untapped resources of talent.

'Will you take a cup of tea if I make it?' I asked.

'No. I just want to lie here. I'll be all right.'

'An iced coffee?'

'No. I don't want anything. Are there any fires about?'

'There's a lot of smoke in the sky, but I think it's all from up country. They're fighting a big burn at Narbethong, just over the Blacks Spur.' What was the use of telling her anything else?

'I can smell burning,' she said with stony disbelief.

'You always can on days like this. There's a bit of an outbreak down at Mordialloc.' Hardening my heart, I took the plunge. 'You didn't do any packing?'

'Are you still harping on that?' she demanded peevishly, as if it were some petty matter I ought to let drop.

'You don't seem to have faced up to the fact that you're going.'

'You're mad,' she said contemptuously.

'Lil, I'm appealing to you not to make a scene, but I'm quite determined. You were the cause of Jean going away. It isn't going to happen again.'

'You think Jean will forget everything, don't you?'

'There's nothing to forget except your lies. And she's forgiven me for losing my temper the other night. She wants to come back. We never had a difference until you came here.'

'She wasn't clever enough to see through you, that's why.'

'Not until you helped her, eh? All right, Mother, have it your way. But you're going, just the same.'

With a grossly exaggerated effort she sat up and pushed back her disordered hair. 'Very good, Jim, if that's how you feel, I'll go. I never stayed anywhere where I wasn't wanted. But some day God will punish you for this. He watches over His children.'

'I'll take a chance on that. You can lie there until I get a bit of lunch ready. It's only a bit after twelve.'

'Don't worry about me. I'll go now.'

She showed no inclination to stand up, so I moved away without answering her.

'You needn't think you'll get away with this,' she burst out as I reached the door.

There was such intense malice in her voice that I involuntarily turned back. 'That sounds almost like a threat.'

'Well, what d'you think all your precious friends are going to say about this?'

'That's something else I'll take the odds on. Anything will be better than losing Jean.'

'I won't go out of my way to cover you up. I have friends, too, you know.' She had, of a kind.

'Do what you damned well like,' I snapped, and went out to water my seed-beds.

By then the general aspect had become quite ominous. It had turned darker even in the short time I'd been at home. The sun was like a ripe pomegranate floating in an inverted bowl of pea-soup. In itself that indicated nothing different from a hundred other north wind days. What did worry me was that there seemed to be some movement in the sky. In the absence of much variation of colour it was impossible to be sure, but over the wilderness of tossing leaves in the direction of Cheltenham and Black Rock, all the heavens seemed to be majestically ascending, like the winding up of an immense back-drop. The smell of burning was more pronounced too, and the wind had reached almost gale force. Twigs and bits of bark littered the lawn, while over the back fence lay the wreckage of a toppled banksia.

Inside again, I drew up the blind of the kitchen window. I must have lingered there for some seconds, looking out, for I was quite startled by the sudden voice of Lil behind me.

'What are you looking for?'

'Just studying the weather,' I replied. I was, as a matter of fact, trying to accept an idea which had just occurred to me: that not only Mother Lil might have to leave the house that day.

'There's fire about?'

I just nodded. Between her and the wind and the heat and the fire I felt myself beset on all sides. There could be no doubt about that movement in the north-west. Southwards and eastwards the sky was a shade lighter and significantly still.

'Far enough away not to worry us,' I lied.

'But I can smell it.'

'That proves nothing. You told me yourself you could smell it in Melbourne when the Dandenongs were on fire in twenty-six.'

'Anyway, I'm not going out in that.'

'If this means anything at all,' I said firmly, 'it means that you might be going sooner than I thought. I might have to get out myself yet.'

Her lip curled contemptuously. 'Trying to frighten me out now, are you?'

'The devil himself couldn't scare you. But since you take that line let me tell you something. There was a fire in Cheltenham Golf Links a couple of hours ago. They must have got on top of it. But anything can happen yet. If it wasn't for you I'd be out now with the other men. There's fire a lot closer than the Dandenongs.'

'You're lying.'

'Go out and look at the sky, you silly old fool! Go out and take a sniff off the back verandah.'

She sniggered in disbelief. 'Are you trying to tell me there's going to be a bushfire in Beaumaris?'

Well, she wasn't the only one who was taken in that day. For the inexperienced it isn't easy to associate wildfire with the suburb of a great city; a suburb served with bitumen roads, electricity, gas, telegraphs, fire brigades and water. Not that the last-mentioned applied to my home. Few of the minor streets then were reticulated from the main on Beach Road. I was still 'on' tank water, the significance of which Lil, who had lived all her life in Richmond, couldn't appreciate.

'All right,' I said, 'I'm just telling you. There's fire —'

'Let it burn. I'm not going.'

She spoke with a rather frightening self-assurance. She hadn't moved from the doorway of the lounge. The dim light from the kitchen wasn't enough to reveal her clearly, but there was an expression on her face which I can only describe as eager. She loved scenes, and I realized with a sinking heart that she was going to exploit the existing situation to the utmost.

'I thought all that had been settled, Lil,' I said quietly.

'No doubt you did. I'm sorry to disappoint you.'

'You're still going.'

'You're very anxious to get rid of me, aren't you?'

'Frankly, I am.'

'I don't blame you. You don't want me here when Jean gets back, do you?'

'That's true, Lil, I do not.' I was trying to fortify myself against a new trick. Something deadly was brewing.

'You're afraid of what I'll tell her, aren't you?'

'I've always been afraid of what you say to Jean.'

'Go on. Pretend you don't know what I'm talking about this time.'

'Lil,' I said desperately, 'the contortions of that thing you use for thinking —'

'Never mind your long words. It isn't what I think with that counts. It's what I see with.'

'What in the name of God are you hinting at now?'

'Just Pearl Powers.'

'What!'

'You heard me. Arnie Powers' wife. You think I'm blind, don't you?'

'My God, Lil —'

'I'm not afraid of you —' Nevertheless she put up her hands defensively as I advanced towards her. This was worse than anything I'd anticipated. Arnold Powers was a fellow gardener living in Mentone. We sometimes joined forces in a laying-out or sizeable renovations job.

'Where were you till eleven o'clock on Wednesday night?' demanded Lil vindictively. 'I know positively that Arnie wasn't home.'

'You wicked old woman!' I shouted. 'I was at a meeting of the Flower Show committee, and well you know it. If you dare to open your mouth outside —'

'I'll open it, don't you worry. There's been other nights —'

'Lil, if you have a spark of decency — this isn't just me, it's Mrs Powers. If a whisper of such a thing got around — you know very well I go there sometimes to discuss work with Arnie. I'm always welcome —'

'You're welcome all right — when Arnie's out!'

Only her age and sex prevented me from striking her. It came to me that I was still underestimating her. That getting rid of Mother Lil called for the exercise of qualities I didn't possess. She was a vixen, a virago, a termagant, and I'd never had anything to do with such a woman.

'You're the wickedest woman that ever God breathed life into,' I said sadly. 'If that slander reaches the ears of Arnie Powers I'll put you through court.'

'I'm not afraid of the law. I know what I'm talking about.'

'Yes, you know exactly what you're talking about.'

And there I left it. Immeasurably depressed, I wandered into the lounge, closed the door, sank into an armchair, and fell to wondering whether I was more or less of a man for not trying the effect of a hearty slap. I heard her fill the kettle and begin to set the table for lunch. There, indeed, lay the very measure of her. For Mother Lil domestic intrigue was the very spice of life. Gone now were all her pains and palpitations. She was happy, revitalized, and without doubt would sit in there now and eat her best meal for a week. She even began to hum 'Lead, Kindly Light', just to show me how completely she was mistress of the situation. Perhaps also to see if there was any fight left in me, because when I showed no reaction she suddenly pushed open the door to ask what I'd like for lunch.

Beside myself with rage, I snatched up a heavy flower-vase. 'Nothing, you old witch!' I yelled. 'You dare to set one foot inside this room —'

'You're mad —' she began.

'Yes, stark, staring, raving mad. Close that door!'

'The heat —'

'Close it — quick!'

She closed it, but in an instant I flung it open again. That was the only time I saw real fear in her face. She retreated against the stove, frantically pulling a chair in front of her.

'And if I hear as much as a whisper from you,' I raged, 'if you dare to hum just one more bar of your infernal hymns, I'll lock you in and start a bushfire of my own — right in the middle of the bloody house.'

She must have believed that, for I didn't hear a sound from the kitchen afterwards except the occasional tinkle of a dish.

And there I sat, committed now beyond redemption. Mother Lil's triumph was complete. Not in the wildest moments of her neurotic dreams had she hoped for such a tale to tell her cronies — and Jean. I'd menaced her life. I'd flourished a flower-vase at her, threatened to burn down the house with her in it. Alone in a house with a madman; how fine it would sound on her practised lips.

Only thin wafers of light slipped in around the edges of the drawn blinds, but gradually my eyes became accustomed to the gloom so that I could see the time by the clock on the mantelpiece. Nearly one o'clock. Physically, such days usually disturbed me little, but the emotional strain of the struggle with Mother Lil was robbing me of both the strength and the will to fight. What more could I do, anyway, that didn't involve leaving her to her own perverse devices? And, of course, leaving my home — and Jean's. Earlier, before going to Mentone, I'd taken what few precautions were available to me: cleared out the dead leaves lying in the spoutings; rammed tennis balls tightly into the downcomers and filled the spouts with water; set out a few containers of water on the verandahs back and front; raked away all the dry vegetable litter from under the tank-stands and around the wash-house; made myself a new beater by nailing a folded wheat-bag to the end of a length of two-by-one. Not that the latter would be of much use anywhere except on the grassed frontage. Only water under pressure, or a burned-off break, could prevail if fire came in through the tea-trees. Men can't work right on the face of blazing scrub.

I wanted to sleep. My head throbbed, and there was a touch of dizziness, with waves of light pulsing across my eyes as when I'd first looked at the white sun early in the morning. And not even my bleak reflections on Mother Lil would drive away the image of that sullen upward-sweeping sky in the north-west. 'It's in the golf links, and building up,' Smailes had said. That one would have been here long ago if they hadn't controlled it. Had they really? And what else was there? Access roads between me and the links were few and rough, with big blocks of land in the hands of speculators and covered by scrub that hadn't had fire through it in years. And there was that deepening black cloud over Black Rock, and the increasing banging of the guelder branch on the wall, like a final imperative summons to action. The breathless calm within the room only added to the menace of what was going on outside; an incessant cacophony of moans, whistles, drummings and whisperings, as if the advance guards of destruction already scurried around the house.

Danger and turbulence. But for a few minutes I must have rest. A little time in which to prepare myself for whatever is in store for me, to get accustomed to the certainty that Jean's homecoming will not be as I'd hoped, to decide where to take her when I meet her at Spencer Street Station, and, more immediately, whether or not to leave Mother Lil and my home and go out to join other men on the nearest fire front.

Every timber in the house creaks and groans, with a perceptible tremor now and then as a particularly strong gust crowds under the flooring boards. The air is warm in the nostrils, and faintly scented by burning leaves. Streams of perspiration run down my chest and lodge along my belt. There's a sensation of lightness and detachment, an illusion of floating, of tilting backwards, of coming out of myself, like the first symptoms of intoxication. And, through it all, the final question: what's it going to be like here tonight when I do come back with Jean? I could, of course, telephone through to Woodend and try to stop her on one pretext or other, but she'd know about the fires and wouldn't be put off. Besides, I want her back in any circumstances. So I'll meet her as arranged. My old parents at Murrumbeena would welcome her, but she'll insist on coming home.

It's hard to accept defeat when every detail of the homecoming was planned with such joy and meticulous care, like a honeymoon. The great moment was not to be at Spencer Street Station, nor at a restaurant where I proposed to take her before leaving the city. It was to be here on the front threshold, when I turned the key in the lock, and took her by the hand, and led her into a silent and deserted house. Perhaps I'd have carried her in, as I did that day three years ago. She's quite a lightweight; a man can hold her easily cradled in his arms, and kiss her like a big baby. Over and over again I'd heard her asking from somewhere down in the hollow of my neck: 'You great fool! What are you laughing at?' And I'd have had to tell her only half the truth, because she will never see her mother through my eyes.

After such dreams it isn't easy to face up to hard facts. I know now that there'll be lights in the house as we come in from the road, and that the instant the taxi doors bang outside Mother Lil will appear on the verandah. Mother Lil on her best behaviour; she can be nice when it suits her. And tonight she'll excel herself. She'll be nice to both of us, but particularly nice to me. For the benefit of Jean she'll make a veritable display of her thoughtfulness. She'll insist on me sitting down to rest my 'tired feet' while she sets out cups and saucers, even though she'll know we've just eaten. I'll be hustled to the cosiest chair as she tells Jean how hard I've been working and what a job she's had prevailing on me to take proper food and sleep. She'll tell me, all within the hearing of Jean, that my lunch is cut for tomorrow, a clean shirt laid out for me, that button sewed on to my overalls, and those trousers parcelled up ready to be dropped in at the dry-cleaner's. And Jean, in her innocence, will think that her going away mightn't have been such a bad thing after all, that perhaps Lil and I have had a heart to heart talk and made peace. Later we'll all retire, and the night will pass without a peep out of Lil. No doubt I'll take Jean in my arms, but the sweetness of possession will be haunted by the spectre of Mother Lil lying wide-eyed in the other room working out how to prepare the ground for a resumption of normal relationships. If only...

Thoughts gradually become retrospective, then disjointed and grotesque, as they usually do when sleep struggles to take over. There was a day last winter when I'd been ill and had got up for the first time to sit here in my dressing-gown. A strong wind was blowing that day also, and although the blinds were right up the light was little better than it is now. But that wind was stinging cold from its journey over snow-covered mountains, and the gloom was the gloom of banking rain-clouds instead of dust and smoke. We had a great log fire burning, and Lil was not yet with us. Jean came in to me with a pot of tea and freshly baked scones, and I well remember the sense of ineffable peace, the deep contentment of two people listening to a storm which cannot touch them.

My eyelids persist in falling, and in the hotch-potch of sounds and images that come before oblivion Jean's voice takes on other tones. The tones of Mother Lil. A spectre, a female figure, is taking shape against the bookcase on the far wall. It keeps moving upwards, yet makes no progress, like a toiler on a treadmill. It turns its head towards me, and I see that it's smiling — and snarling. Smiling with its eyes and snarling with its lips. Its head is thrown slightly backwards so that it's looking down at me. Looking at me with an expression of arrogance triumphant. Altogether, a vision that harmonizes frightfully with the tremendous upward sweep of the northern sky and the flogging of the guelder branch. There's nothing haphazard about that knocking now. It's taken on a rhythm, a thumping staccato beat like the throbbing of barbaric drums...

'You'd better come and have a look at it.'

· North Wind ·

She was indeed there when I opened my eyes. Not close but just inside the door. And not a bit arrogant. Just a twisted old woman.

'Have a look at what?' I asked her drowsily.

'The weather. I've never seen anything like it. There's fire about.'

Half turning towards the windows, I discovered with a shock that one of the blinds had been run right up. 'What time is it?'

'Two o'clock.'

Two o'clock! What, then, had happened to the daylight? Rather foolishly, I asked her who had raised the blind.

'I did. You were sound asleep. I thought I'd better wake you.'

My mouth was dry and sour. It took a few seconds for me to gather my wits. Then a full comprehension of the racket going on outside sent me rushing to the window facing northeast. Other things besides the guelder branch were beating at the walls, and there was an eerie piping under the eaves which distinguished this north wind from all others.

'They're calling for help every few minutes,' said Mother Lil.

No doubt they were. The wind, full gale force now, fairly screamed across the reeling scrub, whilst high in the sandy yellow wastes over the Bay the great ball of the sun hung bloody and dull.

'You should have wakened me before now!' I shouted at Lil as I pushed past her.

In the kitchen the radio was turned low on a Strauss waltz, but the sound was lost as I opened the door and the wind bustled in, rattling the china on the dresser, knocking a calendar off the wall, and lifting an end of a coir runner.

Nothing remote about the smell of burning now. City or no city, this was bushfire. Against the moaning of the scrub the foliage of the nearest trees, brittle from rainless weeks, spattered like rain on an iron roof. Long banners of bark flew from a tall eucalypt beyond the fence. Green leaves littered the lawn, flew through the air like big black insects. Over Cheltenham the yellow haze was smudged with whirling clouds of brown.

The sense of isolation which had troubled me all day was becoming unbearable. There was a longing for human contact. Lil didn't count; she was part of the tempest. I wanted Jean, or men. When, right at my elbow, Lil asked timidly what was going to happen, I snubbed her.

'I told you this morning there was fire. Why didn't you wake me?'

She was going to reply, but froze with her mouth open and one hand uplifted. I, too, had caught the last words on the radio: '— Mentone Fire Station.' Pushing her before me I got inside and closed the door just as the voice began again:

'I will repeat that message. The fire which broke out about noon south of Black Rock is now out of control and travelling rapidly towards Beaumaris. There is danger of it joining up with the other which is burning down from Cheltenham. Some houses have been destroyed and many others are in danger. More men are urgently required. Volunteers are advised to report immediately to Mentone Fire Station.'

Lil stood with clasped hands, watching me. Perhaps for the first time in her adult life she was partly shocked out of her morbid theatricalism. She looked almost womanly.

'Jim, do you think it's very bad?'

'You heard what he said, didn't you? You thought I was trying to scare you this morning.' I sat down and began to lace up my boots.

'Where are you going?' she asked.

'Out to get the strength of things. We can't see anything in here. I don't want to get trapped.'

She didn't reply to that immediately, and when I stood up I was disconcerted to find her regarding me with scowling suspicion. 'It isn't as bad as that,' she said.

'Lil,' I replied firmly, 'I'm going down to the corner, to Beach Road. No further. When I come back I want to find you fully dressed for travelling. Put on all your best clothes and pack a small suitcase. Understand me?'

Her expression hardened even while I was talking. Her lip curled disbelievingly. 'You're still set on getting rid of me, aren't you?'

'You old fool!' I exclaimed, grasping her roughly by the arm. 'Do you want to be roasted? That fire could come right through. Didn't you hear what he said? We've got to get out.'

Shaking me off, she retreated against the dresser. 'I'm not

going, and that's final. You can't scare me. This isn't the bush. We've got fire brigades —'

'Fire brigades? That fire's miles across. Everything's burning. We're in a bad place. Lil, I beg you —'

'You — beg — me!' Leaning against the dresser, she shone her great eyes at me full of hatred. 'Jim Thurgood, I defy you! You'll never get me out of here — never, never, never!'

For the first time it came to me that she was worse than evil; she was mad. Involuntarily I backed away from her. 'You're crazy, Lil.'

'Not on your life I'm not,' she sneered. 'I know what I'm doing. So do you, you cunning beast. It's yourself you're thinking of. As if I couldn't read you —'

'Have a look at the north, woman!'

'I've looked at it. I've been looking at it for over an hour while you slept. That's how anxious you were about it. You went to sleep.'

'Then burn, damn you! Frizzle and fry, you venomous old bitch!' Quite beside myself, I pushed a chair at her so that it toppled over. The sight of her skipping out of the way stirred me to a further pitch of excitement which was nearly my undoing. I leaped forward, but stopped as she reached the door of the lounge and crouched there in a come-and-get-me attitude which would have been funny in other circumstances.

'All right,' I panted, 'you win again. But I'm going myself. And I'm going for good. I'll take my place with the rest of the men. You'll have to work out your own salvation.'

Another bluff, but what else could I do? I went out with a vision of two bright eyes glowing at me from the lounge.

Outside, the wind seized me and rushed me down the garden path just as my neighbour, Bob Burge, pulled up his car at the gate. He was pointed in from the road.

'What's to do, Jim?'

'That's what I want to find out, Bob. What's the score?'

'I'll tell you what the score is; we're in strife, mate. Where's your women?'

'Jean's still away. The old girl's getting ready.'

'She'd better stir it up. I thought you'd have gone. I've been down at Mordialloc, but I heard there's a big burn heading for Rickett's Point, so I shot back to get some gear out. They're in plenty of strife at Cheltenham too. We can't do nothing in here once it gets away from them. Want me to pick up Mrs Pallant?'

'No. Thanks just the same, Bob. I'll see she gets out.'

All the king's horses and all the king's men — but I should have taken him up on that, if only as a witness.

'Please yourself, but don't mess about too long.'

Don't mess about too long . . .

The scene from the end of my street is bewildering. I've worked on many bushfires, including the great holocaust of 1939. This one, in comparison, is only a pigmy, but, raging right in the environs of Australia's second big city, it has a peculiarly terrifying aspect. Along the sea front there is activity such as this road has never witnessed before. Something in the nature of a general evacuation is taking place. Cars and trucks dot the concrete kerb, with a great coming and going at almost every house. Several army transports full of soldiers rumble northwards as I emerge from the scrub. Not far behind them tears a fire-engine, bell clanging for right-of-way. In the opposite direction goes a steel tip-truck loaded higgledy-piggledy with household goods.

At the gate of the house on the corner two spinster sisters stand heavily dressed amid a collection of suitcases. They've lived here for years, but nobody knows much about them. One, holding a cage containing a canary, looks back wide-eyed and open-mouthed at their lovely little villa as if expecting it to burst into flames at any moment. The other stares sulkily up the road towards Black Rock. God help her! She must think the buses are still running to schedule.

Only the surface of the Bay is agitated by this wind off the land, but the white-flecked ripples scurry madly over water which has deepened from green to a dirty brown. In the south little is visible beyond Parkdale's deserted and sand-blown beach. Mordialloc Pier and all the green shore down to Frankston and Dromana have vanished into the weird yellow haze. Northwards, a towering black curtain drapes the sky from Cheltenham right out to the green-mantled cliffs.

Nothing daunts me, however, as much as the activity on the nearest beach. Fugitives. The water is shallow there, and many people, anticipating a blazing foreshore, are wading out into it. More are continually arriving. Invisible against the dark cliffs, they emerge magically on to the pallid sand like ants pouring from an anthill. Little piles of hastily gathered possessions litter the beach. The trembling wail of frightened children reaches me clearly.

Suddenly, something springs on to the cliff-top just this side of the hotel and runs in a long tangent down to the beach. No smoke. No flash of flame. Just a movement, a disturbance, incredibly light and incredibly swift. As if an invisible animal had sped through the stunted scrub. But I know from long experience what it is, and as the first eddies of smoke go up less than half a mile away I turn and run. I'd told her to frizzle and fry, but I'd known all along that I'd go back for her. There were, moreover, certain articles that had to be saved if indeed the house was doomed.

Any woman with a spark of compassion would have reacted humanly in such a predicament. I should have found Lil out on the verandah, fully dressed and packed, eagerly awaiting my return. Instead, she'd been watching for me at the lounge window or a half-open door, ready to resume her macabre play-acting the minute I showed up. This I know, because there wasn't the slightest sound when I entered the house, yet when I came on her she was breathless. Breathless from the sudden exertion of racing to her bedroom as I hurried up the garden path. Once again she was lying just as I'd found her first thing in the morning.

Breathless myself, I stood for a few seconds looking down at her, undecided what line to take. I said: 'Lil, do you realize that this house is liable to go up in flames at any tick of the clock?'

She gave no sign of having heard me. She was horrible. She'd disordered her hair, and placed the chamber-pot conveniently under the bed. That is, where I could see it without seeing into it. This was to be a sickness act. She was without scruples and without womanly dignity.

'Do you hear me, Lil. They're evacuating Beach Road. Can't you hear the fire-bells and police sirens? Yet you lie there! I've come to take you out.'

'You're not taking me anywhere. I'm too ill to move. I nearly died five minutes ago. I nearly reached my heart up.'

Fighting down my disgust, I bent over and shook her by the shoulder. 'Lil, for God's sake don't play with me now! You know very well I'm not kidding you. That fire — come on, up you get. I'll help you.'

She raised her head and looked at me like a dying sheep. She didn't realize that I saw all her tricks against the crude background of that jerry under the bed. 'Jim, I know you mean well, but I can't move. You've got no idea what I've been through.'

'But you must —'

Her skinny hand came up, feverishly groping. 'Jim, you wouldn't hurt me, would you?'

She really did look pitiful. My anger melted just a little, even though I knew by her frantic blinks and face-twisting that she was trying to bring tears. Crying at will was one of her accomplishments.

'Why should I want to hurt you? You've behaved badly to me, but all I want now is to get you out of this house —'

'D'you think I don't know that!' She was on to it in a flash. A spontaneous reaction that she instantly regretted, realizing that it cut right across the dying sheep role. She collapsed again, letting her eyelids fall and her features smooth out.

'Lil, don't go to sleep!'

There was a clatter overhead as a flying piece of deadwood landed on the roof, but she didn't move.

'Lil, get up before I drag you up!'

Her eyes opened. 'What time is it?' She was jealous of the realism of my own awakening half an hour before.

'Getting on for three o'clock. Come on, I'll help you.'

'Tell Jean I want her.'

She closed her eyes again, and all the pity left me. She well knew that Jean wasn't at home. She was in a delirium, not of sickness, but of self-mortification.

'You know very well that Jean isn't here, you damned acrobat. Look here, I'll give you five minutes to get ready. Not a second longer. I'm going to pack a few things, and if you're not off that bed when I get back you can die in it. Nothing will save you if the fire comes through. Do you hear me?'

She didn't answer. She was shamming sleep. Shamming, because from the doorway I looked back and saw her eyelids snap down. She'd never been more alert in her life.

Running out to the back, I let the dog off the chain and kick open the fowlyard gate. I'm caught up in a kind of claustrophobia. There's an impulse to shout, to escape, to run. I feel the weight of the tawny sky, the crowding of the encompassing scrub. At some distance in the east a billow of black smoke suddenly gushes up, as if fire has engulfed an industrial plant of some kind. This, then, is the moment of decision. Alone, I can do nothing here. I have to bet on Lil coming to her senses, however late. I must join the fire front, somewhere. In the event of a retreat to Mentone others will save my house if it possibly can be saved. Homes are the common concern in a bushfire; not one is abandoned without a struggle.

What, then, must I take with me? Valuables? We haven't any in the accepted sense of the term. But how very valuable is everything a working man possesses! So much toil and patient self-denial. Hurrying from room to room I contemplate one precious thing after another: furniture, pictures, books, all the fondly accumulated chattels of an existence which only a few hours ago seemed so secure. Every one a part of me, of Jean, of our ordered lives.

To the devil with fiddling sentimentalities! In our own bedroom I spread a blanket on the floor and fling open the doors of the wardrobe. On to the blanket go Jean's new winter overcoat, a few frocks, my own best suit and overcoat, our best woollens. Into a soft hold-all go Jean's trinkets and cosmetics from the dressing-table. She took little with her; she didn't really mean to leave me. There's a lump in my throat as I strap them all up. It'll be a funny swag if a stranger happens to get hold of it.

Finally some papers in a big envelope marked DOCUMENTS: marriage certificate, war bonds, bank book, title deeds of the land, testimonials etc. Gathering everything up I dump them on the front verandah and go in to Mother Lil.

* * *

She lay just as I'd left her, but a slight flicker of her eyelids and the rigid set of her features betrayed that she was wide awake. No doubt she expected me to approach softly and rouse her with all the caution due to an old woman. I did nothing of the kind.

'Come on, Lil!' I shouted, fetching her a solid wallop on the bottom. 'I'm going now. Up you get.'

She gave a grossly exaggerated start and opened her eyes. Her lips moved in a hardly coherent babble: '... marrer?'

'Matter? The bloody scrub's on fire, that's all. It's just about on top of us. Get moving —'

'Let it burn. Are you trying to murder me? I was in a lovely sleep.'

'You'll be in a lovely sleep all right if you stay here. Come on —' I seized a pillow, but she sank her fingers into it and heaved over to her other side.

'Go away, Jim Thurgood — you can't scare me.'

Bending down, I put my lips to her ear. 'Lil, Beaumaris is burning. Everybody's gone except us. I'm not just trying to frighten you.'

Her shrivelled hand pushed back at me. 'Don't shout at me. It goes through my head like a knife. Can't you leave me alone? I never did you any harm.'

'If I leave you alone you'll die, you crazy fool. God damn you! I'm not going to have murder laid to my account.' Grabbing her by the shoulders I tried to drag her up, but she turned on to her back and pulled at my arms with unexpected strength. When I shifted my grip to her wrists she kicked, bringing her legs right up so that her skirts fell back, exposing pink knickers and part of her blue-veined thighs. Her abominable imagination didn't miss even that. Craning her head forward so that she was bent almost double she surveyed her skinny shanks and actually spat at me.

'You dirty beast! You beast! Just wait till I see Jean —'

Holding her down with one hand I grasped a corner of the sheet and tried to pull it over her. But she was too quick for me, and when I stumbled and fell on top of her her sharp fingernails ripped down the side of my face. That made me release her, and she wriggled over against the wall and crouched there, panting and glowering, and rearranging her disordered skirts as if I'd been trying to rape her.

Passing a hand over my face I brought it away flecked with blood. 'You're not a woman,' I breathed, 'you're a wild animal. Can't you see I'm trying to save you?'

'You're trying to kill me.'

'Lil, for God's sake! Don't commit suicide just to spite me. I'm responsible for you. If anything happens to you —' Too late I realized it was the worst thing I could have said.

'Ah, so that's what's worrying you?' Up to then I doubt if she had fully grasped the potential, for her, of the predicament I was placed in, and she was on to it in a flash. 'You wanted me out of the way, didn't you?'

'I just want you out of this house —'

'Dead or alive, eh?'

I left her. What else could I do? One way or another she had to be got out, and where coaxing and coercion had failed a risky bluff might succeed. The implications of that bluff were daunting, so daunting indeed that I had to put them out of my mind and seek comfort in the reflection that she was more nimble than I'd believed, and could probably move fast enough once she actually saw flames approaching, and when I was no longer there to be tormented. Going out with her taunts ringing in my ears, I picked up swag and beater and set off down the garden path.

It's almost a relief to get back to the brutal lucidity of the north wind. No play-acting here. Under the weight of the swag I go slowly, sucking in the warm air in laboured gasps. Try as I will, I can't shut my mind to the possibility that Lil, in her folly, might decide to call my bluff. How would it look for me, with quite a few people aware of the friction between us? Who would believe me? Certainly not Jean ...

A truck heading northwards pulls up as I reach the road. Some familiar voices hail me:

'There's Jimmy Thurgood. Hi there, Jim!'

'Come on, you old bastard!'

I move eagerly forward. It's good to hear my name on the lips of normal people, to be caught up and carried along on the stream of communal life. Smoke-blackened faces grin down at me from behind the cabin. Friendly hands reach for the swag.

'How did your place go, Jim?'

'This all you took out?'

'Where's the missus?'

I tell them, omitting — to my subsequent regret — all mention of Mother Lil. (Two of us could have bundled her up.) I learn that they've been working since early morning on an outbreak near Dandenong, that it has been contained, and that they've come back in response to calls for help closer to their homes. They tell me there are rumours of lost lives, that there is fire everywhere, that every brigade in greater Melbourne is out, that busloads of volunteers are being carried from the inner suburbs out to Eltham, Diamond Creek, Broadmeadows, Laverton, Strathmore, and a dozen other places on the outskirts. All this information mixed up with the usual tales of misbehaviour by both public authorities and individuals.

'... consequence of this bloody ribbon development. Houses stuck everywhere alongside vacant blocks, and no water laid on.'

'Well, there *is* a war on, Joe. Man-power —'

'Don't give us that. It never was any different.'

'... should have seen the tanker that big chemical company sent out to Noble Park. A beauty. Four-wheel drive —'

'We know all about that, mate. But it did no good. The bloody crew wouldn't take it in off the bitumen.'

'What — scared?'

'I wouldn't exactly say that. They just reckoned that if they got trapped and had to abandon the unit they'd lose their jobs. Some of our blokes offered to take it in, but it was still no dice.'

'... looting going on. Caught one smart bastard getting away from an abandoned house with his car boot guts-full of electrics: vacuum cleaner, radio, toaster, clock, cake-mixer — you name it. Tried to make out he was the owner, but some bloke knew better, and laid him out cold.'

On the sea front only explosions are lacking to make the scene one of war. More trucks with soldiers are moving in from the south. Against us goes the retreat. Every kind of vehicle from heavy industrial trucks to luxury cars, loaded with personal possessions or filled with people. All along the road volunteers are helping residents to get out what they can, just in case. Tables, chairs, beds, bric-a-brac make of front lawns and pavements a long, tumbled furniture mart. They work speedily, but without panic, and without much talk. Indignation over the neglect of public services will come later. In the light of so much experience, adequate safeguards should long ago have been provided against a calamity like this. With water laid on, I would, like so many others, be assured of saving my home, but even the mains are outdated. The building line all around Melbourne always has been miles ahead of water.

Over the din of wind and traffic the voice of authority goes up as a police car equipped with amplifier cruises slowly by: 'All vehicles not actually engaged in fire-fighting must move south immediately. All vehicles not actually engaged ...'

People pause momentarily to stare, some resentfully, some apprehensively. A taxi going in the wrong direction is turned back.

My mates keep shooting questions at me, but only part of me is here. Try as I will I can't get rid of a feeling of guilt. I've left something behind, and I know that now or later I must go back for it. These fellows are aware that I've abandoned my house, but what would be their reaction if they also knew that there is an old woman in it?

In a matter of minutes we reach the scene of action, pile out with beaters in hand, and join a line of men trying to stop flames from getting a hold on the south side of Maroubra Street, another mere dirt track, but less scrubby than mine and a bit wider. The north side, favoured, because of its slight elevation, by a group of the very well-to-do, is being slowly evacuated. Reading back from Beach Road, there's Evans the building contractor, then Jude the barrister, Senator Whitfield, Thoms the wine merchant and retired pastoralist Murchison. The last three houses have already been engulfed; not even their ruins can be seen beyond the raging pyre which was Jude's two-storeyed mansion. Even as we arrive the roof and dividing floor crash in with a prolonged rattle of tiles and furnishings. Hard behind the upflung cloud of glowing debris a cauldron of smokeless flames roars from the jagged shell. Long red tongues flicker from holes that were windows.

All these places have large, mostly 'native' gardens, and through the last of these now skirmishes the advance guard of the fire, rioting up the few eucalypts and in neglected corners, and dying with weary sizzles among the juicy branches of camphors and maples. Sap bubbles on the limbs of Whitfield's magnolias.

All this I take in with occasional glances over my shoulder as I beat with the others wherever the dry verges of the south side catch alight from flying embers. I'm also watching the far end of the street, where, with men falling back from an advancing wall of smoke, the battle seems to have been lost.

But through it all there runs a vision of my own little house, Jean's house — and Mother Lil. Flames haven't reached there yet if I am to believe a man who has just joined us, but it will be a fearful place now with Mother Lil prowling from back to front, trying to measure the approach of fire from one direction and hoping for a sight of me coming from the other. It would be interesting to observe how she behaves without an audience. I can imagine all her senile fidgets, follow much of the meanderings of her wayward mind. Fevered with indecision, she'll wander from room to room, aimlessly moving small articles of furniture, opening and closing doors, messing about with blinds and light switches. Now and then she'll be still for a moment, listening, fingers to lips, eyes cunningly cocked to one side, wondering if the game is worth playing any longer. Most of her mental resources will be concentrated, not on how close is the fire, but on whether I was in earnest when I said I would not return. Nevertheless the fire will increasingly impose itself on her. She'll be plagued by loneliness. There'll be no sound within the house except the imperative banging of branches on the outer walls, and she'll be well aware that no one will hear her even if she screams her head off. If I believed she'd stay there, in real danger of being burned to death, I'd go back immediately. But I've seen so much of these odd people who, in a last effort to get their own way, threaten to kill themselves. If I were to go back for Mother Lil now she'd have the whip hand of me till the day she died. I want her to stay until she gets the fright of her wicked life, and then to run — to run with the flames scorching her very backside. Yet if she doesn't run ...

My bleak reflections are interrupted by a sharp curse from the man on my left, and I stop beating for a moment to rub out a smouldering spot in his singlet where a spark has fallen. It's happening all the time. We can feel on our backs the heat of the burning gardens across the street, and hear the pumping of the fire-engine on the corner. They're trying to save Evans's house, but there's only one line of hose in operation, and the pressure wouldn't be enough to smash in the windows if the place once caught alight. Some men are already dragging what look like antique pieces of furniture out to the close-shaved lawn. Others, one armed with a blow-torch and two with knapsack sprayers, are hurriedly burning a break along the withered grass of the frontage. We'll save the smaller houses on our side if only the fire can be held at the vacant blocks further in.

A man on a motor-cycle comes up and tells us that the fire has got through to Beach Road behind us, but only on a short front and is being held. I ask him what's the position at Mervin Road, which is sealed, and on this side of my street. He replies that they've stopped it there, and are patrolling. 'I wouldn't bet on it, though,' he adds. 'As a matter of fact I wouldn't give a cracker for anything between here and Charman Road.'

Conscience-stricken, I go down to the corner and look back to a point only a few hundred yards away where thin smoke is still going up from a burned-out section of the cliffs. I recall that a feature of the fire that day was the way it ran out here and there in similar long salients. Working on bushfires, I've often seen men behind the main conflagration securing houses and fencing which had just been scorched by the racing flames.

The breaching of the road behind us worries no one but me, because there's no tall timber along there to fall and block us in. I have Mother Lil to think of. It appears now that only the Bay, within the horns of an immense crescent, does not burn. Just for a second the wind eases, and the vacuum created by the terrific heat sucks the smoke upwards. To the north the white road is almost deserted, with only here and there a parked truck or car, and the brighter colours of a lonely fire-engine in the distance. Our own unit at the corner throbs on, with a solitary helmeted man standing by. His immobility is in startling contrast to the frantic animation of his immediate neighbourhood.

I should be beating, like the others, but it's too long since I ate, and an onset of giddiness keeps me from going back into the line. I stand uselessly watching the man in charge of the equipment. He looks exhausted. No doubt that's why he's been given this duty. In a smoke-blackened face his white eyes show up like the eyes of a negro. An agitated woman approaches him.

'Fireman, can't you do something for those?' She's pointing at the few small houses we're trying to protect on the south side. 'They'll all go.'

He regards her wearily. 'Lady, we're doing all we can.'

'But you're wasting your time here. These places are on fire now.'

'Go in and tell the officer in charge. I'm only working here.'

Walking over to the hydrant, he stares absently down at the leaking coupling. She follows after him, agonizingly wringing her hands. I find myself hating some other people besides Mother Lil. No doubt when all this is over they'll call it an act of God. How useful God can be to incompetent and indifferent municipal councillors and parliamentarians! There never was any other answer to the threat of bushfires and floods except the proper allocation and application of public funds. Up-country volunteer firemen have to run dances and raffles to get money for maintenance of equipment.

'But please, mister — they're only little places. The fire's coming up at the back. It would only take a few squirts —'

'Missus, I've got a job to do —'

Another fireman suddenly shows up at Evans's fence. 'Can't you get any more out of that pump, Bill?'

Bill curses softly. 'I told you before it's flat out. It's the mains, Sam. Nothing's been done to them since they hung Ned Kelly.'

Sam turns away and the woman begins pleading again. But Bill pushes her aside as a red roadster pulls up with screaming brakes. A man in a peaked cap puts his head out. 'What station is this?'

'Hampton, sir.'

'Where's Sam Mills?'

'In on the branch.'

'Tell him to let this one go if it catches. Hold it on the front-age and get on to that other side.' The officer is looking up the street to where the last of a few small houses is just visible in the growing smoke haze.

'We're a bit light on —' begins Bill.

'I know. I'm pulling South Yarra back. They'll drop another line off for you. Tell them I said to leave one of their men as well.'

The woman steps forward to the car, but it moves off before she can get a word out.

'Didn't you hear what he said?' demands Bill.

'Not really.'

'We're coming over to your side. Now run along like a good girl and milk the ducks.'

She smiles faintly at the sally, gasps out her relief, and hurries away as if to reassure someone she's left in her home. The fireman looks after her with some sympathy, then scowls to where some men can be seen running back through Evans's garden. I feel flattered when he turns to tell me what's eating him:

'Half those blokes are from a factory. They were rushed down here in a chartered bus to protect one of the joints in the middle. They've been dousing a back garden — a bucket brigade working out of an underground tank. We might have saved all these properties if their bloody boss had put them straight into the firing-line. Serve the bastard right —'

He breaks off to meet the South Yarra unit as it pulls up. Within seconds a wet and roughly flaked section of hose thumps to the ground and the unit speeds on, leaving one of its men standing by the extra line. The new arrival exchanges sardonic greetings with Bill: 'Getting any?'

'Laying the bloody dust, that's about all. No pressure. How's it going back there?'

'Hard to tell. Not too bad in the sealed streets, but we can't go in on these dirt tracks; we'd never get out again. Anyway, there's no head of water even on the mains.'

'Seen anything of the crowd from the Hill?'

'Most of them are out the other side of the city. Old Mick Doyle's with us. He's spitting chips because we're not using sea water. He's right, too. The suction pumps would lift it.'

I glance at the Bay. All that water ...

And now, out of the north, comes the rearguard of the

retreat. An ambulance, two more fire units, trucks filled with exhausted men. Bloodshot eyes look down at us with dreamy detachment as they pass. Less than a hundred yards away it is as if something solid hits the inner side of a cypress hedge. Hits it with terrific force, presses it outwards, leaps upwards, and flickers crazily over the tea-trees on the cliffs. For a split second the whole hedge seems to writhe and contract, then it flares like a torch. Men in a truck crouch low as they pass under an arch of flames that drops right down to the beach. Withered grass at the foot of fences turns to ashes as fast as the eye can follow. Bill, calmly watchful, takes a few paces along the pavement, then comes back. A volunteer close by waits expectantly, but Bill doesn't commit himself until the fence two properties beyond Evans's begins to burn.

'Hop in and tell Sam,' he says quietly.

The time has come for me to go back for Mother Lil, but physical discomfort and the drama of wind, fire, and human endeavour combine to hold me fascinated. A prolonged clatter behind the flurry of smoke tells of the collapse of Jude's house. Almost simultaneously the roof of Evans's spits flame. Groups of men have been congregating on the front of the latter, watching as they would a time-bomb. Coming and going just there has almost ceased. There's an air of tension.

In contrast, and out of a rolling curtain of smoke, men are running towards me down Maroubra Street, with flashes of flame showing up on both sides. A half-grown eucalypt in Evans's garden goes up like a sheet of celluloid, white and fierce and smokeless. In a matter of seconds only bits of dead bark glow and sputter in the forks of its gaunt branches. English trees expire sadly, shrivel and whine, without pyrotechnics. Action returns, there's the glint of a helmet, a bellowed order that sends Bill jumping to his hydrant, a great calling out of other voices, a line of volunteers struggling with a fat hose until it collapses as the water is turned off. On the main road, not twenty yards away, a telegraph post burns at the top like a huge candle. Two legs of the fire have collided there with an explosive puff. An enormous vacuum throwing up a column of red ashes fifty feet high.

The extra man from South Yarra already has his extension laid out towards the small houses, but I'm finding it increasingly difficult to follow all that's going on. I feel helpless, superfluous. What, anyway, can beaters do against this? I'm lost amid a confusion of running men and manoeuvring trucks.

'There she goes!' someone shouts, and through streaming eyes I make out the imposing grey facade of Evans's brick home lit up in the glare of a blazing summer-house. A deep loggia, draped with roses and flanked by pillar cypresses, suddenly vomits fire. Windows crack like pistol shots. The tumbled litter of fine furniture on the lawn begins to burn, apparently without flames actually reaching it. Black smoke swirls down on me in an accelerated rush of wind, making me blink and gasp. In the half-light the shouts of men take on a more urgent note. One voice dominates:

'Come on there, get that bloody truck moving!'

I catch a mention of Mervin Road, and a reply: 'Not yet. We're ordered in there. They're in a bit of strife holding it at the far end.'

Mervin Road, the last line of my own defences. I try to open my eyes, but they also are on fire. The hard rail of a fence at my back steadies me, but at any moment it also might begin to burn. There's the sound of a big engine being revved close by, the clash of a closing door, several voices including one I recognize.

'Hold on, Nugget! That bloke looks crook.'

'I've seen him around. He's a local.'

'It's Jimmy Thurgood. Hey, Jim! Ain't you coming?'

I move forward, and again make contact with friendly hands. 'Up you get, Jim. Your swag's right, Nugget's got it in the cabin.' George Cutler. We go fishing together. He keeps asking me how I feel.

'Lousy,' I reply. 'I've got to get back home.'

'Jeez! You better be careful. Didn't you say the wife's up at Woodend?'

'Yes, but —'

'You'd do better with us, mate. Your joint'll be all right if we can cut it off top of Mervin.'

I'm not thinking clearly, and once again I miss an opportunity to get help. 'I know, but there's a few more things I must get out, just in case. There's the dog —'

'The dog'll look after itself.' George's eyes are full of amusement. Sight has returned, and I find that we've run out of the thick of the smoke. 'Got a wad socked away?'

'Fair dinkum —'

'All right. But for chrissake be careful.'

The heavy vehicle goes fast, lurching dangerously on the curves, but we reach Mervin Road without accident. As we slow down to take the turn I drop off and begin to run.

Right to the last I'd clung to a hope that I'd find she'd gone, but she was still there. I came on her in the lounge, sitting bolt upright as in a trance, her hands gripping the sides of an armchair so tightly that they were bloodless. Her eyes were wide open and fixed with hypnotic intensity on the opposite wall. Loose hair straggled down each side of her wooden face. When I ran over to her and shook her she gave no sign of being aware even that I'd entered the room.

'Lil!' I shouted right into her face.

Her eyes shone right through me. I tried to prise her fingers loose, but they were like hooks of steel. I took her face between my hands, drew down her eyelids with my thumbs, went the length of rubbing my nose against hers. Everything was forgotten except the desperate need for speed.

'Lil! Mother! Look at me! We'll be burned to death!'

She did, with an expression of reproach that momentarily won me. I took heart that at the very last she'd turned out to be just a pitiful and distracted old woman.

'You left me, Jim,' she moaned, as two big tears welled up and rolled down her cheeks. I felt her relax, and seized the opportunity to disengage her hands.

'I know I did, you silly old fool. But you left me no alternative. I begged you to come. Now — stand up —'

'You left me!' she wailed monotonously. More tears came. She began to rock herself from side to side.

'All right, but I came back to get you. We haven't a second to lose —'

'You left me to die!'

I slapped her. I had to. Whether or not she was still putting on an act was beside the point. I'd left the front door open when I came in and the air was getting thicker every minute. Against the howl of the wind I could clearly distinguish the approach of the fire itself. A continuous whirring crackle, like a hailstorm coming over a forest.

'Enough of that!' I shouted. 'I've had a bellyful of your theatrics. Get up, before I knock you cold and carry you out.'

Her eyes widened. All the old cunning flowed back into her upturned face. She really was mad, mad with hatred and self-pity. Mad to a point where nothing else mattered as long as she opposed me.

'What did you come back for?' she demanded.

'I came back to get you out —'

'Liar! You wouldn't have come back if there'd been any danger.'

'Have a look for yourself. Have a look out the back. There's flames —'

'I'll look at nothing. And I'll live, if it's only to tell all the world what you did.'

'You won't live. The fire's taking everything. There's only the two of us left in here —'

'Let it take me, then. Let it take me. That's what you want, isn't it?' She was staring at me with bright-eyed malice. 'Isn't it, Jim Thurgood?'

'You lousy old hussy!' I yelled, and went for her.

The idea occurred to me of hitting her on the head and carrying her out, but it was manifestly too risky a procedure with a woman of her age. I began by concentrating on her arms, trying to get her out of the chair, with a hope of being able to frog-march her down the track. There was some restraint at first, because all a man's instincts rebel at the mere thought of a rough and tumble with an old woman. But that soon passed. She fought with such fury that it was easy to let myself go. She'd anchored herself firmly to the chair, and in the first surge of real anger I pushed it over, grasped it by two of the castors, and dragged it across the floor. I even turned it on its side, but she still hung on. So I fell on my knees and, with one hand on an arm of the chair and the other on the back of her neck, pulled and pushed with all my might. She let go then with a scream of rage just as the dog rushed in and tore in yelping circles around the two of us.

Getting my arms around her waist I tried to lift her off the floor. But she wriggled and spat and scratched like an infuriated cat, fought herself clear, rolled over, and sprang to her feet. We stood facing each other, and in the momentary pause there came a series of short swishing sounds from outside. Everybody familiar with bushfires knows it; the sound of the first flames licking up the lightest and driest growth ahead of the main conflagration. Running through to the kitchen I flung open the back door just as the outriders of the fire swept to the fence. Tea-trees on the other side went up in a hissing sheet of flames, then the fence caught.

I went back to the lounge, and in my desperation actually fell on my knees to her. She was leaning on the table, with head thrust towards me, with drooling lips, with a face contorted in a strange, sick, idiotic smile.

'Lil! Mother! For the last time! Think of Jean — we'll never get out —'

'Burn then! Burn, you murderer! D'you hear me? Murderer!'

A sudden increase of the clamour at the back arrested me in the act of springing at her again. A mounting crackle of dry wood. From where I stood I had only to turn my head to see through the kitchen to the back verandah. Waves of brown smoke were rolling into the house, while tongues of flame from the burning wash-house flickered across to the very eaves.

In one continuous movement I swung around and banged close the door of the lounge-room with my foot.

'Lil!'

But all I saw was an ape-like figure scuttling into the front bedroom. That door also closed, and seconds later I was fleeing down the track with her crazed laughter ringing in my ears. Wind and smoke and flames and searing heat, and showers of sparks that pricked me on like needles. And one long piercing scream as the north wind seized on Mother Lil.

· The Sleeping Doll ·

Someone — I think it was a Frenchman called Parny — has written that 'the wisest of virtues is a calm indifference'. It's a deplorable philosophy, but I once met a man who, probably quite unwittingly, had embraced it and found it the royal road to bliss.

He was a swagman, Bill Boyd by name, and he came to rest on Nullawidgee Station for three weeks in the winter of 1925. I was gardener there, and had a hut a bit removed from the others, and with the only unoccupied bunk on the place. Boyd, taken on temporarily for the lamb-marking, was told to come up and camp with me.

He was the dreariest, weariest thing I'd ever clapped eyes on. Middle-aged, short and tubby, and with the smooth and placid face of a Chinaman. Slightly narrowed eyes, too, but that only came from long habit. His eyelids drooped, like all the rest of him, out of sheer weariness — indifference.

My hut was in a corner of the paddock where the night-horse was kept. I heard someone come in by the gate and stand behind me as I was having a wash one cold evening.

'How are you?' I said when I turned round and got the soap out of my eyes.

His head moved ever so slightly. He was too weary to speak, too weary even to nod. I knew right away what he was and why he was there, but it struck me as amazing that such a man had ever got onto the Nullawidgee pay-roll. Jaensch paid award rates and gave reasonably good conditions, but was an employer who liked every ounce of his pound of flesh and a bit more. And this Boyd had don't-give-a-damn written all over him. Apart from his general air of chronic drowsiness, he was wearing a suit and shoes. And that's a bad sign in a man looking for work in the bush. A brown suit and tan shoes, not at all in bad shape either. Swagmen were plentiful enough in the Riverina those days, but I'd never encountered anything quite like this one. Most of them looked as if they had worked at one time, and might — given sufficient reward — even be persuaded to work again. Boyd looked as if he'd never raised a sweat or a blister since the day he was born.

'Making a start?' I inquired conversationally.

He grunted, a tiny mutter that didn't even part his lips. Without moving his head, he swivelled his eyes so that he could see into the hut.

'There's a bunk in there,' I said. 'Did they send you up?'

'H'm.' His glance moved again, over the screen of hessian I'd rigged to shelter the doorway, over the upturned box with the washing basin on it, over the tin roof of the cookhouse rising beyond the saltbush hedge. Distance seemed to have a soporific effect on him. His eyelids drooped lower still, he swayed slightly. I thought he was going to pitch forward on his face.

'Have a wash if you want to,' I said cheerfully. 'There's fresh water in the tin there. The bell will go for supper in a minute.'

This time he did indeed close his eyes, though only for a moment, as if to add effect to a woeful nod that indicated nothing but blank resignation. The kind of nod a man in the dock might give on receiving a long gaol sentence. This idea was emphasized as his broad back vanished into the darkening hut. I knew then quite positively a few things I'd sensed the instant I set eyes on him — that he wasn't long for Nullawidgee, that he didn't care a hoot whether I liked him or not, and that he would be a bad man to cross.

That first night I made a determined effort to engage him in conversation as we were turning in. I had the measure of him by then, but I wanted to put my conscience finally at rest for whatever period he chose to stay on the place. All efforts by the men to draw him out had failed. He'd sat all the evening dozing over the end of the long table without ever once volunteering a remark. As his hut-mate I felt it was up to me to make some special gesture.

He must have been waiting for me to make a move, for he followed me in just as I lit the lamp.

The Sleeping Doll

'It's nippy when you get away from that fire,' I said.

'Um.' His mutter wasn't a bit surly; it was just laconic, lazy, indifferent.

Hands hanging loosely at his sides, he was contemplating with very little interest the spare bunk, a hardwood frame with four wheat-bags nailed across it.

'How many blankets have you got?' I asked.

'Three.'

'There's an old overcoat behind the door if you want it.'

'Good.'

He didn't move. He was still looking at the bunk, but he wasn't thinking of it. He hadn't got around to that yet; his brain was just beginning to function.

'You'll be going out with the lamb-marking crowd in the morning?' I suggested.

'I suppose so.'

There I rested for the time being, watching him slyly as he turned in. His technique was interesting. First he spread one blanket over the stretcher, then he took off his jacket and folded it neatly for use as a pillow. Then the other two blankets, followed by my overcoat from behind the door. Next he took off shoes, trousers and socks. I thought for a moment he was going to keep his jersey on, but to my amusement he pulled it off, seated himself on the edge of the bunk, pushed his feet into the heavy wool as into a bag and knotted the sleeves loosely round his ankles. Finally, and without having removed shirt or underpants, he shuffled down between the blankets and instantly closed his eyes.

I finished undressing, and had my pipe going and my book opened before I spoke again.

'You don't mind the light, do you?'

I thought he was foxing when he didn't answer, but a moment's consideration of his tranquil face satisfied me that he was indeed sleeping. He was turned slightly towards me, with his lips slightly parted and his breath coming and going in that regular procession of luxurious sighs that no acting can ever quite simulate.

'Bill,' I said softly.

His eyelids didn't even flicker. He was sleeping as soundly as a baby.

In all the time he was with me I don't remember him once asking a question or offering comment or opinion. As often as not he didn't give an audible reply even when spoken to, just a lazy glance or an even lazier nod. He was the same with everybody. Other men would have been twitted or cold-shouldered, but there was something about this one that completely baffled us. You don't take liberties with an unknown quantity, and Boyd was right outside the experience of any of us.

He didn't live life; he tolerated it. Just kept as still as he could and let it carry him along like a piece of driftwood on a river. Nothing ever ruffled him. Nothing ever kindled a flicker of enthusiasm in his cold frog's eyes. Not even food. He ate plenty, as much as most of us, but with no more evident enjoyment than a cow chewing the cud. There was always a clatter of conversation around the dining table, but he took no part in it, didn't even listen. Now and then, when some voice was raised with more than usual heat, his head would come slowly up and he would look at the speaker with mild reproach. Nothing more. Silent himself, you got the impression that he was secretly irritated by any noise out of the ordinary. If he wanted something passed to him he would just name it in a sort of confidential whisper to the man next to him. No 'please' or 'will you'. Just 'jam' or 'sauce' or 'salt', whatever it might be. It was impossible to take offence at him, though, for everything else was implied by his tone. He could say 'salt' with a humility that was almost embarrassing, and there was more real courtesy in the slight nod with which he received it than any dozen words could have contained. He moved amongst us as persistent and as unobtrusive as a shadow. His very restraint kept us acutely aware of him. After a day or two all advances ceased. Nobody spoke to him, but subtle little changes became noticeable in the general behaviour at the big hut. It was like living with an invalid, with an imbecile, with a nagging wife. We began to walk warily, to keep our voices down, to stop joshing each other. Exuberance isn't becoming in the presence of a ghost and we had a ghost with us. Boyd was no lightweight, but he could put his feet down with little more noise than a cat. He had a curious stealthy waddle, reaching forward and getting the feel of the ground at each step before transferring his weight from one foot to the other. Somebody remarked that he walked as if he had a bellyful of cracked eggs. All his movements were the same, careful, smooth, unhurried. To see him stoop to pick something up was a study in economy of effort. He was always last coming down to breakfast of a morning, always last to saunter up to the stockyards for orders, always last in the cookhouse queue at night. In this age of intensive competition, humanity has developed an instinctive dread of being last in anything, an abiding fear that in all good things there may not be quite enough to go around. Boyd took the whole world for granted, confident that, in the final analysis, everything waits for the laggard. He economized in thinking by reducing everything to a routine. Dressing of a morning and undressing at night were performed each day with the same undeviating and trance-like exactitude. I just couldn't imagine him ever stumbling, ever scratching himself, ever upsetting anything. For a man who liked reading at night he was an ideal hut-mate. Sleep came to him the instant he laid down his head, and nothing short of a kick on a kerosene-tin would bring him to life afterwards. The fellows told me he slept at every odd opportunity during the day. He slept on the floor of the wagonette going out to the job of a morning, he slept his lunch-hour away after eating, and he slept all the way home at night. He dozed even during the short spells for morning and afternoon smoke-oh. It was a gift. He could sleep lying on a log, he could sleep sitting on a box, he could sleep standing against a fence-post. They told me he staggered one day while holding a lamb on the board.

At any time other than lamb-marking he wouldn't have lasted one week on Nullawidgee, much less likely three. The fellows were full of stories about him when they came in of a night. They said he was driving Jaensch mad. Efficiency was a fetish with Jaensch; at busy times he used to make the pace himself. He and Collins, the overseer, did all the knife-work — castrating, ear-marking and tailing. They could keep four catchers going. Jaensch liked to see men running; it was part of his conception of efficiency. Collins and he used to dash up and down along the board slashing and snipping and biting as if they were on piece-work. He used to fly into a temper if the board emptied for an instant. 'Come on there!' he'd yell.

'Keep 'em up!' In its own way lamb-marking on Nullawidgee had all the vicious elements of the line in a modern car factory. Each man a cog in a smooth and fast-running machine. Almost as noisy, too, with its bedlam of whistles and barking dogs, and yells of 'Ram!' 'Ewe!' against a ceaseless chorus of scampering, bleating sheep.

But Boyd was one who just wouldn't be stampeded. Against the imperturbable calm of the Sleeping Doll, as the men secretly called him, all the frantic urgings of Jaensch beat in vain. Boyd would neither run nor shout. He must have cut a funny figure. He'd slit three holes in a chaff-bag for head and arms and used it as a smock to catch the blood splashes. They told me he used to waddle out into the middle of the milling sheep, crouch, and wait like a slips fieldsman until a lamb passed within reach. If he missed it he just recovered himself and waited stolidly until another one came along. One of the boundary-riders told me he was a lazy bastard on the job, but I'd have hated to hear anything else about Boyd. It would have been a blemish on a masterpiece. The very thought of him moving out of that magnificent indifference in order to chase a frisking lamb was absurd.

Nor would he shout. Jaensch liked to have the next victim all nicely teed up; he used to keep squinting sideways even while he was operating, his ears pricked for the shouted announcement of sex.

But Boyd would say 'Ram' in exactly the same voice as he said 'Salt' at the dining table.

'What is it?' Jaensch would yell as he came abreast.

'Ram.'

'Then for Christ's sake say so — scream it! It saves my time —'

Boyd might have been deaf for all the notice he took. The fellows were always expecting an explosion. The possibility that he was afraid of Jaensch didn't even occur to them; he was too superbly indifferent. Nothing happened — for three weeks.

Came the last morning.

I knew right away it was the last morning, for long experience of swagmen had made me familiar with all the signs. I wakened Boyd when the first cow-bell rang, but he didn't get up. When I came inside again after washing he was still in his bunk, but fully awake. In the light of the hurricane lamp he lay flat on his back, head resting on clasped hands, his slanted eyes as wide open as they were ever likely to be. It was a bleak morning, and until he spoke I thought he was just struggling with a natural reluctance to turn out.

'What time does the mail-car go through Wanganella?' he asked suddenly.

I positively jumped. It was like hearing a sheep burst into articulate speech — the longest speech I'd ever heard him utter.

'About six o'clock,' I replied. 'Why?'

He didn't answer, except to give that odd little movement of his head which excused him so much. A movement which said as plainly as any words: Don't mind me, old chap. I know I'm a nark, but I can't help it.

I left him lying there, and went down and told the men that Boyd was going to blow the job. I think they all felt as I did; that it was going to be interesting seeing how he did it.

At ten to eight he waddled up to the stockyards, twenty minutes late, and ten minutes after Jaensch had finished giving orders. Everything saddled and harnessed and packed ready to go, with Jaensch puffing furiously at his pipe and casting angry glances along the path leading from the men's quarters. He wasn't going out himself that day, but was too mistrustful and exacting to leave the giving of orders to Collins. The latter also was well worked up, but Jaensch got in first.

'And where the hell d'you think you're going?' he burst out as Boyd strolled up with hunched shoulders and hands in pockets just as he did every day.

Boyd was going to walk straight over to the waiting wagonette. Anyway, he appeared as if he was. Nothing could have been more insolent than the low-lidded stare he gave Jaensch as he came to a halt.

'Eh?'

'I said where the hell d'you think you're going?'

Boyd glanced at the wagonette, then back again at Jaensch. You'd think he'd been asked the silliest question conceivable. 'I dunno. You're boss, ain't you?'

Jaensch dragged out his watch. 'D'you know what time it is?'

'Nearly eight o'clock when I left up at the huts.'

It was exciting just hearing the fellow talk so much. All eyes were on him; we knew something good was coming.

'You're supposed to be here at half-past seven.' Jaensch's thumb stabbed savagely towards the ground. 'Here — in the yards — not stuffing your guts up at the cookhouse!'

Boyd's eyes opened a trifle wider. 'You want me to go out on an empty belly?'

'I want you to turn out with the rest of the men. They've been waiting half an hour. They've got —'

'All right — give us me cheque and I'll beat it.' Still the same unruffled voice. Boyd's hands were still in his pockets. I'd heard Jaensch done over by the tongue of more than one departing swagman, but nothing was ever half as offensive as the Doll's sleepy whisper.

'Give you your cheque? Yes, by God, I'll do that too! I'll give you your cheque!' Jaensch began to stamp and bluster. 'And bloody good riddance!' His darting eyes fell on the crowd in the wagonette and he flung up his arms as at a mob of geese. 'On your way, you fellows! You'll do better without him.'

Collins swung into the saddle to take charge, and Jaensch stamped off towards the gate. 'Come up to the office, you. I'll fix that right away.'

He looked as if he couldn't get the paying off done quickly enough, yet he'd only gone a few paces when he stopped and scratched the back of his head in sudden indecision. I saw him cast a thoughtful glance along the cow-yard fence.

'When did you start here?' he demanded, rounding on Boyd. 'Three weeks tomorrow, isn't it?'

'Three weeks tomorrow's right.'

'Supposing you put the day in and make it a straight three weeks' pay? There's a bit of dummying to do about the yards.'

To this day I can't understand why Jaensch did it. Perhaps it was just a perverse impulse. Boyd was obviously not a bit put out, and Jaensch might just have been looking for a way to provoke him. Perhaps Jaensch didn't want to be bothered working out the pay to an odd day. The cow-yard fence certainly did want some attention, but he must have known perfectly well that Boyd and a crowbar and shovel just didn't make sense. Anyway, whatever his reason he made the offer, and, to my surprise, Boyd instantly agreed.

'I'm easy.'

Jaensch was still thoroughly angry, but I don't doubt he felt the same about Boyd as the men did — that there were depths in the fellow it were best not to plumb.

'All right,' he said with tight lips. 'Go and tell the groom; he knows what's wanted and where the gear is. I'll see you at five o'clock.'

House and garden stood on a slight rise and I was able to observe Boyd all day as he messed about with those dummy posts. He put in three. It was the first time I'd seen him in action, and he certainly was good. No wonder the fellows said he was driving Jaensch mad out at the lamb-marking.

A cold wind was blowing across the plain, and he'd put on his chaff-bag blood-catcher, with a wheat-bag worn as a cape on top of it for good measure. In addition he had strips of bagging wound round the bottoms of his trouser legs, making him look for all the world like a big slovenly brown bear fossicking for nuts. All his mental resources seemed to be concentrated on the problem of keeping his back to the wind. Shovelling obviously distressed him, but the crowbar lent itself in some small degree to his talent for sleeping on his feet. During the process of ramming it was possible to see unconsciousness stealing over him. He'd begin with two or three regular blows, lifting from the elbows and springing slightly from the knees, almost like a human being. Then he'd start to slow down, his knees would bend less and less, his head sag lower, his whole body sway. At that distance he looked far more as if he were operating a vertical pump-handle than a crowbar. Recovery would be delayed a little longer each time, until he finally stopped altogether, like a genteel drunk drooping over an outsize in stalking sticks. He could stay like that for several minutes before coming to life again. He must have suffered the torments of the damned, struggling out there hour after hour trying to keep awake, to keep his hands clean, to keep his back straight, to keep the wind out of his face. In excavating he used to get down on his knees, using more bags as a pad, and holding the shovel short like a big trowel. More than once I saw him pitch forward and steady himself on the edge of the hole as sleep overwhelmed him in the act of bringing up a spoonful of earth.

At lunch-time he fell sound asleep at the table, head resting on folded arms. Jim Tucker, the houseboy, and Neil Batey, the groom, the only men present besides myself, got into a noisy argument over prospects for the Grand National, but Boyd never batted an eyelash. He'd have stayed there all the afternoon if I hadn't awakened him.

'One o'clock, son,' I said as he blinked up at me.

You'd have thought I was a gaoler calling him to execution. He gave a despondent sigh and immediately began to wilt again.

I left him there; it was certainly no business of mine to see he went to work. As a mate I was obliged to see he was informed of the time, that was all. He did turn out, though, for only a few minutes after I got back to the garden I saw him waddle across to the yards. And there he remained — till just after three o'clock.

About that time Jaensch got a telephone message from Pop Rowntree, the boundary-rider out on the back-station, to the effect that the creek had come down overnight and was threatening to cut off some sheep in Two-mile Paddock.

Young Tucker told me about it as he hurried through the garden to get old Bondi, the night-horse. Apart from Jaensch's grey hack nothing else was available. Tucker had been told to saddle the grey, put Bondi into a jinker, and tell me to be ready to go along.

'He's taking me, too,' said Tucker, pleased at being in on a man's job. 'You and me and —' he grinned mischievously '— the Doll!'

'What about Neil?' I asked.

'Neil's got to kill. He's up at the shop now sharpening his knives.'

It took me a few minutes to go up to the hut and put on a coat. When I reached the yards Jaensch was leading out the grey and Tucker was in the act of climbing into the jinker. Boyd, working at the far end of the yards, knew nothing of what was on until we pulled up alongside him.

'All right,' sang out Jaensch, 'you can leave that now. We've got a job to do out on the run. Hop up in the jinker.' I saw his eyes travel disgustedly along the fence-line, taking stock of what had been accomplished.

With all his paraphernalia of bags, the Doll looked funnier than ever seen at close quarters. He was on his knees at the moment, shovelling, and instead of standing up he calmly rolled sideways and sat squarely on his backside, squinting up at us like a man just coming out of a deep darkness.

'Eh?'

'For Christ's sake stand up!' exclaimed Jaensch. 'I want some men in a hurry. There's a job —'

'You're stiff,' cut in Boyd, 'my time's up at five.' His sleepy mutter barely reached us, but there was no mistaking his humour. He actually made himself more comfortable by dropping one leg into the post-hole and resting his shoulders against the bottom rail.

'We'll be back at five,' snapped Jaensch. 'There's only half an hour's work once we get out —'

'Once you get out! But I ain't going out. I'm finishing at five — here.' Boyd wasn't even troubling to look upwards now. He appeared to be lost in contemplation of the grey's forefeet, impatiently stamping the ground only three feet away.

I thought Jaensch was going to have a fit. He shot an angry glance at Tucker and me sitting poker-faced in the jinker. It was a humiliating experience for a man who prided himself on his authority. Goodness knows what kind of a fool he would have made of himself if Neil Batey hadn't come in sight walking across to the killing pen. Batey, with a couple of bags thrown across one shoulder, his hands full of knives and wooden gambrels, and Jinny, his dog, slinking at his heels.

'Hi, Neil!'

Neil came over to us.

'Can you kill?' demanded Jaensch of Boyd.

Boyd's head slowly tilted upwards. He took his time about replying; for a moment I thought he was going to say no.

'I don't know about killing,' he drawled at last without a hint of a smile, 'but I reckon I'd give 'em a shock they'd never get over.'

'Can you kill?' spluttered Jaensch.

'Yes, I can kill.'

'All right, grab those knives and get stuck into it.' Jaensch was so worked up that he was unconsciously swinging his legs, keeping his horse turning in circles. 'Give him the gear, Neil, and get into the jinker. Rowntree's in a bit of trouble out at the Two-mile.'

Neil looked mistrustfully at Boyd, and it was interesting to see a new expression flicker for an instant on the Doll's face. An expression full of friendliness and assurance.

'It'll be all right,' he said softly. 'How's the dog?'

'She'll work for anybody.' Neil laid the bags and the knives on the ground. 'The killers are in the paddock behind the pen. You can leave the meat hanging; there's no blowflies about.'

Tucker and I pressed closer together to make way for the groom, while Jaensch dragged up his hack's head as if he were going to lead a cavalry charge. Boyd hadn't moved. Glancing backwards I saw that he wasn't even watching us. He was idly patting the dog which, at a word from Neil, had seated itself disconsolately on the edge of the post-hole.

Suddenly, as if he'd just thought of something urgent, Boyd's head came up. It was the only time I ever heard his voice rise above a murmur.

'How many d'you want killed?'

Neil turned round to reply. 'Two!' I heard him, and so did Tucker. But he had no chance of reaching Boyd, for Jaensch let off a yell that very nearly put the jinker horse into a bolt.

'How many d'you think you can do — you damned sleeping doll! Keep going till five o'clock; I'll be back.'

Some minutes later, a mile or so out on the plain, I had a last look backwards. The homestead had become a higgledy-piggledy agglomeration of saltbush and tin roofs, but it was still possible to make out a brown blob petrified at a spot half-way along the cow-yard fence. I'd have given odds of a hundred to one that Boyd was already fast asleep.

He was on my mind all the way out to the Two-mile — he and the two unfortunate sheep that were in for a shock they would never get over. Neil's dog could be depended on to see that the mob of killers was efficiently penned, and it was horrible trying to imagine what was going to happen afterwards. Images of that masterpiece of indolence sawing wearily at the throat of a kicking sheep gave me the cold shivers. Neil also was troubled, for the only time he spoke during the journey out was to curse Jaensch. He was silent for a long time, sitting with eyes fixed sulkily on the rump of the grey bouncing up and down along the track twenty yards in front of us.

'What the heck did he go and do that for?' he burst out at

length. 'Couldn't he have brought the Doll and left me to do my own work?'

'Boyd jibbed,' I said sympathetically. 'Anyway, from all accounts Jaensch has had a gutsful of him out on the lamb-marking.'

'That's all right for him, but what about them sheep? That dope'll hack 'em to pieces.'

He wasn't the only one who felt that way, but there was just nothing we could do about it.

At the Two-mile we found an exhausted boundary-rider sitting on a stump waiting for us. A few yards away a backwater of the creek had begun to fill up, isolating several hundred valuable sheep on a narrow strip of land running along the fence-line. In addition, and since Rowntree had sent off the telephone message, another problem had developed. Returning from the back-station, to which he had gone to summon help, he had discovered a small breach in a dam further up, a breach that would undoubtedly widen and cause serious trouble unless quickly mended.

Now Jaensch, whatever his faults, was a quick thinker and a capable organizer. A few shrewd questions to the worried Rowntree and he had the situation fully sized up. He took a look at his watch and at the overcast sky, estimating the weather portents and the amount of daylight left. Then he considered for a moment the mob of scared sheep held at the edge of the water by the dogs.

'We'll have to drag some across to get them started.'

'That break in the dam?' prompted the boundary-rider.

'We'll want bags, shovels, wheelbarrows — more men.' Jaensch cast his eyes over us and picked on me. 'You, Tom, get back in the jinker. Run over to the Ridge and tell Mr Collins to pack up and fetch his crowd here as quick as he can lick. Tell him to give you one man, then go on into the homestead and load the truck up — a couple of barrows, shovels, and all the bags you can lay hands on. Tell Sam to pack you some grub; we might be out late. Two or three lamps as well. Off you go.'

I was seated and on the point of starting when he remembered Boyd and pulled out his cheque-book and pen.

'Hold on, Tom.' I waited while he filled in a cheque. 'Here, give that to Rip Van Winkle and tell him to hit the road. And if he hasn't got those two sheep out of their misery, take them off him. Stay behind yourself in any event. Tell Mr Collins to give you a man who can drive the truck.'

All this suited me very well, for everything indicated a miserable time for the crowd at the Two-mile. Neil Batey shot me an envious glance, and young Tucker was manifestly losing some of his enthusiasm as he watched Rowntree taking off leggings and boots and rolling his trousers up above his knees. The creek water looked black and cold, and no doubt he was already chilled from the drive out. In addition the sheep were wet from the showers during the day. With a fading light it was going to be about ten times worse than pushing a mob of woolblinds up the ramp of a shearing shed.

Dusk was falling by the time I got back to the homestead. Collins had given me one of the teamsters for a mate, and, leaving him to take the jinker on and start getting the truck ready, I dropped off at the yards and made my way over to the killing pen.

I'd been thinking of those two wretched sheep all the way in, and my worst fears were aggravated immediately by the sight of a hurricane lamp beaming weakly from one of the low rafters. As I approached I could see Boyd's head and shoulders. He was standing in the middle of the pen, doing something with his hands, which were out of sight. The place stank like an abattoirs — blood and freshly killed flesh. He heard me coming, gave me a sleepy look, then went on again with whatever it was he was doing.

A wave of relief passed over me; I'd been so thoroughly prepared to find the place a bleating bloody shambles. The fellow looked as if he'd just come to life again after one of his involuntary naps. Over the whole vicinity of the pen there was a graveyard stillness that was different, deeper, than when Neil Batey used to finish his operations. There was the curious sense of congestion, too, that struck me even as I opened the wooden gate and stepped in. It was a large pen, and the light was bad, but I knew the place was cluttered up with something even before I had time to observe what it was.

'How did you go?' I began cheerfully.

'Not bad.' The same old whisper. He was wiping a pair of blood-stained knives on a piece of hessian. Handling them

• **The Sleeping Doll** •

with a dexterity I couldn't help noticing, it was in such marked contrast to the deliberation he brought to every other implement.

Then I saw the pile of skins against the far wall, a pile of skins that reached as high as the wire-netting and tumbled almost halfway out across the floor. And the meat — a row of pale carcases hanging from the rafter and stretching from one end of the shed to the other. A mass of dressed mutton that all the hungry mouths of Nullawidgee wouldn't eat their way through in a month. A heap of heads, bloody and glass-eyed, entrails — no wonder I'd had a sense of congestion.

'My God!' I gasped. 'How many did you do?'

'Twenty-two. There wasn't any more left.'

There wasn't any more left — the very line he had prepared for Jaensch. I saw it all in a flash. Hadn't Jaensch told him to keep going till five o'clock?

'They're all right, ain't they?' he whispered.

I didn't need to look any closer; that line of carcases had the mark of a master craftsman all over it. 'All right? There's twenty too many, that's all. Spare me days, you shouldn't have done the bloody lot!'

'He said to keep going till five,' said Boyd softly. He'd finished wiping the knives; his drowsy eyes came up and looked straight into mine. 'You heard him, didn't you?'

Yes, I'd heard him. So had Neil Batey and young Tucker. Admiration welled up in me and I held out the cheque. 'You've got it all sewn up, son. He sent your cheque in, and I'm to tell you to beat it before he gets back!'

He smiled, for the first and only time in three weeks. Any other man, having gone so far, would have had something to say about it. But not Boyd; he was consistent to the last drop. Whatever satisfaction or amusement he may have got out of the business, I wasn't allowed to see it. It came to me that he would have been good to watch in the past two hours. Only a gun butcher could have put up such a performance.

'Where did you do your killing?' I asked curiously.

'City abattoirs.' Pushing the cheque deep into his inside pocket, he moved towards the gate. 'Somebody else'll have to shift this muck,' he murmured with a dismal sideways nod. 'My time's up — five o'clock.'

I watched him in stupefaction as he waddled away to the hut to roll his swag.

Ten minutes later we shook hands as he was passing the garage on his way out. His clasp was unexpectedly hearty. Next to nothing had passed between us, but he knew very well he had my sympathy.

'Straight along the track there,' I said in answer to his question. 'You'll pick up the road down from Booroorban. The mail-car comes through about six. Take my advice: cash that cheque in Wanganella and go right on to Deniliquin.'

His short figure assumed heroic proportions as it melted into the darkness.

· Quiet Night in Station Street ·

Bored with a documentary following her favorite TV series, she'd stopped resisting her drooping eyelids, allowed the knitting to fall into her lap, and drowsed off.

It was just before ten when he burst into the living-room, closely followed by his girlfriend.

'Mum!' His hand on her shoulder was gentle enough, but the urgency in his voice brought her instantly awake. 'Listen...'

'Billy...?'

'You awake? Listen to me...'

'What's the matter?' Her startled eyes flew from him to the girl at his side. 'I was half asleep.'

'I know. Wake up, listen...'

'Something's happened?'

'Yes, but not much. Only you've got to listen. I've been in a prang.'

'Oh, Billy!'

'Don't worry. Nobody's hurt. But the car...'

'It's only the car, Mrs Dobbs,' the girl's voice coming in.

'You keep quiet, Jill. Leave this to me. Mum, we've got to be quick. And don't look so scared. Everything'll be all right if you do as I tell you...'

'What happened?' She was trying to get up, but his hand held her down.

'Sit still. I don't want you to move. Just listen. I had a few...'

'Oh, Billy!'

'Don't say it like that! I wasn't boozed. Ask Jill...'

'It's true, Mrs Dobbs. My dad opened a bottle...'

'I was stone-cold sober, like I am now.' He reached out to turn down the TV. 'Get a small can out of the fridge, Jill. Put

207

it on the table and pour half a glass, and sit over there and keep quiet. Mum, listen. It was the old gang. They picked me up round in the avenue and chickened me. Ran me through a fence into a garden. The car's stuck there. Jill and me shot through, round the first corner. We had to...'

'Oh, Billy!'

'Don't say it like that! I'm practically off it, and you know it. I had a couple, that's all, but if the coppers had got a whiff of it there... we had to run. It wasn't my fault. The gang's hostile on me since I dropped out. Listen, the coppers'll be here any minute, soon as they check the registration. Now then, I've been here with you and Jill for the past two hours. You got that? You've got to swear blind...'

'Billy...' She was trembling, almost weeping.

'I'm going to tell them the car must have been pinched on me. I'll pretend I think it's still out the front. Jill will back me up. You too...'

'Oh, Bill, they'll know. I'd never be able...'

'You've got to. Pretend to yourself, you'll find it easy. You've got to do it. They'd have put the bag on me if they'd found me with the car. I can't swear what I'd register. And, if they made anything stick, the court would pull that bond on me. You've got to do it, Mum. Where's Dad?'

'He's gone to the club meeting. He'll be late home. It's the election of officers.'

'That means he'll be half stewed when he comes in. They always have a grog-up afterwards. The coppers...'

'Perhaps they won't come.'

'They'll come all right, just as soon as they check the registration.'

He cast a glance at the can and glass on the table, and at the seated girl. 'Right, Jill. Pick up your knitting, Mum, and don't worry about looking upset when they walk in. They upset everybody, but they can't do anything if we stick to the story. I don't think anybody saw us; we shot round the first corner. What was the last program on the telly? Good, they won't catch us on that one. Turn it up again, Jill.'

They didn't have long to wait. He nodded to the girl when the bell rang. 'You go, Jill. Try and look surprised. I don't want them to get me on my own to begin with.'

Little was said at the door, and, when Jill re-entered the

room, she was followed by two uniformed men who could very well have gone by the nicknames of Burly and Slim. Their eyes took in everybody and everything in the room before a word was spoken.

Bill and his mother were on their feet.

'What's all this about?' demanded Bill in a tone of concern cautiously flavored with resentment.

'Oh, Billy!' In the few minutes grace Mrs Dobbs had taken hold of herself and gone through a little silent rehearsal. Jill had moved round the policemen and taken up a position alongside Bill.

'Are you William Dobbs?' Slim opened the interrogation.

'Yes, what's all this?'

'You're the owner of a fawn Holden sedan?'

'Yes'

'Can I see your licence?'

Bill produced it from his pocket.

Nobody spoke while Slim checked it, taking plenty of time. Still holding the licence, his eyes switched to the can on the table, then to the TV. 'Can we have that turned down a bit?'

Bill turned it down.

'Are you his mother?' Slim asked Mrs Dobbs.

'Yes, I'm his mother. And you needn't look at that can. He hardly...'

'How long has he been here?'

'I've been here...' began Bill, but the constable cut him short.

'I'm speaking to your mother. How long has he been here, Mrs Dobbs?' The friendly tone was at odds with the expression of cold suspicion.

'He's been here since tea-time. What's the matter?'

'And the girl?'

'Yes, me too. We...' Jill faltered as the inquisitorial eyes turned on her.

'Now don't you go and upset her,' put in Mrs Dobbs. 'She's a bundle of nerves. She's pregnant.'

Slim couldn't have missed the startled glances that both youth and girl shot at the mother. 'Good luck to her! What are you all looking so worried about?' Then, to Bill, 'Where's the car now?'

It was the one Bill had been waiting for, and he was ready.

'It's outside. You must have seen it. What's wrong with it?'

'You sure it's outside?'

'I wouldn't know, would I? That's where ... cripes!'

The reaction of sudden anxiety was well feigned. He headed for the door, with Burly slipping smartly in front of him and preceding him down the passage.

'So, they've been here since tea-time, eh,' Slim was taking another long look at the licence. 'You were running a bit late, weren't you?'

'There's no need to be sarcastic. Why don't you tell us what it's all about? And you sit down, Jill. You shouldn't be standing around like that.' Mrs Dobbs was well in command of herself now.

Jill, still worried over the dubious glance which the policeman had shot at her figure, immediately sat down. He hadn't replied to Mrs Dobbs when Bill returned, with the silent Burly hard on his heels.

'Mum, the car's gone! Somebody's knocked it off.' He also was settling confidently into the act. To Slim, 'Where is it? You got on to it?'

'Yes, we've got it.' Slim was staring at him with frank disbelief.

'Well, where is it? Is it knocked about?'

'Not much.' Slim kept up the stare.

'What do you mean, not much?'

Mrs Dobbs moved in again. 'Why don't you tell him? What happened? Is somebody hurt?'

'Keep your hair on, Mrs Dobbs ...'

'Don't you tell me to keep my hair on! We're entitled to know. You come barging in here ...'

'All right, all right, all right.' Slim held up protesting hands. 'Cool it. No, nobody's hurt.'

'Where's his car, then? Why don't you tell him?'

'I'll tell him when I'm ready. This is a police inquiry.' Slim's eyes moved back to Bill and stayed there as he said, every word a taunt, 'It's in a garden.' He might as well have added, 'and you damn well know it.'

'They crashed it? Whereabouts?'

'Not far.' With dry resignation, 'Come on, let's have a look at it.'

• **Quiet Night in Station Street** •

Bill, who was clearly beginning to get edgy under the persistent stare, jerked himself loose and again made for the passage, with Burly again neatly getting in front.

Jill started to rise, but Slim motioned her back. 'We don't need you.'

Mrs Dobbs put a restraining hand on his arm as he turned away. 'Don't be too hard on him, constable, will you? He's a good boy. I know who did this on him. It'll be the gang he used to run with. He gave them up weeks ago. You won't keep him long, will you?'

'He'll be all right, Mum.' His voice carried little comfort, though, and she remained looking unhappily into the passage until the street door closed and there came the sound of a car starting up.

Then the girl was at her side. 'What'll they do, Mum? Oh . . . Mrs Dobbs, that just slipped out.'

Mrs Dobbs gave her a wry smile. 'Maybe it isn't before time.'

'I didn't think you knew.'

'That you're in the family way? What d'you take me for? I've had five. How far gone are you?'

'Three months. You angry with me?'

'No, I'm not angry with you, love. But we can't talk about that now. You're going home, quick and lively. I want you out of this house before Dad comes in. He'll be half stunned, like he always is after a meeting. Time enough for him in the morning . . .'

'Can't I stay until Bill comes back?'

'How do I know when he'll get back? I'm calling a taxi for you right away.'

Mrs Dobbs left the room, and the girl heard her at the telephone in the passage. She was back in seconds.

'It's on the way. Now you listen to me, my girl. You say nothing about this to anybody unless you get questioned. Least said, soonest mended. If you've got to answer any questions, Bill's car got stolen off the front of the house, and the police came and told us it was stuck in a garden. That's your story, and see you stick to it. Does your Mum know about the other?'

'The other?'

'The other! You know what I'm talking about.'

'No, I haven't dared yet.'

'How much longer ... anyway, hasn't she got eyes? You've got to tell her. But come round here and have a talk with me first. Come straight from work tomorrow before Dad gets in. Just you and me. What d'you want to do about it, anyway?'

'The baby?'

'Yes, the baby! You're not talking of getting rid of it, are you?'

'Not really ...'

'What d'you mean, not really? How about Bill? You going to get married?'

'We want to.' The girl was watching her anxiously. 'He's going to look for a flat out at Oakleigh if he gets that new job.'

'What new job? What's up with him? He tells me nothing.'

A car tooted outside.

'There's the taxi. Come on. I'll have a talk with Dad tomorrow. And Billy. You and him had better get yourselves married. We might fix you up here in Florrie's room till you get settled. She won't be home till Christmas.'

'Oh, Mrs ... Mum!'

Jill was in her arms.

'All right, all right, I've got nothing against you. You've been good for Bill. He's been a different boy since he took up with you. Leave Dad to me. Come on, he'll be here any minute.'

A few spontaneous kisses of gratitude, and the girl was gone. Mrs Dobbs emptied beer can and glass into the sink and picked up her knitting. But she didn't turn up the TV, and the needles didn't begin to click. She just sat there, waiting ... listening ... thinking ...

It was well after eleven when he came in — a stoutish, rather nondescript man wearing a blue suit with collar and tie in the starchy way of a worker more accustomed to shirtsleeves and open-neck.

'Hello, love.'

''Lo, George. Did you get a lift home?'

'Yes, Sam dropped me off.'

He made straight for a chair, sat down with one elbow resting on the table, and heaved a weary sigh. 'Cripes, what a night!'

'Tired? Want me to get you a cuppa?'

'Tea? I couldn't look at it. Tell you what, give us a glass of milk. I'm going to take a couple of aspirins.'

'You've got a headache?'

'Bit of a one. You know how it is. They wrangle on and on. That Bluey Nichols...'

'And the beer!'

He chuckled. 'Yes, and the beer. I had a few.'

'What about the office bearers?'

'I'm in again. Treasurer for another year. Nobody else'll pull it on.'

She'd got him the milk and aspirins.

He took them, and sat there, blinking sleepily around the room. 'Three nights out this week. I'll be glad when tomorrow comes and I can have a quiet night at home. Anybody been?'

'Just Bill and Jill.'

'Any phone calls?'

'No, nothing. You'd better get to bed.'

'Yes, I've had it. And I got plenty to think about in the next week or two. They want to run a barbecue to raise some dough. We got a club coming down from Bendigo for a game. I always told you the day would come when darts would take off in this country.'

He stood up. Swaying slightly, he bent down and kissed her on the forehead. 'You better give it away too, Mag. I suppose you been sitting there all night blinking at that TV.'

He went off, and Mrs Dobbs sat on, waiting... listening... thinking...

· The Nightshift ·

Eight o'clock on a winter's evening.

Two men sit on the open section of a tramcar speeding northwards along St Kilda Road. Two stevedores going to Yarraville — nightshift — 'down on the sugar'. One — old, and muffled to the ears in a thick overcoat — sits bolt upright, his tired eyes fixed on the far end of the car with that expression of calm detachment characteristic of the pipe-smoker. His companion, a much younger man, leans forward with hands clasped between his knees, as if enjoying the passing pageant of the famous road.

'It'll be cold on deck, Joe,' remarks the young man.

'It will that, Dick,' replies Joe. And they both fall silent again.

At Toorak Road a few passengers alight. A far greater number crowd aboard. Mostly young people going to dances and theatres. Smoothly groomed heads and white bow-ties. Collins Street coiffures and pencilled eyebrows and rouged lips. Creases and polished pumps. Silk frocks and bolero jackets. They fill the tram right out to the running-boards. The air becomes heavily scented.

The young wharfie, mindful of past rebuffs, keeps his seat. He can still see the road, but within twelve inches of his face a remarkably small hand is holding a pink silk dress clear of the floor. He finds it a far more interesting study than the road. Reflects that he could enclose it completely and quite comfortably within his own big fist. Little white knuckles, the fingers of a schoolgirl, painted nails — like miniature rose-petals. He sniffs gently and appreciatively. Violets. His gaze moves a little higher to where the wrist — a wrist that he could easily put thumb and forefinger around — vanishes into the sleeve of the bolero. Higher still. Violets again. Real flowers this time, to go

• **The Nightshift** •

with the perfume. From where he's sitting, a cluster of purple on a pale cheek. She's talking to a young fellow standing with her; her smile is a flicker of dark eyelashes and a flash of white teeth.

Dick finds himself contrasting his own immediate future with that of the girl's escort. Yarraville and the Trocadero. Sugar-berth and dance-floor. His eyes fall again to the little white hand so near his lips, and he sits back with an exclamation of contempt as he catches himself wondering what she would do if he suddenly kissed it. Sissy!

Old Joe's thoughts also must have been reacting to the impact of silks and perfumes.

'The way they get themselves up now,' he hisses into Dick's ear, 'you can't tell which is backside and which is breakfast.'

Dick eyes him with mild resentment. 'What's wrong with them? They look good to me.'

Joe snorts his disagreement, and the subject drops. Dick is only amused. He understands Joe. The old man has shown no disapproval of similar passengers who joined the tram at Alma Road and in Elsternwick. It's the name: 'Toorak'. It symbolizes something. Poor old Joe! Too much courage and not enough brain. Staunch as ever, but made bitter and pig-headed with the accumulation of years. Weary of 'The Struggle'. Left behind. A trifle contemptuous of the young bloods carrying the fight through its final stages. A grand mate, though. And a good hatchman. That means a lot on a sugar job. With the great bulk of the old stevedore at his elbow, and the little white hand before his face, Dick is sensitive of contact with two worlds. Shoddy and silk. Strong tobacco and a whiff of violets. Yesterday and Tomorrow.

Flinders Street-Swanston Street intersection. They get off and push through the pleasure-seeking crowd on the wide pavement under the clocks. Another tram. Contrast again. Few passengers this time. One feels the cold more. Swift transition from one environment to another. Swanston Street to Spencer Street. Play to work. Light to darkness. No more silks and perfumes. Shadowy streets almost deserted. Groups of men, heavily wrapped against the cold, tramping away under the frowning viaduct.

'It'll be a fair bitch on deck,' says Joe, quite unconscious of his lack of originality.

'Yes, you can have it all on your own.'

No offence intended; none taken. They walk in silence. Joe isn't the talking kind. Dick is, but the little white hand and the glimpse of violets on a pale cheek have set in motion a train of thought that makes him irritable. He keeps thinking: 'Cats never work, and even horses rest at night!'

Berth Six, River. Passing up the ramp between the sheds they come out on to the wharf. Other men are already there. Deep voices, and the stamping of heavy boots on wood. The mist is thick on the river, almost a fog. Against the bilious glow of the few lights over on south side dark figures converge on one point, then vanish one at a time over the edge of the wharf.

Dick and Joe join their mates on the floating landing-stage. Rough greetings are exchanged.

'How are you, Joe?'

'What the hell's that got to do with you?'

'You old nark! Got a needle on the hip?'

'I don't need no needle. How's the missus, Sammy?'

'Bit better, Joe. She was up a bit today.'

'Line up there! — here she comes.'

As the little red light appears on the river the men crowd the edge of the landing-stage, each anxious to get a seat in the cabin on such a night. The water is very black and still, and the launch moves in with hardly a ripple. The night is full of sounds. Little sounds, like the rattle of winches at the distant timber berths; big sounds, like the crash of the coal-grabs opposite the gasworks. All have the quality of a peculiar hollowness, so that one still senses the overwhelming silence on which they impinge. In some strange way sound never quite destroys the portentous hush which goes with fog. Dick feels it as he follows old Joe over the gunwale and gropes his way through the cabin to the bows.

'It's quiet tonight, Joe. Can't be many ships working.'

'Quiet be damned. There's four working on north side. Where the hell're you going, anyway?'

'I'm going to sit outside.'

'You can sit on your own, then. This ain't no Studley Park tour.'

Dick doesn't mind that; all the same he isn't left alone. Other men are forced out beside him as the cabin fills. He finds it hard to dodge conversation. Racing. Football. Now if it was politics ... The Struggle! Just a humour, of course. He has no fixed antipathies to nightwork, the waterfront or his mates. Nightwork means good money; three pounds a shift. A real saver sometimes. Many a time he's stood idle for days, then picked up a single night — enough to keep landlord and tradesmen quiet, at least. Two hours less work than the dayshift too. Nevertheless it's all wrong. Surely to Christ the work of the world could be carried on in daylight. So much waste and idleness during the day, and toil at night. Only owls, rats and men work at night.

'What's wrong, Dick? You're not saying much.'

'Just a bit dopey, Bluey. Not enough shut-eye.'

Damn them! — why can't they mind their own business?

The launch travels smoothly and swiftly. Quite safe. The mist is thickening, but there's a bit of light on the river here from the ships working on north side. Small ships, as ships go, but monstrous seen from the passing launch. Beautiful in a way of their own, too, with the clusters of lights hanging from masts and derricks. Little cities of industry resting on towering black cliffs. One can't tell where the black hulls join the black water.

Nameless bows, but still familiar to the critical stevedores.

'That's the *Bundaleera*. Good job. She worked the weekend.'

'The *Era*. She'll finish tonight.'

'The *Montoro*. They say there's only one night in her.'

Strange twentieth-century code of values. A collier which works Sundays is a good ship; a deep-water liner which works only one night is a bad ship.

'They can stick their Sunday work for mine!' Joe's voice.

'I suppose you get more out of the collection-box, you bloody old criminal!'

'That's all right. I only been to church twice in my life. The first time they tried to drown me, and the second time they married me to a crazy woman.'

Dick smiles to himself. A smile of affection for the old warrior. Joe's a good Christian, whether he knows it or not. There's a word for him: 'Nature's gentleman'. A hard doer and a bit of a pagan, that's all. Three convictions: one for stealing firewood during the Depression, one for punching a policeman during the '28 strike, and one for travelling on an expired railway ticket — also during the Depression. Across one cheek the scar of a wound received on Gallipoli. A limp in his right leg from an old waterfront accident. 'Screwy' arms and shoulders from too much freezer work in the days when every possible job had to be stood up for. 'Sailor Joe.' Dick loves him as any healthy youth can love a seasoned guide and mentor. They work together, ship after ship. They travel together, live near each other

With a mutter of deep voices the launch chugs its way across the Swinging Basin. The mist continues to thicken. South side is just visible. Haloes of brassy yellow around lonely lights. Dismal rigging of idle coal lighters — grimy relics of the white wings of other days. North side can be heard but not seen. Beyond the veil ageing winches clatter at the coal berths and railway trucks crash against each other in Dudley Street yards. A man's voice hailing another comes across the water with extraordinary distinctness.

A few minutes later everything vanishes and the speed of the launch drops to a walking pace. Real fog now. Dick's eyes have been fixed on the ridge of water standing out from the bows. Twice since leaving Berth Six it has fallen in height; now it is but a ripple. Voices in the cabin are still cursing the cold, speculating lightly on the chances of reaching shore in the event of a collision. Dick wishes they'd all shut up. He's cold himself, but some of his irritation has gone. Here again is beauty — of a kind, like ships working at night, and the little white hand. Just three feet away the sooty water flows slowly past. It's easy to imagine that only the water moves, that the launch is motionless, a boatload of men resting in the perpetual night of a black river. To port, south side has ceased to exist; to starboard, north side is only the distant clamour of a lost world.

Nine o'clock.

The green navigation light of Coode Island.

Only the light. A bleary green eye, neither suspended nor supported. Green eye and grey fog. They pass fairly close. Too close, they realize, as the launch swings sharply off to port. New sounds come out of the night. Sounds of a working ship. Dead

• The Nightshift •

ahead, and not far away. Yarraville. Conversation, which has languished, flickers into life again.

'What the hell's that?'

'Don't tell me it ain't nine o'clock yet!'

'Just turned. Maybe there's a rockboat in.'

'There is. They picked up for her this morning.'

'We won't be long now — thank Christ! I'm as cold as a frog.'

'Listen to the dayshift howl when we pull in. It'll be ten o'clock when they get up the river.'

In two places, one on each bow, the fog changes colour. Two glowing caves open up, as if a giant had puffed holes in a drop-curtain. And in each cave the imposing superstructure of a ship materializes with all the bewildering play of light and shadow characteristic of ships at night. Rockboat and sugarboat. The *Trienza* and the *Mildura*. The comparatively graceful lines of the bigger ship don't interest the approaching stevedores. Their eyes are all on the *Mildura*, their minds all grappling with one question: how many nights?

'By God, she's low!'

'She's got a gutsful all right.'

'Three or four nights — you beaut!'

Under a barrage of jeers and greetings from the dayshift the launch noses in to the high wharf.

'You were a long time coming!'

'What're you growling at? You're getting paid for waiting.'

'Ho there, Bluey, you old scoundrel!'

'How are you, Jim? Left a good floor for us?'

'Good enough for you, anyhow. She ain't a bad job.'

'How many brands?'

'Five in Number Two Hatch. Grab the port-for'ard corner if you're down there. You'll get a good run till supper. Two brands.'

'Good on you, son!'

The nightshift swarms up the face of the wharf, cursing a Harbour Trust which provides neither ladder nor landing-stage. Dick is last up, for no other reason than that Joe is second last. The strain imposed on the old man to reach the top angers his young mate. Damn their hides! All ugliness again. A man can never get away from it for long. The strange charm of the fog-bound river has gone. The black beams of the wharf, with the shrouded men clinging to them like monstrous beetles, symbolize all the galling dreariness of the ten hours just beginning. Symbolism also in the tremendous loom of the coal-gantry. Toiling upwards, always toiling upwards, with just a little glimpse of beauty now and then, like the mist, and the little white hand, and the ridge of black water streaming away from the bows of the launch.

'Shake it up, old-timer!' someone cries from above.

Joe's big boots are just above Dick's head. One of them is lifted on to the next beam. He waits for the other to move, but the old man is still feeling for a higher grip for his hands. Dick's own fingers are getting numb. The beams are covered with wet coal-dust and icy cold. At either side the dayshift men are swarming down. Noise, confusion, and black shapes everywhere.

A sudden anxiety seizes Dick as Joe's higher foot comes down again to the beam it has just left.

'On top there!' he yells. 'Help this man up!'

Too late. Even as he moves to one side and reaches upwards in an endeavour to get alongside his mate, the old man's tired fingers give in. A big clumsy bundle hurtles down, strikes the gunwale of the launch with a sickening thud, and rolls over the side before anyone can lay a hand on it.

An hour later another launch noses away into the fog. Only two men. Both are within the cabin, one standing behind the little steering wheel, the other crouched near the open doorway with eyes fixed on the grey pall beyond the bows. Coode Island is astern before the boatman speaks.

'He was your mate?'

'Yes, he was my mate.'

'You got him out pretty quick.'

'Not quick enough. He hit the launch before he went into the water, you know.'

After a minute's silence. 'Does the buck know you've left?'

'I'm not worried. I wouldn't work tonight, not for King George. And somebody's got to tell his old woman.'

'I'm going right up to Berth Two. Will that do you?'

'Yes, anywhere.'

Anywhere indeed. And the further and slower the better.

• **The Nightshift** •

Not so much different from an hour ago. Mist, black water, and the crash of trucks over in the railway yards. But no men. One of them embarked now on a longer journey than he ever dreamed of. And in a few minutes there will be lights, and more lights. And voices, and the faces of many people. And not one of them will know a thing of what has happened. Princes Bridge, and the bustle of the great intersection. Trams, and St Kilda Road. And the big cars rolling along beneath the naked elms. The other world — violets — and the little white hand.

The little white hand. Funny. She'll be dancing somewhere now, and the grand old man with whom she very nearly rubbed shoulders —

'What was that?' asks the boatman.

Dick is startled to find he has spoken aloud.

'We don't know much about each other, do we?' he says without hesitation.

'What d'you mean?'

'Oh, nothing . . .'

• Goyai •

It was the most eerily beautiful place I had ever seen. Nailed to a tree, just above head-height, was a board with the crudely painted word: *GOYAI*.

Before me was a track running between walls of manna-gum, casuarina, tea-tree in full blossom, and wedding-bush even whiter. And as I walked on, the whites and the greens and the mellow sunlight all came to an end, and there was the hill, rounded and brown, void of ground-cover, puffing itself up on the lonely heathlands like a great poisoned breast. From foot to summit nothing lived on it except a forest of burned and blighted mealy-gums. From the edge of the surrounding scrub bracken ferns crept out in ever-thinning numbers, faltered, and fell back.

But because there was a dwelling at the top, the first I had seen in several hours of walking, I went on.

A bronzewing pigeon, lurking in the fine sand, whirred away from almost under my feet. The chatter of parrots and honeyeaters died out behind me. A cuckoo, perched on the lowest branch of the last manna-gum, stared at me with strange troubled little eyes, opened wide its pink mouth, and ran wearily up the scale of thirteen melancholy notes.

The air became cool, and the dry-sweet smell of living scrub gave place to an odour of rotten wood tinged with eucalyptus. The deep car ruts in the track lost themselves on a hard sour soil littered with bark and dead leaves, sprinkled with faded sundews, and blotched with patches of moss that had withered in the heat of summer. All the trees staggered northward as if violent winds often blew here. Cinnamon bracket-fungi glowed on trunks charred by bushfires and ravaged by disease.

The large weatherboard hut at the top looked bleak and

furtive. There was no garden, no fowlpen, no outhouses of any kind except the inevitable sentry-box convenience. Only a woodheap, and a sheet of hessian stretched from one tree to another over an ancient car.

But smoke was coming from the chimney, and the door was open. As I got near there came a sound of footfalls, and an old man appeared on the threshold and stood watching me. He had a face resembling that of King George V on English coins, and was dressed in a blue flannel shirt open at the neck, and whipcord trousers held up by a soiled red necktie.

When I got to within a dozen or so paces he descended the steps with astonishing agility, hurried towards me, and grasped me eagerly by both hands.

'From Claire, surely?'

'I'm afraid I'm not the person you're expecting,' I said, 'I'm a complete stranger here.'

The grip of his strong hands relaxed and his face took on an expression of keen disappointment.

'You are not from Claire?'

'No.'

'Then who are you?'

'My name is Quaife. I lost my way in the bush and I thought you might be able to help me. I want to get out to the main road.'

He glanced down the hill to make sure that I was indeed alone.

'How did you find your way in here?'

'I just came on this track. I've been walking for hours.'

I told him where I had come from, where I wanted to get to. He listened suspiciously, never for an instant taking his eyes off mine.

'Seventeen,' he said suddenly, as though trying to catch me out in something.

'I beg your pardon?'

'Seventeen.'

'I don't quite understand ...'

'Does it mean anything to you that this is the seventeenth of November?'

'Absolutely nothing.'

'All right, come inside.'

Frowning, he let go my hands at last and left me so suddenly that he'd gone several paces before he realized that I wasn't following him.

'I don't want to disturb you,' I said. 'If you could just direct me ...'

'Disturb me?' He turned right round and regarded me with what I thought was exaggerated surprise. 'I don't see why you should say that. I was just having my evening meal. You could take a little refreshment before you go on. You have a long walk in front of you.'

He was standing theatrically erect, hands straight by his sides, head thrown backward. I knew then that the beard made him look older than he was.

Not because I stood in need of refreshment, but because he had aroused my curiosity, I thanked him, followed him into the hut, and sat in a rickety cane chair while he put another cup and saucer onto a small table already set for one.

'As regards getting back to the road you have no reason to worry. My track will take you straight to it only a mile from the township. If you had turned left instead of right you would be there now. May I ask what brings you to this part of the country?'

His change of manner was welcome, but transparently deliberate.

'Birds,' I said. 'I'm interested in natural history. I've heard that there is a place hereabouts which is a haunt of the hooded robin.'

He had moved to the stove and had his back towards me. He said something that sounded like: 'Ah, the hooded robin now, eh?' but it was in such a low voice that I let it pass as not intended for me.

The interior of the hut showed that he was living alone. It was a roomy place, unlined, and with a steeply pitched roof supported by paperbark spars raw from the bush. Everything spoke of a man of simple tastes and exacting habits: a single bed made up with military efficiency, a skeleton wardrobe hung with a curtain of sugar-bags opened up and sewn end to end, a coolgardie food-safe, shelves fitted here and there between the hardwood studs of the walls and holding crockery, odds and ends of tins and boxes, and a few books. There was no floor covering and no curtain at the window.

Something of the remote and primitive charm of the place had already seized me. Wisps of blue smoke drifted out from the open stove bringing to me a nostalgic smell of burning tea-tree. Through the open doorway I had a view of one perfectly rounded shoulder of the hill. It resembled nothing I had ever seen in all my years of wandering in the Australian bush. The gloom under the blackened mealy-gums had deepened, while the setting sun touched the canopy of blue-grey leaves with a light that seemed curiously artificial. It was as though night had already fallen and a great lamp were beaming over the tops of the trees. Alongside my chair the window looked out over an unbroken field of scrub ending in a ridge topped conspicuously by a group of pines.

A ragged pepper tree grew close to the hut on this side, and as I looked there appeared a honeyeater feeding on the blossoms of a branch that drooped towards me. Perhaps it was only imagination, but I thought I could hear the leaves tapping together as the bird moved among them. Everywhere else they were perfectly still, and lit up by the sinking sun like slivers of steel.

'So you like birds?' The man sat down opposite me and pushed towards me a plate of biscuits.

'Very much indeed,' I replied.

It had been evident from the first that I was dealing with a chronic eccentric. I felt now that he was secretly laughing at me, and began to wish I had declined his invitation to stay. When he urged me to eat I took the opportunity to remark on the fading light.

'This is very kind of you, but you mustn't think me rude if I go soon. I must reach the road before dark.'

'You can't get lost again, even if darkness does overtake you. Isn't it pleasant sitting here? Listen to it!'

I had indeed been missing nothing of what was going on outside. Every sound of the bush was magnified under the iron roof. Walking up the track a few minutes ago had been like entering a dungeon; now the whole top of the hill had become alive with birds. There was a babel of song and chittering, and through the window we could see the leaves of all the near trees thrown into movement as if a breeze had sprung up.

'They must have followed me,' I smiled.

He pulled a face, as if the remark didn't please him. But the next moment he pointed to where some pardalotes and sittellas were fluttering about the drooping branch of pepper tree.

'It's odd how they all move around together. Except for a golden whistler or a blue jay I never see one bird alone. Sometimes for hours on end there's nothing on the whole hill. Then, suddenly, they are all here. They never stay long, though. They just pass through. Then it's quiet, and I'm all alone again.'

I didn't miss the note of self-pity here, and for a moment thought this was the final lead-in to what he really wanted to talk about. To my relief, however, he went on talking about birds, about the bush generally, about his own particular bit of territory. He spoke of it all with enthusiasm, with wide knowledge, with phrases vivid and well turned though sometimes a trifle extravagant. He talked hurriedly and continuously, like a man in whom a limited number of thoughts have been fermenting for a long time.

I thought at first that I was listening to nothing more than the panegyrics of a cultured and poetic hatter. But after a while I observed that in all his apparent rapture there was an underlying bitterness, as though he were concerned not so much with a precious possession as with the memory of a hard-fought battle by which it had been won.

'And it is all mine. No one ever comes here. No one else wants to set foot in it.'

Suddenly the bitterness came right out, and he was staring at me across the table with a twisted humourless smile.

'Like a prison!'

'Like a prison?'

'Well, what else is it? Does she imagine I don't know what is going on?'

'She ... Claire?'

His smile quickened, became cunning.

'You told me that name meant nothing to you!'

'It doesn't, except that you spoke it the moment I arrived.'

'I'm speaking in enigmas, am I? You don't understand what all this is about, do you?'

He thrust his face nearer, and for the first time a little chill of fear ran through me.

'Or do you?'

'I assure you I haven't the least idea what you're driving at.'

'Perhaps you haven't. But she has. Quaife ... it's no accident to me that your name begins with the seventeenth letter of the alphabet. In all these years I haven't been able to trace one of you back to her. Does the name *Goyai* also mean nothing to you?'

'I saw it for the first time in my life a few minutes ago, at the bottom of the hill.'

'It's an Aboriginal word. It means "Come back". What more can I do to tell her?'

The way in which this was said left me free to answer or not, so I kept silent. Through the window I could see the great ball of the sun now resting lightly on the pine trees a mile or so away. Its flushed beams fell across the summit of Goyai, blazing avenues of long shadow and misty light, and picking out the tufts of seeded sundew like blossoms of tinsel. Everywhere else was receding into night. Some magpies still sang at a distance, but in the vicinity of the hut a deep silence had fallen. I followed the grey gliding flight of a kookaburra under the mealy-gums. On the edge of the scrub, perhaps a hundred yards below, there was a dark object which could have been either a feeding wallaby or the stump of a vanished tree. I became half absorbed in waiting for it to move.

'When I first came here my neighbours used to call on me. Now they shun me. Why?'

'I cannot guess,' I lied. 'You must have been here a long time?'

'Seventeen years.'

'Always alone?'

'Why should I come here if not to be alone? ... Well, until she returns. It took me a long time to find a place like this. When I first came here there were only three other people between me and the road. Now they are all around me. And not one of them can give a satisfactory reason for taking up land in this area. The latest of them moved in only last week.'

'Perhaps it's good country,' I ventured.

He smiled contemptuously.

'Heath country is never good.'

In the manner of a normal man driven to exasperation by stupid questions he raised his eyebrows, hunched his shoulders, and spread his big hands.

'Work it out for yourself, my friend!'

Moving in his chair as it became necessary, he then enumerated his neighbours, beginning in the north and going the full round of the compass:

'Devlin, Morton, Rice, Merrivale, Street, O'Neale, Robb, Kirkwood, Heffernan, the Shapes, Taylor, Rutherford, Davenport, Lanza, Smith, Cullen...'

His voice had gradually risen, so that the last name came with a shout:

'Perrin!'

I waited. 'How many?' he demanded fiercely.

'I didn't count them.'

I knew the answer, though, before he yelled it at me:

'Seventeen!'

'Seventeen.'

'Seventeen! No matter which way I turn now — there they are. Watching every movement I make — like those foul pines!'

He pointed to the distant ridge, now barely discernible.

'How many trees would you say there are in that stand?'

'Seventeen?'

'Seventeen exactly. You can count them easily from here in daylight. Why doesn't she either come back to me or leave me alone?'

'She was your wife?'

'What makes you ask that?'

'My dear fellow...'

'All right, perhaps you are innocent, like the others. But all this talk of coincidence irritates me. You know the podargus?'

'It's a bird. The tawny-shouldered frogmouth.'

'How many times does it call out? I mean, how many separate notes are there in each call? You said you were a naturalist. Come now, don't hesitate, or I'll think you're in it too.'

'Usually about twenty.'

'Not here, my friend. You'll find that nothing is the same here. What have you to say when I tell you there is a podargus on this hill which calls seventeen times? Always seventeen times. You'll hear it for yourself in a few minutes.'

I stood up.

'I'm sorry, but I really can't stay any longer. You've been most kind ...'

Everything else apart, the falling night was indeed beginning to cause me some uneasiness. My directions were simple enough, but I knew from experience how easy it is to get off even a well-defined track in the darkness. All colour had gone from the surrounding bush. The western sky had cooled from a fiery red to a metallic grey. Inside the hut it was quite dark away from door and window.

'Must you really go?' he asked in a voice full of disappointment.

'I must reach the road.'

'I would guide you that far. You might be able to help me. There is so much ... so much ...'

He shook his head as if a sudden rush of thoughts had bewildered him, and placed both hands to his face. Then, to my consternation, he rose, came round the table, and took hold of me by the arms. I got a whiff of perspiration-soiled clothing and strong tobacco, and found myself looking into eyes moist with tears and wild with despair.

'What made you come here?' he pleaded. 'You must tell me. Who sent you?'

'Don't you believe me? I was lost ...'

'No, no, no! Of all the places you could have come to this day ...'

'You're ill,' I said. 'Believe me, I know nothing about your affairs.'

'Of course I'm ill. But I'm not mad, as some of them say I am. Something tells me you understand. You must talk to me.'

He was actually shaking me now, but not in anger.

'Think! Has a strange woman spoken to you? She's tall and fair. She has a lisp ... the kind of lisp you'd never forget. Perhaps you got a letter that puzzled you ...'

'I've had no letter, I give you my word. And no strange woman has spoken to me. You're upsetting yourself over nothing. Please sit down...'

I had nothing to fear from him. He made no resistance as I gently forced him backward into a chair. All strength had gone from him and he suddenly collapsed, folding his arms on the table and hiding his face in them.

'Claire... Claire... if only you would leave me alone! If only you would leave me alone!'

And there I left him.

I tiptoed out, and the cool air, laden with the scents of the sleeping bush, closed around me. In the heavy silence the crackle of dry twigs underfoot unnerved me, and I began to run, stumbling over exposed roots and colliding with trees that seemed to rush at me out of the darkness.

Not until I was at the foot of the hill, and the trees opened up to reveal the friendly stars, did I pause. And in that very moment a frogmouth began calling in the bush on my right. That strangest of all bird sounds, so like the urgent pumping of an old-fashioned car horn: Toot... toot... toot...

Twenty-one.

But I knew positively that in the hut on Goyai a man had lifted his head from a table and counted no more than seventeen, the fatal number by which his disordered mind identified everything with the tragedy of a lost love.

· Dog-box ·

I first became aware of her just before the train pulled in.

Flinders Street Station in the peak-hour is a primitive place. You get pushed at from all sides, and if the pressure from one particular quarter is a bit more persistent than from anywhere else the odds are that you won't even notice it. That is, if you're a regular peak-hour traveller, have a long way to go, and are not as young as you used to be.

I was aware of this particular pressure, though. It turned out afterwards to be the edge of a wicker shopping basket, but it felt more like the lid of a garbage can. However, I held my ground and fought down a temptation to look around, because to have done so would have meant moving more than my head, thereby letting someone else in.

The train came into sight running down from the yards, and a murmur of pleasant anticipation ran along the packed platform. Dog-box! We used to talk of the old dears with contempt, but have changed our attitude since the arrival of the Blue Hussies. It was like seeing the old brown teapot come to light.

It slowed to a stop. Those of us at the front pressed backwards as incoming passengers eased open the swinging doors. I was in a good position, but sensed immediate danger as I felt the lid of the garbage can slide round into my left side. I looked down, frowning, because for all the hurly-burly of the five-to-six rush, there is still a point beyond which most sufferers do not go.

She had Mum written all over her. I was close enough to get even the homely middle-aged smell of her; something of well-preserved clothes, wood-ashes, yellow soap, the stew-pot. Below a comfortable bosom she hugged her garbage can battering ram, a well-filled shopping basket topped with what looked like a folded woollen scarf. Two bright eyes flashed up at me out of a face full of character and rich experience.

'Sorry, mister!'

I gave her a smile, and a few more inches of precious ground, but I knew she wasn't a bit sorry. She was as good as past me, and already digging her basket into the backs of two other women who had moved in from the other side.

Nobody got hurt, but Mum was only fifth in. She was beaten by the two women, a big workman, and a little clerk type of fellow who must have been an old hand at the game, because he seemed to come from nowhere to take fourth place.

When I got in I found the two near window-seats occupied by the clerk and the workman. The three women were on the same side as the clerk, with Mum furthest from the window and apparently none too happy about it. In the fourth corner a tough-looking fellow wearing a black belted raincoat and a cloth cap sat watching us troop in with an expression of sleepy insolence on his unshaven face. On his knees lay what was obviously a bottle wrapped up in brown paper. I sat down next to him before I realized that he was half drunk and that I hadn't noticed him before.

'Flinders Street,' I said amiably. 'This train's going back.'

He turned on me a dull heavy-lidded stare. 'Back where?' he asked with a strong Scottish accent.

'Lilydale.'

'Lilydale.' He gave that a moment's consideration. 'An' supposin' tha's where I want tae go?'

'Sorry. I didn't see you get in.'

'An' supposin' I didna get in?'

Now experience has taught me that the best way to deal with a quarrelsome drunk is to meet him halfway. So I said firmly: 'That's what I was supposing.'

'An' supposin' ye're richt?'

I shrugged my shoulders and looked away from him.

But to my relief he suddenly relaxed and clapped a heavy hand on my knee. 'A'richt, Pop. I been sleepin'. A' the way there an' back. I wanted Nunawading. First thing I know I open ma eyes and there's the bluidy cricket ground flyin' past again, the wrong way.'

'You're all right this time,' I said. 'I'm going to Croydon. I'll have an eye on you at Nunawading.'

In the meantime the compartment had filled up, even with a few standing passengers. During my exchange with Scotty I'd been aware of Mum on the other side taking some interest in the proceedings. But not much. She was preoccupied chiefly with the basket and with the two women on her left. The one in the window seat had lit a cigarette and seemed to want to keep to herself. The other, a stoutish matron in navy-blue overcoat and beret, and laden with parcels, was beaming at all of us, ready to take on anybody who'd give her a fair hearing. She had the air of a woman who has made some bargains and feels she has topped off a good day by getting herself a seat on a peak-hour train going home.

Mum looked as if she were still nursing a grievance over being beaten to a corner seat. Without moving her head she kept darting angry little sideways glances. Her leathery face was grim and anxious as she felt under the woollen scarf to see if everything was still there.

On Mum's right a pale youth in black trousers and pink windcheater had opened up a Superman comic. In the far corner the clerk was reading a paperback. On my side there was Scotty, myself, two mates whose names I soon learned were Bill and Ian, and the workman, of whom all I could see were frayed trouser cuffs and a pair of big blucher boots. The standing passengers were reinforced at Richmond by a man who irritated Mum by flicking her face every now and then with the corner of a *Herald* hanging from a hand hooked on to the luggage-rack.

Bill and Ian were discussing an item in the news: Stanley Yankus, the American farmer who was migrating to Australia because he had been fined for growing too much wheat. Ian, sitting next to me, was doing all the listening, so that I picked up most of what Bill was saying.

'What good will it do him, anyhow? It'll be on here again any tick of the clock. I just heard the other night over the air that hundreds of acres of sugar-cane in Queensland ain't going to be cut this year. My old man told me the best job he ever had in his life was dumping butter during the Depression. He used to work all day carting butter down and tipping it into the Bay. Then go home at night to a feed of snags and fried bread. One of his mates got the sack because they found some butter in his bag . . .'

I began to get interested, but at that moment Scotty came to life again. No preliminaries. I thought he was sleeping until he whispered right into my ear:

'How about a whisky, Pop?' He tapped the brown paper parcel on his knees. 'Nane o' your Australian tack. Real Scotch — White Horse. Have a nip?'

I told him quite amiably that it wasn't my medicine. He frowned contemptuously.

'What do ye drink?'

'Beer.'

'Supposin' I havna got beer?' He stared hard, as if I'd been demanding beer and what was I going to do about it now.

'That's my bad luck,' I said.

'An' ye no want a whisky?'

'No, thank you.'

On my left I caught Bill's voice: 'I saw another case like Yankus only a few months ago. Only it was pigs. A bloke raising too many pigs . . .'

Ian must have moved, for the voice faded. And Scotty was still at me:

'Any objections tae me havin' a nip?'

'No,' I replied, adding impatiently: 'It's your whisky.'

He knitted his brows, and for a moment I thought I'd gone too far too quickly. I tried to appear interested in Mum, but was acutely aware of him keeping me under observation while he decided what to do about me.

Mum had been captured by Mrs Blue Beret. The latter was obscured by one of the standing passengers and I couldn't make out what she was saying, but for the last few minutes her voice had provided a steady overtone to all the other noises in the compartment. Mum was only pretending to be listening. She kept turning her head and nodding sympathetically, but it was plain to me that her mind was never far from her basket. I began to wonder what was in it. She had it hugged close to her stomach, wrists braced against the arched handle, both hands turned inwards and spread out over the folded scarf as if ready to detect the slightest movement of something hidden beneath it.

Bill was flat out on the question of pigs. I'd stolen a peep at him and found him to be a man of middle age with a worried expression on the kind of face that goes with ulcers or a nagging wife.

'Blokes was getting paid for pigs they didn't raise. Now just you get on to it! Say you're a little bloke, just big enough to raise pigs up to the quota. All nicely organized, prices fixed and guaranteed. You get paid for, say, fifty pigs that stink and grunt and make pork. But I'm in it in a bigger way. I've got room for two hundred pigs. And I get paid for two hundred pigs. Only I get told to keep just a hundred and fifty — or else! So I declare a hundred and fifty pigs on the hoof and fifty on paper. And I get paid for them fifty paper pigs just like you get paid for your fifty pork pigs. And people everywhere screaming out for bacon. The game stinks.'

Ian murmured something which was inaudible to me, and nodded his head to agree that the game did indeed stink.

I waited, curious to see where Bill would go from there, but Scotty had returned to the attack on the other side. He must have been brooding, because he took up his grievance exactly where he had left off.

'What ye're tellin' me is: this is a free country, eh?'

I pretended not to grasp his meaning.

'If ye don't want tae drink whisky, ye don't have to. An' if I *do* want tae drink whisky — I drink whisky. That it?'

I smiled. 'That's about it.'

'It's as simple as tha', is it?'

'It was your idea!'

'I didna say it was my idea. I was suggestin' maybe it was your idea.' He tapped the parcel again. 'Supposin' a checker got in just as I cracked this bottle. Ye still say I can drink whisky if I want to?'

'That's a chance you'd have to take, my friend,' I parried, still smiling.

'What ye mean is: this is a free country as long as I'm prepared tae take the odds. Is that it?'

I shrugged my shoulders, and once again he retired into his

alcoholic whirligig. A moment later, under the pretence of identifying a station we were pulling into, I stole a glance at him. Chin resting on elbow, he was staring out through the window with an expression of sleepy triumph.

Mum also was watching stations. We were in Auburn, and she'd been checking off every stop as if on her way to an appointment of life or death. Conversation with the woman in blue had become clinical. I caught the sentence: 'Anyhow, he gave me some tablets for him to take . . .' and guessed that the absent Mr Blue Beret was under discussion.

Mum was showing a little more interest, but still only between stations. Every time we stopped she leaned forward to peer out through the window, remaining like that until we were on the move again. She looked cold. She should have been wearing that scarf. It occurred to me that she had taken it off to protect something in the basket. A kitten? Chicken? Whatever it was she never for an instant removed her sheltering hands. Every now and then I saw the worn fingers spread out, feeling, probing. Next to her the pale youth had been through the comic and was fighting a losing battle with sleep. Mum had had to straighten him up several times with discreet little nudges. But I'm a leftwise subsider myself, and I knew that nothing she could do would make him collapse in the other direction. Motherly type as she was, I believe she'd have let him go to sleep on her shoulder if it hadn't been for the basket. I saw her shift it a little away from him and bring her right elbow forward as a barrier.

Bill was in the full tide of the subject of the paper pigs.

'Them pigs that nobody raises get paid for in real money. The blokes that whistles pigs up say you can't whistle money up — not for pigs, anyway. They say it's got to come from somewhere, and that somewhere always means you and me in the long run. Taxes. Say you're on the basic wage and you got a big family to feed. You'd give 'em all two cackles and a grunt for breakfast every morning if you could, wouldn't you?'

Ian must have agreed with that.

'But you can't, not on your pay. Eggs maybe, but not bacon as well. But, by jeez, you got to pay for bacon! Them paper pigs get paid for with Government dough. And that's you! Now just work it out. You pay taxes to pay blokes to raise paper pigs so that the bloke who raises pork pigs can get a price you can't afford! Now tell me the game doesn't stink.'

Ian evidently was still not prepared to say that the game didn't stink, and a sulky silence fell on my left.

At Camberwell several passengers, including the woman in the corner seat, got off. Nobody got in. Mrs Blue Beret, in full voice on her husband's clinical history, seemed unaware that the corner seat had been vacated until Mum gave her an urgent push. Both of them moved along, and Mum settled herself one place nearer the window with obvious satisfaction. The pale youth lurched violently, collected himself with great embarrassment, apologized, and promptly moved in close to her again. I think he didn't like the look of the passenger who was ready to drop into the empty seat, and felt that if he was going to subside on to anybody it had still better be Mum.

In the commotion Scotty came to life again. I noticed his hand tighten convulsively on the bottle of whisky in the very moment that sleep left him. He shook his head, peered out for the name of the station, relaxed, and after a few seconds' contemplation to thoroughly digest the fact that I was still there, once again began where he had left off.

'So ye think it's a free country, do ye?'

'Look here, my friend,' I began irritably, 'I've done a hard day's work...'

'A'richt, a'richt, a'richt.' I'd been prepared for a different reaction, and was rather disconcerted when he bent on me a dry smile. 'Why don't ye go tae sleep then? Ye're sittin' there wi' your eyes wide open...'

'Any objections?'

'No, no objections. If a man wants tae sleep he's entitled tae sleep. If a man doesna want tae sleep...' he waved his hand in a way that made me want to hit him, 'och weel, it's a free country!' And there he left me again, seething.

I decided to have a piece of him next time, whatever the cost.

Mrs Blue Beret was a foot or two further away from me now, but with the standing passengers gone I could hear more of what Mum had to put up with.

'... little pink ones this time. And do you think I could get him to take them? Not on your life! He said they made everything he ate taste like burned cork. And the doctor had gone out of his way to tell me they didn't have no taste at all. It just goes to show what imagination can do for you.'

Mum, carefully checking the train through Canterbury, nodded shrewdly.

'He was particularly crooked on them spoiling his tea. So he said, anyhow. He's always liked his cuppa. So d'you know what I did? I said to him: if you think they're not doing you any good then you'd better stop taking them. And I started putting them into his tea unbeknown to him! And now he's as happy as Larry. Says he hasn't felt better for years, and that them tablets must have been making him worse. Sometimes I could bust right out laughing at him. He looks at me across the table and winks and smacks his lips. "By God, Sally," he says, "it's good to be able to enjoy a decent cup of tea again!"'

Mum chuckled, nodding vigorously, and, I thought, reminiscently. In other circumstances she might have told a good story back. At the moment she just didn't want to be involved in anything. There was that basket . . .

Bill was still getting a good hearing on pigs:

'The more you look at it the sillier it gets. If you ain't in the pig business you cop it three ways. You don't eat pork, even under the lap. You pay taxes to pay blokes not to raise pigs. And you pay more taxes to pay more blokes to see that the other blokes *don't* raise pork. Because it's like everything else, it's got to be administered. You got to have an office, clerks, paper for forms to fill in so that blokes can say exactly how many pigs they ain't raising. One time farmers just raised pigs, and there wasn't any office anywhere that had anything to do with pig-raising. They just took the little pigs to market. These paper pigs is different . . .'

We had come to a halt somewhere between Mont Albert and Box Hill, and Mum was becoming increasingly worried. I believe she'd have given anything for Mrs Blue Beret's corner seat so that she could open the window and look out to see what was the cause of the hold-up. Mrs Blue Beret rambled on, regardless of the fact that Mum obviously wasn't listening. Mum looked thoroughly angry, as if nothing would suit her better just then than a chance to give the Victorian Railways Commissioners a piece of her mind. For the twentieth time

I caught her withdrawing her hand from under the scarf, and had to fight down a temptation to lean over and ask her if it was still breathing. I wasn't sure how she'd take it.

More pigs ...

'The trouble is, Ian, sooner or later the big blokes is going to take a wake-up to the lurk and go in for it in a big way. They'll monopolize it, get a corner in them paper pigs. They'll have 'em raising litters. They'll be claiming higher prices for 'em because of the rise in costs of all the tucker they don't give 'em to eat. They'll be going overseas trips, tax-free, to study the latest developments in the paper pig-raising industry. They'll get their mates in Parliament to put a duty on imported pork so as to give the home-produced stuff a fair go — struth, we're at Box Hill! We made a quick run tonight ...'

I felt a keen disappointment as the two friends reached for their bags on the luggage-rack. It would have been diverting to see how far Bill would have gone in his dissertation on the controls of private enterprise. I noticed that the moment they were out on the platform he started again.

Some other passengers got out also. More came in. Mostly teenage schoolboys.

Mum had just ridden out another lurch of the pale youth and informed him with a rather tight little smile: 'You was nearly into me basket that time!' He was sitting stiffly now with a red face, trying desperately to find something in the comic that was worth rereading. Mrs Blue Beret announced that she was getting off at Blackburn, and with a new passenger standing against the door I saw Mum gather herself for the slide into the corner seat. With that in prospect she listened quite sympathetically to the final anecdote about Mr Blue Beret's stomach.

'He's supposed to eat brains, you know, but he says he's never sat down to the dirty things in his life and he ain't going to start now. So I give him fish-paste sandwiches in his lunch every other day. That's what he thinks, anyhow. If he's never tasted brains he can't be any the wiser. Sometimes he'll come in from work and say: 'By jeez, Sally, that was a nice bit of fish!' He thinks it's Japanese flat'ead paste ...'

I'd have liked more on that, but just then the tenacious Scot came in again:

'This free country business...'

'How about giving it a rest?'

'No offence, Pop. Ye're an Aussie, aren't ye?'

'Yes, I'm an Aussie.'

'An' ye say it's a free country?'

'Yes, I do.'

'You always cast your vote at election time?'

'You bet I do!'

'An' supposin' ye dinna like ony o' the candidates? You still cast your vote?'

'I can always vote for the one I dislike least.'

The corners of his lips drooped. 'Ye ca' tha' an argument? The real point o' the matter is: ye got tae vote, haven't ye?'

'Voting *is* compulsory, yes.'

Again the pontifically waving hand. 'Tha's jist ma point! A free country — an' compulsion wherever ye turn! In Scotland I never missed ma vote, simply because I was free tae please masel. Oot here the first thing they tell me is: Jock, ye got tae vote! Tha's enough for me. Ma hackles is up. If tha's wha' they ca' democracy they can keep it. I've never used ma vote since I set foot in Australia. I believe in real freedom.'

And with that he retired, supremely confident of having finally flattened me, as indeed he had.

I was still reeling under the blow when we reached Blackburn and Mrs Blue Beret gathered up her parcels and got out. The man in the doorway stepped on to the platform to make way for her, so that Mum had no opposition in taking over the corner seat. I thought for a moment that she was going to open the window, but all she wanted was to make sure that it was in good working order. She just pushed it up a few inches, let it fall again, and immediately had another feel of the mystery under the scarf. If she hadn't looked so homely I'd have assumed then that she had some living thing she wanted to destroy, and was only waiting until the compartment was empty before pitching it out on to the line.

The schoolboys were involved in a lively discussion of TV. It might have been a golden opportunity for me to get an insight into juvenile perversion, but nothing now could divert me from Mum and her basket.

• Dog-box •

Except Scotty, who couldn't resist a final shot during the last lap to Nunawading. I knew for a good minute that he had turned his head and was watching me. I also knew, I don't know how, that he was smiling.

'Dinna let it worry ye, Pop.'

'Do I look worried?'

'No, I'm no sayin' ye look worried. I'm referrin' tae oor wee dispute.'

I said nothing, but was careful to keep a pleasant expression. In spite of everything he had succeeded in making me feel a bit of a nark. We slowed into Nunawading and he took a firm grip on his bottle of whisky and prepared to depart.

'No hurt feelings, Pop?'

'No hurt feelings, Mac. Good luck to you!' I was beginning to like him, but possibly only because he was going.

He lurched out, and, teetering alongside, gave me an ironic salute before banging the door.

'Never mind, Pop, there'll always be an England — as lang as there's a Scotland!'

On again, with Mum and I exchanging understanding smiles across the compartment. I believe she'd have said something but for the fact that, as I noticed with some excitement, she also was near the end of her journey. She was like a cat on hot bricks, measuring off the miles between Nunawading — Mitcham — Ringwood. She must have been feeling very cold. The pinched little neck, where that scarf should have been, was all gooseflesh. Every now and then a shiver passed over her. Her cheeks and the tip of her nose had turned blue. Her feet, which just reached the floor, kept up a ceaseless tapping. But in the keen eyes and on the thin lips there was a smile of joyous anticipation. Both hands vanished under the scarf as if to give added protection over the last mile or two. I must have looked vastly interested, because when she caught me watching her she gave me a you-mind-your-own-business kind of stare plain enough to be embarrassing.

Ringwood. No, she didn't get off. But for all practical purposes it *was* the end of her journey. Everything favoured her.

She must have known every stick and stone of that line, because, sitting with a firm grip on the catch, she shot the window up in the very instant that we hit the end of the platform. Out went her head and a frantically waving hand. A long line of waiting passengers rushed past, slowed down, stopped. Mum was hidden from sight as the door opened, but I heard her urgent piping voice:

'Hi, Bill!'

People were getting off, others crowding around to get in. I got a glimpse of a good-looking young station assistant, his startled face trying to see where the voice was coming from. He stepped forward and was blacked out at the other side of the doorway.

'Spare me days, Mum! Where've you been to?'
'In town. Here, cop this — it's a pie — it'll warm you up...'
'You beaut!'
'How's Elsie?'
'All right, How's Dad?'
'All right. How's Bubby?'
'Fit as a Mallee bull! Got another tooth...'

The changing passengers were clearing and I got a full-length view of him. He stood with one hand resting on the window ledge, carrying on the conversation while casting hurried glances right and left along the train. His other hand held a small brown paper bag with a grease stain on it.

As the last doors banged he stepped backwards, one arm uplifted. The guard's whistle blew. The train tooted. We jerked into a start.

Mum's head was still at the open window.

'Ta-ta, Bill — eat it while it's hot!'

I thought I'd never seen a sweeter sight than that little woman sitting there with a happy smile as she wrapped the woollen scarf around her frozen neck.

Dear old Mum! To hell with the railways! — eat it while it's hot.

• Morning Glory •

The shot was fired about 4.30 in the morning. An hour before dawn, and a little more than an hour before the time set for the rising of the family. Poultry-farming involves early rising, but not necessarily 4.30. Everybody and everything was sleeping. Not a feather had shuffled in the long rows of white-painted pens perched terracelike on the hillside. Not a twitter had come from the starlings and sparrows crowding the cherry-plums and boobiallas behind the homestead.

For several seconds after the shot had broken the silence its echoes rumbled along the shallow valley and crackled back from the opposing slopes. Everybody was awakened, but they kept still for a moment, as people do at such a time, collecting their wits, separating dream from fact, waiting to see what would happen next. There were five of them: Arthur Brady and his wife Margaret, their thirteen-year-old son Lance, Grandfather Brady, and Hugh Griffiths, an itinerant labourer who had been doing some draining and was due to go on his way that day immediately after breakfast.

First reaction came from the Bradys' bedroom, the voice of Mrs Brady in an excited whisper:

'Arthur, did you hear that?'

'My oath I heard it!' There followed the sounds of a man hurriedly getting out of bed, and the click of a light-switch.

It had been a hot night, with all doors left wide open for free circulation of air, and the sudden flood of light in the bedroom dispelled the darkness all through the house.

Grandfather and Lance called out simultaneously from their separate rooms:

'That was a shot, Dad!'

'You awake, Arthur? Joe's had a go at something!'

Only on the back verandah, where the man Griffiths had a shakedown, was there still silence. The house filled with a buzz of voices and the soft swift sounds of people getting into clothes.

'Be careful now, Arthur! Don't go rushing out.'

'Talk sense, woman! What d'you expect me to do ...?'

'We don't know what's happened ...'

'Joe's got somebody, that's what's happened. He got something in his sights ...'

'Can I come, Dad?'

'No, Lance, stop where you are.'

'I'm up ...'

'Stop inside, that's all I'm telling you.'

Arthur Brady a muscular little man in his early forties, came down the passage buckling a belt around a pair of trousers he had pulled on over his pyjamas. His lean brown face was grim and eager. Passing Grandfather's door he almost bumped into the old man, who was just coming out.

'I don't hear nothing else, Arthur.'

'Neither do I. Perhaps he's killed the bastard.'

Arthur hurried on, through the kitchen and out to the verandah, where he stood staring into the darkness, listening with cocked head and bated breath. But all he could hear was the low ceaseless rustling and clucking of a thousand frightened hens in the houses fifty yards away.

'You there, Joe?' he shouted.

A little way down the hillside a torch flashed and a strong voice came back: 'Yes, come on down!'

'Did you get him?'

'Come on down — quick!'

By now Mrs Brady, Grandfather and Lance were clustered behind Arthur at the top of the steps. They all started talking at once.

'Sounds like he got somebody, Arthur.'

'D'you think he's killed him, Dad?'

'Lance, don't you say that like that!'

'But Mum ...'

'You keep quiet ...'

'I'll come down with you, Arthur ...'

'You stop where you are, Dad. All of you stop here. I'll sing out if I want you.'

Arthur Brady went off, running into the darkness. The others remained where they were, following his noisy progress down the garden path, out by the picket gate, across the open space to the fowlpens, and through the dry bracken ferns that clothed the hillside. Halfway down to the road the light of the torch remained on, moving about a little as if the man who held it were examining something. Voices drifted up to the house, but it was impossible to distinguish what the two men said as they came together.

'There's something doing down there, Madge,' said Grandfather. 'Better go in and put some clothes on.'

'What d'you mean?'

He shrugged uneasily. 'Oh, I dunno. There might be something to do ...'

'Like what?'

'Joe's had a go at something, and he wouldn't sing out like that if it was a fox. We might have to get a doctor.'

She didn't move immediately, just stood there staring in the direction of the torchlight, and frowning, as if the detailed implications of the shooting of a poultry thief were only slowly coming home to her.

'Will we have to get the police, Pop?' asked Lance, all boyish excitement.

'Course we will if Joe's hit somebody.'

'I suppose I'd better put something on.' Mrs Brady turned away, but in the entrance to the kitchen she stopped and looked back. 'D'you think he could have killed him?' she asked in an awed voice.

'Kill him — no! Joe would hit him where he wanted to hit him. He had a flashlight rigged — go on in and get dressed. I'll stop here with Lance.'

She went in, and for the first time Grandfather and Lance became aware of the hired man. He had a bag stretcher at the enclosed end of the verandah and had been sleeping without pyjamas. Even in the poor light that penetrated there they could see the white of his legs and short underpants as he put his feet to the floor and stood up.

There was no significance in the fact that he began to dress without speaking. In the two weeks that had passed since he came in off the road looking for work the family had become accustomed to his unobtrusive ways. He was a stoutish commonplace-looking man with an air of mild detached resignation that had baffled them from the first. Only Grandfather, however, really disliked him. He had remarked to Arthur that he always had a feeling that Griffiths was secretly laughing at them. Arthur was satisfied because he was a good worker; Mrs Brady because he was clean in his habits and kept to himself.

He came out now in trousers, singlet and heavy work-boots, and stood beside Grandfather. 'That wasn't a gun, was it?' he asked.

'No, it was a rifle.' Grandfather's reply came quite casually, but the instant it was made he turned sharply on Griffiths as if struck by a sudden suspicion of what lay behind the question.

Griffiths must have been aware of it, but he pretended not to notice.

It was quite warm, but a shiver passed over the old man and he noisily slapped his hands against his skinny stomach. 'Go in and fetch me dressing-gown, will you?' he said to the boy. 'It's hanging behind the door.'

'Did he hit him, Pop?'

'We don't know nothing yet, Lance. We just got to wait till your Dad comes back.'

Nothing passed between the two men while the boy was away. When he came back Grandfather, hugging himself in his dressing-gown, sat down on the top step. Griffiths stood over him, leaning against a post with one thumb hooked over his belt. Even the boy was aware of something in the air besides the actual shooting. His curious eyes moved from his grandfather to Griffiths and back again. He wanted to ask more questions, but the sullen expression on both faces kept him silent, and he went and rested his folded arms on the rail a few feet away.

All three of them watched the light down the hill. It remained fixed now, as if the torch had been laid on a ridge of earth or a stump. Now and then the little beam was broken as something passed through it. A murmur of voices came up

• **Morning Glory** •

almost continuously. It was very quiet, the deep hush that goes just before dawn. In the fowlhouses the frightened birds had settled down again. The three people watched and waited and listened. When a dog rustled out from under the steps and reached up to sniff Grandfather's bare toes he pushed it away with the irritation of a man disturbed in anxious thought.

'Go and lie down, Bob. Go and lie down.'

Suddenly the light of the torch went off and there came again the sound of a man tramping through dry ferns. The voices lifted for a moment, that of Arthur quite clearly:

'Don't you worry about it, Joe. You was there to do a job ...'

All eyes were on him as he showed up on the garden path. He was breathing heavily, and would have climbed the steps without a word had not Grandfather, remaining seated, and moving only his knees out of the way, put out a hand to restrain him.

'What's the score, Arthur?'

'We got a dead 'un down the paddock, that's all.'

'What!'

Grandfather stood up, but Arthur was already past, heading for the kitchen door. Mrs Brady, coming out at the same moment, frocked and combed, stopped on the threshold, fingers clapped to her lips.

'Arthur, did you say ...?'

'You heard me. I told you Joe wouldn't mess about if he got a go. Mind out of the way ...'

He went in, and they heard the tinkle of the bell as he picked up the telephone at the far end of the passage. 'Lil, give us D24 — quick! — yes, fair dinkum ...'

At the back, Lance started to say something, but Grandfather hushed him down with an angry gesture.

Mrs Brady looked beseechingly at the two men. 'Is that true? Joe's killed somebody?'

'Now don't you go getting upset over it, Madge ...'

'He did — my God!' With hands pressed to the sides of her face she walked to the verandah rail and peered out at the scene of the shooting. There was a faint cool movement of air, carrying a smell of dusty herbage. In the east the sky was beginning to lighten. The first cock crowed. From somewhere close by there came the short, dry, tentative cackle of a kookaburra.

Griffiths was at the other side of the steps. He was standing very erect now, his hands gripping the rail, his head thrust forward, his brows knitted in an angry scowl. Grandfather watched him uneasily.

Arthur had finished his call to the police and got involved in conversation with the telephonist at the township. Every word came out clearly to the people on the verandah.

'I've seen too many dead 'uns not to know. What? — yes, of course she is — I am myself — so's Joe. No, Lil, spare me days, you know Joe better than that! Listen — I got to go. They're all out here at the back ...'

He hung up and came out again. Everybody turned to look at him, but he addressed himself only to the boy.

'Get down to the bottom gate, Lance. Somebody's got to pull 'em up ...'

'Who, Dad? The police?'

'You're always talking about D24 — hi, hold on!'

Lance was already on the steps. 'Don't you go out on the road! You hear me? Just open the gate and stand on the side where they'll see you. Them blokes come like hell ...'

Lance was gone. Arthur hitched up his trousers and tucked in his shirt. They were all watching him, but his eyes came to rest nowhere. His manner was ostentatiously defiant.

'This'll stop the bastards once and for all,' he said. He began to roll a cigarette. Mrs Brady was studying his face, but Grandfather was watching his hands, which were shaking.

'Arthur, are you sure he's dead?' asked Mrs Brady.

'Wouldn't *you* know if you was looking at a corpse? Anyhow, Dr Noyes'll be here in a minute. Lil's calling him.'

'Joe stopping down there?' This from Grandfather.

'One of us had to.'

Silence fell, but it was the uneasy silence not of people who are content with their thoughts, but of people who are afraid of saying the wrong thing. Griffiths had moved away from the rail and was sitting on a box against the wall, filling his pipe. Dawn was breaking. The nearest trees were beginning to reveal themselves. A great chirping and rustling was going up from the cherry-plums and boobiallas. Wattle-birds called out in the garden.

Arthur began to pace back and forth across the creaking

boards. Mrs Brady said something to him, but it was in such a low voice that he hardly heard her.

'What?'

'I said: what's he like?'

'What d'you mean? — what's he like...'

'Is he — young?'

'Young — no! Old enough to know what he was up to.'

'Where did Joe — where did he hit him?'

'What does it matter where he hit him? Look, Madge, you'll get yourself and everybody else all stewed up.' Arthur halted and faced her, emphasizing his words with short chopping gestures. 'This has been coming for weeks, and you know it as well as I do. Joe...'

'But I never thought...'

'Neither did I. Nor Joe. Nor anybody else. It's still — oh damn!'

Mrs Brady had covered her face with her hands. Arthur turned his back on her in exasperation, but Grandfather stepped in, and taking the distressed woman by the arm, gently urged her towards the kitchen door. 'Go on in, Madge. This is man's work. It couldn't be helped. Nobody wanted to kill nobody, but it happened. Go on in. Go in and make us a cup of tea. Me and Arthur'll look after this.'

She went in, but no sound of kettle or cups came out to the three men on the verandah.

None of them spoke for a minute or two while the glow of the lighted house began to weaken against the dawn. Then, suddenly, Arthur threw the butt of his cigarette to the boards and ground it with his heel.

'Why the hell do we have to have a scene like this over it! A bloke comes to steal my chooks. He knows I'm hostile on it and I'll do something about it. All right, he takes the odds and he gets shot. What do I do now — sit down and cry?'

'It's just that he got killed,' said Grandfather gently.

'And whose bloody fault is that? Mine?'

'I'm not saying it was your fault.'

'Joe's? We all put in and hired Joe...'

'No, I wouldn't say — don't let's argue about it, Arthur. It's bad enough.'

'What d'you mean — bad enough. I say it's a good job that's

been done. We set out to stop this thieving, and by jeez this'll stop it!'

'All right.' Grandfather, not satisfied, but afraid to take the dispute any further, returned to his position at the rail. The sun had not yet risen, but there was enough light now to reveal the entire landscape: the small roughly tended garden, the dusty track leading past the gate and on towards outhouses and fowlpens, scattered wattles and stringybarks, and patches of brown ferns on a ground of yellow grass.

'Just whereabouts are they?' asked Grandfather after a discreet silence.

Arthur came and stood beside him, pointing. 'See that clump of wattles in line with the corner-post?' he said sulkily.

'Yes.'

'Over to the left — that gum forked at the butt, out on its own?'

'Yes.'

'They're near there. Somewhere near that patch of ferns. It's a bit dark yet. You'll see Joe's head in a minute. He's sitting there...'

Grandfather nodded. 'I heard you telling Lil he was running,' he said cautiously. 'That true?'

'Yes. Joe just let fly...'

'He hit him in the back?'

'Yes. There's a hole in him up towards the left shoulder.'

'Bull's-eye. You know there'll be trouble over this, don't you?'

'Trouble. What kind of trouble?'

'The law says you can't kill a man for stealing a chook.'

'The law says you can't steal a chook!'

Grandfather didn't answer that. He let a second or two pass. Then, with his eyes still fixed on the patch of ferns, he said sadly: 'He might have needed it.'

Arthur gave a scornful laugh. 'By Christ, you're not too bad! How about me? Don't I need 'em? Who the hell am I raising chooks for? Any lousy bastard...'

'Sssh! You'll fetch Madge out.' Grandfather, worried by Arthur's rising anger, held up his hands. 'It's just the killing, Arthur. I got nothing against a charge of shot.'

• **Morning Glory** •

Unobserved by either of them, however, the woman had already appeared, standing in the entrance to the kitchen. She was looking not at them, but at the bowed head of Griffiths, as if she found his detachment puzzling and offensive.

Arthur thought of him at the same moment and turned to him for support. 'What do you say, Griff? Don't you reckon that bloke got what he was looking for?'

Griffiths lifted his head, took his pipe from his mouth, and stared Arthur steadily in the eyes. 'If a man's got property he's got to defend it,' he said quietly.

'My bloody oath! And that's exactly how I see it.'

Arthur, satisfied that his point had been made, resumed his restless pacing, but all Grandfather's attention remained fixed on the hired man. He began to breathe heavily, in the way of an old person caught up in a mounting excitement. His whole body shook, his head stuck forward like an angry parrot. He pointed an accusing finger. Mrs Brady called out to him from the doorway, but he didn't hear her.

'That bastard's laughing at you!' he shouted. Mrs Brady and Arthur moved towards him, but he evaded them, dodging sideways, his stooping body allowing the front folds of his dressing-gown to trail the floor. 'What does it matter to him? He's got nothing. He never had nothing. He doesn't want nothing. He's just having a shot at you. He's one of them blokes that's crooked on the whole world.' Arthur had reached him, hustling him back towards the rail. 'That's all right, Arthur. You didn't see him. I did. He was smiling. That lousy sneering smile. I saw him ...'

'What does it matter — break it up, Dad — I got trouble enough ...'

Griffiths was on his feet, openly contemptuous. 'Let him rave,' he said curtly to Mrs Brady. 'I've got my cheque. I'll eat on the road.'

Arthur heard that. 'What's up with you? I'm handling this. And you keep out of it, Madge ...'

Snubbed on both sides, she stood there, silently watching Griffiths as he walked purposefully towards his bed. She saw him pull off the old grey blankets he had brought with him, spread them on the floor, and begin to throw onto them the few other odds and ends that comprised his worldly possessions: spare shirt and underclothing, a ragged jersey, a pair of worn canvas shoes, shaving gear.

Over at the rail the old man was almost weeping.

'I'm not crooked on you, Arthur. I'm not crooked on nobody. It's this killing, just the killing. I got no time for thieves, but nobody ought to get killed like that. They used to hang blokes once just for taking what didn't belong to them. What do we know about him? He's lying there — take your hands off me mouth! — I know what I'm talking about. I could have got killed myself more than once when you was kids. I never had nothing. I'm glad to see you getting on a bit. But I don't want to see you getting like the big 'eads — walking round what you got with a bloody gun. Your Mum . . .'

'Shut up, will you?'

Mrs Brady rushed over to them, pointing down at the road. 'Arthur, look! Here's a car — the police . . .'

They stopped struggling. In the sudden silence that fell on the house there came only a clink of buckles as the hired man tightened his swag. All the lights were still on, but it was the new day that lit up the rich and peaceful earth and the grim immemorial burden of men.

• The Incense-burner •

It was a one-way trip, and I paid off in London in the middle of winter with twenty pounds in cash, a wristwatch worth fifteen pounds, and a good kit of clothes, half on my back and half in a suitcase. And a fair bit of experience for my nineteen years.

I put up at somebody's 'Temperance Hotel' near King's Cross Station because I was sick of the drunken orgies that had marked every port of call coming over from Australia, and was knocked up at eleven o'clock the first night by a housemaid innocently armed with dust-pan and empty bucket who asked me if there was anything I wanted. There wasn't. That also was something I'd got sick of on the way over.

At the end of a fortnight I had added something to my experience and was down to thirty shillings, a pawn-ticket in place of the watch, and the suitcase, still with contents. So I left the hotel, took a room in a seamen's lodging-house down near the East India Docks, and started to look for a ship home.

I wasn't long in finding out that I'd left my gallop a bit late. In 1929 a seaman looking for a ship out of London needed something better than thirty shillings and a brand-new discharge book. I had only one entry in my book, and Second Engineers and shipping officials weren't impressed. Thousands of good men were haunting the docks every day. Real seamen, with lifetimes of experience behind them, and rubbed old books to prove it. I came to the conclusion after a few days that my book was more of a handicap than a help. I'd had enough of London, and I wanted a ship bound for Australia and nowhere else. And my book made it all too clear. Second Engineers and Second Mates used to flick it open, drop the corners of their lips, and pass it back to me with a dry smile.

253

I had it written all over me — Adelaide to London. They wanted men for a round voyage, not homesick Australians who would skin out at the first port touched.

I lasted two weeks; ten shillings a week for my room and ten shillings the fortnight for food. I did it by getting in sweet with a ship's cook, a Melbourne man, on one of the *Bay* ships laid up for repairs. I got breakfast out of the black pan every blessed day of the fortnight. Sometimes tea, too, until he told me not to make it too hot.

There were some good feeds, but not nearly enough, and it was all very irregular, and I was only nineteen, and as fit as they come, and walking up to fifteen miles every day, and I got hungrier and hungrier. There were days when I could have eaten my landlady. She was a skinny, sad-looking woman with bulging fish's eyes and a rat-trap mouth. I thought she was the toughest thing I'd ever met in my life. I was out all day every day, and on the rare occasions when I saw her she didn't seem to care whether she spoke to me or not. I used to turn in fairly early and lie reading, and until a late hour every night I could hear the thumping of a smoothing-iron in the kitchen at the far end of the passage. She was a widow; with only one other lodger, a pensioner, she had to support herself by taking in washing. It was a dark, silent, dismal hole of a place, smelling perpetually of wet clothes and yellow soap.

I saw the other lodger only once, an old man in a beard and long overcoat, vanishing into his room as I came in one night. I heard him often enough though. Too often. He had one of those deep, rumbling coughs that seem to come all the way up from the region of the stomach. He would go for minutes on end without stopping. He used to wake me up every night. Sometimes I thought he was going to suffocate.

His name was Burroughs — 'old Burroughs' to Mrs Hall. I knew nothing about him — or about Mrs Hall either, if it came to it — until my last day in the house. I had sevenpence-ha'penny left, and the rent of my room was due that night. It was a cold, raw day with skies you could reach up and touch, and a threat of snow. In the morning I did the usual round of the docks, missed out on a last feed on the *Bay* ship, and went back to Finch Street to tell Mrs Hall I was leaving. I'd had to recognize the fact that I was well and truly on the beach; that there was nothing for it now but the Salvation Army 'Elevator', an institution about which I'd heard plenty in the past two weeks.

I was to learn that day that my landlady's forbidding manner was nothing more than a front deliberately built up over years of contact with tough London seamen. She had a heart of gold, but like a lot of good people had become afraid to let the world see it.

She talked to me at the kitchen door, and as I told her what I was going to do she stared past me down the length of the short passage with her grim little mouth tightly shut and an expression of sullen bitterness on her dour face. I felt I was telling her an old and familiar and hated story. She must have seen a lot of defeated men in her time. Behind her was a table piled with washing; two or three ramshackle chairs, a linoleum with great holes rubbed in it, and a stove with several old-fashioned irons standing at one side.

'It's a damned shame, that's what it is,' she burst out with a vehemence that startled me. 'Good, clean, respectable, young men walking the streets.' She sniffed and tossed her head. For a moment I thought she was going to cry. Instead she asked me in for a cup of coffee. 'I was just going to make one. It'll warm you up.'

It was the worst coffee I'd ever tasted, half a teaspoonful of some cheap essence out of a bottle, mixed with boiling water. And a slice of bread to eat with it. Stale bread spread thinly with greasy margarine. But I was cold and hungry, and friendly words went with it. God help her! It was all the hospitality she could offer me. One glance around that wretched room convinced me that I had been living better than her.

I told her I didn't want to take any good clothes into the hostel with me, and asked could I leave my suitcase with her until my luck turned.

'You can leave anything you like. Only no responsibility, mind you.' She went on to tell me that she never knew from one day to another who she was going to have under her roof, and in the middle of it there came a muffled sound of coughing from along the passage. She stopped to listen, holding her breath and pulling a face, as if she were actually experiencing some of the old man's distress. 'I'm not saying anything about *him.* He's all right. I can go out and leave anything lying around. Poor old soul! There's many a time I give him a cup of coffee, and I'll swear to God it's the only thing that passes his lips from morn till night. Where he gets to when he goes out . . .'

'He's pretty old, isn't he, Mrs Hall?'

'Not that old. He was in the war. He's a sick man, that's what's wrong with him. One of these days I'll wake up and find I've got a corpse on my hands. You just ought to be here when he gets one of his foreign parcels.'

'Foreign parcels?'

Mrs Hall finished her coffee, got up, and began sorting the things on the table. 'Don't ask me where it comes from. He never tells me anything, and I never stick my nose into another body's business. But he's got somebody somewhere that hasn't forgotten him. Every few months he gets this parcel. Not much — a pair of underpants or socks, or a muffler — just bits of things. And a little bundle of dry leaves, herbs for his cough I suppose. My God, you just ought to smell them! He burns them in a bit of a tin pan he's got. They stink the house out. And there he sits and just sucks it in. It's beyond me how he can stand it. I've got to get out till he's finished.'

Mrs Hall sniffed and blew, as if the smell of the herbs from the foreign parcel were in her nostrils even then. 'He's been here twelve months, and if it wasn't for that I wouldn't care if he stopped for three years. He never bothers nobody, and he keeps his room like a new pin. I've never yet seen him with drink in, and that's a change from some of them I get here, you mark my words. I know *you're* not the drinking kind, otherwise I wouldn't have asked you in here.'

Poor Mrs Hall!

She wished me good luck and promised to keep my suitcase in her own room until I came back for it.

Travelling light, I walked all the way to the Salvation Army headquarters in Middlesex Street, stated my case to a 'soldier' just inside the door, and was sent over to an elderly grey-haired 'officer' seated at a desk piled with papers. All this happened a long time ago, and many of the details are hazy, but I'm left with an impression of newness, of spacious floors, of pleasant faces, of friendly efficiency.

• The Incense-burner •

The officer asked me what it was I wanted them to do for me. I told him.

'I'm an Australian. I worked my way over as a ship's trimmer. I wanted to see London; you know how it is. Now I'm broke, and I'm looking for a passage back home. I've got to find somewhere to live while I look for a ship.'

'Where have you been living?' Nothing inquisitorial about the question. He was taking quiet stock of me all the time. I had no reason to deceive him, but I felt it would be a waste of time anyway, that I was dealing with a man full of experience.

'In lodgings down in Custom House near the East India Docks. I've got to get out tonight, though; I haven't a shilling left.'

'You didn't jump your ship, did you?'

Only a man who knew sailors would have asked me that. 'No, I've got a clean book.' My hand went to my pocket, but he stopped me with a gesture.

'It isn't necessary for me to pry into your affairs, my boy. You understand that if you go into the Elevator you won't have much time to look for a ship?'

'I know I'll have to work, but that's all right. I could get some time off now and then, couldn't I?'

'Yes, as long as you did your task. But that's the responsibility of the commandant down there.' He reached out and picked a form off a little pile at his side. 'I'll give you a note to take down. I can't promise he'll have room for you, but it's worth while trying. What's your name?'

'Thomas Blair.'

'Do you know where Old Street is?'

They took me in, and for a little over three weeks I earned food and lodging by sorting waste string at the establishment known as the Elevator, down in Spitalfields.

It was the strangest three weeks I have ever experienced, and the most generally hopeless company of men I was ever mixed up with. There were about forty of us, of whom perhaps twenty were professional tramps wintering in. Of the others, fellows in circumstances more or less similar to my own, I got an impression that only a few were still trying to get their heads above water again. Conversation was not primarily around the prospect of finding employment, as I expected it to be, but around the petty incidents of the day, that evening's bill of fare, a certain current murder trial, and every triviality of hostel administration they could think up. At the time I was thoroughly contemptuous of it all, but I understand better now. Those men had had a lot more of London than I had; I was still fresh to the struggle ...

We worked nine hours a day; seven-thirty in the morning until five-thirty in the evening, with an hour off for dinner.

I was never able to find out why they called the place the Elevator, unless because it was intended as an elevator of fallen men. That's likely enough, but I'm not sure that it worked out in practice. I'm not questioning the good faith of the Salvation Army officers charged with its administration, but the prevailing atmosphere was far from elevating. On the first morning a short conversation with my immediate bench-mate served to reveal in a flash the spirit permeating the entire establishment.

'Been in before?' he asked me.

'No.'

'Stopping long?'

'No longer than I can help.'

'That might be longer than you think, chum. Y'ought to try and get on the staff. It's a sitter if they don't know you.'

'What staff?'

'Here, and up at the hostel. Sweeping out, making beds, cooking and serving. They're all chaps that come in off the streets, like you. Not much money in it, but everything's turned on free. All you got to do is get saved.'

'Saved?'

'Go out to the penitent form at one of the prayer meetings. Give your heart to Jesus ...'

And that was it. It was a home for the destitute, largely run by some of the destitute. And if you weren't particularly anxious to move on, and were sufficiently unscrupulous, you could be one of the running brigade. And the way to muscle into the running brigade was simply to get 'saved'. I discovered that some of the old hands got saved every year as soon as the winter winds began to blow and the roads frosted up.

All the charge-hands at the Elevator were such brands clutched from the burning, and a more foxy-looking crowd I never set eyes on. They were on a sweet thing, and in their anxiety to stick to it they took good care that precious little of the spirit of Army benevolence got beyond the corner of the building where the commandant had his little office. Beggars-on-horseback, they ran the place with much of the efficiency, and even less of the humanity, of an ordinary factory.

The Elevator was simply a depot for the collecting and sorting and repacking of waste paper, rags and string. All day long motor-trucks, horse-drawn lorries and handcarts kept coming in heaped with salvage, which was unloaded and dragged to various parts of the great concrete floor for sorting out.

I was put onto the string bench, and each morning was given a one-hundredweight bag of odds and ends of string which I had to disentangle and distribute into a row of boxes marked 'cotton', 'sisal' — I forget the other names.

That was my task for the day, the price I paid for three meals and a bed to sleep in at night. Anything I did over and above that was paid for, if I remember correctly, at the rate of half-a-crown a hundredweight. In the three weeks I was there I earned just enough cash to keep me in cigarettes, carefully rationed, and nothing more. And there was no getting out of it if you wanted those three feeds and the bed. I tried, on the very first day — seizing a moment when I thought nobody was looking, and ramming a double handful of unsorted string into the sisal box. But one of the foxes saw me from a distant part of the floor and made me drag it out again under the threat of instant expulsion.

We didn't live at the Elevator. An old shop next door had been converted into a dining-room, and every day at 12 o'clock we trooped in and received dinners served from hot-boxes brought down from some Army cookhouse. And at the end of the day's work each man was given three tickets on the hostel in Old Street a mile or so away, one for tea, one for bed, and one for breakfast next morning.

The Old Street hostel was one of the biggest in London, and was run on much the same lines, and in much the same spirit, as the Elevator. There was a washhouse with neither soap nor towels, dormitories — barrack-like but quite clean — and a spacious dining-room where the men could sit for the rest of the evening after eating. I understood that most of the food

— 'leftovers' of some kind or other — was donated or bought cheaply from hotels, cafes, shops and bakehouses. But it was priced so low that a man could usually eat plenty; it was dished up with every appearance of cleanliness, and I can't say I ever found it anything but appetising. Meal tickets were valued at 1s 3d, and we could choose what we liked from the bill of fare stuck up at the end of the serving counter: slice of bread and margarine 1d, pot of tea or coffee 1d, soup 2d, roast beef or mutton 3d, stew 3d, kippers 1d each, vegetables 2d, apple tart 3d.

All a bit primitive, if you like, but I had a two weeks' hunger to work off, and they were the most enjoyable meals I ever had in my life. Food was, indeed, the only thing that made life at all worth living just then. I would open my eyes every morning thinking of breakfast, and when it was over I'd grit my teeth and stagger through the next four hours sustained only by thoughts of dinner. And when that was over there came thoughts of tea.

One red-letter day I cashed two tea tickets. My neighbour on the string-bench got on to something better for that evening, and gave me his. When I lined up at the counter the second time the fox in the white apron gave me a cold stare.

'What's this? I've served you once.'

'Don't be funny,' I replied. 'How many tickets d'you think we get?'

Still staring, he became positive, threw the ticket into the tray, and turned to the next man in line, dismissing me with a curt: 'Move on, chum, you've had it.'

He should have known better, because there are two things for which a man is always prepared to fight, and food is one of them. I reached out and seized his wrist.

'Come up with it, Mister! I'm in the Elevator. I worked for that ticket —'

He shook himself free, but I must have looked as savage as I felt because he served me without further argument.

I was like that all the time, hostile on the whole infernal world and ready to take it out on anybody. Each week I got leave off for half a day and went the familiar round of the docks, but a ship seemed to be as far off as ever. I hated London as I'd never hated any place before, began to lose hope, and

The Incense-burner

fell into a mood of gloomy self-pity that made me impatient and contemptuous of everybody around me. Those men didn't talk much about their private affairs, and with the egotism and intolerance of youth I assumed that none of their troubles was as great as mine. A man with youth and good health, and no responsibilities, should find any tussle an exhilarating adventure, but some of us don't realize that until youth is past. I used to try to cheer myself up by comparing my circumstances to those of old Burroughs coughing his life away down in the hovel in Finch Street, but that only made matters worse. Visions of the old man creeping along the dark passage, or crouched over his periodical burning of the herbs, positively frightened me. For he also had had a youth, and somewhere in the past there had been a beginning to the road that led to Finch Street, and that assuredly would go on from there nowhere but to the grave.

The hostel was full of them, shivering watery-eyed old men, who wandered the streets all day, and stumbled in at nightfall to stand for a long time studying the bill of fare with a few miserable coppers clutched in their stiff fingers. Nobody took any notice of them. No doubt they would have envied old Burroughs, for nobody ever sent *them* parcels with mufflers and 'bits of things' in them. All the same, they moved me to horror and fear more than to pity, for were they not lifemembers of a fraternity of which I had become a novitiate?

And if during the day all my dreams were of food, then at night-time all my dreams were of home. The coughing of old Burroughs had nothing on the wheezings and mutterings of that refuge of lost men. Sleep came to me slowly, and was often broken, and in the wakeful moments I would lie with wide eyes and tight lips, deliberately torturing myself with nostalgic longings.

Some building close by had a clock that chimed the hours, and whenever I heard it I would think carefully and call up a scene in Australia that I knew was true and exact of that very moment.

At midnight I would say to myself: it's ten o'clock in the morning, and the hotels down Flinders Street are just opening and the wharfies coming away from the first pick-up are crossing from the Extension and dropping into the Hotham and the

Clyde for a quick one before going home to lunch. And there's a white sky and a smell of dust, and trembling pavements which by noon will be hot enough to fry eggs on. And down at St Kilda beach lazy little waves are lapping in, and some of the Fortunate Ones are crossing the Promenade from the big apartment houses and spreading their towels on the sand for a brown-off. And even though it's a weekday, the Point Nepean Highway down the Peninsula is already lively with cars heading for the bush and more distant beaches. And there's a place down there in the heath country where my mates and I used to go rabbiting on Sunday afternoons. And the big loose-limbed manna-gum where we found the parrot's nest is still there, its thin foliage hard and sharp against the sky in that way that always reminded me of the figures on a Japanese willow-pattern plate. And somewhere on the scrubby slope that runs up to the road a wallaby sits with drooping paws and pricked ears. And the air is full of the scent of the paperbarks down in the swamp, and of the whistlings and twitterings of grey thrushes and honeyeaters and blue wrens. And every now and then, on the breathlike puff of a breeze that comes out of the north, there is another smell that I know well, and over in a saddle of the distant Dandenongs a column of smoke marks where the bushfire is burning...

For three weeks.

Then — suddenly, like most bad things — it was all over.

One morning at breakfast time I got talking with a stranger who turned out to be a sailor. And within a few minutes he knew what I was looking for.

'Why don't you give the *Tairoa* a go?' he asked me. 'Ever done a trip as a steward?'

'No. What about the *Tairoa*?'

'She's leaving for Australia today, and they were signing on single-trippers yesterday. A lot of the New Zealand Company's packets do it. They go out stuffed with emigrants in the 'tween-decks. At the other end they dismantle the accommodation and fill up with cargo for home. They only want most of the stewards one way.'

'How is it I've never heard about this? I've walked those docks —'

'Well, you wouldn't be looking for Chief Stewards with that

book, would you? Anyway, the Shore Superintendent's the chap you want to see. He's got an office down at the East India somewhere. You'll have to look lively if you want to try the *Tairoa* — she's up for noon ...'

She's up for noon — oh, the friendly, intimate jargon of the sea! There was a promise in the familiar phrase that raised my excitement to fever-heat. I never met that seaman again, but I'll love him till the day I die.

It took me two hours to find the Shore Superintendent, and less than five minutes to get the ship. He was a busy man all right. I was at his office by half-past eight, but they told me he had just left for a certain ship, and it was half-past ten before I caught up with him. I can't at this distance of time trace my wanderings in those two hours, but I must have visited at least six vessels at widely separated berths, always just a few minutes behind him. However, I was after something that drew me like the very Holy Grail, and I nailed him at last just as he was about to get into his car. I knew I was on the right track as soon as he stopped to listen to me.

'We don't want trimmers,' he said after a glance at my book. 'We want stewards.'

'That's all right with me,' I replied. 'I want the passage. I'll sign as a steward. I've worked in hotels.'

He passed the book back, taking me in from head to feet.

'Where's your gear?'

I could hardly speak for excitement. 'Up in my room in Custom House —'

'You'd have to be aboard by twelve o'clock.'

'I can do that. Where's she lying?'

He told me. 'Give us your name.' He pulled out a pocket-book. 'Report to the Second Steward and give him this note.'

She's up for noon ...

Finch Street was two miles away, but I'll swear I made it in twenty minutes. There was plenty of time, but I had it in mind there was a suitcase to lug over the return trip, and I wasn't taking any chances. It was a cold foggy morning, but I was sweating from the long chase and the fever of success. And the grey buildings, and the shrouded figures that passed me on the pavement, were like things seen through the enchanted mists of fairyland. All the world had become beautiful, and I strode along puffed with triumph and springing on my toes with physical well-being. I told myself that youth and strength and pertinacity had to tell in the long run. You couldn't keep a good man down. Not when he had something big to struggle for. Those old men of the hostel had lacked the spur, inspiration, a vision ...

No more Elevator. No doubt I wore a silly smile, because more than once I caught a curious glance directed at me as I hurried on. Perhaps my lips were moving too, because the magical phrase 'she's up for noon' rang in my head until it took on the tune of a well-known military march. I could have danced to it, shouted it aloud.

She's up for noon ...

I remember afterwards holding back to let an ambulance pass me as I was about to cross into Finch Street, but the fact that it was an ambulance didn't register at the time — only a car of some kind, and in a hurry.

But I did observe instantly the women out at their doors all along both sides, and the little knot of gossipers in front of my old lodgings.

I thought first of Mrs Hall, then of old Burroughs. But the humour of pitiless superiority was still on me, and I hardly quickened my pace. I'd come back for a suitcase, that was all, and in a few minutes these people ...

They turned their heads and watched me as I came up. I saw Mrs Hall in the doorway, her popping eyes red with weeping.

'It's the old man, sailor. They've just took him off. The poor old soul.'

Some of the arrogance and detachment left me. I wasn't interested in old Burroughs, but this woman had given me a cup of coffee and a few words of sympathy when I needed them most. The other women stood aside, and I moved into the passage, taking the landlady by her elbow and drawing her after me. Something tickled my nostrils, but all my attention was on something else.

'He's an old man, you know, Mrs Hall. What happened?'

'They think it's a stroke.' She began to weep again, dabbing her nose with the lifted end of her tattered apron. 'God help him! He tried to talk to me. He got one of them parcels this

The Incense-burner

morning, them herbs. He's been sitting there — you got a ship, sailor?'

She could think of me too.

'Yes, I'm going aboard in an hour. Where've they taken him?'

But I didn't hear her reply.

Because that something which had been tickling my nostrils got right inside, and I lifted my head like a parched bullock scenting water, and stared along the passage, and sniffed, and licked my lips — and drew in a mighty inhalation that filled my lungs and sent me dizzy with the sickness that had been eating into me for five mortal weeks. I seized Mrs Hall with a violence that made her stare at me in sudden fright.

'Mrs Hall! — that smell — those herbs — where did they come from?'

As if I didn't know!

'Sailor —'

Burning gum-leaves! Oh, shades of the bush and smell of my home!

Pushing her from me, I was down the passage in two frenzied leaps and throwing open the door.

But nothing was left save the belongings of a lonely old man, a wisp of blue smoke rising from a tin set on an upturned box, and a digger's hat hanging on a nail driven into the mantelpiece.

FOR THE BEST IN PAPERBACKS, LOOK FOR THE

PENGUIN

BOOKS BY DAVID FOSTER IN PENGUIN

The Pure Land

Three generations of a family move restlessly from the Blue Mountains of New South Wales to the east coast of the United States and back in search of spiritual fulfilment.

Moonlite

The hero, Finbar Macduffie, driven from his frigid perch on the outermost British Isle by the Clearances, makes his way to the Southern Hemisphere and the grog-soaked goldfields of New West Highlands.

'the most wonderfully individualistic, broad-ranging satire on Australian life ever written' Susan McKernan, *Bulletin*

Plumbum

Australia and New Zealand proudly present the world's most notorious rock band! Featuring the unbelievably beautiful and confused Sharon Scott on vocals and the unbelievably fat and materialistic Roland Rocca on keyboards – the ultimate heavy metal experience.

Dog Rock

Dog Rock, a small New South Wales country town, harbours a dangerous killer. Assistant Postal Officer and Night Exchange Attendant D'Arcy D'Oliveres becomes inextricably tangled in the mystery – and even he is not all he seems...

A marvellous, hilarious murder-mystery spoof, portraying a small Australian town with love, accuracy and much poetic humour.

FOR THE BEST IN PAPERBACKS, LOOK FOR THE

PENGUIN

BOOKS BY JOHN MORRISON IN PENGUIN

Stories of the Waterfront

These imaginative and sensitive stories begin at a time when wharfies turned up at the docks to be picked like cattle, and often went home without work or pay. The events range from personal dilemmas like sharing lottery winnings to coping with pig-headed bosses and the tragedy of sudden death.

John Morrison worked for ten years on the Melbourne waterfront in the 1930s and '40s. His *Stories of the Waterfront*, collected here for the first time, give a realistic yet unusually sympathetic account of the much-maligned wharfie.

This Freedom

These stories are about Australian country and city life. They present people who, consciously or otherwise, need each other; people in love, or in need of love. We meet Rory O'Mahony, who dreams of leaving his wife and job for 'freedom'; Lena, for whom piecework is an escape from an otherwise drab existence; and Geoffrey Oliphant, who feels threatened – personally and professionally – by any change.

These gently-observed stories of struggle, love and human accomplishment make a very rewarding addition to John Morrison's work.

FOR THE BEST IN PAPERBACKS, LOOK FOR THE 🐧

PENGUIN

BOOKS BY GERALD MURNANE IN PENGUIN

A Lifetime on Clouds

The humorous story of Adrian Sherd, a teenage boy isolated in Australian suburbia of the 1950s – in the last years before television and the family car changed the suburbs forever. He dream of orgies with film stars but later renounces these and dreams of marrying his Catholic sweetheart and having eleven children by her.

The Plains

On the Plains the landowning families in their vast estates have preserved a rich and distinctive culture. A nameless young film-maker arrives and chooses the daughter of his patron for a leading role. But nothing in this memorable work of fiction is as it seems.

Landscape with Landscape

A man feels urged to give an account of himself to a room full of strange women. But before he can speak to the women he becomes trapped in his recurring dreams of landscapes and the women in them. Another man spends twenty years searching the hills near Melbourne for a landscape and a woman that no artist could paint. On his last night in the hills he enacts a drunken ritual to make himself and landscape invisible in the eyes of the artists he despises. These two stories and four others make up an elaborate and unforgettable pattern of dreams and reality.

FOR THE BEST IN PAPERBACKS, LOOK FOR THE 🐧

PENGUIN

BOOKS BY DAVID IRELAND IN PENGUIN

A Woman of the Future

The time of this remarkable novel is the near future. The place is Australia.

A Woman of the Future is the diary of Alethea Hunt and her personal odyssey in a harsh society and a world of tomorrow.

Winner of the Miles Franklin Award, 1979 and co-winner of *The Age* Book of the Year Award, 1980.

'a novel of immense originality, wit and gritty wisdom ... David Ireland has reached the top' Patrick White.

The City of Women

The city of women is love, Billie Shockley says. But in the city of women that is her world, love takes strange forms. Arresting, provocative, shocking yet pierced with a sublime tenderness, David Ireland's bizarre symbolism compels the imagination.

Archimedes and the Seagle

'I have to listen to all sorts of crackpot remarks from humans with little knowledge and be thought to agree.' So says Archimedes, from his dog's-eye view of the world. As he marvels at the soaring, solitary flight of the seagle, he recognises how much of his own joy and energy are social. And that even the earthbound can dream of the sky.

Bloodfather

The novel traces the development of a young artist – from birth to the age of seventeen. Davis Blood is a precious child. He asks questions and looks for answers to the mysteries of the world. He falls down stairs, he runs, he draws, he plays cricket. And he has verbal volleys with his aunts – the obsessively punning Aunt Mira and Aunt Ursula who, although confined to a wheelchair, opens up many corners of the world for young Davis. David Ireland plumbs the depths of the obsessions of a young artist and sheds light on the well-springs of creativity.